PRAISE FOR INGRID WINTERBACH

"*To Hell with Cronjé* is a grim, dark, unrelenting book—an exhaustive survey of the sensations of war, from headlice and crippling thirst to grief, suffering, and madness."—Anderson Tepper, *Words Without Borders*

"Winterbach's writing sets the mood brilliantly, and she pitches her blend of characters perfectly to create an uneasy, occasionally frightening feel to her narrative. . . . It is a novel that will stay in my memory for a long time."—Andy Barnes, *Belletrista*

"What makes this novel and its fresh English-language publication so timely is that its themes have become uncomfortably familiar."
—Richard Whittaker, *Austin Chronicle*

"This is an extraordinary story from an extraordinary writer. . . . If you haven't experienced the mind of Ingrid Winterbach yet, she is a writer who clings to your soul."—*Pretoria News*

"This unforgettable novel establishes Ingrid Winterbach as one of the most important novelists writing in Afrikaans."—Thys Human

"An exquisite book, an essential voice."—Antjie Krog

INGRID WINTERBACH

THE BOOK OF HAPPENSTANCE

TRANSLATED FROM THE AFRIKAANS
BY DIRK AND INGRID WINTERBACH

OPEN LETTER
LITERARY TRANSLATIONS FROM THE UNIVERSITY OF ROCHESTER

Copyright © 2008 by Ingrid Gouws
English translation by Dick and Ingrid Winterbach
Originally published in Afrikaans by Human & Rousseau, 2008

First U.S. edition, 2011

Library of Congress Cataloging-in-Publication Data:

Winterbach, Ingrid.
    [Boek van toeval en toeverlaat. English]
    The book of happenstance / Ingrid Winterbach ; translated from the
Afrikaans by Dirk and Ingrid Winterbach. -- 1st U.S. ed.
        p. cm.
    ISBN-13: 978-1-934824-33-7 (pbk. : acid-free paper)
    ISBN-10: 1-934824-33-X (pbk. : acid-free paper)
    I. Winterbach, Dirk, 1951- II. Title.
    PT6592.32.I44B6413 2011
    839.3'635—dc22
                            2011003187

Printed on acid-free paper in the United States of America.

Text set in Bembo, an old-style serif typeface based upon face cuts by
Francesco Griffo that were first printed in 1496.

Design by N. J. Furl

Open Letter is the University of Rochester's nonprofit, literary translation press:
Lattimore Hall 411, Box 270082, Rochester, NY 14627

www.openletterbooks.org

For Liesbeth-Helena Gouws

THE BOOK OF
HAPPENSTANCE

CHAPTER ONE

In March, at the end of summer, I start working as Theo Verwey's assistant. In October, in spring, he is found dead in his office. I am the one who discovers him at six-thirty in the evening. I close the door behind me and move forward cautiously, but there is a threshold I cannot cross.

Everybody is upset about his death, Sailor more so than anybody else. For days on end his eyes are red with weeping and he tells me: He was like a father to me.

Sailor sits in my office. One of his long legs dangles over the armrest of the chair. Under his arms are large patches of sweat. His hair is tousled. His face is red with emotion. Even in his state of collapse he still looks pretty good. Freddie stands in the door. Behind him stands the cleaning woman. (She looks like a cleaning woman, but she is in fact an expert on fossils, more specifically fossils from the Cambrian.)

Sailor says: "It's that Indian dog."

"Which Indian dog?" I ask.

"The margarine magnate," says Freddie from the door.

"It's his father," Sailor says.

"Whose father?" I ask.

"The dog's father," Sailor says.

"The margarine magnate?"

"Yes, he made his money from margarine and cooking oil," Freddie says from the doorway.

"Which one is the dog?" I ask.

"The cunt is his son," says Sailor.

"Sailor thinks he blackmailed Verwey," Freddie says, and grinds out his cigarette beneath his heel.

"Blackmailed," wails Sailor.

"Bad," says the woman.

"He's stinking rich," says Freddie.

"They have a TV screen as big as a wall in their house," Sailor says, "with seats like in a bioscope."

"How does he know that?" I ask Freddie, for Sailor is overwhelmed by a fresh flood of tears.

"How do you know that?" Freddie asks Sailor.

"I was there," Sailor wails.

"Christ Almighty," the woman says, also lighting a cigarette.

"Did the father or the son blackmail him?" I ask.

"The father," Freddie says, shaking his head.

"No, the cunt himself," Sailor says.

"And the cunt is the son," I say.

"Yes," Sailor says, "the fucking cunt with his hot Indian arsehole!"

Theo Verwey and I used to listen to music as we worked. Mahler, Schubert, Cimarosa, Gluck, Strauss, Schütz, Mozart. I helped Theo Verwey with his project. He recorded words that have fallen into complete disuse, as well as words not often used in Afrikaans any more.

A couple of days after his death Mrs. Verwey arrives to collect her deceased husband's possessions from his office. I help her pack the books into boxes.

"Are you willing to complete this task on his behalf?" she asks me. "The project was his lifelong dream and Theo had the greatest respect for your expertise." With my back to her, bending over a box with a small pile of books in my hand, I tell her: "I'll have to think about it; I don't know how much longer I plan to remain here."

CHAPTER TWO

In the last week of May, nearly three months after I started as Theo Verwey's assistant in March, my garden flat gets broken into. When I arrive home late in the afternoon, the flat is in disarray. The cupboards and drawers are open, their contents ransacked, as if someone was hurriedly looking for something before shoving everything back. In the bedroom the bedding looks as if it has been bundled up after being stripped. I do not even take the trouble to see if anything has been stolen—what breaks my heart is my shells!

I brought thirty-seven of my loveliest shells with me. Even the robust conches I packed as carefully as porcelain for the journey. Twenty-one of them I set out in three rows on my bedside table, the other sixteen I displayed on a small table in the lounge. The bedside table is empty. In the lounge a few shells lie on the ground. I go down on my haunches. Only five have remained. The three *Harpa majors* are gone. The periglyptas! Most of the conches. (The irreplaceable conches!) The helmet shell, of which Frans said that its colour resembles his glans when he has lain in the water for too long. The two dramatic murexes. The rare terebras. I did not carelessly pick up these shells during a day or two at the seaside—over the years I have selected and bought them with great care. I hear my own voice moaning: I cannot believe this! The sound comes from deep in my throat, from a place where words are not usually formed. I can feel my throat constricting and the small bones in my larynx pressing painfully against one another. Am I supposed to learn a lesson from this? I wonder in passing.

All my things I view as earthly goods, all of them replaceable—but not the shells. The shells are heavenly messengers! The shells I have been collecting for a lifetime. They are my most prized possessions. Over the years I have taken (with a few notable exceptions) more pleasure in these shells than in people. (My ex-husband said that I was like the dowager empress Tz'u-hsi—more concerned with her silkworm cocoons than with her subjects.)

I move through the house from one room to another, distraught. *Whores*, I think. Whoever did this. Barbarians.

In the small back room there is a large wet stain on the carpet, as well as a large piece of human excrement. I instinctively draw back from the smell and the substance. Someone actually urinated and defecated on the carpet! The feces look dangerous—black, solid, shiny, coiled like a snake. (What must be ingested to produce a thing like that! What relentless thoughts can direct a turd like that?) Menacingly it lies there, a warning: Be careful, or you will get to deal with me, and I do not show any mercy. The humiliation, the naked intimidation of this deed.

My own spiritual need is urgent. It takes a great deal of energy to sustain this high level of psychic need. Meditating on the shells is one way of centring myself and lowering my levels of anxiety. These shells are a source of infinite beauty and wonder to me. I can rely on their beauty to divert me from vexation and discontent.

I move into top gear; some kind of hysteria, surely. Carefully I lift the feces with a wad of tissues and flush it down the toilet. I soak the carpet in Dettol. The water in the bath turns a murky black. (It is a carpet of which I am very fond; I bought it at a time when my ex-husband, the child and I were still together.) I cannot afford to be intimidated by a turd. Having done this, it occurs to me that there may be techniques these days for determining the identity of criminals from their excrement. Too late for that. I phone the police. I should probably leave everything as I found it, but I do not have the heart to leave the violated shells lying on the ground. I put them back on the table.

The doorbell rings. Two constables announce themselves: a Constable Modisane and a Constable Moonsamy. Constable Modisane makes a sympathetic clicking sound with the tongue while surveying the scene of the disaster. He is the younger of the two. He has smooth, youthful cheeks and a domed forehead.

"Do you like these things?" he asks, looking at the shells on the table.

"Yes," I say.

Mr. Modisane, Constable, how can I begin to say how I regard these shells? I have not led an admirable life, and there is not much I can change about that. I have been irresponsible and inconsiderate in most of my relationships. But concerning the shells, sir, I am and have been all reverent and devout attention. It is my way of acknowledging the wonders of creation. My meditation on the shells has been one of the very few things I do to tend my spiritual well-being.

"Why do you like them?" he asks.

"Because they are beautiful," I say. "And because God made them."

Constable Modisane casts a last sceptical look at the shells and exchanges a surreptitious glance with Moonsamy.

"Can you sell them?" he asks. "Are they worth any money?"

"I'm not interested in selling them," I say. "And if necessary I will pay money to get the stolen ones back."

"How much?" he asks.

"I've not had time to decide yet," I say.

"O-kay," he says amiably.

"What is that smell?" I ask. "Do you recognise it?" For the first time I pick up the sweetish smell of aftershave in the room. Constables Modisane and Moonsamy both sniff the air suspiciously. Constable Modisane a trifle more energetically than Moonsamy.

"It's Boss," Constable Modisane says. "Hugo Boss aftershave."

•

The next day I encounter Sof Benadé at the Sand Dune. She works as a language advisor and translator at the museum. She translates from Afrikaans to English, and from German and French to Afrikaans. I think of her as the curator of languages. She is sitting with a copy of *Die Kerkblad* in front of her. "My father subscribes to this for me every year," she says, "although my family knows that I have turned my back on

7

salvation. They have long since accepted that I shall burn for all eternity in the fires of hell. The Reformed Hell." She gives a little laugh—half apologetic and half provocative.

"Is it that bad?" I ask.

"It's much worse," she says. "I thought that I could get away from the pastorie. I was wrong. Deluded. A deluded doos."

(Deluded doos. I like that.)

Sof has a disarming awkwardness and narrow hands and feet. She is younger than I am. Dark hair, with the first signs of grey, and a small gap between her front teeth. She is shy, her eyes defenceless. Fine, soft grey-green eyes, withdrawn behind her glasses—but painfully observant.

"They broke into my place yesterday and stole most of my shells," I say. I have a sudden need to tell this woman of the loss I have suffered, although I hardly know her.

"They urinated and defecated on one of my carpets. It's a carpet of which I am really fond. I found it an intimidating gesture. But the real loss is the shells."

"The one who did it should have his hand chopped off in public," says Sof and gives a small cough.

"If only I could get the shells back unharmed," I say, "I demand no drastic measures of retribution."

"Who would want to steal someone else's shells?" she asks.

"I would want to," I say. "But I can hardly use myself as the norm."

"What else was stolen?" she asks.

"Nothing that I've really noticed," I say. "What matters to me is the missing shells. It breaks my heart."

That afternoon I drive out along the South Coast to contemplate my loss. We used to come here during the July holidays, when it was cold in the Transvaal, and rent a house on the sea. My father started sunning himself weeks in advance. He sat on a chair in our back yard with a towel around his waist and a hat on his head. In this way he acquired a gradual tan and his skin never peeled. On holiday my brother and I made little trains from the stems of banana leaves. We ate some liana and it made us sick. A little friend came to play and we offered her some as well. I drew in a book I was given by my grandfather—my mother's father, who had abandoned his family and had recently returned after an absence of twenty years. It was a Croxley Pen Carbon book, ten and three-quarters of an inch by eight and three-eighths of an inch in format. The pages were numbered, and every alternate page was lined. My father drew a train for me with a red ballpoint pen. (More pink than red.) I drew ballerinas, brides and bridegrooms with flower girls and bridesmaids. I traced my playing cards. I painted an ocean scene with a pirate ship in the background, which I copied from the lid of my box of watercolour paints. My sister Joets drew a mermaid on the back cover. It was beautiful. I was five or six, she was eleven or twelve. Our mother remained as white in her bathing costume as she had been before the holidays. She was afraid of the waves. The dunes in front of the house were unspoilt. They were covered with indigenous scrub and a creeper with small leaves and red berries.

I look in vain for that unspoilt coastline, for the whole coast has since been converted into a pleasure resort, densely built up with blocks of flats and time-share units. The coastline offers no consolation today. Which hardly improves my mood.

Since I arrived here, I have begun to write again. A young woman steps out onto a stoep; she is wearing a soft, flowered dress. For this woman it will never be possible to find happiness. She keeps her gaze fixed unremittingly on a man in white flannel trousers and a white shirt with rolled-up sleeves. His fine arms are tanned and he is smoking a cigarette. Another man descends into the copper mines at Messina. He does not know where he comes from nor where he is going, and he seeks refuge in the pursuit of fleeting pleasure.

•

Very late that evening a man phones me. His name does not ring a bell.

"I'm thinking back tonight to an evening in 1978 in Braamfontein, in Felix du Randt's flat. I would like to continue the conversation we had then."

"Twenty-seven years later?" I say.

"You and I had a very enlightening conversation that evening," he says.

9

"Is that so?" I say.

"You spoke with remarkable insight about Plato. How well you explained to me that we are lost in this world. That what we experience here is but a pale reflection of the real world, and that all the knowledge we possess is but the memory of an existence in a prior world."

"You mistake me for someone else," I say firmly. "I did not on that evening, nor any evening before or after, speak about Plato."

"Oh, no," the man says. "I could never confuse you with someone else. Never. I want to take the liberty of saying that I could not confuse you with someone else for all eternity."

"For all eternity?" I say, with a scathing laugh (thinking of Sof's Reformed Hell).

The man also laughs, a jolly chuckle.

"What did you say your name was?" I ask.

"Freek," he says. "Freek van As."

"I'm sorry," I say. "I still can't place you. You are confusing me with someone else."

Freek van As continues, unperturbed. "You arrived there late that night with Marthinus Maritz and Herman Holst."

"That I remember," I say. (I lost my head that night; I was drunk, my conduct was reprehensible.)

"Listen, Freek," I say, "I can't speak to you now. I had a burglary yesterday. I'm still recovering from the shock."

The line suddenly crackles and his voice is almost inaudible. I consider replacing the receiver softly. Herman Holst, the editor, was there that evening; Marthinus Maritz, overzealous and misdirected, he was there. We were visiting Felix du Randt, a former lover of mine. Very vaguely I recall the presence of a fourth person, but I cannot be certain. A dark man? Pale.

"I have to go," I say. "I can't continue this conversation now. I have too many other things I have to attend to at the moment."

"No problem," Freek says. "I'll be in touch again."

"Rather not," I say, and put the phone down. So much for the nebulous phantom of Freek van As, and also the intrusive memory of an evening in Braamfontein nearly thirty years ago. I can return to that when I am less unsettled by my loss.

I drink a whisky and go to bed. I still lack the courage to make a list of the missing shells. What made Freek van As decide to get in touch with me after twenty-seven years? Do I owe this man something?

.

Theo Verwey is smooth-shaven and rosy this morning. Schütz on the CD player. We discuss this specific recording.

"I used to be a member of a Schütz choral group," Theo says.

"It must have been a singular experience," I say, "to sing Schütz."

"It was," he says. "I attended a performance of the *Symphoniae Sacrae* in Berlin in 1996. It was excellent."

"Seven years after the dismantling of the wall," I say. "Schütz in Berlin. Do you like Berlin as a city?"

"A truly exceptional city," Theo says. "It has a feel different from the rest of Europe."

"An anarchic energy, I've heard. I've not yet been there myself."

"You should really go," he says.

I shrug.

"We've received an additional grant for the project," he says.

"That's good news," I say. "Who from—a benefactor?"

Theo looks surprised. "How did you know?"

I say that I took a guess; I made a joke.

"A member of the Commission for the Promotion of Afrikaans. The *Derde Afrikaanse Taalgenootskap*. A high-profile individual. A substantial amount of money. This person is generously sponsoring your appointment for the first six months as it is, but with this grant we can extend your contract by another six months."

Theo stands in profile, gazing out of the window. He is a good-looking man. I cannot fault any of his features. All in perfect harmony, the mouth perhaps a trifle too sensual. His complexion is rosy—a sign of good blood circulation and a healthy diet. His dark hair is lush, beginning to grey. A face suited to sensual abandon. Had the expression in his eyes been different, it could even have been called a passionate face. His eyebrows form a high arch, lending his face an expression of permanent surprise. For a moment he pauses reflectively with a card in his hand.

I have things weighing on my mind, pressing issues, and this man evokes a need in me to pour out my heart to him. Inexplicable. Is it perhaps because I know that this is not permissible? Does the prohibition sharpen the desire? What would the appropriate (decorous) words be for the feelings that rise up urgently in my throat from the region of the heart? For the time being I do not know how to clothe them fittingly.

"I read a very fine book recently," I say.

He glances up from his work. Politely. "Oh, yes?" he says.

"It's about a man who is very rich. Fabulously rich. It appealed to me," I say, "that kind of wealth. Among other things, he wants to buy a chapel with Mark Rothko paintings. His agent advises against it. But he insists with a kind of perversion."

Theo Verwey still looks at me politely; he is waiting for me to continue.

"The man's agent and advisor—a former lover of his—one of a series of advisors, in fact, says that he owes it to the public not to acquire the chapel for his private use."

Theo looks interested.

"But the man persists. He wants it for himself. Simply because he is *able* to have it."

I pause for a moment, listening to the music. I find the instruments lovely; I associate the sound with complex colours today—tertiary, not primary colours.

"Although it's more than his wealth that appeals to me in the book," I say.

"Yes?" Theo says.

"This man moves from one point in the city to the next in a limousine, speaking to his various advisors along the way. He encounters a variety of delays and obstructions, among others a funeral procession—one of the loveliest parts of the book. Once or twice he gets out of the car and has a meal with his wife. They've been married for only two weeks. She's enormously rich herself. At the end of the book he's dead."

"Is that so?" Theo Verwey says, raising his well-proportioned eyebrows a little higher.

"Yes," I say. "Alas, yes."

"Do you recommend it?" he asks.

"Oh, yes," I say. "With all my heart. The book, or death?"

He smiles.

•

That afternoon I phone Constable Modisane to enquire whether they have caught the villain who stole my shells.

"No-ho," the Constable says, with a hesitation in his voice that makes me suspect that they have not yet made the slightest effort to do anything about the case.

"It's causing me much, much grief," I say to him, "the loss of those shells."

"Ye-es," the man says, not unsympathetically.

"I trust you will do your best," I say.

I hear other voices in the background; the constable is talking to someone over his shoulder.

"Well, goodbye," I say.

"Goodbye," the constable says, distracted.

That evening I drink two whiskies before I make a list of the missing shells. The three *Nautilus pompilius* shells are gone—two small specimens and a large one. Both *Murex nigritus* shells are gone. The *Terebra maculata* and the *Terebra aerolata* are gone. The three *Harpa major* shells are gone. The *Conus marmoreus*, the *Conus geographus*, both *Conus textile* shells, the two *Conus betulinus* shells and the two *Conus figulinus* shells, all gone. The two *Periglypta magnifica* shells are gone. The top shell, *Trochas maculata*, is gone. The bride of the sea, *Argonauta argo*, is gone. The two white cowries (*Ovula ovum*) and the tiger's-eye cowrie (*Cypraea tigris*) are gone. All the tonnas and the helmet shells are gone. The *Marginella mosaica* and the blushing *Marginella rosea* are gone.

I lie down on the couch in the lounge. I have contradictory thoughts. The three *Harpa majors* were among the most beautiful of my shells. Their form and colour are moving—the delicate vertical ribs like the strings of a harp; the delicate light-brown wavy patterns between the raised ribs resembling the thin lines drawn by a seismograph. These three shells I have recently been looking at with great attention. I would even call the attentiveness with which I looked at them a kind of meditation, for there are few other things that I give the same selfless and painstaking attention. (Reverent attention.) But although I meditated without ego on these objects, these shells, and even saw God in the detail (in a manner of speaking), I was still attaching myself excessively to them. Should I have had my heart less set on them? Should I have tried to bring about the salvation of my (eternal and immortal) soul in a different manner? Should I have allowed their beauty to nourish me, but renounced the pleasure of ownership? Should I have invested less in lifeless things over the years and more in relationships? I told Theo Verwey about the rich man today. Why? Fragments of memory of the evening in Braamfontein, nearly thirty years ago, come to me. Who is this Freek van As, who comes to me after nearly thirty years like a dog with a dead bird in its mouth?

Of that particular evening I recall first of all that I drank too much. I remember that the young editor Herman Holst was there—a neat, inhibited fellow, who has since vanished into the void to seek his happiness in America. He and the poet Marthinus Maritz often hung out together at the time. I went to Felix du Randt's flat with the two of them. I regretted having ended my relationship with Felix some weeks previously and wanted, at least, to restore something of our relationship of trust. If I remember correctly, the poet and the editor were more than keen to accompany me. Starved for a little action. It was late when we arrived at Felix's flat. I was in a worked-up and overemotional state. Sexy Felix du Randt, with his sharp, sly, foxy face, received us politely, but was icy cold towards me. From his side, reconciliation was not an option. Never could I have foreseen that foxy Felix, with his warm, freckled skin, who just a few months before had regarded me with such passion, such tenderness, such loving certainty, would turn his back on me so implacably. The more he distanced himself from me that evening, the more hysterical I became. What did I want from him? That he should take me back into his arms? That he should smile on me tenderly and intimately as he had done in bed some weeks before? That he should promise eternal fidelity, after I had made it clear that he was not the right man for me? Felix revealed a different side of himself that evening, the existence of which I had never suspected.

Marthinus Maritz is dead. Felix I never saw again; he had been head of some language institute or linguistics department somewhere up north before dying in a car accident in his early forties.

The poet Marthinus Maritz, filled with grim and misguided yearning, walked with a slight stoop. His torso was fleshy, his feet pointed slightly outwards; his heavy, dark, bearded head was too large for his body. His gaze was at once challenging and bewildered; in his eyes was the light of poetic possession. His first volume of poetry was a huge success. He was passionate about poetry, ambitious, intellectually energetic—even indefatigable—but an emotional cripple. A despairing, tormented man. His childhood had been difficult, his mother had neglected him shamefully, her lovers had mistreated him. He was married; we attempted something sexual once or twice, but we were verbally attracted to each other, not physically. His first volume of poetry was hailed as a gift of God to the language. Where else in Afrikaans is there another debut—a comparable volume, in fact—in which pain, uncertainty, and emotional abandonment are expressed equally poignantly, where there are as many heart-rending poems about youthful illusion and despair as in that first collection of poems by Marthinus Maritz? He could not equal that again. Wallace Stevens was one of his favourite poets. The motto in that first volume was a quotation from a poem by Stevens. Marthinus was an incongruous figure, and he felt himself increasingly disregarded and isolated. He abandoned poetry, tried to make money. Succeeded. His business enterprise was a huge success; he became very wealthy, took up poetry again, but could never write anything to match his first volume. Perhaps he thought that if he became a fat cat like Wallace Stevens, he would be able to write like him.

Marthinus was a man with a penetrating intelligence and an uncontrolled aggressive streak that ran like a faultline through his personality. His aggression was mostly directed at women, though. I did not realise it then. That evening, when I ranted hysterically and deliberately spilled wine on Felix's new white mohair carpet, Marthinus slapped me on both sides of my face with abandon. I recognise the intensity only now, thirty-odd years later. It gave that man great pleasure to slap me publicly, on both sides of my face, so that the fingermarks were visible, ostensibly to calm me down. Felix du Randt, my ex-lover, looked on expressionlessly and fetched a cloth to mop the red wine from his expensive new carpet. It was clear that everything he had previously emotionally invested in our relationship he had now reinvested in that costly white woven mohair carpet. He regarded the wine stains with abhorrence. I doubt if he would have intervened if Marthinus had treated (punished) me even more roughly.

But besides Marthinus Maritz, Felix du Randt, and Herman Holst, there appears to have been a fourth person present, the indistinct Freek van As, who observed everything that evening and had a conversation with me about Plato, if I am to believe him. The editor has disappeared, the poet and the former lover are dead, only Freek van As remains. After twenty-seven years he strides forth from the nebulous regions of the past to remind me of an incident that occurred in my late twenties. Am I still interested? It is over and done with, that period of delusion and poor judgement.

•

"The most arresting part of the book I began telling you about yesterday," I say to Theo Verwey the next day, "is perhaps the description of the funeral procession of the dead rap singer. A spectacularly extended procession. The rich man gets out of his car to watch it. The body of the deceased is exhibited in the hearse, somewhat tilted, if I remember correctly, so as not to lie flat, and his voice on cassette—immensely amplified—accompanies the procession. Just imagine. In this extended funeral cortege there are also dervishes. What would that be in Afrikaans again?"

"A *derwisj*, a Muslim mendicant monk," Theo says. "From the Persian *darvish*, meaning poor."

"The mendicants dance," I say. "They whirl round and round. It's one of the most exquisite moments in the book, the description of the whirling, turning dervishes."

Theo Verwey nods politely.

"The rich man then fantasises about his own funeral," I say. "He has about five chance sexual interactions with women during his journey through the city, and he fantasises about the role that each of these women will play at his funeral. Although it's hardly a journey—rather a slow progression. He sees his wife a couple of times—from the moving car he sees her walking past on the pavement, he sees her passing him in a taxi. They eat together once or twice. He asks her during one of these casual meetings when they will have sex again." I look down at the tip of my shoe. "At the end of the book they have a brief sexual encounter. In a standing position, somewhere."

Theo Verwey looks surprised.

"She clasps her legs around his body," I say. "It's a passionate rendezvous."

Theo's eyebrows arch even higher.

I speak with averted eyes, my tone of voice slightly ironic.

"His wife is a poet," I say. "Although the man doesn't think much of her poetic abilities. They've been married for only two weeks. She's also very rich. I've mentioned that already. Heiress to an astounding banking fortune. In the course of the day the man trades ever larger sums of money, against the counsel of his financial advisors. He loses everything. His wife's money as well, which he steals in a deceptively simple—astonishingly simple—digital or cyber transaction. I'm not sure exactly how."

Theo Verwey is now listening with undivided attention.

"He tells her that he's lost her money, but she doesn't really believe him. Before he left his apartment that morning, he first talked to his dogs."

Theo Verwey gazes at me wordlessly for some seconds. "Do you recommend it," he asks once again, "to wager everything you have knowing that you might lose it?" He smiles. Something ironic in his voice as well? "To steal your wife's money only to lose it in some risky transaction?" He is still smiling.

I also smile. I get my breath back. This is further than I have ever gone with anybody in one morning. This is further than we have ever gone with each other.

•

That evening I lie on the couch in my garden flat as on the evening before. I am renting the smaller ground floor of the house, the owners occupy the large upper storey. I had my landlord replace the locks on the front door and install a sturdy security door immediately. They were out on the day that the burglary took place. According to him, they have never had a burglary before. Ever since the incident I have been feeling uneasy.

I contemplate the event. What kind of thief leaves behind clothes, jewellery, shoes, a CD player, CDs, and a television to steal shells? A disturbed thief with perverted needs? A thief with a secret agenda? A thief whose left hand does not know what the right hand is doing? A Dr.-Jekyll-and-Mr.-Hyde thief? Dr. Jekyll carefully enters the house, Mr. Hyde pulls the clothes out of the cupboards and sweeps the shells from the table with a single movement of the arm. Dr. Jekyll, the aesthete, steals the shells, Mr. Hyde, the thug, urinates and defecates on the carpet. Dr. Jekyll bundles the clothes back and carefully packs the shells into a box. I do not like this—besides being bitterly upset about the loss, I do not like the idea that someone specifically targeted my shells. The event rests like a dead weight on my chest. My chances of getting them back are slim, judging by Constable Modisane's tone of voice. The recovery of stolen shells is hardly a priority for the police anyway.

I need to talk to someone, but I do not know to whom. I can picture my ex-husband's reaction if I told him about this. I can imagine his condemnatory silence at the other end of the line, his slightly laboured and admonishing breathing. In his view of the world the loss of shells would count as hardly anything. I do not wish to burden my child with this. (Do I expect some degree of censure from her as well? An impatience with my stubborn clinging to my loss? She travels light—casting off much as she moves along.) Neither do I wish to involve Frans de Waard, my lover and companion.

But my shells! The paper nautilus, *Argonauta argo*, related to the nautilus, fragile, papery thin, lustrous—one of my most exquisite shells. A shy bride! A prancing little caravel on the open sea! A thirteen-year-old girl! The *Conus betulinus*, smooth, spiral-grooved around the base, a heavy, ochre-coloured shell, whose cool weight I can still feel in my hand. As I can likewise feel the weight of the two heavy *Conus figulinus* shells, and clearly recall the day when I bought them in a town on the Cape coast. The *Conus marmoreus*, of which Rembrandt made a series of etchings. The two dramatic *Murex nigritus* shells, a rare bounty, all the way from the Gulf of California—white, ornate, capriciously imagined, with dark markings over the shoulder region and dark-brown protrusions. The light *Tonna variegata*—delicate as a Japanese paper lantern! The *Mitra mitra*, largest of the mitres—a heavy, spiral-shaped shell resembling a bishop's hat (the Latin *mitra* from the Greek *mitra*, turban). The small marks on it are a deep orange, slightly paler in the smaller shell. The *Marginella mosaica*, with spiralling rows of dark-grey or brown markings like sand drifts on its pale, milky surface—as if time itself has woven its marks into the surface.

I do not even want to think about the loss of the three nautiluses— the two smaller ones and one larger one. Two proud knights and a queen, standard-bearers of the striped blazon, little cavorting horses of the deep seas! Perhaps the closest to my heart of them all (except for the two brown *Figulinus* conches). The last remaining genus of the primeval order *Nautiloidea*—an ancient shell, smooth on the outside, coiled on the inside, with thirty-six chambers, of which only the outer ones are inhabited.

How did the thief know, with what unfailing instinct did he take the loveliest, the most valuable ones, those dearest to my heart? How should I explain this? Or should I see in it only the fickle hand of Mrs. Fortuna?

In my distress I appeal to my mother, my father, and especially to my deceased sister, Joets. It is not that I address them, but rather that I turn my imploring face in their direction. As if to say: See me. Here I am. What am I to do?

Now that I no longer have to take their corporeal existence into account—with the subtle intervening shifts and irritations that mark a relationship—I think I am able to see each one of them with greater clarity.

I have not thought of Marthinus Maritz for a long time. Freek van As caused me to remember him again. Although my acquaintance with Marthinus was short-lived, he made a deep impression on me. In the presence of my former lover—sexy, foxy-red and seductively freckled Felix du Randt—the editor Herman Holst and the nebulous Freek van

As, he slapped me hard on both cheeks, but even with those two robust clouts he could not succeed in making me change my ways.

•

"The man you told me about yesterday," Theo Verwey says the next day, "you mentioned that he talks to his dogs. What does he say to them?"

"It's not clear," I say. "I don't recall that his exact words are given. His apartment has walls reaching two or three storeys high, and I picture the dogs in a black marble cage."

"What breed of dogs are they?" Theo asks.

"I can't remember. White borzois, perhaps. Russian wolfhounds. Dogs cared for by his staff, I suppose. With that kind of money people can probably be employed for the sole purpose of caring for the dogs and taking them for walks. Although they are still glad to hear the voice of their master. They are referred to again at a later stage in the book, which makes you think that the rich man values these animals highly."

Theo Verwey gazes pensively into the distance. Does he want to say something? Something he finds hard to say? I wait, while he picks up a number of cards from the desk and arranges them in a neat pile. He does not look up. I wait, sensing his hesitancy.

"The ransom of a man's life is his wealth, but the poor hears no rebuke," he quotes reflectively. I wait. Is that a dismissal or a prompt to continue?

We continue our work in silence for a while. This morning we are listening to Monteverdi madrigals. Two male voices are singing "Mentre vaga Angioletta," about the miracle of love. An ecstatic intertwining of voices. But I find the music somewhat depressing. "O miracolo, miracolo, miracolo," the men sing. I wonder what Theo makes of this ecstatic celebration of love. I watch him covertly. He shows no sign of being transported.

"Do you remember the poet Marthinus Maritz?" I ask.

"Yes," Theo says, surprised. "Why?"

"I was thinking of him the other day," I say.

"He had a beautiful voice," Theo says.

20

How could I have forgotten! His voice was one of his most distinctive features. Memory is selective. I remembered the high rump, the rather thickset torso, and the dark, bearded head. His aura of danger and defiance I remembered, the vengeful glint in his eye, but not his voice. Why?

"I've begun to write a novel," I say.

"Oh, yes?" Theo says.

"It's set in the Forties," I say.

"What is it about?" he asks. He looks interested, or is feigning interest.

"The outlines are still tenuous," I say, "the storyline is still undefined."

(A young woman emerges onto a red cement stoep. She is wearing a floral dress. She is in love. She is about to be married. She is filled with anticipation about the new life that she is about to embrace. She wants to leave the sorrow of the past behind her. She has set her heart on fulfilment. She believes that this fulfilment of the heart is possible. She wishes only to make good the tears, the despair, and the uncertainty of the past.)

"I'm thinking of rereading C.M. van den Heever," I say, "even though a vocabulary for emotional nuance hardly exists in the prose of his time." His eyes are large behind his glasses. He reflects on what I have said, holding the stack of cards loosely in his hands.

"No," he says. "You're right. You won't find what you're looking for in the early prose." We are interrupted by a light knock on the door.

His wife closes the door behind her. She is pretty. She is also a successful businesswoman, and self-satisfied. She has a madonnalike beauty—fine features, large, bright eyes, softly curling hair, and small, sharp teeth (a feral sharpness). But this morning I detect in her presence (her trail, her wake) a slightly unpleasant feminine odour, associated with menstruation. Could the woman be careless about personal hygiene? Someone in her prominent public position? I find myself blushing, not for her sake, but for that of Theo Verwey. I am nervous that his wife's intimate odour will embarrass him in my presence. As soon as I have greeted her, I leave Theo's office.

I hurry to the tearoom, where we regularly have tea with the museum staff. I enjoy their conversations; they interest me. I am a lexicographer by profession (though not by initial training) and have not had much exposure to science during my career, although it has always interested me.

The tearoom is small. Boxes are stacked against one of the walls, there is the pervasive smell of bone. There is a table with a kettle and cups. Old easy chairs are arranged in a wide circle around a low coffee table. Freddie Ferreira is here this morning, and Vera Garaszczuk and Mrs. Dudu. A while later Sof Benadé, Sailor, and Nathi Gule also show up. For years I have not given death much thought, and now I am suddenly obsessed with it again. Obsessed: *behep*, from the Dutch *behept*, derived from the Middle Dutch *behachten*, or *beheept* (of which the origin is uncertain), in the sense of being stuck with, or troubled by. This is how Theo Verwey explained it to me.

CHAPTER THREE

We continue with the letter *D*. It is the beginning of June. The obsessive, almost perverse proliferation of summer is abating. Like someone coming to the end of a manic episode. A paradisiacal peace begins to descend. The days are cooler, with the occasional leaf fluttering down. The poinsettias are beginning to flower, as well as other plants in my landlord's autumnal garden. In the early morning and at evening the colours are turning richer and deeper. The earth is becoming more fragrant. The threatening lushness of summer is cast off like a psychological affliction; there is a new commitment to decorum in the air. There is the promise of maturation. Even in this province, where the approaching autumn and winter are so different from where I come from.

Theo Verwey rocks back and balances on the rear legs of his chair this morning. Don't, I want to say, you will fall over backwards. I have never seen him sit like that. He is deep in thought. The palms of his hands are pressed together tightly and his index fingers rest against his mouth. Keeping guard of his mouth this morning? Does something want to slip out? He is not that kind of man. I do not read him like that. Although I admit that I do not read him well.

I am sitting with the bulky stack of cards in my hand, the dictionaries open before me. The first card in the stack is *da*. The last card is *dyvelaar*.

"*Da*," I say, "where does that come from?"

23

Da or *dè* is probably an abbreviation of *daar* (there) and was noted for the first time in Afrikaans by Pannevis as *deh* and in the *Patriotwoordeboek* as *dé*, he explains.

"*Dyvelaar*," I rhyme teasingly, "as in *twyfelaar?*"

"*Dy-vel-aar*," he spells out, "or *dy-huid-aar*." A vein in the lower leg, the vena saphena, he explains. "Not to be confused with the femoral artery, the arteria femoralis."

"What would the *dermbeen* be? And the *dermbeendoring?*" I ask.

"The *dermbeen* is the topmost, flat part of the hipbone, the ilium, and the *dermbeendoring* is any of its peaked protrusions."

"*Dermbeendoring*," I say. I repeat it a couple of times to feel the uncommon sequence of sounds in my mouth.

We are still listening to Monteverdi madrigals. *Madrigali guerrieri e amorosi*, performed by the Taverner Consort and Players on historical instruments, conducted by Andrew Parrott. This is not my favourite music by Monteverdi, but I do not object. The next track is exquisite, though, and we listen to it in silence. "Su pastorelli vezzosi. Su, su, su, fonticelli loquaci." (Arise, comely shepherds. Arise, babbling springs.)

Theo leans back in his chair, his hands behind his head, and it must be the effect of the music, for I am unexpectedly overcome—overpowered—by a sexual receptivity to him in a way that I have not experienced before. The sensation is so intense that I feel slightly nauseous and have to bend forward. God forbid, I think, I could slide my hands under his shirt, over the chest, and let them nestle in his armpits.

It takes a while to regain my concentration. I continue to page through the dictionary. I read the definitions of "death" and "life." This morning I rose with a heightened sense of mortality. The soft armpits, the powerful male stomach, the tender groin and instep of the foot. What would it be like, carnal love with this man? A day or two ago I told Theo Verwey about the passionate meeting between the man and his wife at the end of the book. I mentioned that they have sexual relations standing up. I told Theo that she clasped her legs around her husband's body, but did not mention how ardently she kissed him. In the small hours I dreamt of a seducer—someone focusing obsessively on me. Something threatening in the man's attentions. In the soft, compressed space of the dream he forced himself on me with an offensive licentiousness. I woke up and too soon lost the mood and content of the dream.

This morning I am inclined to think that it was death who had fawned upon me and flattered me like that last night. Why not? Would I not be able to clothe death in this way in my subconscious?

Their dictionary definitions hardly shed an adequate light on the mystery of either life or death. As a child I would often sit and watch dead insects. Or I would kill an ant to observe the difference between the living ant and the dead. I see now that I tried to probe the secret of life with my child's mind.

"Do you have a clear conception of what life is, and how it originated?" I ask of Theo.

"That you will have to ask Hugo Hattingh," Theo says.

"Will he know?"

"He will know, I presume. He should know how life first originated."

"What kind of man is he?" I ask.

Theo Verwey makes an odd little gesture with his head and shoulders. Disparaging, dismissive? I cannot say.

"I don't know him," he says. "Have you started to alphabetise the cards?"

No, I have not. I glance through the cards in my hand. On the greater majority of these cards are words formed with or containing *dood* (both death and dead). Often descriptive, often to indicate the intensive form "unto death"—to the utmost. *Doodaf* (tired unto death), *doodbabbel* (babble to death), *doodjakker* (gambol or frolic to death).

"*Doodlukas?*"

"Regional. Dead innocent."

"Nice," I say.

Doodluters as a variant of *doodluiters* (blandly innocent or unconcerned), I read, *doodmoor* (murder, torture, or strain to death), *doodsjordaan* (crossing the river Jordan as a metaphor for death), *doodsmare* (tidings of death), *doodswind* (wind bearing death), *doodswym* (total unconsciousness), *doodboek* (register of deaths), *doodbaar* (death bier), *doodbus* (death urn), *dooddag* (day of death), *doodeens* (agreeing completely), *doodellendig* (miserable to death), *doodgaan-en-weer-opstaan* (die-and-get-up-again, aromatic shrub *Myrothamnus flabellifolia*—so called because it appears dead in dry times but revives after rain), *doodgaanskaap* (sheep dying from causes other than slaughtering), *doodgaanvleis* (flesh of animal that has not been slaughtered), *doodgeboorte* (stillbirth), *doodgegooi* (very much in love; literally thrown dead), *doodgeld* (money paid out at death), *doodgetroos* (resigned unto death), *doodgewaan* (mistakenly assumed dead), *doodgooier* (heavy dumpling, or irrefutable argument), *doodgrawer* (grave-digger, or beetle of the genus *Necrophorus*), *doodhouergoggatjie* (descriptive name for any of various dark beetles of family *Elateridae* that keeps deathly still as self-protection), *doodhoumetode* (method by which an animal mimics death).

"They are endless," I remark, "the words formed with death."

"There are many interesting words," Theo says, "but a large number of them have been lost."

"The world is changing," I say. "We don't relate to death as intimately any more. I have never seen a winding sheet. Or felt the wind of death blow. Actually the mere thought of it makes me shiver a little."

Theo smiles. "The wind of death, yes. An unpleasant thought."

"An indecent thought," I say. He smiles.

I continue looking through the cards. *Doodkiskleed* (black cloth covering a coffin), *doodkisvoete* (feet as large as coffins), *doodknies* (to waste away by continual moping), *doodlallie*.

"*Doodlallie!*" I say. "Where does that come from?"

"Very prosperous. A regional word."

Some of these unusual combinations I have not encountered before. "*Doodop?*"

"Totally exhausted."

Doodsbekerswam (also *duiwelsbrood*—devil's bread, poisonous mushroom *Amanita phalloides*), I read. *Doodsbenouenis* (distress unto death), *doodsdal* (valley of death), *doodseën* (blessing for the deceased), *doodsgekla* (moaning associated with death), *doodsgraad* (degree of death).

"Degree of death. As if death has degrees."

"The degree of heat or cold above or below which protoplasmic life can't exist."

"Protoplasmic life," I say. "Would that be the first, most basic form of life?"

"Ask Hattingh that as well," Theo says.

"Would that be the primal slime?"

"It could be that, yes."

Doodshemp (shroud), *doodshuis* (house of death), *doodsjaar* (year of death), *doodskamer* (room of dying or death), *doodsklok* (death knell), *doodskloppertjie* (little knocker of death—deathwatch beetle, family *Anobiidae*), *doodskopaap* (death's-head monkey), *doodsvlek* (any one of the coloured spots found on a body twelve or more hours after death), *doodsvuur* (ignis fatuus: foolish fire, because of its erratic movement).

"I clothe myself in my shroud, my shirt of death, lie down in the room of death at the appointed hour and hark the death knell tolling," I say.

Theo Verwey smiles.

Doodsrilling (shudder as if caused by death; fear of death), *doodsteken* (sign of approaching death; in memoriam sign), *doodvis* (to fish to death). *Doodtuur* or *doodstaar* (gaze to death).

"*Doodtuur,*" I say. "A strange word."

"To gaze yourself to death at what is inevitable, for example."

"Like the hour of death," I say.

"Like the hour of death," he says.

"To fish to death I also find interesting. To think a stretch of water can be fished to death."

"Yes," he says. "A particularly effective combination."

I ask about the origin of the word *dood*.

"Probably from the Middle High German *Tod*, the Old High German *Tot*, from the Gothic *daupus*, of which the letter *p* is pronounced like the English *th*—probably based on the Germanic *dau*," he says. "Compare the Old Norse form *deyja*, to die."

I would like to ask him how he feels about death, now that we are covering the terrain of death so intensively. But it is too intimate a question. Dead intimate. As intimate as death. Intimate to death. Highly improbable that we will ever know each other that well.

I continue looking through the cards. *Dader* and *daderes* (male and female doer, perpetrator). (Theo Verwey and I? And in what context would that be?) *Dadedrang* (the urge to do deeds). *Daarstraks* (obsolete for a moment ago), *dampig* (vaporous; steamy—after the joys of love?). *Dries* (archaic for audacious), *dageraad* (archaic for daybreak; *Chrysoblephus cristiceps*, daggerhead fish).

"Dactylomancy," I say, "you probably know . . ."

"Divination from the fingers," he says, "from *daktilo*, meaning finger or toe, as in dactyloscopy."

"Looking at fingerprints," I say.

"For purposes of identification," he says. "Based on the fact that no two persons have the same skin patterning on their fingers—and that this pattern remains unchanged for life."

•

I weep for my shells as Rachel weeps for her children. I am alternately murderously angry and depressed. I phone Constable Modisane regularly to enquire if anything has been found. What do I care if he thinks there is something amiss with me? A woman going on about shells as if she has nothing better to mourn. I have much to mourn, but at the moment I am mourning for the shells.

I have a child, a daughter, and I have a companion, someone with whom I have had a relationship for the past seven years. Although my daughter is already a young woman, with a life of her own, she is constantly in my thoughts. I often recall with painful intensity her form in all the phases of her life—as an infant, as a young girl, and now as a grown-up woman. The smell of her hair close to the scalp, the silky skin and barely noticeable transition from neck to jaw, the delicate meandering of veins in the area just below the collarbone, her particular tone of voice—when she is pleased, or anxious. The heat of her breath when she is feverish, or when she says something close to my ear. All this I recall clearly. I have great affection for Frans de Waard, the man with whom I have a relationship. He gives me much pleasure—edifying as well as erotic. He is a many-faceted man, solid as well as sexy, attractive, intelligent, and virile. Prompt—receptive to the giving and taking of pleasure. But I have been less open to him over the past months. I have been more focused on my immediate circumstances—the project with which I am assisting Theo Verwey, the book that I have begun writing, and the recent loss of my thirty-two shells.

And now, out of the blue, when I am least expecting it, Marthinus Maritz insinuates himself into my thoughts—although I have little reason to believe that the impetus is coming from him. Freek van As (whom I still cannot remember clearly) reminded me of him. My most vivid and immediate recollections of Marthinus Maritz are of his side-long glance, the powerful, somewhat fleshy torso, his emanation of both aggression and neediness, and a restless impatience that determined the pace of his physical movements as well as his mental activity.

I keep thinking about the dead—those who were close to me that I have lost, and a few others, like Marthinus Maritz. I keep communing with them in my thoughts. I think I see them with greater clarity—my mother, my father, my sister, Joets. I recognise more clearly the ways in which each of their lives was thwarted. All this I could have mourned, but I choose to focus my grief on the missing shells instead.

Her name is Judit, but I call her Joets. During the December holidays our family visits my aunt on their smallholding in the Orange Free State. I am nine, Joets is fifteen. By day we take long walks in the veld; sometimes we catch crabs in the dry banks of the spruit. In the afternoons I play by myself in the front garden. Everyone is sleeping and in the enclosed stoep behind me there is a constant low humming noise, like a whirligig moving very slowly. (At night this noise scares me.) I play in the shade on the grass, close to a small round rock garden. I play an imaginary game with a little celluloid doll. I am totally immersed in the game. At night Joets and I sleep in a room full of unpacked boxes—my aunt and her husband have only just moved in. These boxes are stacked all the way to the ceiling. There is no electricity yet. Joets wakes me up with a candle one night and threatens to burn my toes if I do not tell her what presents she will be getting for Christmas. The rooms have low hessian ceilings, there are always flies, the kitchen smells of milk, and during the long summer afternoons it is hot and dead quiet in the house.

•

Nine days after the burglary I get a call from Constable Modisane.

"Your stolen goods have been retrieved," he says.

"Where?" I ask.

"In Ladybrand," he says.

"Ladybrand in the Free State?" I ask.

"Yebo," he says. "Ladybrand in the Free State."

"Who took them?" I ask.

"A Mr. Patrick Steinmeier," he says. (He pronounces it Pah-trick.)

I hesitate for a moment before I ask if Mr. Steinmeier is white.

Constable Modisane enquires over his shoulder. In the background a hubbub is audible.

"They don't know," he says.

"Where is Mr. Steinmeier now?" I ask.

"Mr. Steinmeier is dead," he says.

"How did he die?" I ask.

"Mr. Steinmeier hanged himself," Constable Modisane says.

"I see," I reply. "Where did he hang himself?"

"In Ladybrand. When can you come in to identify and claim your stolen goods?" he asks.

"I can come immediately," I say.

"When you come, I will show you the photographs," says the constable.

I am confused. Photographs of the shells? "What photographs?" I ask.

"The photographs that were taken of Mr. Steinmeier when they found him," he says.

"I don't want to see them," I say.

"Okay," the constable says jovially. "I will show them."

I report at the counter twenty minutes later with a thumping heart.

Constable Modisane is a genial fellow. He obviously does not hold my obsessive telephone calls over the past few days against me. I notice only now that his hair is cut in a kind of crew cut, a style similar to those I have seen depicted outside barber shops downtown. As he turns around, I notice the exuberant swelling of his rounded buttocks and thighs.

He places a small cardboard box before me on the counter. It feels as if I am receiving the ashes of a deceased person. I pick up the box and shake it lightly. It feels about the right weight. I am so nervous that I struggle to open it.

The shells are in a small hessian bag inside the box. The bag has a strong, unplaceable odour. It is slightly moist. With shaking hands I unpack the shells one by one on the counter. Thirty-two shells were stolen, nine have been recovered.

One of the periglyptas is back, the smallest *Harpa major* is back, as well as the *Trochus maculata*, the smallest *Conus figulinus* and the *Conus geographus*. Two tonnas and a helmet shell. And one of the two small nautiluses.

Constable Modisane makes soft, sympathetic noises: ". . . eh heh, eh heh," he says, when not engaged in conversation over his shoulder with one of the other constables.

The shells are dirty. They are covered with soil, and something greasy. I do not want to sniff them in front of the constable. What has happened to them? Have they been used for a ritual? A divination? Have they been gambled with, did they land in a fire? I gently stroke the surface of the small nautilus. It looks damaged. My eyes are tearful and I feel a lump forming in my throat.

"Are these your goods?" he asks.

I nod. "There are still twenty-three missing," I say.

"Sorry," says the constable, and clicks sympathetically with his tongue. He turns around and lifts a large brown envelope from a shelf behind him.

"These are the photographs," he says.

"I don't want to see them," I say.

He nimbly slides the photographs from the envelope anyway. In spite of my firm resolve, I cannot help but look. The photos are folio-sized and printed in black and white on glossy paper. There are a number of shots from different angles of Mr. Steinmeier hanging by his neck from a beam. Luckily the images are somewhat out of focus. It is nevertheless no pleasant sight. It is in fact a most shocking sight—it is horrible, I look at it with horror. There are a couple of close-ups of the dead man's face, probably taken in the morgue, for he is lying on his back. His eyes are swollen, his mouth half open. Mr. Steinmeier appears to be of mixed descent, but what does that have to do with anything these days anyway?

"Is this the man who came into my house?" I ask.

"We cannot say that with certainty," the constable says. "But we found the stolen goods with him."

"How long had he been dead when they found him?" I ask. It probably will not help to ask if the deceased was smelling of Boss aftershave.

The constable is becoming impatient. He replaces the photographs. I receive a form to fill in and sign.

At home I wash the shells carefully in soapy water. The sand and ash come off more easily than the greasiness. None of the shells are broken, but the surface of most of them are scratched, and one or two have small cracks in them. At first glance they appear unharmed, but for me they have been irreparably damaged. Violated.

•

I inform Sof about the recovered shells. The next day I phone Constable Modisane to find out where the deceased (the dead thief) is from; perhaps even to obtain his home address. But if the constable had been accommodating a day of two before, happy to supply information, he is now unwilling to do so. He must have been reprimanded; he was probably not supposed to have given any information in the first place.

"What am I to do?" I ask Sof.

"Bribe him," she says and gives a small cough.

(I remember Aunty Jossie, a friend of my mother's, asking a traffic policeman who had stopped her if he liked chocolate cake. As a child I appreciated her unconventional manner. She was less predictable than the other women I knew. My introduction to an irreverent female character? Gertjie would be sitting in the back of the car with a maid when she came to visit. Gertjie was her younger son; he was retarded. He was so pale his skin seemed to have a greenish hue.)

"What with?" I ask. "With chocolate cake?"

"Why not?"

"The days are gone when one could bribe servants of the law with home-made cakes," I say.

"Try biltong," Sof says.

"Which I will find where?"

"At Checkers. What is this information worth to you? How about two crisp hundred-rand notes?"

"And if he exposes my attempted bribery in front of everyone?"

"Then you say you want small change for parking."

"Small change for two hundred rand?"

"Why not? What do you want to do with the information?"

"I just want to know."

I decide to go and see Constable Modisane at the charge office. The first time he is out on patrol duty, the second time I find him behind the counter.

Where did the man who hanged himself come from, I enquire of him.

"I cannot disclose his identity," the constable says. He is wearing his cap today and he keeps his eyes averted, busying himself with paperwork.

"But you've already given me his name! You told me that his body was found in Ladybrand," I say. "You showed me the photographs! I didn't even want to see them!"

"I cannot give you more information," he says.

"Just tell me where the man came from," I say softly. "Was he from Ladybrand as well?"

"Why do you want to know?" he asks suspiciously. He is copying information from one book into another. The upper joints of his fingers are plump, as exuberantly rounded as his thighs.

"Because it will give me peace of mind," I say.

Constable Modisane glances fleetingly over his shoulder (anybody keeping an eye on us?) and without looking up says softly: "He came from Ladybrand. Same place where his body was found."

"Thank you," I say, and turn around.

The man comes from Ladybrand, I say to Sof the next day and I want to go and see where he lived. Sof is more than willing to go there with me.

•

I enjoy having tea with the museum staff. Their conversations interest me. I see it as an unexpected perk that Theo Verwey's office is located here (on account of his involvement with the Department of Regional

Languages, also housed in this building). An added benefit is that I would otherwise not have met Sof Benadé.

Freddie Ferreira is the curator of mammals. He is small and wiry, with straight, oily hair and small, lively dark-brown eyes. I take him to be no older than forty-five. He is an impatient and at times unpredictable man. It is hard to determine the content of his inner life, but about mammals he knows everything.

This morning he is in conversation with Hugo Hattingh, a palaeontologist. At first glance Hugo is an attractive man, but surly, not inclined to make contact of any kind. He appears to be in his mid-fifties, about the same age as Theo Verwey, possibly younger. Brilliant at his subject, Sof maintains, with a taste for child pornography. Boys. How does she know that? I ask. She shrugs: Whatever—heard it from Sailor or Vera, she says. What does she mean by whatever? I ask. Whether it's child pornography or paedophiliac tendencies, she says, his knowledge is extensive and always at hand, and, unlike most other people, he is mostly worth listening to.

This is the man who, according to Theo Verwey, can explain what life is, explain the phenomenon of life more comprehensively than any dictionary definition could. (A man who can account for life down to the matrix, the Ursludge, the primal slime.)

He and Freddie Ferreira are disagreeing this morning about the geological time frame in which bone evolved. Sof Benadé wants to know why bone originated and what its function is. Hugo Hattingh puts forward some hypotheses for the early functions of bone. Amongst other things it had to serve as protection against aquatic predators: water scorpions and nautiluslike cephalopods. (Simply hearing the word nautilus upsets me.)

Sailor enters the room. His name is Johannes Taljaard, but everyone calls him Sailor. Why that is so I do not know. He looks like Flash Gordon—like Sam Jones in the leading role of the film version. A comic-strip hero, with high cheekbones, a powerful jawline, blue eyes with blond, curly eyelashes, a broad chest, long legs, and slim hips. He is responsible for the exhibits of the museum. He is the curator of exhibits.

Freddie greets him with a stylised gesture of the hand; they seem to be good friends. Hugo glances fleetingly at him before continuing his exposition. He refers to the occurrence of endochondral bone in extinct stickleback sharks. Freddie explains that they are not real sharks, but resemble sharks only superficially. "Howzit?" he asks Sailor, without looking at him. He grinds out his cigarette butt under his heel.

"Is there no cake this morning?" Sailor asks.

"Why should there be any?" Freddie asks.

"What *is* bone?" Sof asks.

"Bone is a compound of inorganic calcium phosphate crystals, hydroxyapatite, and organic collagen fibre. A bone like the femur of a mammal has a minimal content of approximately sixty-seven percent. This provides rigidity and the collagen offers resistance to pressure," Hugo says.

Of this I take note. This too is valuable information.

"Isn't it someone's birthday today?" Sailor asks. "Isn't there something we can celebrate?"

"Why do you always want cake?" Mrs. Dudu wants to know.

Sailor has a wide smile and his teeth are surprisingly small, I note, for a man of his height, of his heroic proportions. Small, strikingly square and polished, like freshwater pearls.

"Mrs. Dudu also likes cake," he says, and stretches his arms contentedly above his head. He is wearing a water-blue silk shirt and Diesel jeans.

Mrs. Dudu laughs roguishly. Her hair is braided artfully. It reminds me of the braids of wool I made for myself as a child.

"Did the vertebrates originate in sea water or in fresh water?" Sof asks Hugo Hattingh.

If Freddie Ferreira seldom looks at the person he is talking to, Hugo does so even less. He has a heavy head—a stalwart lion's brow—with sharply chiselled diagonal planes. He is not tall, but he makes a solid impression: powerful in the shoulders. There is something stiff, something rigid to his movements. His greying beard is neatly trimmed, his hair darker, boyishly short.

Only one of my father's four brothers had black hair. I remember its texture—thick, hard hair, like a brush. His voice had a strange, raspy sound. He liked young boys. That my mother told me much later. He stayed in a rondavel in the Lowveld and he collected things: aloes, stones, maybe even shells. As a child this fascinated me, as did his manner of speaking (slightly scratchy) and his sense of humour (dry, cynical, somewhat whimsical). He and my mother got on well, but when he visited with a friend, she would strip off the sheets and wash them as soon as they had left. I am suddenly reminded of him this morning.

Hugo Hattingh starts explaining that the chief proponents of the freshwater theory are Alfred Romer, a palaeontologist, and Homer Smith, a renal physiologist, but Freddie interrupts him by saying that these arguments are so dated that they are hardly relevant any more. Hugo Hattingh nonetheless continues, unperturbed, to expound Romer and Smith's arguments, whereupon Freddie, who is still sitting with his elbows on his knees and looking at his feet, cigarette in hand, remarks that it seems as if Hugo Hattingh is convinced by Romer and Smith's arguments. Hugo Hattingh still takes no notice of Freddie's objections and concludes that the evidence favouring a marine origin is more convincing than Romer and Smith's freshwater theories (the theory that Freddie had been insisting on all the while). As conclusive evidence, Hugo cites the fossil record, which is now much more complete, and which indicates that all known fossils from the Cambrian and the Ordovician have a marine origin.

"Now you understand, don't you?" Freddie says half mockingly to Sof.

"Yes, thank you," Sof says. "I see now that we crawled with great effort from the sea onto dry land."

"By the sweat of our brows," Sailor remarks. I am surprised; I did not expect biblical references from him. I had mistakenly assumed that for him everything centred around the exterior—the body beautiful and cheap thrills.

"What makes you think it was so hard?" Freddie asks.

"The Bible," says Sof, and gives a little cough.

Hugo is not listening any more. It is difficult for me to imagine the nature of his thoughts and preoccupations. I would have liked to be able to place myself in his position through some manoeuvre of the imagination. I cannot. I envy him his knowledge. To see the drama of evolution played out before you like a film—to see it unfold like a flower before your eyes—that I find enviable. To know how bone developed over millions of years. To be intimately acquainted with the origin and inception of life. Valuable knowledge! That is not enough for him. He longs for more, for something else. The psyche has different needs. Knowledge is not enough. This man has a taste for child pornography, he has paedophiliac longings, his desire is after young boys, if it is true what Sof alleges.

It is not the first time that this knowledge interests me, but for the first time it interests me so emphatically. I sit up straight, in a manner of speaking, and prick up my ears. Loose facts, shreds of knowledge (unsystematically acquired), and an old interest come to life again. I have an urgent desire to learn about the circumstances that were needed for life to originate on earth. Hopefully I will also gain a better understanding of the nature of man—a mammal that developed how many millions of years ago. Seeing humans in this context must shed light on how consciousness developed and functions, and thus on the existential dilemma of an animal with a developed intelligence and an awareness of its own mortality. A consciousness which, if I understand correctly, developed around an anus at one end, a mouth at the other, and a spine connecting the two.

·

The nine retrieved shells I have packed away for the time being. I still cannot look at them without being reminded of the loss of the others. What happened to the missing twenty-three? Why were they separated from the others? Are they still lying somewhere in the room where the dead man was found? Of what value could they be to anyone? Have they been sold somewhere for a pittance, traded for tobacco, for bread, for liquor, for a gun, or do they perhaps grace someone's display cabinet? Did the person who took them want them for himself or as a gift for his wife, for his mistress, for his mother, perhaps? How did the thief—or thieves—know about the shells? Did they break in with the purpose of stealing the shells, or did they come upon them by chance and decide that they were more useful loot than the other apparently more valuable possessions in the house? All equally improbable. Why did he—did they—select the shells with a discerning eye and then defecate on the carpet? Shit on the carpet, to be precise. What conclusion must I draw from this, what hidden warning lurks here? What message? Why did the man, poor Patrick Steinmeier, hang himself? Is he the culprit, who took his own life out of bitter remorse, or are those who left with the rest of the shells the guilty ones?

Over lunch I ask Sof what she thinks. Maybe the thief or thieves were looking for something specific, she says. Maybe they confused your place with someone else's.

"And then the shells caught the eye of one, while the other was shitting on the carpet," I say. "For good measure."

I am uneasy. The man with whose corpse the nine shells were found (Dr. Jekyll?) may be safely laid out in the morgue. (Hard to judge on the basis of a few black-and-white photographs, but the poor deceased hardly had the appearance of a thug.) But what if Mr. Hyde is still roaming free? Or Mr. Hyde and his henchmen—his unscrupulous gang of house defilers. As soon as I get home, I phone Constable Modisane again to find out if there could possibly have been more than one burglar.

"Because you did not report anything else missing and your stolen goods have already been retrieved, we have closed the docket," he says.

"They have not all been retrieved," I say. "There are still twenty-three missing."

"Eh heh," Constable Modisane says, the last syllable ending low and melodiously. In the background I hear a terrific noise.

But I do not want to say goodbye! I do not want to let him go! I want to talk about the hanged man, I want to know exactly where they found the shells, I want to know all there is to know.

"Constable Modisane," I say hesitantly, "I'm worried . . ."

The constable speaks in Zulu to someone over his shoulder.

"What is it that you're worried about?" he asks patiently.

"I'm worried," I say, "because I don't know what happened precisely. Who came into my house. Who took the shells. What he was looking for. If there were more than one person. I would like to know all these things."

"Yee-hes," says the constable, not unsympathetically.

"I would like to know everything that happened," I say.

"O-kay," the constable concedes in his soothing bass.

"Are you sure you have no more information? Were there no other burglaries in the neighbourhood at the same time?"

"No," the constable says. "Nothing else." Again he calls out to someone in Zulu, and laughs heartily.

"Well, then," I say. "Thank you."

"O-kay," he says jovially.

•

My heart remains heavy and it is not only about the loss and defilement of the shells. Ever since the burglary I have been finding it hard to fall asleep at night. I sleep with the bedside light on, for the moment I switch off the light the darkness comes to rest on my chest like a dead weight.

When I was five years old, the devil appeared to me in a dream one night. We had just moved into our new house, and the room I was sleeping in was painted blue. My bed stood against the wall, facing the window. The devil in his full demonic glory materialised full-length at the foot of my bed. I was panic-stricken and screamed so loudly that my father stubbed his toe badly against some obstacle in his haste to come to my aid. As a child I never doubted that I had indeed been visited by the devil.

The last time I gave credibility to the devil was when I was nine years old. One day I earnestly remarked to my father that from that day on I would never listen to the devil again. We were in the dining room, standing next to the tea trolley that my mother had inherited from her mother. This remark caused my father genuine mirth. He laughed silently. He laughed as he laughed only at someone else's expense. In this case it was at my expense. I remember his face in profile as he laughed. When I laugh the corners of my mouth draw up in the same way. I was devastated. From that day on I banned the devil from my frame of reference and wrote off my father as a confidant.

After forty-odd years, one evening I suddenly have a strong aware-ness of the devil again. I find it surprising. He is neither evil nor threat-ening, but a melancholy character, who has come to the end of his road. Together this devil and I stand on the brink of an abyss. We have equally little say over our allotted fate. Moreover, in my current state I find his presence strangely reassuring.

CHAPTER FOUR

I want to go to Ladybrand, I tell Sof, I want to pursue that link with my stolen shells. She asks if I would mind her coming along. I say: With pleasure! By all means! We decide to go over the weekend.

On Friday morning Theo and I listen to Cimarosa. Andrew Riddle is the conductor, Theo says. At first I suspect he is pulling my leg. Riddle, as in riddle? I ask. Yes, as in riddle. Riddle left the London Symphony Orchestra to join the Berlin Philharmonic Orchestra, Theo says, and succeeded in getting it back on its feet again.

The music hardly speaks to me this morning. I bend over my cards. Where should I begin? I have urgent matters on my mind, urgent issues for which I cannot find suitable words.

For a while we work side by side in silence.

I am busy with the word *dool* (roam, rove or wander). *Doolgang* (labyrinth). The cavities in the inner ear, hollowed out of the substance of the bone, are called the osseous labyrinth. The figurative meaning of *doolgang* is an errant way: the labyrinths, warrens or networks of the criminal's life. Error is from the Latin *errare*—to stray. *Ronddool* (rove, or roam about). Spiritually or morally on the wrong track; to deviate from the way of virtue.

"What do you understand by the virtuous way?" I ask Theo.

He raises his eyebrows enquiringly.

"Virtue is the tendency to what is good, and the virtuous way is a metaphor for a life in which the good is pursued," he says. He has clear eyes. He is impeccably polite. His gaze rests on me evenly—without curiosity or demand. That does not prevent me from watching him closely, from pointedly focusing my attention on him. Do I wish to provoke him? Besides his interest in words, he has a great appreciation for music. I have no objection to listening to his music with him. Here, too, I can learn from him.

"Labyrinth, or maze, I find a beautiful word," I say. "It speaks to my imagination. It is poetic, it has resonance, I can visualise it. But I have difficulty with the virtuous way—as a concept it means little to me."

He nods politely. "As a concept and as an expression it has probably long since lost its validity," he says. He gazes reflectively in front of him for a while, before returning to his work.

"How did virtue become *deug*?" I ask.

"Virtue comes via Latin to the Old French *vertueux*; *deug* is of Germanic origin," he says (without looking up from his work), "from the Dutch *deugen*, from the Middle Dutch *dogen*." He is also a discerning man, I have noticed. He likes beautiful things. I have seen him unobtrusively lift a cup to look at the name underneath, and turn a teaspoon to check the hallmark. I noticed that the day Sailor treated us to cake at teatime. Sailor had brought along his own tea service, teaspoons, and cake forks. No half measures for Sailor—only the best for him, Sof remarked to me.

Doolhof, I read. Maze. Where one cannot find one's way; place where one can easily get lost; bewildering network; labyrinth. The figurative meaning of the word is a complex situation or set of circumstances, in which it is difficult to follow the right way; a situation that makes no sense. Anatomically the word refers to the passages and spaces in the temporal bone of the skull, where the senses of balance and hearing are situated.

Deug and *deugdelik*. Virtue and virtuous. I see Theo Verwey as a virtuous man—a considerate husband and a loving father. He is reserved. He keeps things to himself. What he holds back, I do not know. I have my own assumptions about his inner life. I imagine it to be as ordered, as filed as his extended card system. I would be very surprised if I were to learn that he is given to excess. This is a man in whom the will—or the virtuous impulse—keeps the appetite, the pleasure-seeking instance, thoroughly under control. This is how I read him. I may be wrong.

•

On Friday afternoon Sof and I leave for Ladybrand. We travel through a landscape of uncommon beauty, but I am distracted and do not take in much. From the corner of my eye I see the wintry poplars, the muted, ochre fields, and the misty dales flash by; I see the majestic cliffs of the mountains in shades of deep, pale and pink ochre, but the beauty leaves no lasting impression. I am nervous, for I have a plan and it may be a foolish one. I have the address of the only Steinmeiers in town, and I intend paying these people a visit tomorrow. I have no idea what I will encounter there.

We stay in a guesthouse in town—sumptuously fandangled, but fundamentally unattractive. That evening we eat in an Italian restaurant-pizzeria, decorated like a Roman villa—or the owner's idea of such a villa. There are painted fountains, painted statues, and a painted curtain, drawn to the side with a flourish to reveal the vista of an Italian garden with cypresses.

At the table next to us six Chinese men are devouring their food in complete silence. Sof clears her throat, leans forward and says softly: "I wouldn't be surprised if they are the Chinese Mafia, said to be very active here in Lesotho. They may have something to do with the disappearance of your shells." Thanks, I say, I will bear that in mind. I eye the men covertly with some displeasure. When they have finished eating, the staff appear with a cake topped with burning candles. Everyone congratulates Charlie, one of the men; the cake is cut and devoured as wordlessly as the main meal. Afterwards the remains are sent back to the kitchen.

What do I really know about Sofia Benadé, I wonder during the meal, except that she grew up in a pastorie, that she is married, has twin sons, and that she has an annual subscription to *Die Kerkblad*. We are still sounding each other out, looking for common ground. But tonight I am off balance. My attention is elsewhere. I am not trying particularly

43

hard to establish an understanding. This does not seem to be a problem. Sof strikes me as someone who would not oppose the flow of events too much. She drinks her wine and smokes her cigarettes and observes the people.

After our meal Sof says that we are now going to explore the night-life of Ladybrand. I think: If she has a clear idea of what we should do, I am more than willing to go along. It is cold outside. A biting cold, and the night sky is high and wide. There are more stars here than in the city. We walk up and down a few streets in the nearly deserted town, until we get to a place called the Red Lantern, across the street from the Spar. In front of the window hangs a brown bead curtain.

"This looks like a nice enough little place," Sof remarks.

Inside there are a couple of tables and a fancy cane bar counter as well as cane bar stools. The place is still half full.

"By day the local branch of the Women's Agricultural Association meets here," Sof says.

It is pleasantly warm inside. A waitress with prodigiously rounded thighs in tightly fitting pants takes our order. I look around. At one of the tables a man and a woman are seated; at the rest of the tables there are mostly young people.

"They all work in the local bank," Sof says.

A man and a woman enter. A respectable couple, sound of character and upbringing. The woman has short, dark hair which she touches self-consciously. With his hand against her back, the man guides her lightly to their table in the corner.

"The lawyer with the Latin teacher's wife," Sof says. "They met at the tennis club."

"Where's her husband tonight?" I ask.

"He's marking essays," Sof says. "They have two sons. The elder is quiet and serious and the younger has pale green eyes and too much energy."

The waitress with the rounded thighs asks: "You girls still okay?"

"We're waxed, sista," says Sof, and gives a little cough.

"And the lawyer's wife?" I ask.

"She has a headache tonight, but that's only an excuse, because she hopes the magistrate will come by in her husband's absence. They have two little daughters, two thin, pale little girls."

The place fills up gradually. The music starts. Donna Summer sings "Hot Stuff." Sof mouths the words silently: "I need some hot stuff baby tonight." Her expression betrays nothing, only her mouth forms the words. She does this with the next song as well. "I will survive," she sings wordlessly, making small, accompanying movements with her shoulders. A cool customer, Sof, even if she calls herself a deluded doos. We order more wine.

A slight young man with close-cropped, curly hair, particularly dark eyebrows, intense eyes, and an evasive glance enters. He looks uneasy. He sits down at a table in the corner and orders a beer. He has a dark-blue sports bag with him. He seems to be waiting for someone, as he keeps checking his watch. He takes a small notebook out of the bag and writes something in it. He puts the notebook away and checks his watch again. He glances around him restlessly for a while. Then he takes out the notebook again and writes something in it for the second time.

"Hasn't yet learnt to hold a pen properly," Sof says.

I observe the young man surreptitiously. There is something compelling about his face, especially his eyes—ever so slightly squint. It is a face that can be read as either underhand or mischievous. His beard seems sparse, not yet firmly established: dark but downy. An attractive young man, if one could trust him; if his manner were not so agitated.

"He clearly suffers from attention deficit syndrome," Sof, who has also been watching him, remarks. "A course of Ritalin will do no harm."

"Or he suffers from a bad conscience," I say.

"Es war spätabends," Sof quotes, "als K. ankam. Das Dorf lag in tiefen Schnee. Vom Schlossberg war nichts zu sehen, Nebel und Finsternis umgaben ihn, auch nicht der schwächste lichtschein deutete das grosse Schloss an."

"Do you think Kafka had such a lightweight, skittish young man in mind?"

"Probably not," Sof replies, "but this is the African version of K."

"Wet behind the ears and of mixed descent?"

"Why not?"

"Actually the story should have ended there for poor K.," I say.

"At fifteen I loved Kafka," Sof says. "I read his biography and deeply mourned his death."

"That I can well understand," I say.

The Latin teacher's wife gets up to go to the toilet, behind a second bead curtain. The lawyer makes a call on his cellphone.

"I remember friends of my parents' when I was a child," I say. "They lived in the same small town as my grandmother. The man was an Afrikaans teacher at the local school. He took remarkable photographs. We sometimes went on holiday with them to the South Coast. They were friends with the Dippenaars; the two couples played tennis together. On holiday I played with Engela and Moetsie, the two Dippenaar girls. Later it turned out that for years Mr. Truter, the teacher, had been having an affair with Mrs. Dippenaar. I don't remember Mrs. Dippenaar as a particularly attractive woman. Her legs were hairy and too wide apart. Mrs. Truter, Santie, on the other hand, was lovely. Warm and easygoing. What drove her husband into the arms of plain Mrs. Dippenaar? I still can't make sense of it. Santie Truter later had a stroke and shot herself. I remember her in her bathing costume on the beach, looking over her shoulder at the photographer. Her husband. He had moles all over his body. What exactly made him sexually attractive to his wife as well as to Mrs. Dippenaar is not clear to me."

"The ways of people are unfathomable," Sof says. "My father always abhorred the hypocritical piety of his congregation. They were constantly indulging in all kinds of bizarre infidelities. Then he would be expected to provide pastoral counselling to them as well as the aggrieved husbands and wives."

"Whereupon the miscreants would have the best of resolutions until the next time around when once again they could not keep their hands off one another," I say.

Not much later the young man with the furtive glance gets up, pays, and leaves his beer half finished.

"Now his adventure starts," Sof says, as he exits through the door, like K., into the cold night.

•

I sleep restlessly. The bright passage light worries me all night. I have a dream about Felix du Randt. We are together in a garden. We have a row. There are tears, but the next morning I cannot recall the exact circumstances of the dream.

Sof and I eat breakfast in the dining room together with seven men who are attending a course for railway officials. The guesthouse decor is as kitsch inside as outside. There are artificial flowers on the tables. We are served scrambled eggs, bacon, and a sausage as pink as a dog's pizzle. At the table next to ours there are four men, their skin colour varying from Van Dyck brown to a deep bluish brown. They speak Afrikaans with a South-Sotho accent. At another table one of the three men has earrings, a reddish moustache, and hair cut in a mullet. He wears off-white trousers, a white belt, white socks, and white shoes. The smallest of the three has watery eyes. "He had ringworm as a child, and his brothers and sisters bullied him," Sof remarks dryly. She takes two Panados, for she has a headache this morning. Smoked and drank a bit too much last night, she says, and laughs her small, exculpatory laugh.

Two women serve us. One is tall, with a small head and a broad behind. She is clad in shades of beige—from her tight-fitting stretch pants to the colour of her lipstick and powder base; the two spots on her cheekbones are a warm blush-pink beige. She has a small, resolute mouth and her hair, fringe flat on the forehead, is teased up behind her head in a seething, russet-red nest. The other woman is petite, a shy beauty, her skin of a yellowish hue, her features resembling the comely girl-women of hunter-gatherers.

I am nervous. Sof and I discuss our plan. It is a shot in the dark, but we are going to risk it.

"Maybe it's crazy," I say anxiously.

"Relax," Sof says. "What could actually go wrong?'

"What if we end up in a den of thieves?"

"We first check out the scene before we move in," Sof says, and gives a little cough.

The men are conversing with gusto. Every now and then they call out remarks to one another, from table to table—remarks like echoes that bounce lightly from cliff to cliff, with a densely forested valley between them. Against the wall hangs a copy of a Thomas Baines painting in a large, gilded frame. It is a depiction of Bloemfontein from Naval Hill. In the foreground a rocky hill offers a view of a sprawling plain and of a small town far in the background. Oh, says Sof, the charms of the metropolis. Sof, I say, I trust that you will support me today.

•

There is only one Steinmeier in Ladybrand. I looked up the address in the telephone directory. The house is on the boundary between the white and coloured neighbourhoods, a distinction that clearly still applies in this town. It is an old house, but well kept, with a wide red cement stoep and pillars supporting its roof. The house—like most of the houses in the more affluent white neighbourhood—is of an ochre-coloured sandstone. The front garden is small, but neat, the little lawn is withered, and to the side of the house are a number of bare fruit trees. On the stoep there are potted plants in tins.

I knock.

"Fu-uck," Sof says softly behind me.

An elderly woman opens the door. I greet her with enthusiasm, but my heart is thumping fiercely. She regards me somewhat suspiciously. Would this be Patrick's mother?

Behind her a young woman appears with a baby on her hip. She reminds me of Hazel, a young girl who worked for my parents more than twenty years ago.

Sof and I have decided to use false names. (That we have to deceive these people like this!) I introduce myself as Dolly Haze, and Sof introduces herself as Anna Livia. (Anna Livia Plurabelle. O / tell me all about / Anna Livia! I want to hear all about Anna Livia.)

I ask the older woman if she is Mrs. Steinmeier and she says yes, she is Rosie Steinmeier and this is her daughter Alverine, and she gestures at the girl behind her, who transfers the baby to her other hip with the same movement Hazel would have used twenty years ago. I say that we are from the Durban Bible Society, that we were in the vicinity and that we have come to deliver the parcel that Patrick Steinmeier ordered from us. (At Cum Books in the large shopping mall near us I bought a Bible and two spiritual booklets. I had a great deal of difficulty with the choice of titles, for what would be suitable titles for the dead?) The parcel I made up neatly and pasted a label on it with Patrick's name.

The two women exchange a quick, furtive glance.

"Patrick Steinmeier doesn't live here any more," Rosie Steinmeier says.

"That's strange, for this is the address that he gave us," I say.

Again the two women exchange a quick glance.

"Patrick died not long ago," Alverine says, and her intonation is so much like that of Hazel twenty years ago that I experience a moment of total confusion. (Could it be her, unchanged, after twenty years?)

I say that I am truly sorry to hear that and respectfully ask the older woman if she is the mother of the deceased. Rosie Steinmeier brings her apron to her eyes and nods. I hear other voices in the house, behind them.

"Then I must let you have the parcel," I say hesitantly, "with the compliments of the Bible Society."

Suddenly I do not know how to proceed (that we have to deceive these poor innocent people like this), but over my shoulder Sof asks if we may come in for a moment.

The two women look at each other. The older woman moves aside and we enter. We step into a cool, dusky passage. My heart is beating violently. I have no idea what I can expect to encounter here. Four of my shells on the display cabinet? I may be wide of the mark; Patrick Steinmeier had probably long since stopped having any contact with his family. That we have to enter the house under such false pretences!

The lounge leads off the passage. The room is furnished with heavy ball-and-claw furniture, a lounge suite with a subdued floral pattern and a plethora of ornaments and little crocheted coasters and armchair protectors. The curtains are drawn. On the sofa and one of the easy chairs there are two large stuffed toy tigers. In the darkened room I back away—taking one of them to be a dog or something. Fright of my life. Heart thumping in my chest. Against the walls are prints, some in ornate frames. In one corner of the room is a shiny dark-wood display cabinet. I do not want to look around too much, but I can hardly help myself. Trying not to stare too openly, I take in every detail of the room with a burning gaze.

I sit on the edge of the sofa, next to the large stuffed tiger that keeps a fixed and glassy eye on me. Sof sits opposite me, prim and erect, her legs crossed at the ankles, under a large print of a landscape in glowing synthetic colours, framed in a gilded, excessively elaborate frame.

Rosie Steinmeier offers us a cup of tea and tells Alverine to go and make it.

I am completely flustered and can think of nothing to say except to compliment Mrs. Steinmeier on the appearance of the room, although my enthusiasm sounds most insincere to me. At this point, however, Sof's pastorie persona comes to our rescue. She leans forward in her chair, clears her throat and asks firmly, though sympathetically, like one accustomed to doing the rounds daily, if Patrick died after a long illness.

"No, mevrou," his mother says, "the circumstances of his death are *very* sad."

"How come?" Sof wants to know.

"He took his life by his own hand, mevrou," the woman says.

Sof says that she is bitterly sorry to hear that; it must surely be a great shock and a time of trial and tribulation for the whole family.

"Just so, mevrou," says Rosie Steinmeier.

At this point Hazel-Alverine enters the room with a tray, and behind her, without a doubt, the young man that we saw in the Red Lantern last night. Herr K., on his way to the castle. The unsettled young man with the evasive glance.

Sof and I exchange a brief, though urgent glance. The mother introduces him as Jaykie, her youngest child. "And this is now Miss Dolly and Miss Anna from the Bible Society in Durban," she says. "What is the surname again, Miss Anna?" she asks Sof.

"Livia," Sof says, and clears her throat slightly.

"Unusual, mevrou," Alverine says (with Hazel's intonation exactly—the first syllable of "mevrou" considerably higher than the last).

Jaykie's hand is cool and damp and his handshake not very firm. For a brief moment our eyes meet. Unusual eyes. Dark-brown, cunning. Darker, almost blackish-brown around the outer rim of the iris and a somewhat warmer brown towards the centre. A slight, very slight squint. Curly eyelashes; dark, lush eyebrows. And he smells of aftershave. At half past ten in the morning in Ladybrand this young man smells of aftershave. Could it be he? If he smells of aftershave this morning, and the shells were found at the feet of his brother's corpse—could it be that he was involved in the theft too? Does he possess information about the burglary? Does he know about my stolen shells? Could it be this young man who either took my shells, or shat on my carpet? That was no innocent gesture. It was a deed of aggression and intimidation. Does he know who I am, does he see through our bluff?

"Yes, mevrou," the mother, Aunty Rosie, says. "It's a terrible thing that came over us."

Alverine pours the tea. "Hold the tray for Miss Anna and Miss Dolly!" she tells Jaykie. With exaggerated politeness he first draws two small ball-and-claw coffee tables closer for Sof and me. Then he holds the tray with tea, his bearing submissive. Without sniffing too obviously, I lean forward slightly to catch his smell again. But the moment is too charged—I cannot identify it. When I take the cup from the tray, I spill tea in my saucer. This man may have been in my house. Worse still, this man may know who I am. He has long since seen through our false pretences.

"Do you have any idea, Mrs. Steinmeier," Sof asks in her pastorie voice, "what exactly happened?"

I bite into a Lemon Cream. Jaykie sits with his eyes cast down, his hands pressed together between his knees, his whole demeanour betraying barely suppressed restlessness. I take a sip of the weak, milky tea.

"He was in trouble, mevrou," Hazel-Alverine says, "we think he got mixed up with gangs."

"Did he work in the city?" Sof asks.

"Yes, mevrou," says the Hazel-sister, "then he mostly came home weekends. But the past few months not so often any more."

The landscape in the gilded frame behind Sof depicts a peaceful scene with a stream, lush banks, and shady trees in synthetic sea-greens and lurid, autumnal oranges. My eyes roam to the display cabinet with photographs in the far corner.

Sof clicks sympathetically with her tongue. She takes a delicate sip of tea. I dare not catch her eye.

"Show Miss Anna and Miss Dolly Patrick's photo," his mother tells Jaykie.

Jaykie jumps up, fetches a framed photograph from the cabinet, and hands it to me. Again our eyes meet for a moment. His eyes are roguish and cunning in equal measure. Cunning priest's eyes. I have seen eyes like those in religious portraits. The eyes of saints or confidence tricksters. Swindlers. Or epileptics.

I study the photograph.

"It's a picture of Patrick on his wedding day," she says.

Head-and-shoulder portrait of the bride and groom. The bride has a stiff, obstreperous head of hair, one lock artfully brushed over her left eye. Her short veil, blooming behind her, is covered in confetti. Patrick wears a pale, sand-coloured suit. His hair is short and curly, like Jaykie's, but he has a long nose, much longer than that of his brother. His eyebrows run to his temples in a strong downward arch. I strain to see a resemblance between this man and the photographs of the corpse that Constable Modisane showed me. I think I see something, a vague similarity. The corpse was also that of a tall, lean man, but I can't remember the nose. The photographs were not particularly flattering.

That I have to deceive these trusting people like this! The man in the wedding photograph (which I am still holding in my hand) has nothing to do with the man who took my shells! Or with the photographs of the hanging corpse that Constable Modisane showed me. The constable was mistaken! There is a huge misunderstanding somewhere. This will not be the first time that the police have been misguided. What are we doing here, on a Saturday morning in Ladybrand, in Mrs. Rosie Steinmeier's house? If anyone here has anything to do with the disappearance of the shells, it is probably Jaykie, with his aroma of aftershave and his seductive fraudster's eyes.

These thoughts go through my head as I sit on the sofa alongside the stuffed tiger with the glassy stare. While Sof keeps the conversation afloat, Mrs. Steinmeier—the bereaved mother—wipes her eyes with her apron every now and then, and Alverine rocks the baby on her hip in the exact way Hazel would have done twenty years ago, in my parents' house.

"He was a good man, mevrou," the mother says. "He would not have harmed anyone. He was a Christian too. But he was led into sin! He was led into sin by crooks and skelms!"

"Skollies!" his sister says. "They *made* him do it!"

"Do what?" I ask. I am distracted, I am flustered. I am not certain of my case any more. I am overwhelmed by the resemblance between Alverine and Hazel. I am flooded with strange associations and memories. I have a sense of unreality.

There is a long moment of silence.

"They made him commit crimes, Miss Dolly," Alverine says softly. "We think he got mixed up with gangs in the city."

"It's in the city where he was led into sin," his mother says. "That's where he lost the way."

"Did he have children?" Sof asks. (My support and succour in this bewildering hour. How grateful I am that she accompanied me here.)

"Yes, mevrou, he has children, but his wife left with them long ago," his mother says.

"We saw the photos," the sister says softly. "The police came and showed us the photos. As they found him there."

"Do you know for sure that it was him?" I ask.

"It was *him*, Miss Dolly," Alverine says, and the mother wipes her eyes again.

"Up to this day we don't know what happened, mevrou," the mother says. "The police just came and told us."

"And showed us the photos," the sister says. "We don't understand it, Miss Dolly! One day he's still here, the next day the police bring us the pictures!"

I clear my throat. "Did it happen here," I ask, gesturing vaguely with my hand, "here in the vicinity?"

"Yes, mevrou," the Hazel-sister says. "There just before the turnoff to the highway, there mevrou will see a little brick building, that's where they found him."

Jaykie sits with his hands between his knees, moving restlessly on his seat. It looks as if he might jump up at any moment. I ask if I may use the toilet. The bathroom is a large room with an old-fashioned bath and an old-fashioned medicine cabinet against the wall. I glance into it rapidly. No sign of Boss aftershave. Nor of any shell. I sit down on the rim of the bath for a brief while. The photographs that Constable Modisane showed me, the recovered shells returned to me, the rest of the shells, the crime, my complex feelings of loss—all those have nothing to do with these people this morning in this house in Ladybrand. I am entirely on the wrong track. And that I have to lie to these unsuspecting people like this in the process! Except Jaykie. Him I don't trust. If there is a link, it has to be this young man. The chances are good that he has some knowledge of what happened to my shells.

When I return, I ask if I may look around the room. There are more framed photographs on the display cabinet, as well as a number of plates decorated with painted pink flowers, a clock hand-mounted on a sawn-off section of tree trunk, two glasses with artfully folded blue serviettes, copper coasters, and two identical glass fishes supported by glass waves. No sign of a shell.

As we get up to go, I ask Jaykie if he also works in the city. Before he can answer, his mother exclaims: "Jaykie is the artist in the family, mevrou! Jaykie, go fetch your artworks, show the mevrou!"

Jaykie returns with a small art folder. Dutifully he presents his works of art. They are mostly pencil drawings, mostly of women, both nude and clothed. Jaykie is regrettably not very skilful with the pencil, and why does it not amaze me? Does he not find it difficult to sit still for any length of time, and did Sof not remark on his ineptitude even at handling the pen the previous evening? The drawings are decidedly sugary in theme and touchingly clumsy in execution—like that of a much younger person. In one of them a girl turns her eyes dramatically towards the heavens—Saint Teresa of Avila with a Barbie hairstyle. Sof and I make appreciative noises, but dare not look at each other.

"Do you study art somewhere?" Sof asks.

"No, mevrou," Alverine says proudly. "He taught himself. He's saving his money to go and study at the tech in the city next year."

After this we take our leave. We are seen off at the door with much flourish. We are thanked from the heart for our visit and for the parcel. We are thanked for our trouble and our sympathy.

In the car I ask Sof: "Where on earth do they get those stuffed tigers?"

"You get one free when you buy a Sealy Posturepedic," she says.

•

I tell Sof that I do not want to stay in this town any longer. I want to go home immediately. This place makes my skin crawl, I say. I want to go home and reflect on everything that has happened. "So much for Herr K. on his way to the castle," I say. "It's not out of the question that that sanctimonious youth either took my shells or shat on my carpet. Although," I say, "I have my serious doubts about the latter. There is something disarming about him after all, and he doesn't seem quite the type to defecate on a stranger's carpet. But he's hiding something. Of that I'm sure. It would not surprise me at all if he knows something about the shells."

I tell Sof that she will have to distract me. I will drive, it will do me good to keep my eye on the road, but she must talk. The whole fucking episode, I say, has unsettled me and made me even more on edge.

Before taking the turnoff to the national highway we come across the small brick building, resembling a small electrical substation, where Alverine said that Patrick Steinmeier had hanged himself. Presumably it is there that the bag of shells was found. (I had assumed all along that the bag was found at his feet.) I want to stop and look inside, but there are no windows, and the place is closed off from the road by a sturdy wire fence. I nevertheless insist on getting out and taking a couple of photographs.

Speak, I say to Sof, and don't stop before we are in Durban.

•

"When the war breaks out in 1914," Sof says, "James Joyce and his family move from Trieste to Zürich. Had he stayed on in Trieste, he would have been in danger of being interned. During the seven years he spends there writing *Ulysses* he has fits, ulcers, and countless eye problems—there is a daily build-up of fluids in his eyes, his eyesight deteriorates by the day. In the evenings he writes in a room with a suitcase on his lap. He works ten hours a day. After each episode he breaks down and Nora nurses him back to health. He writes to everyone he knows to send him information about Dublin. His gargantuan imagination brings a thousand and one disparate things together. Songs, maps, sailors' jokes, idioms, and phrases. He asks his Aunt Josephine to write things down on scraps of paper. He is on the lookout for anything, for there is nothing that he cannot use. His head is like a factory. Imagine everything that is going on in there!"

But I interrupt her.

"Who would have done it?" I say. "Am I totally deluded here? Do the Steinmeiers perhaps have nothing to do with this? Neither of the two brothers—not the poor dead one nor Jaykie. Judging by his drawings he doesn't have a particularly sensitive eye, and I'm not sure that he has it in him to produce a turd like that."

"Human nature, like the human digestive system, is unfathomable."

"Unfathomable?"

"Well. Unpredictable," Sof says, and gives a little cough.

"Of one thing I'm sure," I say. "The same person couldn't have committed both deeds. I can't see how anybody with such a fine eye for beauty could commit such a coarse and violent act."

"It's not impossible," says Sof, and coughs dryly.

"It's not impossible, but it's highly improbable!" I exclaim. "No, actually it is impossible. It is out of the question. I cannot reconcile it with my conception of the world."

"It won't be the first brute with a refined eye," says Sof. "Take the Marquis de Sade as an example."

"Of what?"

"Of someone with a refined literary sensibility who wouldn't have hesitated to shit on someone else's carpet."

"He did not shit on carpets as far as I know."

"Whatever," says Sof. She keeps her eye on the road. We are taking turns to drive.

"I speak under correction," I say, "but no one in De Sade shits on carpets. They defecate on one another."

"The male characters probably defecate on the female characters," Sof says. "Although I cannot say with any certainty. I haven't read De Sade in a long while. Probably not since high school."

"In the pastorie?"

"Wherever. Maybe not in the pastorie, maybe at university."

"But Jaykie knows something about the matter," I say, "because he couldn't look me in the eye, and the shells were found with his brother."

"So?" Sof says.

"And he smelled of aftershave this morning. You must have noticed it too."

"That doesn't prove anything," Sof says. "You can't assume that it's the same man who was in your house just because he smells of aftershave."

"At ten o'clock in the morning in Ladybrand? Who uses aftershave at ten o' clock on a Saturday morning in Ladybrand?"

"Jaykie Steinmeier," Sof says, "because he's an artist."

"Sof," I say, "don't taunt me."

But it is right here, I suddenly know, that our friendship is sealed.

•

Back home, I am deeply disturbed. My thoughts move restlessly from one thing to the next. I had better not entertain the thought that the youth with the seductive squint might have shat on my carpet (improbable), or even worse, that he wilfully deceived me, and that he is hiding the rest of the shells somewhere, or knows where they are being hidden (more probable). In my mind's eye I see flashes of the beautiful landscape through which Sof and I travelled. The sister of the hanged man—the reappearance of Hazel after twenty years—has deeply touched me. And what has become of *her*, that lively young woman? I remember her with my child on her hip, how she would stand listening, silent, as if waiting for an answer. I remember Marthinus Maritz's brutal sidelong glance. How do I remember my mother, and my father, and Joets? What residue of them remains in me? I ceded them to death with great sorrow: my mother even more than my father. On the way back Sof kept telling me about Joyce. She said that Joyce's mother always returns in his fiction to persecute him. "Thou hast suckled me with a bitter milk," Joyce said of her. I listened with divided attention and gazed with unseeing eyes at the lovely wintry valleys and dales that Sof pointed out to me.

I cannot sleep. I phone Frans de Waard, the man, my companion, with whom I have had a relationship for the past seven years (sexual in nature and intention). He keeps late hours.

"Do you have any idea," I ask him, "if characters defecate on each other in De Sade?"

"Yes. It does occur at some or other stage."

"What exactly happens—who defecates on whom?" I ask.

"I can't remember. I read it too long ago."

"You don't want to take a guess?"

"No," says Frans, "why would I want to take a guess? Let me rather not say anything of which I'm not sure. All right?"

"Yes," I say, "all right."

Do I hear someone coughing softly in the background, or am I imagining things? Have I caught him out—caught him out in flagrante delicto? No, this has more to do with my own fantasies than with reality. No man has ever suited me better. He is older than I am, ironic, erudite, and full of surprises in bed. This man is the best that I will ever encounter—I realised that soon enough. He is more deserving than anyone I have ever been in a relationship with. He is as much as I could ever expect from a lover and companion. That did not deter me, however, from applying for the assistantship when Theo Verwey advertised it. Even if it meant that we would be parted for a while and would not see each other regularly. He has already given me much pleasure, and I count on it that he will continue to do so in the future. And I believe that I, in turn, have pleased him well and shall continue to do so.

•

On my spool I have five photographs of the small building in which Patrick Steinmeier hanged himself. Although I did not particularly focus on the landscape, I took four photographs of the magnificent sandstone cliffs, as well as a picture of Sof next to the car, with the mountains in the background, and she in turn took one of me. (Sof, of whom I actually still know little, who accompanied me to Ladybrand on the spur of the moment, and whose pastorie persona made the visit to the dead man's family home considerably easier.) Eleven photographs on a spool of twenty-four. Before I hand it in for development I should perhaps fill up the roll. I bought the film because I intended to document the exact arrangement of the shells next to my bed. But I never got round to that.

For many years I have had a preference for a heavier, larger kind of shell, especially for the conches—that wonderfully large variety of solid forms from tropical waters. But in the past four or five years I have been looking with more interest and appreciation at other, lighter shells, and have begun to augment my collection with tonnas, helmet shells, and harpas. The twenty shells next to my bed were all medium-sized. (The heavier conches and dramatic murexes I displayed in the lounge.) Their colour varied from sandy whites, muted ochres, and pink ochres to the darker brownish pinks of the harpas and the delicate blues of the *Tonna perdix*. I set them out next to my bed in three rows. Sometimes the light fell in such a way that they were lit from beneath, so that they glowed and appeared almost weightless—with an otherworldly beauty, like the host of angels, the ranks of the saints. These shells were the last objects that I would see at night before switching off the bedside lamp, and the first that I would rest my eyes on in the mornings when I awoke. By looking at them, I felt myself strengthened within. Their beauty restored my trust in all of creation. I felt myself at one with the immense variety of life forms on earth, a small link in the immeasurable chain of coincidence that binds us all together.

I hand in the film spool as it is. I can think of nothing else I want to photograph.

I do not tell Theo Verwey about my visit to Mrs. Rosie Steinmeier in Ladybrand. I do not tell him about the hanged man and the photographs I took of the small building. I fear he will find it laughable. Maybe it is laughable—my efforts to follow the trail of the lost shells. After the burglary I mentioned briefly that my shells had been stolen and left it at that.

I sit with the cards in my hand. We are still busy with the letter *D*. *Dorskuur*—cure brought about by restriction of fluid intake. *Dorsnood*. Suffering from the throes of thirst? I ask. Similar to other less commonly used word combinations like *dorsbrand* (burning caused by thirst*)*, *dorsdood* (death from thirst), *dorspyn* (pain caused by thirst), Theo explains. Shall we go and have a drink? I ask. (Theo smiles.) *Dos* (decked out). (How charming he looks this morning, decked out—*uitgedos*—in that fine, cream silk shirt.) "Gedos in die drag van die dodekleed," Leipoldt says. Decked out in the apparel of the shroud. *Doteer* (donate). *Douig* (dewy)—not a word particularly suited to this province. *Douboog* (rainbow formed by dew), *doubos* (dew bush—word used in West Griqualand

59

for the shrub *Cadaba termitaria)*, *doubraam* (bramble bush of which the fruit is covered with a thin waxy layer*)*. The many word combinations formed with *draad* (wire), with *draag* (variant of *dra*—carry), and with draai *(turn)*. Who would have thought, I say to Theo, that simple words like these could be the basis for so many combinations? *Draaihaar* (regional word for hair crown). Has it been your experience as well that people with many crowns in their hair are unusually hot-tempered? Theo smiles and shakes his head. *Draaihartigheid* (disease caused by a bug found in cruciferous plants whereby their leaves turn inward). The word sounds like a character trait, I say, a twisting and turning state of the heart. Theo nods and smiles. *Draais* (the word used by children when playing marbles, yet sounding so much like a synonym for *jags*—horny). But it is especially *droef* (sad) that interests me. Woeful. Indicative of sorrow. Causing grief or accompanying it. Evoking a sombre or doleful mood. *Bedroewend*—saddening. Also in combination with colours, to indicate that a particular colour is murky or muted and can elicit sadness, sorrowfulness, and dejection. *Droefwit* (mournful white). And *droefheid* is the condition of being sad, sorrowful, or mournful; inclined to dejection, depression, and despondency; something gloomy, cheerless, and downcast, as opposed to joy. Is that all? I think. So few words for an emotion with so many shades? The complete colour spectrum—from *droefwit* (mournful white) to *droefswart* (mournful black), from *droefpers* (mournful purple) to *droefrooi* (mournful red). (*Droeforanje, droefblanje, droefblou*—mournful orange, mournful white, mournful blue.)

CHAPTER FIVE

Twice Constable Modisane is not there when I look for him at the
police station, but the third time I find him and luckily Moonsamy with
his pained face is not there to keep a hawk's eye on us.

Constable Modisane greets me in a friendly manner, but promptly
sees to it that he busies himself with some or other document in front of
him. This woman, he probably thinks by now, means trouble.

"Are you sure you found the shells, the stolen goods, with the hanged
man?" I ask. Should I not get straight to the point?

"I was not involved with the case," the constable says. (The emphasis
on the first syllable of "involved.")

"Would this be the house where his body was found?" I say, placing
the five photographs before him on the counter, fan-shaped, like a deck
of cards.

At first he does not look. Then he looks, reluctantly. Then he says:
"Where did you find these?"

"I took them myself," I say. "Last weekend. I also met his family.
Mister Patrick Steinmeier's family."

Constable Modisane glances rapidly over his shoulder. He shakes his
head, disapprovingly.

"What is this?" he says. "Why do you do this?"

"I told you," I say, "those shells are important to me. I want to know
what happened to them."

He shakes his head. "You must stay out of this," he says, not looking up from the ledger in front of him. "You are meddling in the affairs of the police."

"I am not meddling. If possible, I want the other shells back. There are still twenty-three missing. Otherwise, I am not interested in the affairs of the police," I say.

He shakes his head again. A young man, the upper joints of his fingers fleshy and rounded, like his thighs and buttocks.

"These shells are like my family," I say. "They are like my ancestors."

In evolutionary terms, I suspect, this is not completely correct, for the shells are invertebrates, molluscs, and this young man with the smooth, dark-brown skin and I share a vertebrate primal ancestor. In one of our first evolutionary incarnations, approximately four hundred million years ago, we sucked food off the ocean bed through our primitive, armoured, fishlike mouths.

Constable Modisane emits a strange sound—a rather high, soft and throaty sound, something like a suppressed, pained exclamation, like the call of some or other wild bird—an indication that what I say is beyond comprehension.

"I met his family," I say, "because I wanted to see what kind of man would take my shells. They are good people. Although I don't know about his brother."

He shakes his head. He does not want to hear any more.

"He has a younger brother. I don't know if he had something to do with the burglary. He smelt of aftershave at ten in the morning. I couldn't tell whether it was Boss or not."

Constable Modisane has now had enough. From this information he wishes to distance himself.

"You must stop this," he says. "It is not your task to maintain law and order, it is the task of the police."

"I don't want to maintain law and order," I say. "I want my shells back."

He looks up for the first time, a heavy frown on his smooth, youthful face.

"Why do you like these things so much?" he asks a little despairingly, as if he knows that he will never get to the bottom of it.

"Because when I look at them, God's creation makes sense to me," I say.

Again the strange, high sound from the constable's throat, expressing extreme bewilderment.

In vain, I think as I walk out of there. This is a futile and useless search. It will yield nothing. I should be grateful for the recovered shells and let the others go.

My ex-husband accused me of being heartless. Cold and heartless, he said. I care more about things than about people, he said. (He was constantly reaching out to people; he concerned himself exclusively with the upliftment and welfare of others.)

As I emerge from the cool interior of the police station, my eyes blinded by the intensity of the sunlight, I think about our last major confrontation. I recall how my ex-husband and I stood facing each other on the lawn, how he snatched off my dark glasses, beside himself with rage and frustration, how he turned red in the face, and how he—that soft-spoken man who never raised his voice—called out in a hoarse, pained voice: Now I know what you are worth! In human terms you are worth nothing! I shudder, he said, to think that you are the mother of my child! I left him shortly afterwards, leaving him behind to continue with his unstoppable humanitarian mission.

I do not see myself as heartless. I have a particularly heavy and sorrowful heart: dark, heavy, and saturated with blood. A hairy sack, like the sun in Revelations.

•

I cannot sleep at night. Sometimes I play a computer game. I drink a small glass of milk with whisky, as my father used to do. I read. I read the book of Ruth in the Bible. Ruth bending over the sheaves of corn. What am I looking for? I reflect upon my shells. I reflect upon the different phases of my life. I reflect upon the people who have crossed my path. Did I ever come to the realisation that I am at the crossroads, from where my life could proceed in two different directions? Or in one of four, or one of eight different directions? Did I think: Here I can make a choice, here I have eight options (hypothetically): four options

63

for the broad or four options for the narrow way? Felix du Randt was a good man. Warm, eager, freckled, sexy Felix du Randt's only sin with regard to me was that he hardened his heart (for self-protection, without doubt) to such a degree that he could watch expressionlessly as Marthinus Maritz slapped me on both sides of my face—the red fingerprints visible afterwards.

Did Felix's betrayal (let me call it that provisionally) drive me into the arms of the next man? It is quite possible that it happened that way. On a Thursday morning in my twenty-sixth year I found myself in the bed of a man who would engineer, without the slightest hesitation, the downfall of anyone opposing him. Another whim or quirk of my memory is that I can recall the compass points of any room I have ever found myself in. The bed in that bedroom was on the east-west axis, with the headboard facing east. The sheets were light-blue, of a synthetic, drip-dry fabric. The woman of the house was gone with her children (three girls), on a visit to her parents. The wall-to-wall carpets muted all sound. The blinds and curtains were drawn. Outside it was hot, but inside the house it was cool and dusky. Abel Sonnekus. At ten-thirty in the morning, more or less, behind a suburban fence and drawn blinds, that man could have his way with me and not a soul would know about it.

Was the improbability of an erotic liaison with him in itself an incitement? Sexually arousing? Instigating? Was it a provocation? Bony head, frizzy blond hair, duck's body—complete with oil gland at the arse. Duck's beak and webbed fingers. Short, blunt nose like that of Thomas Mann's harbinger of death in *Der Tod in Venedig*. Short, thick penis. Hairless body, as if the hair had been shaved off, or stripped off with hot wax. The sparse pubic hair frizzled and yellow, like dried seaweed.

On that scene I draw a curtain. It is long past. I leave Abel Sonnekus and myself behind in the violated nuptial bed, wrestling with our respective demons. Past tense. Left behind. I prefer to let that sleeping dog lie.

•

My ex-husband was a tireless campaigner for the welfare of lame ducks, a defender of every lost cause. During the ten years of our marriage he provided shelter to countless flounderers, depressives, rehabilitators, subversives, and other fringe figures. Black, white, and brown. On the day of our final confrontation on the lawn in front of our house I told him that I refused to accommodate two of his friends. I don't like them, I said, they have unhygienic habits, I don't feel like preparing meals for them and making their beds. I don't want them at my table and in my house for an unspecified period. They encroach upon my space and disturb my peace of mind. (One was a jazz pianist and the other a free-floating anarchist.) I have been doing that long enough, I said, and I don't feel like making this sacrifice one day longer.

You are inhuman, he said, you are an inhuman woman.

You have no idea, I said, how inhuman I am. Or how much more inhuman I can still become.

In that marriage I came to close my heart to the needs of others, out of self-preservation.

The more radically my ex-husband took pity on one and all, on widow and orphan, fledgling anarchist and political suspect, the more I cordoned off and protected my private space.

During the last years of our marriage my shell collection was consolidated and significantly extended. I set out the large conches in rows on the table at my side of the marital bed. Like chess pieces I set them up—an army preparing for battle, all the heavy conches, row upon row.

It was at this time that my husband remarked in our bedroom, his eye on the shells, that I care more about things than about people, that I remind him of the dowager empress Tz'u-hsi, who was more concerned with her silkworm cocoons than with her starving subjects.

That is so, I said, every one of these shells means more to me than any one of your many needy friends.

(My back against the wall, as vicious as a cornered snake.)

My husband merely gave a small, bitter (joyless) chuckle, before leaving the room.

My mouth was stopped in the last years of our marriage, or so it seemed. My emotions were blunted. I did nothing worthwhile. Time passed.

After the divorce I left for another province, taking along our child. In Cape Town I started working as a lexicographer. My ex-husband remarried soon afterwards. His new bride had been standing in the shadows on the day of our last confrontation, awaiting her opportunity. She had a formidable revolutionary agenda. She was a lawyer, irreproachable in her sentiments, and she had independently established and managed a legal aid centre for the destitute.

Perhaps he and his new wife gradually tired of all and sundry to whom they gave shelter, tired of all those continuously knocking on their door for help. Perhaps his new wife's insatiable social and political fervour exhausted even my ex-husband. (He had no need to convert her, for she was no renegade, like me.) A year later he left her. I could well imagine him raking leaves or stones somewhere, as he had always raked the leaves in our garden in autumn. I could picture the expression on his face. Completely absent, completely self-absorbed, cut off from what was going on around him, his thoughts turned inward. What would he have been preoccupied with—painful memories of his youth, Utopian fantasies? All his life he paid for sins he had not committed. Hereditary sin. The sins of the fathers visited upon the children. A man who did not himself know how heavily he was burdened. Occasionally he sent our child a postcard, to put her at ease and to confirm that he was still alive, and from that I concluded that he had renounced much of his previous life, but not all of it.

I recall that he indicated to me quite early on, at the start of our relationship, that I had a limited emotional register. You are clever, he said, you are very clever, but you have little aptitude for emotional complexity. At the time it upset me, for I admired him—he was to my mind a man with an extremely refined sensibility and a rich emotional register. Now, after all these years, I am once again beginning to think that he may have been right, that my emotional scope is not particularly extensive, and that this is why I have had more success as a lexicographer than as a writer.

•

In this manner we come to the end of June, and my twenty-three missing shells have not yet been recovered. I do not worry Constable Modisane any longer. Theo Verwey and I bend over the cards. We are still busy with *D*, with combinations formed with the word "death"—the *doodsverbindings*—of which Theo remarked that they never seem to come to an end. We listen to music as we work, sometimes we talk, but never much. He seldom initiates a conversation.

I have to make the best of a bad situation, I decide. I have to make peace with the loss of the shells. I read about dissociation; the phenomenon suddenly interests me. The pathological condition during which aspects of conscious experience become inaccessible to memory. Dr. Jekyll and Mr. Hyde are the classic example. Although I have to admit that neither Patrick Steinmeier (as far as I could judge from the police photographs) nor Jaykie Steinmeier (in spite of his sly, hypocritical glance) resembles a Dr. Jekyll/Mr. Hyde character. I had fantasised summarily, but unjustifiably, that Patrick Steinmeier, the man who hanged himself and with whose corpse my shells were found ("your stolen goods," according to the constable), represented the Dr. Jekyll figure, but the Mr. Hyde figure seems less applicable to him. I am beginning to think that someone else is guilty—the miscreant, the dissociating villain is probably roaming on his own, or he is on the run with his small band of accomplices. Fighting fit for a second and third round.

CHAPTER SIX

"This morning I'm thinking of a scene from another book by the same writer," I say to Theo Verwey on a morning in July. "The same writer as the one who wrote the book about the rich man."

This is the theme I am introducing today. For whatever reason.

"This novel starts off," I say, "with the main character deciding on the spur of the moment to change his flight, hire a car, and visit a woman with whom he had a short-lived erotic relationship in his youth."

"Oh, yes?" Theo Verwey says, and turns towards me slightly, an indication that I may continue.

"The main character is fifty-seven years old. The woman he is on his way to, is an artist. He finds her at an enormous air-force base in the desert, where she is busy with an art project. He was seventeen when he saw her last, she was thirty-two. That was forty years ago. She is now seventy. Some forty years later, and in the older woman he still sees the young woman. He can lift the younger woman from the older one, so to speak, and make her stand before him. Night has fallen by the time he reaches the place. Everything is dramatically lit. She recognises him immediately. Someone is conducting an interview with her. She explains that the landscape forms part of the artwork—the desert forming a central element of the work. It frames the work. The project entails the painting of aircraft used during and after the Second

World War—deactivated bombers. First the paint is removed from the planes by scraping and sandblasting them. Then their surfaces are coated with a base and sprayed with oil paint, enamel, and an epoxy resin. Paintbrushes are also used for a less industrial effect. The volunteers executing the project have tanks fastened on their backs and they wear gas masks. These people stand on twelve-foot ladders with their spraying equipment."

I stop speaking for a while to order my thoughts. To catch my breath.

"It's a massive project by its very nature, financed by grants amounting to tens of thousands of dollars, and donations of materials by various manufacturers. Some of the planes are B-52 long-distance bombers, each a hundred and sixty feet long."

Theo Verwey is still turned expectantly towards me.

"Imagine," I say, "hundreds of painted bombers in the vastness of the desert. Improbable. Immoderate. It speaks to me. The unboundedness of it speaks to me. It is the opposite of the enclosedness of the labyrinth. It is unrestricted, excessive, larger than life, much like the life of the rich man in the other novel I spoke about. The desert features in that novel as well—the rich man fantasises about the desert when he fantasises about his death. He wants to have his body—along with the bodies of his dogs—crashed down into the desert in an airplane."

Theo Verwey nods politely. He is still half facing me with a slightly surprised expression. I continue.

"After this reunion of the man and the woman, the novel peels off layer by chronological layer to their first meeting and sexual relationship forty years previously."

Once again Theo Verwey nods politely.

"That is all," I say. "That is what I was thinking about this morning."

"In the desert?" he says.

"Yes," I say. "In Arizona, in the desert."

He nods again, musingly. Then he turns away from me and continues with his work. I fix my attention on the cards in front of me. I should not expect the impossible from him. A man with an enviably comprehensive knowledge of words—a man who knows everything about words and their origins, of their genesis, their ascendancy and their decline—and so incapable of having them serve him. I see his hesitancy. I see how he does not find words. Or keeps himself in check. A natural reticence? Certainly. His lips sealed in the interests of decorum? That as well. A wariness? An insecurity? But at the same time more than the sum of all of these. I sense a lack in him. An inability. A man who has so many words at his disposal, and yet is so unable to apply them for his own benefit.

We are still busy with the letter *D*.

Nearly all our conversations to date have dealt with deviations, or excesses of one kind or another. Yet it is left to me to articulate the subtle undercurrents that I pick up in his presence, because he cannot, or will not, do it.

First we listen to Richard Strauss's "Vier Letzte Lieder."

"The piccolo at the end," I say. "One would want to be able to play it simply for the sake of those last notes."

Theo Verwey smiles and nods.

Then we listen to Mahler's "Kindertotenlieder" and "Lieder eines fahrenden Gesellen." I see, from the corner of my eye, how he closes his eyes for a moment, as if the beauty causes him pain. An erotic gesture, and for a moment this man is superimposed on a man of whom I dreamt the night before.

"Beautiful," I say. "Beautiful enough to sing at a funeral."

"The wedding song?" Theo asks.

"Why not?" I say.

And furthermore we have not had a single conversation without some reference to death.

•

I encounter Hugo Hattingh alone in the tearoom one morning and decide to make use of the opportunity.

"I want to know what life is," I say, "and when the first life on earth originated."

For a moment Hugo Hattingh's gaze flutters over me with scant interest. His expression is dismissive. He takes a sip of tea, replaces his cup on the saucer, and asks, without looking at me: "What exactly is the question?"

(I take it he finds it difficult to use the personal pronoun "you.")

"What is life?" I ask.

"Life is the presence of DNA," he says.

"And what is DNA?" I ask.

(While Freddie Ferreira, the curator of mammals, enters, pours himself a cup of tea, and sits down with a magazine.)

"DNA, deoxyribonucleic acid," Hugo Hattingh explains, "consists of amino acids linked together to form proteins. It consists of two very long molecular strings, twisted around each other to form a double spiral."

(Freddie pages through the book; something about his body language, about his hard-boiledness, his crabby remoteness, his mute misery, suddenly reminds me of an uncle of mine, one of my mother's brothers.)

"The lateral chain of the spiral consists of sugar and phosphates; nucleotides form the cross rungs—complex ring-shaped units, consisting of adenine, cytosine, guanine and thiamine."

(Nathi Gule enters, Freddie does not look up, but they greet by pressing the palms of their right hands together: a swift, well-coordinated movement. Nathi brings, as always, an air of expectancy along with him.)

"The two strings are enabled to separate from each other and to form corresponding strings by means of the messenger RNA, ribonucleic acid."

(That I like, the fact that a messenger, a mediator, is necessary.)

"That is the simplified answer to the question," Hugo Hattingh says. "Life can also be defined as a complex, self-organising phenomenon that sometimes occurs in places where energy flows from a warmer to a cooler object. Without this flow of energy it cannot occur. It is an essential prerequisite for life—although not the only one."

Freddie looks up and asks if I now understand what life is. (Slightly mockingly?)

"What were the conditions," I ask Hugo Hattingh, "for the origin of life on earth?"

"The laws and constants of the universe were conducive to the evolution of life," Hugo says.

"In what way?" I ask. "And while we're on the topic of the universe, I would like to know how I should picture the single point of infinite density and infinite heat where the universe apparently began."

Hugo Hattingh looks at me as if to say he doesn't care a hoot how I picture that starting point.

Meanwhile Sailor has entered. Flash Gordon. Gorgeously dressed in white—does he *work* in these clothes? He and Freddie are bantering with each other on the left. When Sailor enters the room, I have noticed, everyone responds to him. Everyone except Hugo Hattingh, who is still sitting cup in hand, gazing intently in front of him, explaining that the Big Bang occurred approximately fifteen thousand million years ago, that it had extended between 10^{-36} and 10^{-32} of a second thereafter—the so-called inflation period—to a radius of a hundred billion kilometres. That the temperature one hundredth of a second after the Big Bang was a hundred thousand million degrees Celsius, and that one second thereafter it had already cooled to around ten thousand million degrees Celsius. He explains that it was still too hot for the formation of atoms, and that the universe consisted of a chaotic but homogeneous mixture of radiation, hydrogen and helium.

"All elements known to us today," he says, "issued from that."

(Nathi, Freddie and Sailor are paging through the book that Freddie had been looking at and are laughing about something.) Hugo continues unperturbed. "After half a million years the temperature was approximately four thousand degrees Celsius, equal to that on the surface of our sun. Atoms were formed from subatomic particles. Matter began to condense as a consequence of the attraction exercised by gravity. Radiation subsided and the universe gradually began to darken. After some thousands of millions of years, vast gas clouds of matter began to cluster together, and the stars and galaxies were formed."

Sailor and Nathi have finished their tea, only Freddie remains seated. Hugo Hattingh places his cup on the table before him and says, without looking at me, that as far as the nature and origin of life are concerned, laymen always ask these types of questions—the large, unanswerable questions—whereas science is concerned with hypotheses that can be tested, and only with the use of well-defined facts. (Freddie is sitting with his elbows on his knees, his gaze fixed on the ground before him. I can see that he is listening, although he gives no indication of doing so.)

"Actually," Hugo Hattingh says, "it cannot be stated with any certainty what life is, nor where it began. Darwin wrote his last book on worms. Not a grand reflection on life and evolution. On worms."

Freddie is intently contemplating the high ceiling.

"A year before his death," Hugo Hattingh says, "a book on worms. An important book. Enlightening. He uses worms as a metaphor for the important role that small changes and adaptations play over a very long period."

Freddie casts a casual, ironic glance in my direction, as if to say: There you have it. He stubs out his cigarette and gets up to leave. I also get up. I feel somewhat rebuked by Hugo Hattingh, rapped over the knuckles, but this hardly diminishes my zeal. I am excited, I am impassioned. I have been given a new framework within which I can situate the phenomenon of life.

Hugo Hattingh remains seated for a moment. "This is how Darwin sees evolution," he says musingly, "the distribution of small changes over a long period."

That evening I lie in my bed and I think: After the Big Bang it took the universe half a million years to darken. I must never forget this. If I always bear this in mind, I shall live in a state of constant wonderment.

•

But alas, *laes*! The small details of my daily life rapidly crowd out the bigger picture. I do not succeed in keeping my eye on the fifteen thousand million years that the universe has been in existence. The chaotic appeals of my inner life rapidly jostle these remarkable facts away. (My shells. My relationship with Frans de Waard, the man I left behind. Other losses. The countless small, hardly detectable psychic shifts from one moment to the next.) The days are becoming cooler and shorter. I am deeply under the impression of the transience of our days. Every day I realise that every hour may be my last. Every morning I get up with the knowledge that I am one day closer to the end of my life. I ask Sof to quote a fitting text, surely she has one for every day of the year, after how many days in the pastorie?

"All flesh is grass," says Sof Benadé in the tearoom, "and all the comeliness thereof as the flower of the field."

"What else?" I ask.

"The grass withereth, the flower fadeth but the word of our God abideth for ever."

Sof is gentle, compliant, there is something awkward to her movements, something almost childlike. But behind this exterior, I begin to notice, abides an unwavering will. Our friendship is gradually assuming a discernible shape.

She visits me one evening. I am surprised to see her. She hopes that she is not disturbing me, she says, she was in the vicinity. No, I say, not at all, I am glad to see her. I pour some wine. Because I do not know much about her, I ask what her childhood was like.

"When I think of my childhood," Sof says, "I think of subdued light. I think of a silence that is never broken. I think of my sombre, tormented father and my pious, unspeaking mother. I think of a house with a long passage and closed doors. I think of the eye of God penetrating all surfaces. I think of myself sitting on my bed in my room with my hands folded in my lap, following the passage of God's eye as it penetrates all obstacles and finally comes to rest on me."

She sits hunched forward. I notice she has narrow feet. They are placed firmly together.

"The idea of infinity gives me the creeps," she suddenly says. "It gave me nightmares as a child, and it still does."

"What is eternity?" I say.

"Eternity is God's time," she says. "It is when our time has run out."

We sit in silence for a while.

"What do you understand by the virtuous way?" I ask (my conversation with Theo Verwey in mind).

She reflects for a moment. Tips cigarette ash on the carpet by mistake. Spits on her finger and picks it up. She has narrow hands too, I see. Her concentration is visible in the line of her eyebrows.

"I see the virtuous way as a high, narrow mountainous path. Actually little more than a ledge of rock, with great chasms on one side. And immense, whirling mist clouds and sheets of icy mist that virtually obliterate visibility."

Sof sits hunched forward, cigarette in hand, focusing intently on the narrow tip of her shoe.

"My life is a mess," she says out of the blue. She says it without emphasis, soberly and level-headedly. She has not said anything in this vein before. Her personal life has not yet cropped up in our conversation in this way.

"In what way?" I ask. Uncertain, cautious, aware that I am treading on dangerous terrain, the treacherous psychic undergrowth.

"Messy," she says. "Chaotic. Disgusting, for the most part."

Disgusting, I think. Causing disgust. Repugnant. Disgusting is not a word with which I would describe my own life, but it is certainly not wholly inapplicable in some instances. I would go so far as to describe some of the people with whom I have associated, even intimately associated, as repugnant. So, I think, Sof, you do not have the monopoly on a disgusting life. Or at least on episodes and liaisons that evoke feelings of intense repugnance in retrospect.

Sof still sits hunched forward. I say nothing.

"My life is going nowhere," she says.

"Did something happen?" I ask.

"No," Sof says. "Nothing in particular happened. Except that I married the wrong man and wasted my time."

"What with?" I ask.

"With harbouring illusions," she says, "and delusional notions. All my life I've suffered from gross self-deception and misjudgement."

Delusional notions. A delusion is also a false impression. A notion is an idea, a belief, conception, conviction. Sof grew up in a pastorie, where the Bible—as ultimate truth—must certainly have warned against all manner of false and delusional notions. Her face could be described as open (directly readable), honest (without deceit), and intense (a heat of conviction to be read in it). An Israelite in whom is no guile would not be an unfitting description of her.

I do not ask her when she came to realise these things, or about the nature of the illusions she harboured, or what misconceptions and false impressions she suffered under.

"What is wrong with your husband?" I ask.

"He's a doos," Sof says. "I sometimes consider bumping him off."

"Would there be a method of preference?" I ask.

"Yes," she says. "I would stab him in the heart with a carving knife while he's watching rugby."

"I see," I say.

"But I am the *real* doos," Sof says. "I should never have married him. I've been spineless. Lacking in will. I actually deserve him—I took no control of my own life."

"Your husband is a doctor," I say.

"Yes," she says. "He is a psychiatrist with as much insight into the human psyche as a mole. For that alone he deserves to die."

After that we drink a few more glasses of wine and Sof smokes numerous cigarettes, although she claims to have given up smoking the day before. When she has left, I cannot sleep. I have never really slept well since the disappearance of my shells. At night I am plagued by dreams, which are often most unsavoury and in the main bewildering in content. (Perplexing. Disconcerting.) Bewildering indeed that the unconscious can come up with such images. Come up with? What precisely *does* the unconscious do during the dream? Freddie Ferreira, curator of mammals, will probably know the evolutionary function of the mammalian dream. On the internet I look up the geological periods. I print out the information and begin to memorise it. These periods will form the framework for my new knowledge, for everything that I hope to learn from Hugo Hattingh.

•

One afternoon in the first week of July, approximately six weeks after the burglary, there is a knock on my door. It is Constable Modisane, cap in hand, dressed in his police uniform. In his hand he holds a small brown paper bag. For one vertiginous moment I think that he is returning the rest of my shells.

He greets, eyes averted, and I invite him in.

We are both uncomfortable. He does not immediately reveal the purpose of his visit. I ask if he would like to sit down and he draws out a chair at the dining-room table. I offer tea and he accepts.

As I enter with the two mugs and take a seat facing him, he pushes the bag towards me. Through the paper I can feel that it is a single object and that it is not shaped like any of my shells. My heart sinks into my shoes.

It is a large abalone shell, one of those commonly used as ashtrays. Not a shell that I would ever consider for my collection.

"It's a gift," he says. "For you."

I am taken aback. Does this man want to use this shell as a gift to get me in bed? What am I to make of this?

I thank him profusely. "It's very kind of you," I say. "And it's very beautiful."

"Eh heh," he says with eyes averted.

We drink our tea in silence, the shell on the table between us.

At last he says: "There's been a mistake. We got two files mixed up. Your stolen goods were not retrieved in Ladybrand."

"So they weren't found with the body of the dead man. With Mr. Patrick Steinmeier?"

"No," the Constable says. "It was a mistake. Wrong file."

"I see," I say. "Where did they find them?"

Constable Modisane looks uncomfortable. "It's confidential," he says.

"Then why are you telling me about it?" I say.

(Aunty Rosie and her children led up the garden path.)

Constable Modisane just shakes his head. He looks subdued, not his usual exuberant self.

This man wants to get me off the Steinmeier case, I suspect.

"They were found in a stolen car," he says reluctantly.

"And where was the car found?" I ask.

"It was abandoned on the banks of the Umgeni River, just off the M4."

"Why was it abandoned?" I ask.

Constable Modisane looks increasingly uncomfortable. Apparently he dare not look up to meet my gaze. On the other hand it might be his manner of showing respect. How would I know.

"The car was stolen," he says. "The driver was killed; the three passengers managed to escape."

"I see," I say. "Did the police find other stolen goods in the car as well?"

"Ye-es," the constable says.

"Will the case be reopened now?" I ask.

"I'm not too sure," he says. He drums on the table with his fingers. Long, lively, bouncy fingers, fleshy at the upper joints, darker at the knuckles. His skin is a fine, healthy, even brown, warm, with a hint of copper in it. The planes of his face run seamlessly one into the other. His forehead is round, the bone visible under the skin; his nose has a small, unusual fold at the tip, indented as if formed of wet clay. His lips are fleshy, well formed and expressive, darker than the rest of his face, with more blue in them.

He gets up. Only once do our eyes meet. His are a deep, warm brown. (I would even go as far as calling it a poignant brown, although that is not the way in which colour is usually described.) The iris occupies a large section of the eyeball, the white is tinted brown, as if the colour of the iris has seeped into it. Am I imagining it, or is there something entreating in his expression? I thank him again for the shell. "If you could still keep your eyes open for my missing shells," I say as he is leaving, "I would be most grateful."

My own face in the mirror is joined together differently from his. The planes are less continuous, the colour less pronounced.

I am upset when he has gone. On one hand Constable Modisane's story is plausible. On the other hand I suspect that he wants to divert my attention from the Steinmeier trail because I have interfered with the case too much. He has provided me with too much confidential information. It could land him in trouble.

Be that as it may. Whatever the story may be. I do not want to let Patrick Steinmeier go. Even Jaykie, his brother, delightfully squint-eyed (the lustrous whites of his eyes like those of a saint), even him I do not want to let go. I could never again *not* think that my recovered shells were found in a little bag at the dangling feet of Patrick Steinmeier's corpse. Although I could never suspect him of doing the evil deed, I will nevertheless always *associate* him with it. (His wedding portrait finally convinced me of his innocence—unless that man was so beside himself, had taken such leave of his senses that he was completely irrational, he would never even have considered stealing a shell.)

Patrick and Jaykie Steinmeier, even Aunty Rosie and Alverine, the hanging corpse, the little brick building outside Ladybrand (of which I have five photographs)—all are inseparably associated with the loss of my shells. It has become a single given. Perplexing, for certain, but a single reality. Patrick Steinmeier's long eyebrows, arching sorrowfully downwards to his temples (lending his face a mournful expression); the disturbing photographs of the corpse on the bier in the mortuary; Alverine, who so closely resembles Hazel of long ago; Jaykie, with his dark, sly priest's eyes and youthful, winsome glance—all have become part of the constellation of loss. All of these form the matrix within which the loss of the shells is embedded.

•

Mrs. Dudu (assisted by two ravishing Indian princesses) is in charge of the library of the Museum of Natural History. As member of the Department of Regional Languages she is also employed as a consultant by the city library on the ground floor. The department concerned has ordered a drastic pruning of the Afrikaans books to create more shelf space. She would appreciate it if I could advise her in this matter.

What kind of book is she intending to throw out? I ask her. She says that she doesn't know yet. Her instruction is that everything that was published before 1990 will have to go, and for the rest she will let herself be guided by the popularity of books. She will probably retain those that are most widely read.

"Where does that leave the serious student of Afrikaans literature?" I ask.

"If the department notices that books are not being read, they throw them out anyway," she says.

"Do the Afrikaans books occupy that much shelf space?" I ask.

Mrs. Dudu shrugs. "There's nothing I can do about it," she says. "It's a decision of the department."

"Isn't it an ill-considered decision?" I ask.

Mrs. Dudu shrugs again.

"What will happen to the books that get thrown out?" I ask.

"No decision has been taken yet," Mrs. Dudu says in her impeccable Afrikaans. She has small, delicate hands, her hair is woven artfully in little braids, and when she smiles, her gums are visible.

"Will they be sent to deserving organisations?" I ask.

"We can't say with certainty yet," Mrs. Dudu says.

"Maybe to rehabilitation centres for drug addicts in the Natal midlands?" I ask. "They would surely welcome such a gift?"

"No," Mrs. Dudu says firmly. "No decision has been taken yet."

We have a cup of tea at the Sand Dune. We each eat a banana muffin, wrapped in Cellophane and sparsely spread with margarine.

The Sand Dune is a small restaurant on the first floor, the same floor as the Museum of Natural History. The city library is on the ground floor and the art gallery is on the second floor, above the museum. The basement serves, among other things, as storage space.

In its heyday the building must have been imposing, for it is grandly conceived and constructed. A broad marble staircase leads to the entrance of the building. The floor of the entrance hall is laid out with black and white marble tiles. Two flanking staircases with red carpets lead to the first and second floors. The light shaft formed by this winged staircase culminates in a high glass dome, through which natural light streams into the building from above.

I ask Mrs. Dudu about the history of the building. It appears that it was initially designed to serve exclusively as a cultural and historical museum, but the cultural-historical section was later moved to another building in order to accommodate the library and art gallery. Over time, she explains, the space available to the museum, as well as to the library and art gallery, has been cut back. And now the library space is due to be cut back even further to accommodate the offices of the Department of Regional Languages.

I ask Mrs. Dudu where she gained her impressive mastery of the Afrikaans language. Oh, she says, she grew up in a small town in the Natal interior. "There we were still taught proper Afrikaans," she says. "But that was in bygone days," and she laughs exuberantly, her lovely, meticulously braided locks shaking.

"Now we have other troubles," I say.

"Yes," she says. "Now we have other troubles."

Little has remained of the original grandeur of the building. The carpets have become worn over time, the wooden thresholds have been trodden through, unattractive wooden partitions have been erected in the entrance hall and elsewhere to convert the large spaces into smaller, more practical units.

"It's no longer a priority of the local administration to maintain this building, is it?" I say.

"No, it isn't," Mrs. Dudu agrees and adjusts her spectacles on her nose. (These have a small gold decoration at each corner.)

The Sand Dune is small and dark, surrounded by exhibition cases, separated from the adjacent locale by a wooden partition. Behind us are display cabinets containing fish and crabs. The specimens, I notice, are all dusty, slightly eroded and worn down, their initial lustre gone. (Like that of the building itself.) Perhaps that is the fate of all specimens, of everything that is maintained artificially. As I glance upwards, I meet the eye of the giant reconstructed dinosaur (resembling a huge, plastic toy).

Because of all the many subdivisions and temporary partitions, the museum appears overfull, as if the space is too small for everything it has to accommodate.

I ask Mrs. Dudu if her parents are still alive. No, she says, they have both passed away.

"Did they spend their entire lives in the rural areas?" I ask.

"Yes," she says, "they always lived there."

"What did you read at school in Afrikaans?" I ask.

She reflects for a moment. "We read *Swart pelgrim*," she says, and *Geknelde land*, and *Offerland*, and *Uit oerwoud en vlakte. Rabodutu* and *Fanie se veldskooldae.*"

"So you know everything about the Afrikaner's struggle for the land?" I say.

"Everything," Mrs. Dudu says.

"And about the black man's place in the great dispensation?"

"Everything," Mrs. Dudu says. "Everything." We laugh.

We drink our tea. She is probably a few years younger than I am.

I ask about her children. They are still at school, and she complains about the price of a school education, but I am no longer following the conversation with particular attention; I am thinking about the novel I have begun to write.

CHAPTER SEVEN

I stand in front of the Afrikaans fiction section in the city library on the ground floor in a state of shock. There are nine shelves of not quite a metre long available for Afrikaans, and this shelf space has to be reduced by half. Because most of the titles here are popular fiction, not half a shelf will probably remain for serious literature published since 1990.

I tell Mrs. Dudu: Choose someone else for this task. Do it yourself. I had no idea what I was letting myself in for. I do not want to be guilty of this misdeed. I do not want to be the one responsible for getting rid of most of the already meagre collection of Afrikaans books.

This causes Mrs. Dudu great mirth. She laughs heartily. She thinks I am joking. *You* don't have to pack the books and send them off, she says.

"On what basis should I choose?" I ask. "And should my choice be representative of Afrikaans literature for the benefit of this English city?"

Mrs. Dudu laughs so much, her braids shake. She does not see the gravity of my objections.

I stand dejectedly before the sea of titles. The writers I am familiar with present no problem, but how do I choose between *Die afgrond van Mammon* (The abyss of Mammon), *Seën van erbarming* (Blessing of grace), *Liefde in die laning* (Love in the lane), *Die Engelse dreig* (The English are advancing), *Verskroeide verlange* (Scorched yearning), *Melodie van begeerte* (Melody of desire), *Blinde voordeel* (Blind advantage), *Bruid van die oerwoud* (Bride of the jungle), *Skyn van waansin* (Semblance of madness), *Wraak in die aandskemering* (Revenge at dusk), *Suster Mandie* (Sister Mandie), *Versperde steë* (Obstructed alleys), *Die toring van liefde* (The tower of love), *Wie erf Rietvlei* (Who inherits Rietvlei), *Vlam van vervulling* (Flame of fulfilment), *Verrukking in die vroegte* (Ecstasy at daybreak), *Die vertes wink* (Beckoning horizons), *Onstilbare hartstog* (Unquenchable passion), *Vlammende karavaan* (Flaming caravan), *Weerkaatsings van weemoed* (Reflections of wistfulness), *Staan by my beminde* (Stand by me, beloved), *Vuur van verlange* (Fire of longing)—to mention but a few of the titles. On what basis do I select? Where do I begin?

"Is this your revenge for being forced to read *Fanie se veldskooldae* at school?" I ask.

Now Mrs. Dudu is really laughing boisterously.

"Oh, no," she says. "I liked that book. I liked *all* those books very much!"

"Should I separate the more serious literature from the popular fiction?" I ask.

"No, don't bother," Mrs. Dudu says. "Rather keep it alphabetical, the way it was."

All right, I think, I shall do it like that. *Onweer op Vlakmanshoogte* and *Verbete vreemdeling* by Sanet Sadie go in a box with *Uit oerwoud en vlakte* by Sangiro. *Verterende vlam*, *Naakte aanvalligheid* and *Vertroude aarde* by Nonnie van Schalkwyk go in the same box as *Bart Nel* and *Verspeelde lente* by Johannes van Melle. *Suster Martie*, *Dokter Gysbrecht* and *Verskrikking in saal sewe* by Melanie Malherbe go in a box with *Hans-die-skipper* and *Die meulenaar* by D.F. Malherbe. It breaks my heart, but Etienne Leroux's Welgevonden trilogy has to go with Elsie Lessing (*'n Bruid vir Welgelegen*, *Soos die dobbelsteen val*, *Sal ons paaie skei*, *Die hart van 'n vrou*) in a box. Henriette Grové, a few early Karel Schoeman novels, Elsa Joubert, all in boxes, together with *Moord in die malhuis*, *Gekneusde bloeisels*, *Spore van haat*, *Onraad op Olienfontein*, several omnibuses by Sofie Wesley-Winton and Janetta de Waal-Hanekom. (I consider leaving a few seminal titles published before 1990 on the shelf, but I suspect Mrs. Dudu is watching me like a hawk. She is a thorough and methodical woman, she will see to it that every assignment gets carried out to the letter, is my impression.)

I ask Mrs. Dudu if I can set apart a few books for myself. I assure her that no one is going to miss them—no institution for rehabilitation in the Midlands, no convicts in maximum security prisons, no school libraries for the previously disadvantaged, no members of the city library. At first Mrs. Dudu looks sceptical. What about those serious students of literature? she asks. (It takes me a few moments to realise she is pulling my leg.) My choice is idiosyncratic, I tell her, it is based on a small reading list I have compiled for myself. They are mostly books that are hardly in great demand any longer, and for once the serious students will have to manage by themselves. The small pile I keep out for myself includes some old Afrikaans works written in the Twenties, Thirties and Forties, such as *Die sewe duiwels en wat hulle gedoen het* (The seven devils and what they were up to) by Ou Oom Jan, prose works by Eugène Marais and Louis Leipoldt, *Verspeelde lente* (Forfeited spring) by Johannes van Melle, *Somer* (Summer) and *Laat vrugte* (Late fruit) by C.M. van den Heever, *Die meulenaar* (The miller) by D.F. Malherbe and *Die Sprinkaanbeampte van Sluis* (The locust officer of Sluis) by Jochem van Bruggen. With these I can amuse myself when I am unable to sleep at night. Especially the adventures of the seven devils in Ou Oom Jan's book promise a great deal of amusement.

I pack the books. It takes me two days. I close the flaps of the boxes. With a koki pen I mark them A–M, N–R, S–Z. I inform Mrs. Dudu that I am done, my task is completed, I wash my hands in innocence. She laughs with heartfelt pleasure, rubs her hands together in satisfaction and suggests that we have some tea and muffins at the Sand Dune.

After I have completed my task, there are four and a half extra shelves available for the Department of Regional Languages to use at their discretion. I tell Mrs. Dudu I fully trust that the department will make good use of the additional space. She laughs again, shakes her head, takes me gently by the arm, leads me firmly to the first floor, and says that she cannot thank me enough—she could not have done it better herself.

Yes, I say, and this way the fate of *your* immortal soul need not be at stake.

It is the end of July, and it is cold. Even by the standards of this region, where it is mostly very hot. Compared to the rest of the country, bleached and wintry, it is still green here. I find it lovely, the sultry lushness of this province. I find the climate sensual and the colours rich and varied, though sometimes a little too rich, bewilderingly rich, almost strident. I like this city, yet would never want to settle here. Theo and I are nowhere close to the completion of our task, but sometimes in an unguarded moment I fantasise about the milder region where I come from.

•

My next conversation with Hugo Hattingh is less chaotic. I am better prepared. At least I am now familiar with the sequence of the geological periods. I have a clear image of the way in which the Archaean and the Proterozoic aeons—the period of invisible life—precede the Phanerozoic aeon—the period of visible life. I know now that the Palaeozoic is divided into the Cambrian, Ordovician, Silurian, Devonian, Carboniferous, and Permian; the Mesozoic into the Triassic, Jurassic, and Cretaceous; the Cenozoic into the Palaeocene, Eocene, Oligocene, Miocene, and Pliocene (the latter two forming the Tertiary period), and that the Quaternary period consists of the Pleistocene and Holocene. I am well aware of how primitive and rudimentary my knowledge is—no more than an elementary scheme, a first ordering principle.

It is often difficult to have a serious conversation in the tearoom. The talk is sometimes quite boisterous, especially when Sailor is there, and although this does not appear to worry Hugo Hattingh, I get distracted. There is much that I want to ask him, but the other conversations also interest me. I am keen to hear what Freddie Ferreira, young Nathi Gule, and Vera Garaszczuk, the expert on Cambrian fossils, have to say. Sof Benadé is at the museum only twice a week, and Theo Verwey does not join us for tea that often. Only when there is cake, he has remarked laconically.

"Does Darwin maintain," I ask Hugo Hattingh this morning, "that there is a tendency to progressive development in evolution?"

I have waited until Hugo has poured his tea and taken his usual seat. Diagonally opposite him Sailor is sprawling in his chair, one leg over the armrest. He is chatting to Mrs. Dudu and Vera. Freddie and Nathi are not here yet.

"No," Hugo Hattingh replies. "Darwin's theory is based on localised adaptations. It does not necessarily imply progress. It is generally assumed that human beings are the most successful life form on earth," he says scornfully, "the result of billions of years of evolution through natural selection, with the consistent improvement of each new species and a final goal in sight. That is not so. Evolution is not about progress. Biological evolution does not favour any descendants, and there is no ultimate destination for any form. The most successful life forms on earth are single-celled organisms, microorganisms that have not needed to change their basic form for millions of years."

"I see," I reply.

"In every phase of the evolutionary process there are successful species that are exceptionally well adapted to their ecological niche, and they remain unchanged. We are descended from a long line of evolutionary maladaptives—individual species that were unsuccessful in certain niches and had to find new ones. Take the transition from sea to land. The successful fish remained in the sea. There was no pressure on them to change. The less successful fish were forced into shallow waters, where they found a new way of life by becoming amphibians. The less successful amphibians, in turn, were forced from the water to become reptiles.

"I see," I say. (I am beginning to see that the worm is the crowning glory of creation and that the human line is the result of an extended genealogy of outcasts.)

"Mammals therefore did not survive because they were inherently superior," he says.

"So why did they continue to survive?" I ask.

"The dinosaurs lived for a hundred and fifty million years. They were particularly well adapted. For a hundred million years the mammals were an insignificant group because the dinosaurs were the dominant group. It was only after the dinosaurs had become extinct sixty-five million years ago that the mammals could begin to come into their own," he says.

"I see," I say.

"As far as humans are concerned," Hugo adds, "we are the descendants of unsuccessful primates, driven from the shrinking forests of East Africa and having to find a new way to survive."

Freddie and Nathi turn up. "Howzit, my man," Freddie says to Sailor, shaking his hand in passing, without looking at him directly. (Freddie forever elsewhere in his thoughts; Freddie of tribulations.) Upon which Sailor, following him with his eyes, leg still draped over the arm of the chair, his designer sneakers hypercool, asks if he has the keys to the taxidermy workshop with him, and Freddie says: "Hang on, I'll check for you right away," and cup of tea in one hand and cigarette in mouth searches in his trouser pocket, whereupon Nathi points out that he is looking in the wrong place, doesn't he recall that Sailor asked him for the key yesterday already? Whereupon Freddie, putting down his tea, cigarette still in mouth, both hands in the air as if surrendering, says: "From you I have no secrets." And Nathi at the tea table, pouring his tea, shaking his head, Rasta locks swinging, moves aside nimbly with his thin, agile body so Mrs. Dudu can pour her tea as well, quipping something in Zulu to her so that they both laugh. Whereupon Sailor, still idling in the chair, turns to Mrs. Dudu and asks where she bought her lovely shoes, and Mrs. Dudu, holding her small foot with the pretty shoe slightly aloft for all to see and exclaim over admiringly, savours the moment and the appreciative comments. All except Freddie, by this time seated with tea and a cigarette, in his customary mode of elbows on his knees and head between his shoulders and his gaze fixed on the floor. (Oh, once again so much like one of my uncles—my dry and cynical uncle, weighed down by cares at too tender an age.) "Mrs. Dudu and I are going dancing tonight," Sailor claims, "and she's going to wear those little shoes." Mrs. Dudu finds this great fun and laughs with her head thrown back.

Freddie and Nathi have a bantering relationship. Freddie, as curator of mammals, refers to Nathi as the curator of stones. I am replaceable, Freddie says of himself from time to time (wry, shaking his head, his gaze focusing intently on the floor before him), my time has run out,

I am soon to be replaced by Nathi and his friends. Yes, Nathi says, you will be replaced and posted off to the bundu. Cast into outer darkness, Sailor says. This kind of talk causes Mrs. Dudu great merriment, and she laughs, her braided locks shaking. (Nathi's Afrikaans is good, but not as flawless as that of Mrs. Dudu.)

I once again fix my attention on our discussion and ask: "Could it have turned out differently, could the dinosaurs, had they survived, also have evolved a more advanced intelligence?"

"No," Hugo Hattingh replies without any hesitation.

"Would you say it is coincidence that we have developed the intelligence we have?"

"We are mammals and mammals developed from the vertebrates," Hugo Hattingh says. "Among the first mammals there is but one vertebrate ancestor. Vertebrates occur on land only because of a relatively unknown group of fish of which the fins were connected to a strong central axis that could be adapted to a weight-bearing limb on land."

"One of the group of ill-adjusted fish," I say.

"Yes," Hugo Hattingh says. "Most other fish have a different fin shape. None of them became land animals. Three hundred and fifty million years ago one would not have thought this one, deviant group significant. One would have thought this group rare, with no future. Not going anywhere."

"One would have thought them on the way out," I say.

"To answer the question, then," Hugo Hattingh says, "yes, our intelligence and sensory consciousness developed the way it did as a result of an extensive series of coincidences."

•

This morning we are listening to *Alceste* by Gluck, with John Eliot Gardiner conducting the Monteverdi Choir and the English Baroque Soloists. Theo Verwey has great appreciation for Gluck. I notice, as I glance at him covertly, how transported he is by the music, how his face softens as he listens. It is clear that the music has a beneficial influence on him, for he looked troubled when he arrived at the office. We have begun working on the letter *E*.

"*Erbarming*," Theo says. "How often does one still come across this word?"

"It's not a word I often use," I say. "Or come across regularly."

"Indeed," Theo says.

"What would be its origin?" I ask.

"The German verb *erbarmen* is probably derived from the Old High German *armen*, to be poor, and *abarmen*, to be freed from poverty or need."

"Would compassion be the best English translation?" I ask.

"Probably," he says. "Derived from clerical Latin, from *compati*, to identify with suffering, to feel sympathy. *Erbarming* is already entered in the Patriot dictionary of 1902."

"Only to be rejected in the ensuing rounds as a useless word."

Theo smiles. I can at least achieve *that*.

This morning I have difficulty concentrating on the cards. Fortunately *E* is a less comprehensive letter than *D*.

"I've asked Hugo Hattingh what life is," I say.

"And?" Theo turns towards me, his eyebrows raised in anticipation.

"To begin with, life is the presence of DNA," I say.

Theo Verwey nods wordlessly.

"I still don't understand how DNA came about," I say. "He pointed out to me that laymen are inclined to ask the big, unanswerable questions, whereas science occupies itself with smaller, testable hypotheses."

Theo Verwey still does not reply.

"I felt myself somewhat reprimanded," I say.

"That is understandable," he says.

"I can't help thinking again this morning," I say, "and I can't really say why, of the funeral of the dead rap singer I told you about. Of the dervishes, the mendicant monks, whirling so ecstatically at the end of the procession."

•

I ask Vera whether the museum has other shells in storage, for there are relatively few on display. She takes me to the section of the Natural History Museum, inaccessible to the public, where the unexhibited specimens are kept. The storage room is an enormous L-shaped space at the far end of the wing housing the offices of the museum staff and the large taxidermy workshop.

The door opens onto the short leg of the L. Against all the walls are either built-in cupboards that reach up to the high ceiling, or wooden shelves. In the middle of the room there are small freestanding cabinets—arranged to form a smaller L within the larger one. Most of these cabinets are small, chest height and no more than fifty centimetres in width, with many drawers. Vera pulls out one after another, displaying moths and butterflies, birds and insects of all and any description.

The wall at the far end of the room is lined with built-in cupboards. Vera uses a stepladder to open one of these. She hands some boxes down to me, all of them containing shells. With these we can't do anything, she says, these specimens have not been labelled with a name, date, or location, and are therefore of no value for scientific purposes. The place smells of insecticide. She hands me a couple of smaller boxes. I place them carefully on the table; I will look at the contents later.

Leading off the large L-shaped room is a smaller one. Against its back wall are two large cabinets, each a metre in width. She opens the doors of the first one (there is a table in front of the second one) and pulls out the drawers one by one. There are fifteen drawers. Each one is filled with shells. They are stored in small stapled boxes of about ten centimetres square. This collection is properly classified—each shell has a name and a date.

"May I look around on my own for a while?" I ask.

"Certainly," she says. (Vera Garaszczuk has a Polish father and a Dutch mother, but she grew up in Kenya. The Cambrian fossils of the Burgess Shale are her special area of research. She is a tall, athletically built woman with strong calves, high Slavonic cheekbones, a slightly upturned nose, and she needs only a feather duster to make her look like a somewhat louche—but very seductive—cleaning woman.)

When she leaves, I go through all the drawers again slowly. The conchologist responsible for these classifications has left, Vera informed me. (Shall I undergo training and offer my services?) Quite a few super-families of the class *Gastropoda* (phylum *Mullusca*) are represented here, as well as the classes *Bivalvia* and *Cephalopoda*. But the shell kingdom is immense: *Mullusca* is a particularly large phylum, with approximately a hundred thousand species, and this collection could not come close to covering all the families, genera, and species residing under each superfamily.

Roughly half of all shells are found in salt water, the other half live in fresh water or on land. Compared to shells from colder regions, warm-water shells are generally more colourful. (Pale Arctic shells?) Molluscs have a brain, a digestive system, and a reproductive system. They lay eggs, which in many seawater species undergo a veliger phase before changing into miniatures of their final form.

Slowly, one by one, I go through the fifteen drawers. To build up a scientific collection molluscs must be collected live. I find the idea distasteful. I do not want to have to kill the animal inside. A shell collection is of no value if the location, date of collection, and habitat are not noted. My own collection is therefore without value. It is of no value to anyone except myself. (Whoever the thief was, he certainly was no collector.) Reference collections must, like this one, be stored in the dark. I prefer setting out my shells (in neat rows, as attentive as members of a congregation), even if it means that over time they will fade. Why should I stow them away in light-free cabinets when I want to look upon them daily to derive joy and consolation from their presence?

In the first three drawers are the superfamilies *Neriaticea, Cerithiacea,* and *Strombacea.* I do not particularly like these shells. In the fourth and fifth drawers is the superfamily *Cypraeacea,* the cowries—popular because they are glossy and colourful. Like other shells, they grow spirally, but as soon as they mature, the outer lip turns inward, and thickens to form teeth on the lip as well as on the columella. I pick up one of the white cowries: *Ovula ovum.* The aperture folds chastely inward, enclosed and marblelike. When my mother was dying, I bought two of these and placed them next to my bed along with a few other white shells. Cold and motionless this shell lies in my hand this morning. Cool against my cheek.

In the sixth and seventh drawers is the superfamily *Tonnacea*—the tonnas and phaliums (helmet shells) that I have more recently started adding to my collection. The helmet shell, of which the siphonal canal folds vertically upwards, is a heavier shell than the thinner, more fragile tonna. There are a few fine specimens here of the *Phalium glaucum*. I gently stroke the surface of one of them with my finger—its texture so different from that of Frans's velvety glans. How pleasing the proportions of this shell, with its wide apex and relatively small, sharply pointed base.

In the eighth drawer is the superfamily *Muricacea*—represented here by a large variety of specimens, but none as fine as my two stolen *Murex nigritus* shells. In the ninth drawer is the superfamily *Buccinacea* and in the tenth and eleventh drawers the superfamily *Volutacea*—to which a number of my favourite shells belong. The exquisite harpas, believed by some collectors to be the most beautiful of all shells. Active, carnivorous animals found among coral reefs, with a varying amount of axial ribs (folds). Between these ribs are fine marks, as if the animal has seismographically registered the most minute previbrations and vibrational frequencies, the subtlest indications of movement on the ocean floor. Pinks and browns—my mother's colours—with sometimes a bluishness woven in.

In the twelfth and thirteenth drawers is the superfamily *Conacea*, which includes the families *Terebridae* and *Conidae* (the conches). The genus *Conus* exhibits a particularly large variety of colours and patterns, but little structural variation. The conch shell is formed through a process whereby each whorl very nearly covers the preceding one; the outer lip is thin and the aperture long and narrow. Like the harpas, the conches are carnivorous animals, inhabiting tropical waters. Their sting can be fatal to humans.

I cannot look at these lovely specimens this morning without feeling the loss of my conches weighing heavily on my heart. I remember the day I came across the two *Conus figulinus* shells in a shop in a small Western Cape coastal town. My mother was on holiday with us. While we were swimming in the morning, she sat on a bench overlooking the sea. Her sun hat was fastened under her chin. She wore dresses of a light material with a floral pattern. Her state of mind was soft and heavy. My father had just died. As she gazed out over the sea, she was perhaps reflecting on her loss, or on the early days of her young womanhood. Of all my shells the larger of the two *Conus figulinus* shells was possibly the loveliest. A heavy shell, and when resting in the palm of my hand my thumb and index finger could barely encircle even the tapered base. Fitting in my hand as if fashioned for it—a perfectly finished hand tool, and yet so exceptional in form and conception that it surpasses human skill and imagination. The apex has a virtually flattened spire, the base colour is a soft bluish brown, deeper around the wide shoulder and gradually turning lighter and greyer down to the narrow base. Across the whole surface run fine, darker-brown horizontal lines, which seem to be woven into the surface. A cool, perfectly balanced shell. Whorl upon whorl completely folded in upon itself. Consummate.

In the fourteenth drawer there are shells from the class *Bivalvia*—the double-valved shells. (Among others, some stickle oysters—a deep, melancholy orange—and fanned shells.)

In the fifteenth drawer are shells from the class *Cephalopoda*—which includes the octopuses, squids, spirulas, and the nautiluses. The nautilus differs marginally from its prehistoric predecessors and is the only surviving genus of nautiluslike cephalopods (with limbs attached to the head) that flourished approximately a thousand million years ago. A living fossil. A predator that keeps to deep waters by day and moves closer to the surface at night to hunt. Ninety small tentacles around the parrotlike beak, and next to that the eye. Head and foot close together. In the male, four of these tentacles have been adapted for copulation, transmitting the sperm parcel to the female, who attaches the fertilised eggs one by one to the ocean bed, where they hatch. I know what the eye of the nautilus looks like. I have seen it depicted. It is an eye without a lens—it does not resemble a human eye, nor that of a fish or a shark. It is a ponderous eye—stark and not inclined to forgiveness; not sympathetic.

When I have gone through all the drawers, I carefully open the boxes that Vera took down from the top of the cupboard. As she pointed out, these shells are of no value to anyone. In one of the boxes I find five shells I can identify as belonging to the genus *Busycon*. I have coveted these for a long time. Be that as it may.

After having looked at the contents of the boxes, I look around some more and come across a smallish cabinet with two bronze sea horses for handles. A private collection, I notice as I open the small doors. Donated to the museum by Miss M. Eva. What an apt name for a shell collector. (Perhaps an alias, an assumed name, perhaps she was also a Miss Dolly Haze.) There is an unclear photograph of her with windswept hair. Every shell in her collection is meticulously named and dated. There are many shells from the Durban bay area, like the exquisite *Cypraea chinensis* cowrie and the *Lamellaria nigra*. But many are from elsewhere, presumably acquired through bartering or buying—conches from the Indian ocean, a few *Harpa majors* from the Caribbean (paler than those stolen from me). Attractive phaliums from Japan and the Mediterranean ocean, and sought-after volutes from New Zealand and Australia.

In some of the larger shells the strip of paper with information has been folded and slipped into the aperture—like a message in a bottle. The handwriting, in ink on the yellowed paper, reminds me of the letters that my father's widowed sisters used to write to him. These letters to their youngest brother speak of a changing small-town and rural world, the gradual disappearance of the old way of life. An account is given of the demise of loved ones and friends, the troubles of children and grandchildren, and once, almost too terrible to mention—news of the death of a sister's beloved younger son by his own hand. The letters are hesitant, laboriously formulated, suffused with a melancholic resignation. That is the world my father left behind when he boarded the ship, sailed up the coast of Africa, danced with strange women on deck in the evenings, disembarked to buy a cowrie, a fan, an embroidered tablecloth.

As the sisters were writing the last of these letters, Miss Eva awaited the boats with their rich finds on the quay. (Would she sometimes lie down for someone, in exchange for a valuable specimen?) I tell Sof about her that afternoon. The Durban bay area was paradisiacal before it was developed, she says. There was a huge variety of birds: pelicans, flamingos and many more. There was any plant you could think of. And there was Miss Eva, I say, our primal mother, who collected and documented all the shells in this opulent bay.

That evening I reflect on what I have seen. I used to focus exclusively on the shell, but these days I tend to think more often of the animal that inhabited it, forming its shell layer upon layer through slow secretion. As the animal grows, so does the shell. A more or less regular process, depending upon light, temperature, and the food supply of the animal—a being with a brain and hence with a consciousness—however limited.

But tonight I have to think about the nautilus in particular. How I turned cold when I saw a picture of that eye for the first time. A primeval eye—the first thought of an eye, the blueprint of an eye. Maybe that was what God had in mind at the beginning (in his mind's eye) with EYE. When in his omniscience He conceived the idea of an eye. Perhaps the idea came to God like an intimation, like a tiny bubble on the void, a quantum fluctuation, moments before the beginning of time. Perhaps that eye was indeed created after the image of God—wholly eye: intrepid, inexorable.

·

An evening or two later I once again get a phone call from Freek van As, about seven weeks after the first call that he made shortly after my shells had been stolen.

He wants to know how I am, he so much enjoyed our brief talk on the previous occasion. At first I say nothing. I find it unsettling that I still fail to place him.

"Are you sure your memory is not deceiving you?" I say. "Are you sure you're not confusing me with someone else?"

"My dear," Freek van As says, "how could I ever confuse you with someone else? That evening at Felix du Randt's flat stands out in my memory as if it happened the day before yesterday!"

"Nearly thirty years ago, and it feels to you like the day before yesterday," I say.

"Like yesterday," Freek van As says.

"Then you must have a remarkable memory," I say.

"That I have," he says. "But you were a very special young woman."

"Did we meet socially only that once?" I ask circumspectly.

"No," Freek says, "we met on quite a number of occasions. I recall a second time, for instance, at the home of the publisher Tobias Achterberg."

"The evening at Felix du Randt's flat I misbehaved, to say the least," I say. "My behaviour was reprehensible, improper, and scandalous. It is not an evening I like to be reminded of."

Freek van As gives a little chuckle.

"It is in fact a whole phase of my life I don't like being reminded of," I say.

This time his chuckle is slightly more mocking.

As we talk, I am trying to recall that evening, any evening in fact, at the home of Tobias Achterberg. There were a few such occasions, but in none of those hazy contexts can I conjure up the person of Freek van As. A tall, pale, dark man?

"There was also a third occasion," he says. "At the home of Abel Sonnekus. It was on the evening of the publication of his book on fin de siècle Dutch poetry. We had an illuminating discussion then as well."

"What about?" I ask mistrustfully, for I vaguely recall the occasion. It was during the time that Sonnekus and I were involved with each other. Although our short-lived liaison could hardly be characterised by mutual feelings of tenderness and regard.

"You had just begun reading Henry James and said that *Portrait of a Lady* was a moving novel."

"It is a moving novel," I say.

"You told me about a novel you were intending to write," he says. "You sketched it to me in broad outline. It was grandly conceived. I thought: This young woman will go far yet—she has no lack of writing ambition. I thought—"

I silence him. I resent being reminded of my youthful impetuosity.

"That evening you—"

"I don't want to hear anything more about what I did or said on that or any other evening," I interrupt him. I am beginning to suspect that I misbehaved on that occasion as well.

"You were out of sorts," Freek van As continues, unperturbed. "Something clearly upset you."

"How do you know that?" I ask.

"At one stage you were in the bathroom for a while, and when you came out, you looked disturbed."

(This man's memory!)

"Were you spying on me?" I ask admonishingly. "How else would you know how long I remained in the bathroom—or wherever?"

"Did I assume correctly that your displeasure was related to the person of Dr. Sonnekus himself?"

(In the green bathroom with the unappetising floor tiles. Sonnekus neighing as from a shot of something up the arse. Diabolically jolly. His incessant fits of laughter coming in spurts—high and hysterical. He was going on about his wife, whom he despised, about his guests, whom he likewise despised. He was never in such high spirits as when he could be so at the expense of someone else. His knees worn through on the coarse bath mat. I went along, neither an unwilling nor an unappreciative audience. And yet I got up there and thought that I was invincible. I could be a match for him, any day.)

Enough for one evening. These things belong to the past. I do not want them forced on my attention in this way. I certainly do not like the man's insinuating tone of voice.

"What have *you* been busy with these past thirty years?" I ask.

"Oh," he says, "I'm still with the newspaper."

"Which one?" I ask.

"First I was with *Die Vaderland*, then with *Die Transvaler*, and now I am with the *West Rand Daily*."

"I see," I say.

"But to return to Dr. Sonnekus," he says. "Now there is a man of character and integrity. I shall never be persuaded of the contrary."

"I have to go," I say. "Goodbye."

Tobias Achterberg. For many years I have not given him a thought. Large and morose, a heavy, dark man with a cynical, roving eye. An able businessman, who started his own small publishing company. Our paths never crossed erotically and for that I am grateful. I do recall one occasion, though, when he rubbed himself hot against me in someone's kitchen. Not two words were exchanged between us, but he pressed himself urgently against me, his breath in my neck. (His wife was attractive, dark-haired, and well-bred, an honourable, refined person.) Could that have been one of the evenings Freek van As was referring to? Did he observe us from some doorway? Is he going to make a point of continually confronting me with some or other compromising situation I found myself in at the time?

Tobias Achterberg shot himself later, when he discovered that he was suffering from an incurable disease. So many half-forgotten figures coming to my attention again lately. Or brought to my attention by the enigmatic Freek van As (dark hair, skin pale as wax?). Felix du Randt and Marthinus Maritz, Tobias Achterberg and Abel Sonnekus.

Surely this man wants something from me? Why would he suddenly announce himself as the self-appointed facilitator of my memory now, after nearly thirty years of silence, if he does not stand to benefit from it himself?

To the devil with Freek van As, whoever he may be, who hoisted up Abel Sonnekus, along with the others, as from some deep well.

.

When I arrive at the office two days later, Theo Verwey shows me a small report in the newspaper. Dr. Abel Sonnekus is recuperating after a stroke. His condition is no longer critical, but he is not yet out of danger.

(Abel Sonnekus—so recently hoisted from the well!)

"A great campaigner for the cause," Theo Verwey says. "His contribution to the preservation of Afrikaans language and literature is incalculable."

"He hates women," I say. "He hates people."

Whore, I think. *Whorer.*

Theo Verwey raises his eyebrows even higher. He clearly did not expect this reaction.

"Do you know him well?" he asks.

What do I say? Knew him? Knew him carnally? My body surrendered to him for his unbridled sexual pleasure? My tender and unformed, my youthful spirit exposed to his dishonourable and offensive presence?

"I knew him well enough, but not that well," I say.

The lover with the webbed toes and bony head. Am I now liberated at last, on the eve of his demise?

"Abel Sonnekus," Theo says somewhat accusingly, "is the benefactor who donated the large amount for the project. He is the one sponsoring your assistantship."

I am taken aback. I did not expect this. I knew about the sponsorship, but could never have guessed that he was the person behind it.

"Had it not been for Dr. Sonnekus's generous donation, I would not have been able to appoint you," Theo says.

"When he made the donation, did he know who it was for?" I ask.

Theo is a little uncomfortable. "No," he says. "At that stage he didn't know."

"And if something should happen to him," I ask, "who will then sponsor me?"

Theo Verwey shrugs. "Then we will have to see," he says. "I should think he would have provided for that."

Here our paths cross again. On a morning, nearly thirty years ago, I wittingly got into Abel Sonnekus's bed in a suburban house with drawn blinds and wall-to-wall carpets. My relationship with Felix du Randt had very recently come to an end. I had already befriended Marthinus Maritz. Do I owe it to Sonnekus then, that I find myself in a strange province with my shells gone? Has he been instrumental in the loss of my shells? Should I see it like that? Are we dealing with coincidence here, or with convergence? Or merely with the whimsical hand of Mrs. Fortune?

CHAPTER EIGHT

I could divide my life into five phases. Childhood. Turbulent youth. Misguided twenties and early thirties. The unhappy phase of my ill-fated marriage. And at present the advent of the final phase: the beginning of the end.

The presence of my sister, Joets, dominated my childhood and youth. I focused my attention on her as a child, even more than on our mother.

Felix du Randt (warm, sexy, freckled Felix) dates from the phase of self-deception and foolhardiness. So do the poet Marthinus Maritz, the editor Herman Holst, Tobias Achterberg with hangers-on (the whorers and adulterers), and Abel Sonnekus. In retrospect it seems as though I found myself endlessly in a deserted scrapyard—in an environment of unspeakable desolation. Or as if I roamed the streets of the city burning, with the raging Marthinus Maritz on one side and the silent Herman Holst on the other, my hair a brood of teeming snakes.

The phase of my unhappy marriage I associate with my ex-husband, a man I loved and admired, but who found me insufficiently humane and compassionate—and limited in my emotional register. From that marriage our child was born, and although she already has a life of her own, far from here, I think of her every day. I recall the exact texture of her skin as a child, the smell of her hair, and the delicate wrists where the beating pulse was faintly visible.

•

My sister, Joets, is brilliant. She is six years older than I am. She excels in everything at school. She writes exemplary essays; they appear in the school yearbook year after year. She is always first in her class; she is always held up as an example to everyone. I am also clever, but I go my own way. I am a wilful child, on the lookout for adventure. Joets is not always friendly towards me; she does not want to play with me. She teases me. She reads avidly; hour after hour she lies on her bed and reads. I stand in the door and watch her eyes moving across the page.

I prefer to play games of the imagination. I roam in the garden alone, or with friends as imaginary characters. We are horses on the lawn in front of the house—Elsie Haarhoff (who always breathes through her mouth) and I. We rest under the small wattle tree with the yellow flowers. Elsie is feeling ill; her parents come to fetch her. On holiday in the Free State, in Moetsie and Engela's back yard, we pretend that I am Tarzan, Moetsie is Jane. (I do not remember the faces of the two little sisters, but I do recall their back garden with the sparse fruit trees, the soft summer light, and the sense of being utterly transported into an imaginary world, of my pleasure in the game.) Often I play on my own. I play with little dolls outside in the garden, in the rock garden— the rocks are mountains, the plants are trees. On the lounge carpet I play with small Plasticine animals I have made. They trek in a group across the large surface of the carpet; they have many adventures as they proceed.

I am also an ill-tempered child, and I often feel lonely and anxious, but there are specific moments in my childhood, times I can still vividly recall, when I experience a sense of profound contentment that I am well aware of, even at the time.

I love climbing trees. Our neighbour's daughter and I spend entire afternoons in the large tree in front of their house. My father says I am *balhorig*. I find that a strange word. It means that I am stubborn. I have eczema and scratch myself until I bleed. I often have nightmares; every evening I pray that I will not have bad dreams. From a very young age I have periods of intense fear of death. As a young child I listen to my father singing to our little brother in his pram. Some of these songs make me sad. When he sings a song like "Wat maak oom Kalie daar," it brings a darkness over my child's mind; it makes me think of dying.

I also read, but not as much as Joets. Only later, when she has left home, do I start reading with fervour and abandon.

Joets goes to university at sixteen. She excels at her undergraduate studies. In her honours year she falls pregnant. She will heed no advice, she terminates her studies because she wants to get married. This breaks my father's heart. At twenty Joets is burdened with a child and an irresponsible husband.

Between Joets and me there was another child, a boy. Three years younger than Joets, three years older than me. He was a few months old when he died. There is a photograph of my mother holding him. He is wearing a knitted baby outfit. She holds him away from her and aloft, towards the camera, as if to say: Here he is, my little boy, this is what he looks like—the light of my life. As a child, I sometimes imagined him crying at night.

•

Joets is twenty; she is sitting in the back of the car with the baby. I am sitting in front with the man. I am fourteen years old. It is winter. I am wearing a blue dress and a duffel coat. I have been visiting Joets in Port Elizabeth; we are getting a lift back with a friend of Joets and her husband's. He is probably in his late thirties; he is a child psychiatrist. His name is Bernard Nell. He is a tall, dark man with glasses and a beard, and he speaks with a slight lisp. We are on our way to our parental home. (Joets merely to visit.) He is on his way to Johannesburg to meet his bride—he is on the point of getting married.

He wants to know how old I am.

Seventeen. (Untrue.)

Have I ever slept with anyone?

Yes, I say. (Not true either.)

An organ concerto by Bach is playing on the car radio.

Will I put my hand between his legs? he asks.

Yes, I will do so.

The road is long. A strange sensation, my hand between the man's legs.

We spend the night in a hotel, somewhere in a town between Port Elizabeth and Johannesburg. In our room I help Joets with the baby. She is distracted; I know she is not happy. She does not talk much. I do not know whether she saw where I put my hand. Later that night the man kisses me in the elevator. He is a big man, with an urgent physical presence. I am surprised by his fervour; all this is new to me. He teaches me to kiss. Breathe in, he says. I find it a strange kissing technique. Breathe in while you kiss, he lisps. I learn fast. In his room he slides his hands under my dress. When he tries to penetrate me, he is unable to. At that point he must realise what the true state of affairs is. He is indignant, he is greatly angered. Why did I give him the wrong impression? he asks.

The next day we travel the rest of the way in silence. I do not tell Joets or my mother about anything that happened.

A child psychiatrist, I think later (much later)—you could easily have convinced me of the opposite.

●

On one hand I feel myself moved by the drama of evolution, and on the other by the drama of my stolen shells. Between these two poles my emotional life swings like a pendulum. I feel strongly inclined to take up contact with Rosie Steinmeier and her family again. The unreliable younger brother with the skittish glance and the eyes of a Spanish priest; the deceased older brother—the alleged thief—with the sad downward curve of the eyebrows; Aunty Rosie and Alverine (so uncannily like Hazel of twenty years ago)—each of them has a role in the small psychic drama of my missing shells.

The night here is different from what I am used to in the Highveld, where I am from. The night sky has a different shape here—it is elliptical, not round. I sometimes imagine that I can see its narrow point when I sit outside in the garden at night. This ellipse makes me think of the shape of my life and of the orbital paths of the dead. I hear the fruit bats; their dark, flitting shapes are visible somewhere in the dark mass of leaves and branches. Who could have guessed that the subtropical heavens could be so sparse, so nebulous and pointed; even the moon is more modest here. And for what reason? The air is too heavy, too damp, the humidity obstructs the visibility of the stars. It is the rank earth and the heavy foliage that dominate here. The gaze is forced downwards, it is earthbound. Compared to the gravitational pull of the earth, the thin strip of sky has no substance—it is pale and weightless. Here the heavy air enfolds one, funguses invade even the body. And for nights on end the penetrating rain can be heard on the huge, shiny, tropical leaves.

What did that man actually do to me? The fellow with the colourless pubic hair and the bony death's-head. The lover, Abel Sonnekus. My benefactor, I am told. Nothing tangible that I can think of. And yet my rancour towards him has increased over the years, even though we have never had any contact since. I called him a hater of women and of people, a misogynist. Theo Verwey was surprised, as if he wanted to ask: From where the vehemence? Yes, I thought, from where and for what reason?

•

I have only just fallen asleep one night at the end of June, when my phone rings. It is Freek van As.

"Do you know what time it is?" I say.

"You've never been overly concerned with time," he remarks.

"It is a quarter past two," I say. "I have just fallen asleep."

"I followed your career with interest," he says, "but I have to confess, also with some disappointment. You showed plenty of promise, back then."

(I struggle to emerge from a dream. The mood is still strongly present, but the content is rapidly fading. I am trying hard to recall it. It was important.)

"The book you eventually published was rather small in format, if I'm not mistaken."

"You're not mistaken."

"Why the long silence? Why not a single thing written in all these years—all of seventeen years, is it not?"

Is he drunk? I can hear him lisping slightly. A sly, insidious lisp.

"It is."

A tail-wagging, insinuating lisp. (It was a dream in which Joets featured. I could not see her. She sat apart from me in a hall full of people.)

Whisperer.

"What became of Judit, your sister? Also greatly talented. A beautiful woman, I recall."

"She is dead, Freek. Goodbye."

"Wait. Not so impatient. You and I have a lot to talk about."

Still for the life of me I cannot place him. A dark man, an unhealthy pallor. A minor physical aberration of some kind? *Had ek van die een en twintig vryers nog maar een / Jan Piet of Klaas met die rotteskeen.* (Had I of the twenty-one suitors left but one / Jan, Piet or Klaas with the rotten shin.) A rhyme of my father's.

"I have a few thoughts I want to share with you. I came upon some passages tonight and I thought, if this is not something for Helena Verbloem. Would this not help her to break free from her constrictions: from everything that restricts and handicaps her, everything that curtails and obstructs her, that hinders and hamshackles, curbs and cramps her—"

The line suddenly crackles as if there is too much static in the air.

(I am aware of Joets's presence. I have said something wrong. A shudder of revulsion ripples through the audience. I whisper something in her husband's ear.) What is this man driving at?

"Hallo," he says, "are you still there? I have a couple of particularly useful quotations about the fundamental principles of fiction. Can I read them to you quickly? I am of the opinion that they will really be of use to you—to direct and guide you, to prepare the way, in a manner of speaking—"

I quietly put the telephone down.

Two minutes later it rings again. I ignore it. My sleep has been banished. The man's meddlesome remarks have disturbed me thoroughly. Wagtail.

When the phone rings yet again, I pick it up to tell him to go to hell, with his useful quotations and all—to the real hell, not the watered-down Reformed version.

It is Sof.

"Helena," she says, "am I disturbing you?"

"No," I say. "I've just been woken up by a man who claims that we knew each other twenty-seven years ago. For the life of me I still can't recall him. Is something wrong?"

"My husband and the children have gone to visit his parents, and I've just had a horrible vision of all three of them plunging down some abyss. It's the children I am worried about."

"Drink something," I say. "Nothing will happen to them. Read something."

"I've been reading all night," she says.

"Sof," I say, "can we talk tomorrow? I'm suffering from sleep deprivation."

"I'm so sorry," she says. "I don't want to disturb you. You need your sleep. But I've just spent a devastating couple of hours. I think my family is right when they assume that I've strayed so far from the righteous path that I've forfeited all chance of redemption. They probably think that I voluntarily turned my back on salvation through my obstinacy and my depraved nature. But," and she gives a small laugh, "it's possible that I was never destined to be a recipient of grace. It's probably not even through any fault of my own that the fires of hell are in store for me for all eternity." (Again the little laugh.)

"Accept that you have sinned and go to bed," I say. "We've all sinned. We've all strayed from the path. We'll talk again tomorrow."

CHAPTER NINE

From Vera Garaszczuk I obtain a key to the large storeroom. I want to have a quiet look at the treasures there on my own. Vera says it is fine, I can go at any time, I will not disturb anyone. One morning I come in especially early. The door to the large room is locked, but when I enter, the lights are on. Perhaps they always remain on. I linger a while to defer my pleasure, looking at the birds, moths, and the dune mole skulls. The previous time I was here, I concentrated on the cabinets with shells; today I want to move the table in front of the second cabinet in the smaller back room out of the way, to have a look at those shells as well.

The door leading to this smaller room is half open, and as I am about to enter, I notice movement at the far end of the room. Sailor is bending over, with his back turned to me, and behind him is Hugo Hattingh. He is moving with robust and rhythmic thrusts, while Sailor is energetically manipulating himself with his right hand. The only sound in the room is that of the table, on which Sailor is supporting himself with his other hand, banging regularly against the cabinet (with shells). The light has been switched off, but Hugo Hattingh's naked buttocks are clearly visible. I look up. The ceiling here is of the same height as that of the first room. There are blinds in front of the windows, filtering the light and bathing the room in a bluish hue. There is the odour of mothballs and bones. As I am on the point of retreating, Sailor turns his head and half glances over his shoulder.

This is clearly not an appropriate time to view the shells. I do not know if Sailor saw me during the brief moment that I hesitated in the half-open door. I make a quick and silent retreat, closing the door of the first room softly behind me, making sure that it is locked again. Sailor and Hugo should consider a *Do Not Disturb* notice. Who would have guessed? Those two? I was under the impression Hugo Hattingh's preference was for young boys.

Later that morning I say to Theo Verwey: "Would you have guessed that Sailor and Hugo Hattingh find consolation in each other's arms? Although I would hardly call it consolation," I add (considering Hugo Hattingh's forceful thrusts).

Theo, standing at his desk with his back towards me, turns slightly in my direction.

"Consolation?" he says with a slight frown, apparently not quite understanding.

"Yes," I say. "Consolation—whatever, in a manner of speaking. I caught them in the act this morning, in the heat of the act, in flagrante delicto. In the room where the unexhibited material is stored. The shells and so on."

"Consolation?" Theo says and laughs scornfully. (I have never heard him laugh like this.) "Hugo Hattingh is one step removed from autistic."

"Does that mean," I say, "that he is not capable of sexual contact?"

Theo turns away from me. He places the stack of cards on the desk before him, his hands resting on it lightly, his gaze focused fixedly ahead. He does not answer me.

"Did you get all the cards sorted yesterday?" he asks, slightly irritably.

I look at the card in my hand. *Doodjakker*—to gambol, frisk, cavort, and caper to death. Sailor and Hugo Hattingh gambolled themselves to death this morning and Hugo Hattingh fucked Sailor good and solid. This I had better not mention. The card after *doodjakker* is *doolhof*— labyrinth, maze. No, I have not yet alphabetised them. Theo and I have already discussed the different meanings of labyrinth. I said that I have a clearer picture of the passages and spaces in the temporal bone of the skull than I have of the virtuous path. *Doolhoftandiges—Labyrintho-dontia*; something for Freddie. Theo sits down and turns his back on me. So named because the dentine of the type of tooth, found in the

Labyrinthodontia and *Crossopterygii* species, has a large number of folds, forming a complex structure. Theo turns his back on me as if I am the one to have strayed from the virtuous way. I should have kept quiet, I now realise.

We do not listen to music this morning. Until teatime we work in complete silence. Sailor and Hugo Hattingh are both in the tearoom. Sailor has a healthy glow on the cheek, he is coquettish with Freddie, he sweet-talks and flirts with Vera. Hugo Hattingh drinks his tea; he is in conversation with Nathi Gule, although he hardly looks in his direction, but stares in front of him as is his manner. Not a glance is exchanged between him and Sailor.

Hugo Hattingh is holding forth on the evolution of the eye. Nathi, with his broad face, slightly convex towards the centre, high cheekbones, and semi-oriental eyes, sits bolt upright on the edge of his chair, eager to learn.

"It is estimated that in the animal kingdom the eye evolved independently between forty and sixty times. There are nine recognised independent optical principles, and all of them evolved more than once. It would seem that there is a powerful impulse in evolution towards the formation of an eye," he says.

(To contemplate the glory? I wonder.)

"The human eye evolved out of something that had not been a recognisable eye before. It's not a particularly good design, for the blood vessels run in front of the retina, in contrast with the eye of the octopus, for example."

Sailor takes a large slice of Vera Garaszczuk's cake. She baked it herself—a rich, dark, moist cake with poppy seeds inside, a Polish recipe, she says. Sailor praises the cake enthusiastically. He eats one slice after another. Vera's sallow cheeks are flushed with pleasure. She keeps offering him more. Nothing wrong with his appetite. Great jollification in the tearoom. The cake is a feast de luxe, Sailor says. Yes, festive, exclaims Vera. What is it called in Polish? Sailor wants to know. It's called makowiec, Vera says. Everyone tries to pronounce it. Ma-ko-veets, Sailor says. Again everyone tries to pronounce the word. (Hugo looks away, irritated.) Ma-ko-vee-yets, Vera repeats. But where is Theo Verwey, she wants to know, she told him yesterday that she is bringing cake today. She knows how much he likes this poppyseed cake—she baked it especially with him in mind. Yes, Sailor asks, why is he not having tea with us today, and he looks directly at me, smiles, and in the highest of spirits takes another slice of cake. He may be here later, I say, he has something to attend to urgently.

Back at the office, Theo informs me that he has to leave; he has an appointment. Will I continue to alphabetise the cards, the death combinations? (No problem, Theo, I will have them done in the blink of an eye. I will not allow myself to be handicapped, hampered, encumbered, or cramped. Certainly not by the death words.)

•

Theo returns only much later in the afternoon. (I have in the meantime made good progress with the cards.) He seats himself at his desk and stares ahead of him. He sits like that for a long time.

"What happened to your stolen shells?" he suddenly asks, without turning towards me. For a moment I am taken aback. I did not expect this question.

"Thirty-two were stolen," I say. "I got nine back. The other twenty-three are still missing. A Constable Modisane of the SAP put me on the trail of someone in Ladybrand who allegedly had something to do with the theft. Sof Benadé and I paid the man's family a visit. The police had found him hanged. The nine recovered shells had been in a bag next to the body. I took a photograph of the small building where it had happened. The information was probably a false lead. Although I suspect that the man's younger brother knows something about the disappearance of the shells. I have not abandoned hope of finding them—of finding the shells."

Theo Verwey says nothing. He is still gazing ahead of him. "Ladybrand?" he asks after a while.

"Yes," I say. "There are lovely sandstone cliffs on the way there."

Theo nods. "I am well acquainted with that area," he says.

Doodjakker, to gambol to death. I am still sitting with the card on my lap. Theo is so dead still, so dead silent, so dead absent that I begin to sense trouble.

"Is anything wrong?" I ask.

"No," Theo says. He shakes his head slowly. "No," he says, "nothing is wrong," and he puts on his glasses and bends over his work.

Everything dead jolly. All unsettling thoughts silenced to death.

He is in the final phase of his great word project. The many thousands of words he has transferred to cards over the years have only to be catalogued and alphabetised finally before their eventual consolidation in book form. This large-scale collection of words has been compiled from meticulous research, including field work, extensive questionnaires, and consultation with other etymologists and language experts. With this project, Theo Verwey aims to gather into a single book all the words that have become obsolete in Afrikaans, all expressions no longer in common use, and to record their etymological origins. A large, ambitious project. I sometimes have to think of Mr. Casaubon in *Middlemarch*, with his key to all mythologies. Theo Verwey employed me as project assistant on account of my experience as a lexicographer. As I am currently not bound to the routines of schoolgoing children or a permanent job, I can afford to spend a number of months—my provisional contract is for six months—on a project like this.

I regret having told Theo about Hugo Hattingh and Sailor this morning. I will not refer to their early-morning romp again. *Doodjakker*, according to the dictionary definition, is total exhaustion due to excessive cavorting. Neither Sailor nor Hugo seemed exhausted, Sailor not in the least. More blond, more arch, more winsome than ever. In this case, neither of the two involved sported themselves to death, or into a state of near terminal exhaustion, and there had been no need to inform Theo Verwey about the incident.

•

The next day at teatime I turn my attention to Hugo Hattingh again. Nathi and Freddie have not arrived yet, and neither has Sailor. Last time we spoke about coincidence in evolution. Only one branch of lobe-finned fish moved onto land and that was the start of an unrepeatable history. That is how coincidence operates. The smallest difference—however insignificant—can change the course of history. I am self-conscious in Hugo's presence today, as if I am the one who was caught in the act.

We speak about coincidence again. "People proceed from the premise that what is important, or what they deem important, is also inevitable, but that is not so," he says. "Billions of contingent events eventually led to *Homo sapiens*. The form of no single species known to us today was predictable at any stage. Every species is the result of coincidence, of countless preceding events."

My next question is about consciousness. (I am impatient, I want to proceed by leaps and bounds.) I want to know how the sense of self came about. What its possible evolutionary function could have been.

For a brief moment he seems irked. These lay questions again. Too bad, I think. He looks different this morning. Could Theo Verwey's scornful remark of the day before have anything to do with the way I perceive Hugo this morning? It has not struck me before how soft and rasping his voice is—as if projected with difficulty from a small balsawood construction in his throat.

Theories about the nature and origin of consciousness fall outside his field of study, Hugo says. "People like Dennett wrote on the significance of language for the structuring of consciousness and the development of self-reflection."

Something is amiss with him this morning, unless I am imagining things. His mouth is an uncommonly deep red—it looks like a thin-skinned fruit, the blushing (bleeding) flesh visible underneath. I judged him too rashly. He is not as impenetrable as he appears to be. His hands holding the cup are shaking lightly, he has trouble controlling them. I can see that his extensive knowledge cannot shield him this morning from some appalling intimation of terror. He is off balance and I do not know why. I do not know if the incident with Sailor has any bearing on his mood. This man, who seldom displays any trace of emotion (and if Theo Verwey is right, is barely capable of experiencing emotion), today looks as if he is helpless against some sense of inner turbulence. His face is blotchy, the skin red and swollen in places.

I can tell by the way he turns away from me, drinking his tea, that he is not inclined to continue our discussion. (Self-reflection. The word echoes disturbingly in the silence between us.) We finish our tea without further speech, but as I get up to leave, he repeats that the essence of science is testability—for which the detail of the observable world is often of cardinal importance.

"I am ashamed," I say, "that I keep coming with these irresponsible lay questions. I must learn to channel my enthusiasm better."

He looks at me for a moment, as if the remark is registering. Then he removes his glasses and slowly runs his hand over his face. A sigh, a shudder almost, seems to go through him before he puts on his glasses again.

•

Two nights later the telephone rings late in the evening again. It could be one of four people, I think. It could be Sof, harried by thoughts of eternity; it could be my lover, who (cautiously) wishes to enquire how I am; it could be my child, calling from another country (seldom taking time difference into account). Or it could be Constable Modisane, to report the recovery of the other twenty-three shells.

It is Johannes Taljaard, also known as Sailor. Can he drop by, he is in the vicinity. I think: Perhaps he wants to talk to me about Hugo Hattingh and himself.

He looks battered. I invite him in. His hand is covered with a bandage. There is blood on his shirt. He asks if I have something to drink, something strong. I offer him whisky. His lover walked out on him, he says. They had a fight. The man slashed his canvases, broke his glassware. He had to throw him out of the flat. His hand was cut in the process. He had to have stitches. (That explains why he was in the vicinity—the hospital is nearby.)

How did he know where I live?

Sof once told him.

Sailor drinks heavily. The more he drinks, the paler his eyes become, the more cheerless his gaze, the more noticeable his eyelashes, the wetter and weaker his mouth. The less he resembles Flash Gordon. I can picture him in middle age—his eyes puffy and his jawline undefined. He keeps running his hand through his hair. He talks of his lover's tantrums and destructiveness. Never once does he refer to Hugo Hattingh.

Late at night, when he has downed the entire bottle of whisky, he suddenly says: "And on Sunday afternoons my father fucked my brother."

He gives a small snicker, puts his hand before his mouth.

"Oops," he says, his eyes pale as two marbles, "that slipped out accidentally."

CHAPTER TEN

In primary school my little friend Elsie Haarhoff and I both read *Die gesel van Namaland* (The scourge of Namaland). We argued about where the emphasis should fall in *gesel*. She thought it should be on the last syllable (which would have changed the meaning to companion, or escort). We also read *Die metamorfose van Pietman Mol.* I did not understand the meaning of the word metamorphosis and she wanted her book back before I could make out what had befallen Pietman Mol. Of neither of these two books do I remember anything. But I clearly recall the mood of two other books, belonging to my mother: *Die volstruiswagtertjie* (The little ostrichkeeper), and *Kees van die Kalahari* (Kees of the Kalahari). Two scenes in particular in these books upset me deeply—an ostrich kicking someone to death, and vultures pecking out the eyes of the mother baboon. (A short 35-millimetre nature film we saw at school at the time, of a lion killing a buck, profoundly upset me in the same way.)

When I was fifteen, and Joets had left home, and I no longer felt compelled to follow her eyes as they moved across the page of the book she was reading, I began to lose myself with passion in my own reading.

In my middle thirties I wrote a novel. It was received well; it was a minor success. After its publication Joets turned her back on me for a considerable length of time. She made it known to me that she found it a good book but that she did not want to speak to me again. (She was never one for half measures.) She stuck to her resolve and had no contact with me for months. We were eventually reconciled again, but between us no reference was ever made to the book again. I suspect that she read herself and our mother into the characters of the sister and the mother, and resented the way these two characters were portrayed.

Sof and I take a drive after work one day. It is a fine day. Clear. We sit in the car at a beach to the north of the city, overlooking the sea stretching endlessly before us. We certainly do not sit like Mrs. Curren and Vercueil—for Sof is not Vercueil, and I am not as old as Mrs. C, nor am I dying. As a character, I am not as sorely tried as she is. My shells have been stolen, but this is hardly anything compared to the losses she has to endure in the course of that novel. My mother would have said this as well: It is nothing, she would have said. The loss of a few shells is nothing. They are worldly goods, not of any importance. Life and death, that is what is important, that alone. (She could say this only at the end of her life, when she was dying. Earlier on she had dreamt of being loved—*adored*, like Isobel Archer in *Portrait of a Lady*. The novel that Freek van As brought to my attention again just recently.)

I find it beautiful, the way Mrs. C speaks of Thucydides to the black child in the hospital. I am moved and overcome by it, it leaves me breathless—the leap the writer takes there. How much he risks by making a dying white woman in a hospital explain Thucydides to a black child—a child whom she does not even like all that much; one she feels she has to learn to love, for otherwise her love for her daughter would not be valid.

Mrs. C says that she has "grief past weeping." "I am hollow," she says, "I am a shell." I am not there yet. I am not yet a shell. I am still inhabited by an ego, as if by the animal in its shell. It binds me—as muscle tissue attaches to bone—to my child, even though she is far from here; to my lover, on whom I depend for the satisfaction of my physical and emotional needs; and to my shells, on which my heart is set and of which twenty-three of the stolen thirty-two are still lost.

Sof says: "The very day I married my husband I began to fantasise about leaving him."

"Why did you marry him?" I ask.

"I was young. I had no inner life. I had no will as yet. I was as lacking in will as a snail."

"A snail has a will," I say.

Sof and I are sitting next to each other, looking out over the sea. The sea is calm. On the horizon is a ship. Our paths have crossed over the past couple of months, but what do I really know about her history—about the complex course of her life, about the convergences and meanderings that have led her here, to sit next to me today with her particular troubles and vexations?

"By no means a complex will," I say, "but a will nevertheless."

That evening I get a call from Frans de Waard, my lover and companion. When will we see each other again? "I have been patient for a long time," he says.

"Don't pressurise me," I say. "I'm still dealing with the loss of my shells."

"The loss of your shells," he says. There is a cutting edge to his voice, as if his patience is wearing thin.

"Yes," I say.

"Your shells," he says.

"Yes," I say, "my shells."

"Perhaps you should consider a few therapy sessions," he says, "to help you deal with the loss." And with that he puts the phone down. I am not particularly upset by his words.

Therapy I do not consider. I have no need of someone guiding me with a firm hand through the labyrinths (mazes) of the psyche. I should rather resist the temptation to phone Constable Modisane. He sees the case as closed. His visit to me and the gift of the shell were a token, a request: Let us leave it at that. More than a request even—a plea: Do not concern yourself with this matter any further.

But I want to! I cannot resist the temptation to concern myself with the matter. I do not wish to let it go, and Constable Modisane is the last remaining link with my missing shells. Every day I have to withstand the temptation to phone him. I waver between different options. I could tell him that I am offering a cash reward for every shell recovered. That should be sufficient as an incentive. But because I do not want to pressurise him, because I like him, I urge myself to show restraint. Give him a chance, I think, on his own he may take more trouble to find out about the missing shells than if I breathe down his neck and compromise his position. If I harass him continually, he may get annoyed with me; if I am patient, something may yet come of it.

But what can come of it? Will an overworked, underpaid policeman go to any trouble to recover twenty-three missing shells? No. I have to let them go. I have to let every single one of them go. Even the *Argonauta argo*—little caravel of the open seas! Even the heavy *Conus figulinus*, perhaps the loveliest of my shells, which I can still feel resting in my palm, cold and heavy. Even the papery thin *Tonna allium* from the warm Indo-Pacific coastal regions, and the two *Nautilus* shells—proud standard-bearers! I have to let each one go.

I know what a therapist would say. Behind every loss lies an earlier loss. The loss of my shells is a pretence (an evasion, a cloaking and veiling), an attempt of the cunning psyche to obscure earlier, more painful losses.

At night, when I cannot sleep, I immerse myself with a zeal nearing obsession in my new knowledge. Sometimes I find it hard to unravel and make sense of all there is to know. I have to keep my eye firmly on the intricate course of the earth's history of origin and evolution, and focus hard to order the information systematically.

CHAPTER ELEVEN

When I speak to Hugo Hattingh again, I stick to my resolution to temper my impatience. I have been too hasty, too zealous up to now. This field of knowledge has to be approached methodically. I have to make sure that I understand everything from the beginning.

"The earth was formed approximately ten thousand five hundred million years after the Big Bang," I begin. "Do I understand correctly that the earth in its earliest state was probably completely molten, that it gradually became bigger through the agglomeration of asteroidlike debris—attracted by the earth's gravity—and that in this phase it was continually subjected to the bombardment of planetesimals—"

"Whose heat caused the melting," Hugo says.

"And that this earth, molten during the first million years after its formation, cooled gradually and differentiated into various concentric layers, with a core of nickel iron—"

"These layers were stratified according to their density," Hugo Hattingh says. "With the denser material continually sinking downwards."

"So that the crust of the earth has a lower density than the core?" I say.

"Correct," Hugo Hattingh says.

"And do I understand rightly," I continue, "that this early crust was almost completely destroyed by the constant assault of asteroids and comets, attracted by the earth's gravitational field?"

"The parts that were not destroyed," Hugo says, "were later taken up into the mantle."

I keep my eye on the ball. I am trying to get a clear picture of the early formation of the earth. But how should I conceive of this young earth during the chaotic period of its formation? The so-called Hadean era? (A hellish, otherworldly time?) How should I conceive of this half-molten planet in the making, this wild and empty, turbulent and inhospitable, half-formed cluster of elements—exposed to enormous gravitational and radioactive energies, as well as the bombardment of solar debris? I find this almost impossible to grasp. I persevere nonetheless.

Freddie Ferreira, the curator of mammals, has turned up in the meantime.

I try and visualise as clearly as possible the processes happening on earth over billions of years, but I keep my gaze averted from Hugo Hattingh, because it unsettles me to look at him this morning. As before, I am struck by the turbulence beneath the surface of his skin—erupting in red spots and angry weals. His mouth as dark red as a contused fruit, the blood close to the surface.

Freddie is listening, sitting with his elbows on his knees, as usual, and looking at the floor in front of him.

"And is it correct to say that the earth was initially too hot for the formation of oceans? That it was able to cool down and solidify only when the solar bombardments diminished? And that the early atmosphere was gradually replaced by an atmosphere formed by volcanic degassing?

"Correct," Hugo Hattingh says. "It isn't possible to analyse the exact composition of the initial atmosphere. The noble gases helium, neon, argon, and xenon were still abundantly present in it—as in fact also in the rest of the universe."

"Good," I say. "I understand that the current atmosphere developed from volatile gases released during volcanic eruptions in the early stages of crust formation."

"It's more complex than that," Hugo Hattingh says. "The atmosphere was bound by gravity and over time repeatedly changed in composition. Some of these changes were caused by biological processes.

The atmosphere does not have the same chemical buffer as the ocean, preventing changes in its composition."

Freddie is still sitting with his elbows propped on his knees, his head hanging between his shoulders. He is tapping softly and rhythmically with the tips of his shoes, keeping the heels on the floor.

"Be that as it may," I say. "Broadly viewed then, the cooling of the earth's surface caused water vapour to condense in the atmosphere and rain helped to form the early oceans."

"Correct," says Hugo Hattingh. "In broad outline that may be assumed."

"And, most crucially, the earth has retained an atmosphere as well as oceans—in contrast with Mercury, which is too small and too hot, Mars, which is too cold, and Venus, which is too hot for an ocean."

"Correct. The occurrence of stromatolites—stroma, algae—dating from about three thousand eight hundred million years ago," Hugo Hattingh says, "is an indication that the earth's surface had cooled down to less than one hundred degrees Celsius, whereas it had been much warmer during its early formative phases."

"And these stroma are the first signs of life?"

Hugo Hattingh nods briefly. "Those are the first fossil indications," he says, "although life probably originated earlier." Freddie is looking the other way. A flash, a fragment of a dream I had the night before, comes back to me. As if my mother died a second time. Never again, never again, I said, I shall never see her again.

"But," I say, "before we get to the first signs of life—the blue-green algae, the primordial slime—I first want to make sure that I understand the earth's early formative phase properly, in order to picture the stage on which everything is about to be enacted, so to speak."

"The geological history of the earth and evolution cannot be separated from each other," Hugo says.

Upon which, despite his visibly increasing impatience, he briefly explains how the different prevailing rock formations succeeded each other during the formation of South Africa specifically: the Kaapvaal Craton and the Barberton Greenstone Belt three thousand one hundred million years ago, the Limpopo Belt and the Witwatersrand Supergroup two thousand seven hundred million years ago, the Ventersdorp

Supergroup two thousand six hundred million years ago, the Bushveld Complex and Transvaal Supergroup two thousand million years ago, the Waterberg and Olifantshoek Supergroups and the Ubendian Belt one thousand seven hundred million years ago, the Namaqua-Natal Belt a thousand million years ago, the Pan-African Belt five hundred million years ago, and the most recent, the Cape and Karoo Supergroups, laid down sixty million years ago. The rocks in the Barberton Greenstone Belt are therefore the best exposed and best preserved rocks in the world, he says, and among the oldest on earth.

But I have stopped listening with undivided attention, for I have complex, though fleeting associations with some of these names: Barberton and Ventersdorp and Olifantshoek. The bygone world of my father. It would have given him much pleasure to know that the rocks where he came from were the oldest on earth. He would have said, yes, that makes sense. He would have been proud. He would have related a few of his adventures as a young man. He would have told of the patches of mist so dense that you could not see your hand in front of you as you came down the mountain pass. He loved that world. To him it was paradise. He always hankered after it.

This time I proceed slowly. I am ashamed of the way in which I swamped Hugo Hattingh with rash and silly questions. It is the first week of August, ten weeks since my shells were stolen, six days since I discovered Sailor and Hugo Hattingh in the storeroom, too long (three weeks, a month?) since my lover and I lay in each other's arms a whole weekend long.

•

In our house there were two *Cypraea tigris* cowrie shells, a species not commonly found in South Africa. Perhaps my mother had inherited one of them, perhaps it had been part of her inheritance—a cowrie from Ceylon, where her grandfather had been a prisoner of war. Perhaps she and my father had been on holiday and had bought it from a woman exhibiting her wares on a pavement at the beachfront. Perhaps every Afrikaner home in the Fifties boasted a cowrie shell, for these shells are commonly found in Mozambique, and had probably been travelling down some trade route to Durban for many years. Perhaps my father had bought the other on one of his boat trips up along the coast of East Africa. Those shells were cool and smooth against the cheek, and it was a strange sensation to let one's tongue glide over the ruffled, teethlike opening underneath. The shells made me think of ivory when I was a child, it reminded me of the ivory keys of the piano—which my mother had also inherited, and which no one ever played.

On holiday along the South Coast we would pick up shells. My mother too. She seemed distracted as she did so. Bending over, she made me think of the picture of Ruth in my Children's Bible, picking up loose sheaves of corn in Boas's field. When I think of my mother picking up shells, it is as if she was surveying her whole life while doing so. As if she was weighing up everything that had ever happened to her. My mother had much to reflect upon. She had been wronged at an early age. Perhaps picking up shells like that, with only the droning of the ocean in the background, brought her a measure of equanimity. Her father had abandoned them, he had gone down a mine, and had emerged above ground only much later.

Perhaps it was the overlapping of our histories, the shared point of reference, that had drawn the poet Marthinus Maritz to me, and me to him. Both my grandfather and his father had been miners, and both had left their families to descend into some mine in Messina, or elsewhere in Africa. We had that in common, besides a taste for adventure.

On the prowl in the city at night, in the company of the raging Marthinus and the silent Herman Holst. The more Marthinus drinks, the more he quotes from Ezra Pound, Isaac Bashevis Singer, Allen Ginsberg, Wallace Stevens. But especially Stevens. The more dangerous (unreliable) the glint in his eye, the more he fulminates, rants and rails. God help us. The more he goes on about his alcoholic mother and his lost father, and the series of abusive, substitute fathers. About the injustices he suffered and the scars he sustained. His second volume of poetry has just been published, but it has not been as well received as the first. He resents this deeply. He is convinced that his poetry is underrated, that no one understands what he is attempting to do, that the public is uneducated and the critics sell-outs. It was Abel Sonnekus who was most critical of the volume, dismissing it as virtually worthless, and Marthinus does not want to hear his name mentioned—his contempt for Abel Sonnekus is boundless. He goes white around the nostrils and the corners of the mouth, the expression in his eyes turns murderous when he speaks of Abel Sonnekus. We are sitting in a large beer hall somewhere in Hillbrow. It is exceptionally rowdy and the air is heavy with cigarette smoke. We drink brandy and Coke. Next to me Herman Holst drinks in silence. Nobody knows what he thinks, for he never speaks. Marthinus sits facing me, he holds me hostage with his fanatical gaze, with the urgency of his grievance. His father left his mother when he was a baby. He probably disappeared down the copper mines of Messina, although he could also have come to the end of his known history further north, in the tin mines of Namibia. "Who will ever know?" Marthinus asks, stubbing out his cigarette, drinking his brandy, and staring at me with a grim light in his eyes—blue, as flammable as methylated spirits. His sleeves rolled up, large sweat stains under his arms. His mother was always involved with rough types. At four he taught himself to read; he read anything he could lay his hands on as a child. One of the mother's lovers burnt his books. At the age of eight he became very ill. He was dying. His mother promised that she would stop drinking if his life was spared. He survived, but his mother did not stop drinking. She took in one man after another. They lived in a caravan for a while. His mother became involved with a church sect. "We were actually white trash," he says. "Trailer trash." Gradually his shoulders become more hunched, as if the burdens of childhood increasingly weigh him down; his shirt strains over his fleshy torso. "My mother would hit me with a belt when she was drunk," he says, "and then she would weep and try to get into bed with me in her maudlin state. Even when I was no longer a child."

Marthinus is drunk with resentment, aggression, thwarted ambition, loss. He is furious because not enough is happening, because the pace of his life is too slow; he is frustrated with the restrictions of middle-class life; he is ambivalent towards his material success, he craves recognition. He has feelings of guilt, he is consumed by remorse: he did not make his peace with his mother before she died, he let her down, turning his back on her at the end. He betrayed her. He is full of self-justification: she never gave him what he needed, she did not grant him a life. "She was a whore, she was a drunk." Herman Holst listens in silence. Marthinus is white around the nostrils, pale with emotion. His father didn't give a fuck. His father left him and his mother intentionally. He could not get far enough away from them, from him and his mother. In his twenties Marthinus spent some time in a psychiatric ward. "I lost it," he says. "What do you expect?"

He wrote moving poems about Johannesburg in winter—in the early morning, at dusk. Poems in which loss leaps up from the paper and seizes you by the throat, wrings your heart. He ingested the desolation of the city with mother's milk and brandy, he maintains, "and when the breast dried up, or was laid claim to by one of her lovers, only the greyness remained." On his mother's side his genealogy goes back to illustrious Boer heroes, but his father was of obscure descent: a Scot, an Irishman, or a Lithuanian. A Jewish refugee. A miner. After his father had left, he took his mother's name: Maritz, a solid Boer surname.

It is on a night like this, after hanging out in beer halls and pubs, that I suggest the visit to Felix du Randt. From Hillbrow to Braamfontein in the car, Herman Holst silently at the wheel, with Marthinus next to him in the passenger seat, and me in the back. Herman silent and Marthinus singing; he is singing all the way, but his gaze is that of a stalker—I do not have to see his face to know that, I can read it off the back of his head. His shoulders are hunched forward with a homicidal slant. He sings Chris Blignaut songs, he sings Yiddish songs and Scottish ballads. In the back of the car I listen to his voice; it captivates me. It speaks to me erotically in a way that his physical person never does. After the visit to Felix du Randt neither of us seem to find it necessary to refer to the incident again.

I moved to another province. Months, maybe even a year or two went by. The last time we saw each other was in a bar in the Western Cape. He was overweight. Even more solid. I found him too fleshy, somewhat repulsive. His face had an unhealthy cast. His eyebrows were heavier than I had recalled, the pallor around the corners of his nose and mouth was more pronounced. His hands were sweaty. He told me about a homo-erotic incident in his youth, with a man in a shower. I never saw him again. A few months later I learned of his death. He was still young, in his early forties. Hard to believe that death could silence such a refractory soul.

Eventually I yield to the temptation and pay the police station a visit. Luckily Constable Moonsamy with his hawk's eye is not there. I ask where I can get hold of Constable Modisane.

"Constable Modisane is not here any more," the constable on duty says (attractive in an oily, Bollywood sort of way), without looking up from his business.

"And where is he, if I may ask?" I say.

"He has been transferred," the unhelpful servant of the law says.

"Where to?" I ask.

"To another province," the man says.

"And which province may that be?" I ask.

"He has been transferred to Limpopo province, to Musina," he adds reluctantly.

Messina. I do not believe it.

"Why Messina?" I ask.

"Musina," the man says.

"It used to be Messina," I say.

"Now it is Musina."

"I know," I say. "Why Musina?"

The man shakes his head, does not look up.

"Is this a temporary transfer?" I ask.

"Lady," he says, and looks up briefly, "this is a confidential police matter. It is not of any concern to the public."

"I am not the public," I say.

"You are family, perhaps?" he asks.

"Yes," I say, "why not?"

He must have decided against taking me up on that. He continues with his writing.

"Please," I say. "He has helped me a great deal. I want to thank him."

"Then you must do so in your personal capacity."

"I do not have his address."

"Ask the other members of your family," the man says cuttingly.

"Just tell me, please," I say, "is this a temporary transfer?"

"No," he says. "It is not temporary."

I cannot believe it. Constable Modisane gone. Gone to Musina. Messina. Gone to Messina, where my grandfather and the father of Marthinus Maritz had disappeared to. Down into the mines. Ostensibly. Be warned. It could have been a fiction, a falsification. It could have been a fabrication, a misrepresentation, it could have been a counterfeiting of the truth. It is possible that it never happened that way. Is Constable Modisane dead? He was transferred to Musina: is that a euphemism, cryptic police speak? Or has he been elevated, exulted, promoted to a higher rank for distinguished service, and posted to Musina?

To Messina of the silvery ring, the baobab tree, and the heat. All my life I have dreamt of Messina. Now Musina. Messina at the end of the known world, where my grandfather was swallowed by the earth and later spat out again—to my mother's eternal chagrin and despair.

Or is Constable Modisane being punished for unbecoming conduct, for too readily supplying information, allowing the public to view confidential documents? Constable Modisane put me on the trail of Patrick Steinmeier, which took me to Ladybrand, to the house of Aunty Rosie, Alverine and Jaykie, the house with the two stuffed tigers, and although the visit yielded nothing, it brought about a broadening of possibilities, it extended the network of probability, which I prefer to my shells vanishing without trace into the void.

I do not have a good feeling about Constable Modisane as I walk out of that charge office. Not about him, nor about my shells.

I go home and sleep. I dream restlessly of Messina, the town with the mines, which links together Marthinus Maritz, Constable Modisane and me.

•

The dead move along their own orbits, like planets. Like celestial bodies they encircle me in their elliptical courses. My mother, not urgently present in my thoughts for a long time, now appears in my dreams night after night. Her soft, elliptical path is at its point of closest proximity to me, and each of her appearances ushers in a great sadness. I see her lying in a small room, with only a bed and a tiny window. She is sleeping. She is abandoned, she is sick or dying. There is something indescribably desolate about her sleeping form under the blanket. There is something about the blanket which lends it an unbearable emphasis. I cannot hold on to the dream to reflect on it. Even worse is when I know that I have dreamt of her, but cannot remember the dream.

If Marthinus Maritz should describe an orbital course, it would be that of a distant, cold planet. Would he be one of the outer planets? Neptune with its howling winds? Uranus with its aeons of darkness, where time gets infinitely extended? Saturn, so light that it could float on an enormous lake? Or Pluto, the smallest, coldest, darkest, and most distant—the only solid outer planet, with its surface of ice and methane, a frozen rock?

Sof phones again late one night, shortly after we had sat in the car looking out over the sea in the manner of Mrs. C and Vercueil. At least this time I am not asleep. I am still immersed in my unravelling, in my laborious journey through evolutionary and geological history. I am still trying to make sense of the magma ocean, of iron pools, of the cooling earth crust, of the crystallising of the earth's mantle. (How in God's name should I conceive of all these processes?) My eyes are burning. Much more than a therapist (and here I have to differ from my lover), I need a geologist to guide me step by step through this inaccessible and treacherous terrain.

"Am I disturbing you?" Sof asks.

"No," I say.

"I'm thinking of taking a lover," she says and clears her throat slightly.

What can I say to this? Have you anyone particular in mind? Who is the lucky man, or woman? Nowadays anything is possible, and I am not yet familiar with the ambit of Sof's sexual preferences.

"Who is it, Sof?" I ask.

"It is my children's paediatrician," she says, and gives an exculpatory little cough.

"I see. What does he look like? She? What kind of person is this—a kindred spirit, a concordant fellow being? Is there a future in it for the two of you?" I am tired, the nightly acquisition of complex knowledge is taking up much of my energy.

"He's a cripple. I think he had polio as a child. He has reddish hair. He has heavy eyelids that flutter slightly when he speaks, as if he can open his eyes only with great effort," she says with the unmistakeable tremor of erotic excitement in her voice.

"That has to be irresistible," I say.

I know the type; I am familiar with the erotic persuasiveness of a russet complexion. (Perhaps I should never have terminated the relationship with Felix du Randt.) As regards the other afflictions, I do not need much convincing, since I have been beguiled by a variety of aberrations and deviancies—physical as well as psychological—myself. Consider the bony brow and the blunt death's-nose. I should have remained true to Felix du Randt. He would have been a good man for me. He would have kept me on the straight path, the virtuous way. I would have been less exposed to temptation and spared many woes. My impressionable spirit would have been less contaminated. I am suddenly under the impression of the lifelong burden of emotional sullying (from the French *souiller*, to soil, Theo would have pointed out).

"It is!" Sof says. "It was the fluttering, half-mast eyelids that finally did the trick."

"When was the deal clinched, so to speak?"

"This afternoon."

"What is the next step? Where will you meet? Will you go dancing? No, sorry, I guess that's not an option."

"I'm meeting him in his consulting room on Friday afternoon after five. We will take it from there."

"Sof," I say, "this is unexpected. I don't know what to say to you. I wish you luck. Happiness, ecstasy if needs be."

(If I had the choice now between the bitter excitement of a drawn-out erotic intrigue and the grind and risk of writing—to which Becket refers as the "bitter folly"—which would I choose?)

"I've just read an interesting article," Sof says with a little cough. She is embarrassed; she wants to change the topic. "All writers are actually pursuing a single ideal, namely the universal."

"I've always thought the universal to be suspect."

"It is," she says, "but it does not make the striving of writers less valid. All writers intuitively know this—the one who gets a grip on the so-called universal attains the upper hand. The trump card. Whatever. I thought it would interest you."

●

During this time Theo sometimes leaves the office in the afternoon for an hour or two to attend auctions. He returns with a feverish glint in his eye. In this state of heightened excitement he listens to Schubert's piano sonatas to calm himself down. He breathes deeply, closes his eyes, and surrenders himself to the music. Only then can he resume his work.

Did you see lovely things? I ask cautiously. (What is the ironic undertone doing in my voice?) Beautiful, he says, but does not elaborate.

Enamoured of something? His heart set on objects of beauty? With that I am well acquainted.

His hands are not small, but well-formed, like his wrists. His nails are somewhat fan-shaped, the way I like them. He is no longer a young man. The well-defined, youthful male form has begun to soften. The eyelid is softer, it looks more vulnerable, as does the skin of the neck—I know how desirable I find that in my lover. The hair on his chest (what is visible of it) is beginning to turn grey. All these things appeal to me. I am here to assist him. The documentation of words no longer commonly used, that is our shared purpose.

I return to the cards. *Eindera*, regional term for *eintlik*—actually. *Eindjie*—archaic form of *entjie*—a little way (*stap 'n eindjie met my saam, my lief*—walk a little way with me, my love). *Einste*, originally *eienste*—decidedly the same. *Eindtyd*—the end of time, end of the earthly dispensation. *Êit!*—restraining exclamation: *êit, kêrel, nie so onverskillig nie*—easy, lad, not so reckless! *Elkedaags* and *elkedags*—outdated variants of everyday. *Elkelike*—regional term denoting regularity. *Elkaar* and *elkander* (each other); *elkendeen* (everyone); *elkendeur* or *elkensdeur* (time and again); *elkenkeer* or *elkenmaal* (every time)—all of them outdated forms. *Ellend* (variant of *ellende*—misery).

"*Die ellende staan blou in die blom,*" I say. (Misery stands blue in the bud.) "A lovely expression. What would be the origin of *ellende*? Of the word, I mean."

Theo explains that the Dutch *ellende* is derived from the Middle Dutch *ellende*, which means another country, or exile, also a disastrous condition, grinding poverty, and privation. This may be compared to the Old Dutch *elelendi* from the tenth century, the Old Saxon *elilendi*, and the Old High German *elilenti*, of which the *el* was abbreviated from *elders*, *alja*, and *lende*, *landa*—which literally means land elsewhere, that is to say, sojourn in a foreign country, exile, and its accompanying feelings of uprootedness.

"Thank you," I say. "Now I understand that our earthly existence is essentially wretched."

Theo smiles, but will not take the bait. I wonder how often I am mistaken about him.

We often listen to Schubert during this time. When Theo is relaxed, he sometimes whistles softly to the music.

A day or two later he shows me a ring that he has bought at an auction. It is an antique Indian ring, white gold, inlaid with countless small amethyst stones. He must have paid a fabulous sum for it.

"Is it a gift for someone?" I ask (cautiously).

"Yes," he says.

"For your wife, perhaps?"

"Yes," Theo says, "yes. It's a present for my wife."

"Then she is a lucky woman," I say.

"Do you think so?" he says, and looks at me searchingly for a moment.

He holds the ring in his left hand with the tips of four fingers and a thumb. I notice that his fingers are trembling slightly. He is under the impression of the beauty, of the costliness of the ring, his face suffused with blood, his eyes gleaming with gratification. I can see that it gave him pleasure to buy it. He turns the ring ever so slightly for the stones to catch the light. He slips it on the little finger of his left hand and spreads his fingers. He looks at it as a woman would look at it. I have seldom seen him so pleased, elated even.

At the end of July we have completed the letter *D*. From *doodbabbel* (babble to death), to *deurween* (to thoroughly bewail). From *dadedrang* (the urge to act, to do the deed), to *dabbeljasgras* (edible grass, on which the man from Amsterdam survives in the riddle). From *diepborstig* (deep-chested) to *donkerbloedig* (dark-blooded—with or from blood of a non-white, sic). From *droeflik* (a sorrow-filled state), to *duiwel*, sometimes *duwel*: the devil incarnate and carnal, the real, the one and only, undisguised and palpable, Beelzebub and Belial, the Foul Fiend, old Nick, old Scratch and Harry, the Evil One, lord of the evil kingdom and underminer of the salvation of our soul. All his folk names we have written up: *Asmannetjie* and *Bokbaard* (Ash Goblin and Goatbeard); *Bokhoringkies* and *Bokspoot* (Little Goat's Horns and Goat's Hoof); *Broesa, Damoen, Drietoon* (Threetoe); *Gratebene* (Fishbone Legs); *Herrie, Horrelpoot* (Clubfoot), and *Hans Jas* (Hans with the Coat). *Jasbok, Jonkers, Joos, Josie. Kantvoet (*Lacefoot) and *Klamhandjies* (Little Damphands). *Knakstert* (Snaptail); *Kopertoon* (Coppertoe); *Oortjies* (Smallears); *Oupa langoor* (Grandpa Longear); *Ou Vale* (Old Grey); *Penkop* (Peghead); *Pikhakskene* (Tarheels); *Pylstert* (Arrowtail); *Stofjas* (Dustcoat); *Swart Piet* (Black Piet); *Vaaljas* (Old Drabcoat); *Vaalkaros* (Greykaross); *Vaaltoon* (Greytoe); *Veinsaard* (Trickster); *Vuilbaard* (Dirtbeard); and *Woltone* (Wooltoes). All the devil combinations we have written up.

"*Duiwelsnaaigare?*" I ask. Devil's serving thread. Also called *monniksbaard* (monk's beard), *nooienshaar* (maidenhair), *perdeslaai* (horse salad), or *duiwelstou* (devil's rope), Theo Verwey explains. *Duiwelsloënaar* (devil's denier), and *duiwelsprenteboek* (devil's picture book). *Duiwelstuig* (devil's instrument), and *duiwelstoejaer* (jack of all trades—my role as Theo's sidekick and factotum).

The endless death combinations have been rounded off and written up. The cards have been alphabetised, brought up to date, catalogued. We move on, the devil and death and all the possible names and combinations we leave behind us. Too long we have tarried there.

•

In this way then, I found myself in Abel Sonnekus's jolly, suburban bed. I do not recall how long our erratic sexual liaison lasted, or the exact course it took—neither its chronology, nor its emotional shape. (Shallow, I would say it was, shallow as a saltpan.) I do, however, recall a weekend we spent together in the Eastern Transvaal (now Mpumalanga).

We are sitting on a cool stone stoep under a grass veranda. We are looking out over the beautiful orange groves, over papaya and avocado-pear plantations. It is my father's world. It is the Lowveld. The earth here is very old. It is the paradisiacal world of my childhood, but on this visit my childhood is far from my thoughts. Sonnekus is at the summit of his literary career; he is nearly twenty years older than I am. He is an authority on early Afrikaans prose (D.F. Malherbe and C.M. van den Heever in particular), although he obtained his doctorate (in the Netherlands) on the poetry of the Tachtigers. His public manner is correct and formal. His rollicking ebullience is reserved for behind the scenes, for the inner room. There he can gambol and cavort himself to death. Behind the scenes, so to speak, out of the public eye, in the bathroom, in the bedroom, on the road—there his manic quest for all manner of gratification knows no end.

With a glass of brandy in his hand, the ankle of one leg propped up on the knee of the other, gazing out over the lovely Lowveld landscape, his exuberance knows neither limit nor confine. In contrast with his sober, uninspiring prose style, his verbal diatribes are entertaining, diabolically inventive. He is going on about Felix du Randt. (Felix's betrayal, his heartless conduct towards me, is still fresh in my memory, I have not come to terms with it yet.) Sonnekus refers to some inane remark or other that Felix made. He laughs himself silly about it. He elaborates on nonsensical remarks that his colleagues are supposed to have made. He expands with relish on the shortcomings of Marthinus Maritz's second volume of poetry. (I see no reason to contradict him.)

He is a brilliant raconteur whenever his story is to the detriment of his subject. The greater his malice, the more intense his exuberant enjoyment. As on the evening in the bathroom of his own home, his manic laughter rises increasingly higher, his merriment coming in overwhelming volleys. After a while he calms down. He wipes the tears from his eyes with a snow-white handkerchief. He quotes the Dutch poets Kloos and Gorter, and long passages from D.F. Malherbe and C.M. van den Heever. In a more sober mood he confesses to his ascetic side, claiming that he often feels the desire to withdraw from the world. "But first," he says, "I'm going to fuck you nice and hard in the rondavel."

During this time his wife is admitted to a clinic for depression. Their three daughters are left in his care. The youngest is mentally disturbed. This only becomes apparent during her adolescence. Like James Joyce's daughter, Julia, she is gone beyond recall, and eventually she will be committed to an institution. An angelically beautiful child (I am always reminded of Nicole Warren in *Tender is the Night*). She is the apple of Sonnekus's eye, were his eye to have an apple, for the iris is a shallow disc, like a shard of glass. And keep in mind the frizzy, colourless pubic hair (albino duck), the sharp edge of the corner of the eye, and of the glans. And the blunt nose, like that of the man that Gustav von Aschenbach encounters before undertaking his journey to Venice and to his death.

But Abel Sonnekus is my lover, after all, and I regard him with a measure of tenderness and trusting benevolence. And elatedly (immorally and indecently) we travel together through the lovely Lowveld landscape.

•

The Eastern Transvaal is my father's world. That is where he comes from. As children we visit his relatives in Louws Creek, Barberton, Sabie, where the mist lies thick on the mountain pass, the roads meandering down between aloes. We play in the orange groves with our cousins. It is another world, far removed from our daily existence. But here the road comes to an end; it does not go as far as Messina—of which our father only tells us, never taking us there. Years later our grandfather attempts to indicate to us children the circumference of the baobab with awkward, ponderous gestures.

Although Messina can be shown on a map, it is also a place that exists only in the imagination. It is a place outside the boundaries of the conceivable world.

•

If my human form, the nature of my consciousness and of my senses are the result of a thousand and one coincidences, how can I not reflect on the role of coincidence in my own life?

If, according to Hugo Hattingh, the minutest difference—however insignificant—can change the course of evolutionary history; if everything here—in its ostensibly solid and immutable form—is purely the result of coincidence; if countless contingent events eventually led to *Homo sapiens*, then my life could have assumed a different course at a host of other junctures. Should I understand it like that?

Then it would not be my life to begin with, for had my father begotten me at another hour, on another day, had my mother turned herself away from him on the day of my conception, overwhelmed by the burden of her past (also the result of an infinite series of coincidences), then it would not have been I, but a different child conceived in her.

Is it correct to assume that if my grandfather had not left his family to go down into the copper mines of Messina, my mother's life would have taken a different course, and at the hour of my conception, perhaps—quite likely and in all probability even—she would have found herself in the arms of another man?

Simply because I (and all other things) exist, I think that my existence is inevitable. That everything is the way it is supposed to be. But that is, of course, not so. In evolutionary terms that is the first of many erroneous assumptions.

CHAPTER TWELVE

One afternoon in the middle of August the telephone rings as I arrive home. It is a cool, windy day, my mood is sombre, Joets had pointed out something in a dream that morning, but when I woke up I was none the wiser.

"Miss Dolly," Alverine says, "I know who took your shells."

A great many thoughts go through my head at once. They make my ears hum. Where did she get hold of my number? If she has my number, why is she using my false name? How does she know that my shells have been stolen? How does she know who did it? I am caught off guard—too many things to be reckoned with simultaneously.

"Alverine," I say, "where did you get my number?" I am cautious; I do not reveal my true identity for the time being.

"Jaykie got it, mevrou," she says.

"And where did Jaykie get it?" I ask.

"I can't say, Miss Dolly, I think it was from a friend."

"The friend who took the shells?"

(Did Jaykie know who the culprit was at the time Sof and I went to Ladybrand?)

"I can't say, Miss Dolly, I think it's from a friend of his in the city."

Sailor, I suddenly think. The thought leaps into my head, irrationally.

"Does the friend know me?" I ask.

"I can't say, Miss Dolly, it's better to talk to Jaykie himself. He's actually the one who knows who took Miss Dolly's things."

"Where is Jaykie? Why doesn't he phone me himself? For how long has he known this?"

"No, Miss Dolly, I can't say myself . . ."

"Alverine," I say, "did Jaykie know who took my shells on the day Miss Anna and I came to visit you?"

(I was clearly not the only one guilty of subterfuge and counterfeiting that day.)

"I can't say, mevrou," Alverine says. She sounds somewhat flustered.

"Why doesn't Jaykie phone me himself?"

"Jaykie is *scared*, Miss Dolly," Alverine says, with exactly the same rhythm and intonation that Hazel would have used twenty years ago. I am instantly transported back to that time. I feel the cold wind of time brushing against my face.

"What's he afraid of?" I ask.

"He has a bad conscience, Miss Dolly, he wants to keep a low profile."

"What does he have a bad conscience about?" I ask.

But now Alverine is clearly unwilling to talk any further. I think I hear shuffling and noises in the background. Conferring.

"Alverine," I say, "does Jaykie know that you are phoning me?"

She hesitates for a few moments before saying: "He *knows*, mevrou."

"Can I come and see you again?" I ask.

"That's okay, Miss Dolly," she says.

And with that our conversation ends. When I put the phone down, my cheeks are ice-cold and my ears are burning hot. I am not quite sure what to make of this.

•

I want to go to Ladybrand straight away, on Friday, if possible. But I want Sof to come with me, and on Friday she has her first appointment with the man with the droopy eyelids. The polio victim, the man on whom she has set her heart erotically. Her erotic heart. Erotic, which refers to sensual love, and sensual, which satisfies only the senses. As if the senses have a life and discernment of their own. I spoke to Sof on Monday; today is Wednesday.

I phone her. "Sof," I say, "are you still seeing your children's paediatrician on Friday afternoon?"

"I've been having second thoughts," Sof says, "and I think I'm going to let it go."

"Why?" I ask. "On Monday you still had your heart set on that man."

"Yes," Sof says, "but my life has taken enough of these wrong turns. I've decided to resist the temptation."

"In that case," I say, "do you feel up to going to Ladybrand with me again?"

She feels up to it. She could see that nothing good would come of the Jaykie character. Her husband will see to the children. He is a doos, but he is not averse to spending time with them. Although she thinks that he probably writes them up as case studies. It would not surprise her at all, she says, he has no fucking conscience.

"He's a psychiatrist, Sof, surely he had to meet certain ethical standards to qualify for the profession?"

"His patients are too disturbed in any case to realise he's a doos."

"Heavens," I say.

"You know what my fantasies are," she says, and gives her little laugh.

"Sof," I say, "I don't recommend it."

"Why not?" she says, and coughs.

"You will have to pay dearly for those few moments of intense gratification."

"It's worth a lot to me," she says, again with the laugh.

"How much? Half a lifetime in jail? Think of the effect it will have on your parents, on your children."

"That's all that keeps me from doing it."

"Why don't you rather leave him?"

"That's a long story," says Sof.

I need Sof by my side, with her pastorie skills. Should my own social abilities desert me in the heat of the moment (as happened the previous time in Aunty Rosie's lounge), I know that I will be able to rely on Sof—her life has prepared her well for that. I have not met her husband or seen her children yet, I do not know what her house looks like.

From the subdued background of her pastorie past she has emerged, in a manner of speaking, to accompany and guide me on my errant path.

•

On Friday afternoon we drive to Ladybrand. I informed Alverine that we would visit them on Saturday morning. "Just see to it that Jaykie is also there," I said.

On the way I ask Sof about Sailor. She tells me what I know already, and also what I have surmised—that he is irresistibly attractive to men as well as women (I have seen him wind Mrs. Dudu and Vera Garaszczuk around his little finger), that she does not know why he is called Sailor, that he is generous, but that his integrity is not always above suspicion, that he is probably emotionally damaged and hence dangerous, and that he constantly lives beyond his means.

I tell her that his father apparently molested his brother regularly. Then you may be sure, she says, that he was molested as well. (Molest I know is derived from the Latin *molestare*, to hinder, to trouble, or annoy.) I would not be at all surprised if that is indeed the case. (Recalling again the expression in his eyes when he visited me some time ago—late in the evening, when he had already had too much to drink.)

Sof tells me that he likes beautiful, expensive things: silk sheets, Lalique glass, designer furniture. I ask how he is able to afford such things. She suspects he selects his lovers carefully. She wouldn't know, she suspects that he is capable of anything: blackmail, emotional extortion.

I ask if she knows who his lover or lovers are.

"One of them was this scrawny, temperamental little guy."

"Someone like Jaykie Steinmeier—like Herr K.—for instance?" (Remembering my sudden hunch that Jaykie had obtained my number from Sailor.)

"Yes," Sof says. "It could well be someone like that."

"Are you sure it isn't the little Steinmeier guy?"

"No," Sof says. "It isn't him, but it could easily have been him. Same type."

"Someone who would steal your shells and defecate on your carpet?"

"Yes," Sof says. "Why not?"

I tell Sof: "When we returned from Ladybrand last time, you were telling me about James Joyce. Joyce in Zürich, writing *Ulysses*. I cruelly interrupted you. Will you please continue?"

I turn my head slightly to the left. How beautiful is the winter landscape speeding past, and how little solace it offers today, for my mind is turbulent and my eye restless.

"After the outbreak of the First World War," Sof says, "Joyce and his family move to Zürich. That I've already mentioned. That is where he works on *Ulysses* for seven years. In the little room, on his lap. With all his physical afflictions. With his eyes regularly giving in. Everything he knows, everything he remembers, everything he's ever heard, everything he's ever read—and he has read everything—he puts into that book. He knows everything and he has read everything. He speaks five languages. He consults rhyme dictionaries, maps, history books. He makes use of anything that comes to his attention. Jokes, ditties, bawdy sayings, all flotsam and jetsam—anything his gigantic imagination can appropriate. Everything he puts into that book. His sight deteriorates irremediably during this time, but later he considers the years spent writing *Ulysses* as the richest of his life."

But, like the last time, I cut her short. "I have boundless respect for Joyce, but I don't want to hear anything more. You must stop immediately. I have other things to think about at the moment. What if Jaykie isn't there? What if he refuses to talk to me?"

"Take it as it comes," Sof says. "Don't precipitate events."

We drink tea at a Wimpy on the way. We are served by a pretty young girl; her name, printed on the payslip, is Latoya Joyce.

"Talk about coincidence," Sof says.

"Wouldn't it be beautifully apt," I say, "if she were one of Joyce's descendants? The child of an illegitimate child, for instance. The transplantation of Joyce. The Africanisation of Joyce. The browning of Joyce. The miscegenation of Joyce."

"Anyway," Sof continues when we are on the road again, "Joyce in Zürich. Engaged with the mammoth task. That virtually superhuman labour. With that book he wants to—"

But once again I do not want to hear any more. To the devil with Joyce and his encyclopaedic imagination. I am on a mission of my own and I am tense. I do not know what awaits me at the home of Aunty Rosie. I do not know if Jaykie will clear up the mystery of the missing shells.

We do not stay at the same guesthouse again. They have closed down. The obscene pink sausages for breakfast did not go down well. The passage light shone too brightly in the eyes of the guests at night. The winsome hunter-gatherer girl fled with the print of the Thomas Baines painting under her arm, and the woman with the seething nest of hair offered her services elsewhere.

We have supper at the Italian restaurant again, but this time the six Chinese are not present. During the meal Sof receives an SMS. And another. From the paediatrician? She laughs bashfully, a blush on her cheek. After the meal we visit the Red Lantern again. Outside it is bitterly cold. The mountains are clearly etched against the vast, open sky. If it was cold in June, it is piercingly cold now, in August. A cold that banishes obsessive thoughts, that clears and empties the head, that purifies the resolve. We drink a glass of wine. In a corner sits a morose man.

The guesthouse in which we are staying this time is solid, old, built of sandstone. It looks like the kind of house where the president of the Orange Free State might have spent the night on his way to signing the peace treaty of Vereeniging. The rooms are spacious, and a broad stoep runs along three sides of the house. Because the rooms are so large, Sof and I share one. There is a hearth, but no fire. I say to Sof: "We've had it. We'll bloody die of cold here tonight."

She sits on the bed, her delicate knees pressed against each other. She gazes intently ahead of her. Despite the somewhat ironic cast to her mouth, the strong chin, and the first indication of sharp downward lines from nose to mouth, her eyes are soft, half hidden behind her glasses, her appearance deceptively defenceless. How this strikes me again tonight.

"I don't know if I should do it," she says.

"What?"

"If I should go for the man or not."

"I can't decide for you, Sof."

"Oh, what the hell," she says, and swings her legs into the bed.

I have difficulty falling asleep. Sof sleeps restlessly, talking in her sleep. Probably grappling with different options. When eventually I fall asleep, I do not sleep well either. I dream of insects. I crush an insect under my heel. It could well be a cockroach, but it is smaller. It doubles under my foot—a small, black, strange double insect. Not squashable.

In the very early morning, before sunrise, I suddenly wake up from a dream. The room is icy, the cold seeming to seep through the stone walls. I had phoned my mother's number. She answered. She sounded irritated. She had been sitting there long, waiting for me. On my way to her I sat in the car and looked out over a stormy sea. The car's windscreen was completely steamed over. The waves were crashing onto the beach. They were ominously close and green as glass. Even the steam on the window was green as glass.

We stamp our feet and blow into our hands in the large dining room. We are served by an overfriendly Afrikaans-speaking woman and her sullen Sotho-speaking maid. The food is unpretentious.

"At least we don't have to cope with Boer Baroque this morning," Sof remarks softly, and gives a civilised little cough as the woman brings our eggs.

In vain I attempt to hold on to the dream. Where was my mother? Where did she come from? Where was she waiting for me?

At eleven o'clock we stop in front of Aunty Rosie Steinmeier's door, ten weeks after our first visit.

Alverine opens the door. This time Aunty Rosie welcomes us heartily. Again we sit in the lounge with the two tigers, the one next to me on the couch still fixing me with a cold, glassy stare. Patrick's wedding portrait is still in the same place on the display cabinet. I feel a little sick; I have an unpleasant foreboding.

Aunty Rosie immediately starts talking animatedly. She tells us about Patrick's wife and his children. The wife works in Bloemfontein, and the poor kids stayed with her, with Aunty Rosie, for a while. "They miss their father terribly, Miss Dolly." Apron in front of the eyes. Alverine looks at the floor at her feet. The previous time she was talkative; today she keeps silent. What is she thinking about? Aunty Rosie tells us about her other children as well—her married daughter in Fouriesburg, who has a good job at the municipality, but whose child was brain-damaged at birth and with whom her daughter has great difficulty. "He'll never be able to learn, you understand, Miss Dolly? He can actually do nothing for himself. But she *loves* that child, Miss Dolly, she cares for him with her own hands."

Pale Gertjie sitting in the back of Aunty Jossie's car, so pale as to be green, his mouth half open. The memory suddenly strikes me like a wedge of light falling through a half-open door. Whatever happened to Gertjie? Did he survive his mother? Gertjie sitting at the back of the car with the young black maid who looks after him. The car is parked in the street in front of our house. Aunty Jossie comes in at the front door without knocking and announces herself cheerfully. Leentjie, she calls out to my mother, your little friend is here! This morning it suddenly comes to me—forty years down the line I realise something I sensed as a child but could not explain—Aunty Jossie's frenetic cheerfulness, her constant joking was a way of hiding her great sorrow about her child. She whirled, she whirled like a dervish around the abysmal emptiness in her heart to relieve the burden of Gertjie's painful presence in the back of that car. Gertjie. *Gertjiewert weer snertelpert in die worteltitseltjies / Kry Gertjie gotsgedagtetjies in die blinkbloublitseltjies?* One of Joets's little rhymes. A first warning, a gentle sign. Something pushing up in my throat. Linked also to Alverine sitting so withdrawn.

But to begin with, I owe these two decent women an explanation, whatever the extent of their knowledge of the state of affairs.

"I have a different name, as you probably know," I say. "And Anna too."

"No, really, Miss Dolly!" Aunty Rosie says.

"My name is Helena Verbloem. And Miss Anna's name is Sofia Benadé. Her father is a minister."

"*Mevrou!*" Aunty Rosie exclaims, pleasantly surprised, her hand before her mouth.

"It was wrong not to give our real names," I say.

"And as it is, I'm a Christian woman, Miss Dolly," Aunty Rosie says.

(I have to think of the real Dolly Haze. Of one of the most beautiful opening sentences in twentieth century literature: But in my arms she was always Lolita.)

Sof is sitting at the edge of her chair, opposite me, as on the previous occasion. But today she is not going to rush to my aid or my support. Today I am on my own, I can see that from the corner of my eye. For today Sof is absent, she is completely given to the weighing of possibilities. She wavers, she urges herself to caution, and at the same time she is already unreservedly turned to the russet half-cripple, the paediatrician, and to the fantasised possibilities that present themselves. The first intimations of erotic bliss. Of abandon and rapture.

"It was not our intention to deceive you," I say. "I'm sorry, I hope that you won't hold it against us."

"No, it's all right, Miss Dolly," Aunty Rosie says. "I can see you are respectable people."

When Jaykie Steinmeier enters the room, I feel the hair at the nape of my neck rising. I am suddenly intensely irritated with him.

He looks younger than I remember him from the previous time, and he is wearing a woollen cap. Against the cold? Why the strange indoor headgear? Is he hiding something? A shorn convict's head? A tattooed gang number on his skull? Was his manner quite as sweetly apologetic last time? He cannot look me in the eye. Only once, fleetingly. Winsome, dark eyes, slightly squint, but an evasive, guilty glance. I regard him with resentment, with growing anger, as if he is the culprit, as if he is not only responsible for the disappearance of my shells, but also for the horrible death of poor Patrick Steinmeier, his brother with the sadly sloping eyebrows.

Stop your game-playing! I want to say. Come out with the truth! Enough of your deceit and evil-doing! Confess! Admit to your complicity or guilt! You have led me up the garden path long enough!

It is through your doing, I want to say, that poor Constable Modisane—a fine and honourable man, about whose welfare I have grim forebodings—has been banned to Musina. Posted to Musina—whatever that may be an euphemism for. Because he felt obliged (under pressure from me, granted) to supply confidential information.

But this morning Jaykie is all adroit sidestepping and self-justification. He talks of this and that and his prattle is neither here nor there. He bounces off the wall like a rubber ball, hardly able to sit still for a minute, fidgeting and shifting. His eyebrows lift expressively as he talks, one eye starts to wander slightly, from time to time his eyes roll dramatically to the heavens, the whites visible. So like a Spanish saint, the dusky skin and smouldering eyes, and the gleaming whites of the eyeballs. I would not be at all surprised if he were inclined to seizures. He actually has nothing to do with anything, he claims, he is in fact not the one Miss Dolly (sic) wants to speak to. Tonight he will take Miss Dolly and Miss Anna to the right people, to the people who will properly explain what is going on.

Aunty Rosie, clearly not informed about the whole matter, nervously sits with her apron before her mouth. Jaykie wants to exonerate himself and at the same time he does not want to give his mother any indication that something may be amiss. I realise that I will not be getting much information from him here, in his mother's lounge.

We drink a cup of tea. Alverine enters with the tray, and Jaykie leaps up to take it from her. As on the previous occasion, he draws up coffee tables for Sof and me with exaggerated politeness.

I am upset. My cup rattles in the saucer when I put it down. To think that I have to sit here in the lounge of this unsuspecting old woman and make smooth talk with this wheedling youth with his obsequious little ways. This young man, who may be party to the disappearance of my shells, and who may have been present when my favourite carpet was pissed and shat upon. For I had unmistakably caught the scent of aftershave again the moment Jaykie Steinmeier entered the room.

I have little desire to take his evasive prattle into account this morning. Involuntarily I am reminded of the insect that I was unable to crush under my heel. His presence disturbs my mood. For Alverine is still looking at the floor in front of her, her face turned away, trapped in the vortex of her own thoughts. A second admonition, the announcement of a feeling rising up within me, when I see her sitting like that. I have to think of Hazel sitting at the table in my kitchen twenty years ago, her face turned away in the same manner. Hazel with the headscarf, fine and upright, proud and gallant in the abandon of her youth. Memories of that time suddenly flood me with unexpected intensity, as if the whole morning, no, the past few weeks, have been a preparation for this. The past, the life of my parents, the time of my earlier self. What has become of us? What inscrutable series of coincidences gave rise to this moment?

It hardly matters any more, I suddenly think, here in Aunty Rosie's lounge with its abundance of trinkets and ornaments, fancy frills and trimmings. The shells are gone. My parents are dead. Joets is dead. A life is over so soon. It was an illusion, even when I was holding the heavy shells in my hand, it was an illusion that they are solid. Even shells, if they are immersed deep enough under water, will dissolve.

The loss of the shells and the circumstances of their disappearance have become disconnected, this I realise as I let my hand glide over the synthetic fur of the stuffed tiger, and Jaykie strains forward in his chair, pent-up and restless, his dark glance nervous, full of smiles and explanations, as piously hypocritical as they come, and Alverine keeps her head averted, and Aunty Rosie tries in vain to make sense of the conversation, and Sof perches on the edge of her chair, attention elsewhere.

The loss of the shells has been taken up into the configuration of a greater loss. The circumstances of their disappearance, this cunning young man's possible complicity, all are actually of little or no importance, and completely arbitrary. It does not matter a damn any more who took the shells.

Dust to dust. Element to element. Time is exerting pressure on us; our eventual destination is to be united with the elements from which we came. I have great sadness for my parents and Joets, whom I shall never see again. We are a unique and fleeting, and above all an accidental configuration. From the darkness and the void we emerged, and thence we shall return. We shall never be embodied in this way again, in the aeons of time it could happen in precisely this way but once. And so it is with my child. Child, you whom I love so dearly. Your form more dear to me than any other on this earth can be, or ever will be. From now to all eternity. And with that I challenge the great silence. I bend my head. I place my hand on my heart, on my midriff, as if I have been fatally pierced. My throat is constricted with emotion. I cannot speak.

It is quiet in the room. Outside a bird is singing its sweet song.

I straighten up. Sof looks at me strangely. Forward then with the business at hand.

"All right then," I say to Jaykie, "where can we meet tonight?"

I have considered coming up with some explanation for Aunty Rosie, but think better of it. Let this young man explain the situation to his mother in whatever way he wishes. We get up to leave. I embrace

147

Aunty Rosie and hold her small form pressed to mine for a moment. She looks up at me questioningly.

"Everything's okay, Aunty Rosie," I say. "There's nothing to trouble yourself about."

I indicate to Jaykie that he must accompany us to the car. That gives me leeway to negotiate briefly with him (under the watchful eye of his mother, standing on the stoep with Alverine).

"Is it a good idea," I ask, "that we go to these people? Why don't you just tell me what you know?"

"It's a *good* idea, mevrou," Jaykie says. "I don't know all that much."

"How do I know these people are not thugs?"

"No, mevrou, they're not thugs. Never."

"Gangsters, then."

"No, Miss Dolly, never."

"If they're not thugs or gangsters, how come they know about the disappearance of my things?" (The word "shells" I cannot get across my lips.)

"They're informed, mevrou, trust me, they know, they have contacts." Jaykie is still guiltily trying to avoid eye contact.

"Do they have contact with the police?"

"Yes, mevrou, they have police connections."

"And what is your connection with them?"

"No, mevrou, we're actually just friends."

We say goodbye. I get into the car. I wave to Aunty Rosie and Alverine on the stoep. I still know as little as when I came here this morning. But at the same time I realise, as we drive away, that although this youth and these people and this town are once and for all part of the extended network of my lost shells—which is how I have viewed the situation up to now—neither they nor anyone else actually has anything to do with it. The whole matter is but another coincidence, another small link in a vast, dense but invisible web of coincidences, which spins my own and every other life together.

"What does that young man smell of this morning?" I ask Sof.

"Of Clicks' Mother's Day perfume special," she says, and gives a dry little cough.

If I have already half suspected it, it now becomes clear to me. I now know clearly and beyond doubt that Jaykie Steinmeier is not the one who took my shells, or violated my carpet. That he knows about the matter, that may well be. Of that I am sure. But he is not the culprit. I know that now. He may be predisposed to a Jekyll-and-Hyde duplicity, but I can hardly picture him as someone who would urinate and defecate on a carpet. And I strongly doubt if he has the necessary artistic sensitivity to select the most beautiful shells—his drawings were simply too inept for that. He may know what happened, but he is not the one.

I tell this to Sof. She agrees that it makes sense. He does not give her the impression of being a hardcore thug. He is too much of a lightweight, and his taste in aftershave is far too common.

"And yet there is something about him," I say, "that I find moving. However much he may irritate me."

•

At half past six we drive to where Jaykie said we should meet. On the way Sof says: "Do you know the thirty-second canto of the *Inferno*? After the noise and raging of the preceding parts everything becomes very still here. Very still and very cold. It is the part where the traitors have become embedded in ice."

We stop in front of an old house. Like Aunty Rosie's house, it is situated on the border between the coloured and white areas of the town. But the house is not well kept like Aunty Rosie's, and it sits virtually on the pavement, with no fence or garden, only a dense shrub next to the postbox.

We wait in the car until Jaykie eventually turns up, the woollen cap pulled down low over his ears against the cold.

He leads the way. He rings the doorbell, but there is no reaction. He rings again. A girl appears and unlocks the safety gate without greeting us. Her hair is dyed pitch-black. Her complexion is exceedingly pale, her eye make-up is dark (the so-called drowned or destroyed look?).

Against one wall of the entrance hall is an abandoned, old-fashioned porcelain washbasin full of sand, with a withered succulent in it. On the other wall hangs a poster of a man who looks like Ravi Shankar.

We turn right into a narrow passage, a closed door on the right. The passage opens onto the lounge, a large room, lit by a single light bulb in the centre. In the far corner is a tiny television set.

There are five people in the room, and only two glance briefly in our direction as we enter. Two men are seated on either side of the doorway leading to the kitchen, one of them no more than an arm's length from the television on his left. Two other men are sitting on a couch opposite them, to the right of us. The couch is badly worn. Next to them on the couch lies a sleeping dog. He is wearing a small knitted coat. Even he does not deem us worthy of a glance. On the divan to the left of us a man lies sleeping. He lies on his back, his cap pulled down over his eyes.

Indeed an unconventional seating arrangement, for each one of those seated is positioned at such an awkward angle to the television set that it seems highly unlikely that they are able to see anything—considering the size of the screen as well.

As no one takes any notice, the three of us hesitate in the doorway. I look around. The room is filled with all kinds of bric-a-brac. A white plastic garden table and chairs in the far right-hand corner faces the television. On a thin wooden ledge above the couch is a dead potted plant, an empty bottle with a plait of hair in it, a male doll in combat gear. Behind the white table is a small built-in bookcase containing various objects as well as a few books. Against the walls are several posters. On the floor is a threadbare but once attractive Persian carpet. Next to me Sof softly clears her throat.

The girl with the black hair appears in the door leading to the kitchen. She is wearing donkey or rabbit-shaped slippers. Grey and blue.

"Help yourself to tea," she says to Jaykie.

We cross the threadbare carpet to the kitchen. Jaykie is obviously familiar with the setup. The kitchen looks as if it has not been cleaned for a while. In the sink are unwashed dishes, the breadbin is open, with half a loaf of bread and half a tomato on a breadboard next to an unwrapped block of margarine. The surfaces are unwiped. A cat leaps onto the small kitchen table. Another one is eating from a saucer on top of the fridge. Next to the breadbin is a small fish tank. I take a closer look. A single goldfish is swimming restlessly inside. The water is amber-coloured. A few green aquatic plants stir murkily at the bottom. I take an even closer look. Against one wall of the tank a water snail is moving slowly, probingly up the glass wall, its shell the same deep amber colour as the water.

While we are standing around with mugs of weak tea in our hands, the man who has been sitting closest to the television appears in the doorway.

"Ahowzit," he says.

"This is Sparrow," Jaykie says.

"Aha ahahemem," Sparrow says. He is wearing a knitted cap. His blondish beard is bristly. His eyes look in different directions. "Aha," he says, and "Ahem."

"No, it's okay," Jaykie says, without looking at him.

"Aha," Sparrow says. And: "Ahawaha," and "ahamenem." And: "Aha. Ahahahem."

He is softly beating the fist of one hand in the open palm of the other and rocking back and forth on his running shoes. Jaykie busies himself with the tea and does not look at Sparrow. I wait.

The young man who has been sitting on his other side also appears in the doorway. He has lively, dark eyes and a considerable gap between his front teeth. A jovial young fellow. "Howzit," he says chattily.

"This is Alvin D," Jaykie says. (Dee or D?)

"Howzit," Alvin D says again. He looks interested.

"Ahem," Sparrow says. And: "Aha." And: "Ammene, ammene, aha, ahem, amenne."

Next to me Sof is again clearing her throat. I address myself to Jaykie's back, under the eyes of the roguish Alvin D and the speech-impaired (speech-encumbered, speech-burdened) Sparrow. These two merry fellows hanging around in various degrees of attentiveness and expectation.

"Your sister phoned me earlier this week," I say. "She said that you know who took my things. In your mother's lounge this morning you promised to take me to the people who know what happened. Here we are now," I say firmly and without hesitation.

151

Sparrow looks at me askew and askance—each of his eyes fixing me from a different wind direction. He seems to have difficulty taking in the whole of my person with a single, embracing glance. He rocks backward on his soles and says: "Aha. Amenne. Ahek. Ahei." Then he stands aside slightly and gestures towards the lounge for me and Sof to go through.

"Ammene, amenne, ahem," he says.

Alvin D darts ahead and gallantly draws out the two plastic garden chairs on either side of the table. Sof and I sit down.

Sparrow and Alvin seat themselves on either side of the doorway again. Jaykie stands in the doorway. I can see that he is tense. It is quiet in the room except for the sound of the television. Some sitcom or other is on.

The two men on the dilapidated couch next to the sleeping dog are still sitting exactly as they have since we arrived—both collapsed against the wall, chin on chest. They sit there like Rosencrantz and Guildenstern. Like Malone and Molloy. (Where now? Who now? When now?) Like my long-lost brother and his friend, years ago. Both of them bearded, both with downcast eyes and a hint of a smile around the corners of the mouth—like initiates, in deep contemplation of some Kabbalistic revelation.

Guildenstern slowly rolls a cigarette, lights it, takes a deep draw, and hands it to Sof. Sof hesitates for a moment before declining amiably—like one declining the offer of a bowl of pudding at a bazaar. She hands it to me, our eyes do not meet; like her, I am tempted momentarily, before passing it on to Sparrow. From there it does the rounds, although Jaykie, like us, also declines. The sweet, herbal smell fills the room.

"It's not yet September," says Rosencrantz. I assume the remark is addressed to Guildenstern, although he does not look in his direction.

"When can we expect them?" asks Guildenstern.

"The future is dark." They both laugh.

"Have we decided?" asks Guildenstern.

"Plan A, B, and C. In reverse order," says Rosencrantz and laughs.

"Plan C if plan B does not appear auspicious."

I refuse to look at the television set behind me. Alvin D and Sparrow are watching as if hypnotised. Jaykie is still leaning nervously against the doorjamb. The black-haired one is moving to and fro between bedroom (assumedly) and kitchen in her donkey slippers. From the corner of my eye I see Sof sitting expressionlessly. Unperturbed. Well schooled. From having been exposed to all and sundry at the pastorie.

Now and then Sparrow mutters appreciatively: "Ahemmemene aha."

As the girl appears for the umpteenth time in the arch leading to the rest of the house, she suddenly stands still and with her slippered foot kicks lightly against the feet of the sleeping man. Next to her against the wall is a poster of a whale. It is hanging askew. The man wakes up, removes the cap from his face and sits up straight.

The moment he does so I know immediately: this is the man. I feel it in my kidneys. He is the link. He is the one who possesses the information. I feel it in my gut, in my neck, in the hair rising on my scalp.

The girl hands him the cigarette. He draws deeply on it. My heartbeat accelerates, my hands are moist. I dare not look at Sof. A wrestling programme has replaced the sitcom. I hear the crowd cheering.

"This is Fish," Jaykie says. "And this is Miss Dolly and Miss Anna— from the Durban Bible Society," he adds lamely.

The man gives a brusque laugh. He has an unhealthy complexion and long, straight, dark hair. He looks at the wrestling scene for a couple of moments (he must have remarkable eyesight to make out anything at that distance) before fixing his attention on us. With the palm of one hand he cracks the knuckles of the other—a habit I detest.

"So, ladies?" he says.

"My shells were stolen," I say. "Twelve weeks ago. Thirty-two were stolen, I got nine back. Twenty-three are still missing. I want to know if anyone here knows what happened to them. They are of no value, except to me."

"Shells," Fish says. "What's your case with shells, Doll?"

"I don't have a case with shells," I say. "I collected the shells over a long period. They are important to me."

"Wha-now, easy now," Fish says, his hands up in the air in front of him, his face dramatically averted: "Not so aggro, lady."

He lights a leisurely cigarette. Behind him, high against the wall, is a tiny A4 watercolour painting of waves.

"Just say it again, what is the story with the shells?"

To gain time, the fucker. Jaykie stands in the doorway with hanging head.

"Ahem. Ahemmeneha," Sparrow says.

"I want to know what happened to my twenty-three missing shells," I say.

"Twenty-three," the man says. "Twenty-three shells in the sunset. Oh something something my darling, home safely to me."

Next to me Sof is moving uneasily in her chair.

"Doll," he says, leisurely, "I tell you what. You and your friend from the Bible Society go back to the city tomorrow. Go wrap up your Bibles or whatever you do with them." He cracks his knuckles. He looks at the television screen again. One huge man throws another on the ring floor and jumps on him with his entire weight. Alvin D groans. The crowd cheer. Next to Fish stands the girl with the white face and the black hair—the dyed black bush—as in a vision, an apparition. His silent guide. So lovely and blest a lady.

"My guess is," Fish says, and he blows out a trail of smoke, "that the stolen goods have been traded in long ago—twelve weeks is a long time. I can give you the name of a contact in Durbs. Where the sun never sets. Where the fun never ends. He's the guy the boys usually take stolen goods to. My guess is, the boys have moved on. If your shells are anywhere, they're at that address. His name is Ozzie. O-zed-zed-eye-ee. Indian dude. He's got a second-hand shop somewhere in town. Point Road somewhere. And that's as far as I can help you."

And with that he leaps up, remarkably agile—the lean dog—draws his fingers through his long hair, draws his cap down over his head, and disappears through the arch down the passage. Shortly afterwards loud rock music can be heard from the room further down the passage.

Guildenstern again offers a rolled cigarette to Sof. "The Grateful Dead," says Rosencrantz. Sof again declines with the resigned pastorie smile and a little cough. "Jefferson Airplane," says Guildenstern. "Quicksilver Messenger Service, Gary Snyder, Timothy Leary, and Allen Ginsberg," says Rosencrantz. "Our main man, Quicksilver," says Guildenstern. "If plan C fails, consult the *I Ching*," says Rosencrantz and gives a short, explosive laugh.

"In the third line," says Guildenstern, "it does not profit one to stare blindly."

"Shoulder to the wheel," says Rosencrantz. (Again the short laugh.) "In the bottom line, obstruction in the face of danger. Avoid sudden movements."

"The slow man," says Guildenstern.

"Shows circumspection," says Rosencrantz.

"To the highest degree," says Guildenstern.

"He checks the scene out clearly," says Rosencrantz.

"Before crossing," says Guildenstern.

"In the fifth line," says Rosencrantz, "he concerns himself neither with profit nor with loss."

"Nevertheless," says Guildenstern, and carefully tips his cigarette ash into an empty beer can. "And never too much."

"The seventh hexagram. The sixth line," says Rosencrantz, "the seventh configuration. Evil is overcome." (Still with the ironic smile. Not once did he look up while speaking.)

"Ahememne ah," Sparrow says.

"Good God, no," I say. "Enough of this." I get up, Sof and Jaykie following me. The white dog lifts his head once, stretches himself and sleeps on with his paws stretched out in front of him. I nod a greeting in the direction of Rosencrantz. So much like my brother thirty years ago. So unsettlingly like him.

The house inside has not been warm, but outside it is piercingly cold. The night sky—suddenly stretched out above us so cold and so vast—gives me a fright. So boundless in its scope and brilliance. The starry abundance makes my head reel.

At the car I grasp Jaykie by the shoulders and turn him firmly towards me, my teeth chattering in the moonlight, my pupils opening up like caverns, every hair, so it seems, standing on end on my head, my breath hanging in a little white cloud before me.

"Jaykie," I say, "look me in the eye for once. Were you in my flat the day the shells were stolen?"

For the first time Jaykie looks me squarely in the eye, his dark priest's eyes bathed in misery. Filled with miserable remorse.

"No, Miss Dolly," he says. "I swear I wasn't there."

"Do you know if Fish, or Flesh, whatever, if he was there?"

"Neither Fish nor Flesh," Sof says, blowing her nose.

"Fish. I can't say, Miss Dolly," he says.

"Can't say or dare not say?"

"I can't say, Miss Dolly," he says again, miserably.

"Why did you bring us here?" I ask.

"I wanted to help you," Jaykie says softly.

"Yes," Sof says next to me, "out of the frying pan into the fire. You felt guilty, but did not have the guts for the truth."

"Aren't you afraid that I will ask the police to pick up your friend Fish or Flesh and ask him a few questions?"

"No, Miss Dolly," Jaykie says. He looks away. "Fish is a tough customer, but he isn't one of the gang who . . ."

"Who did what?"

Jaykie does not answer. He is still looking the other way. Did he let the cat out of the bag?

"Who came into my house and took my things and pissed and shat on my carpet and put the shells in a bag next to your poor brother's body to make it look as if he took them?"

Jaykie's expression is pained, as if I had struck him in the face with a small whip.

"Jaykie," I say, "you know who the gangsters are."

"Yes, mevrou," Jaykie says softly, hoarsely. "I know about them."

"You dare not tell me who they are."

"They will kill me, mevrou."

"You deliberately led me astray. You wanted to deceive me. You wanted me to believe Fish." Jaykie nods.

"You won't tell me who the gang members are. I'll never know who really did it."

"It's better so, Miss Dolly," Jaykie says softly, his head turned away.

"Did Patrick belong to that gang?"

"He was never a gang member, mevrou! He would never have worked with them, Miss Dolly, Patrick was a good man."

Tears are streaming down Jaykie's cheeks.

"That was my impression of him as well. Although I saw only a photograph of him. He did not want to cooperate, and then he was killed."

Jaykie weeps softly. Poor youth.

"They thought he had info they wanted," he says.

"Good," I say. "I accept it that way. I'm not taking the matter any further. I'm leaving it here. What has happened, has happened. I have to accept it. Maybe I have to learn something from this. Nothing belongs to us. We come into this world empty-handed and that is the way we leave it. My shells are gone, I won't see them again. I cared more about those shells than about most people. I attached myself exceedingly to them. Their beauty was a source of strength, encouragement, and joy to me. I cannot begin to describe how lovely they were. The precious *Harpa majors*, the *Periglypta*, the *Argonauta*. The nautiluses. To mention but a few. Everything passes, in a moment everything is gone. Our lives also. In the greater scheme of things our lives don't represent much. The universe is not well disposed towards us. You will notice that, if you concern yourself even a little with evolution. Evolution teaches us that everything could have been different—one different move and we wouldn't have been here now. Neither you, nor I, nor the shells. Coincidence and transience, bear those in mind. Everything we bind ourselves to excessively will eventually cause us pain—that way lies madness, and grief."

Jaykie keeps his head turned away, but I am not to be stopped.

"Especially grief. Afrikaans unfortunately doesn't have enough words for grief. Grief, heartache, woe, sorrow—not sufficient. Not sufficient to express all the nuances of grief. Maybe there are languages that have enough words. There must surely be such languages. We may not bind ourselves to anything or anyone, not even to those we love most. A difficult brief, but there is no other way."

Jaykie is still standing with downcast eyes and averted head.

"Just tell me one more thing," I say. "One last thing before we go and leave you in peace. How did you get hold of my telephone number?"

Jaykie sighs. He casts his eyes slowly upwards, with that long, shuddering, heaven-directed gaze that leaves the whites of his eyes clearly visible—like an epileptic, God knows, like some saint. I see that he also has his woes. I see his troubled young man's gaze. I see that there are things he knows that he would rather not know.

"Through the grapevine, Miss Dolly," he says.

"Did you know it already the last time we were here?"

"Yes," says Jaykie.

"Okay," I say. "Goodbye, Jaykie. We will leave it at that. I won't disturb you again." I embrace him fleetingly, my cheek for a moment against his cheek, warm and wet. I expected him to be averse to contact, but something in him gives way. Poor youth, poor child.

We get into the car. As we are about to drive off, Jaykie indicates something to us. I roll my window down.

"Miss Dolly," he says, "they weren't after your shells. They were at the wrong address. It's drugs they were after. They had the wrong address." He hesitates for a moment. "It was drugs also, but actually it was revenge."

•

The whole of that evening Sof and I lie on our beds in the large, cold room. The woman has taken pity on us and given us a small heater.

We lie on our backs and look at the ceiling. Later Sof goes for a shower in the large bathroom at the end of the passage.

That night I cannot sleep. All night I lie on my bed, staring at the ceiling in the dark. In that huge, freezing room. I hear Sof tossing about restlessly, and I hear her muttering in her sleep again. It gradually turns so cold that I feel frozen to the marrow. I put my clothes on and get back into bed, fully dressed. Still later it becomes very quiet. Quieter than quiet, a silence like glass. Only much later do I fall asleep.

In the early morning, at the crack of dawn, I wake up from a dream state in which I fell like an earthworm down a black hole, a thin void in which I was infinitely and wormily extended, my head at one end and my rear exit at the other. Like the first vertebrates—a mouth and an anus, connected by a rudimentary nerve: with, on either side of me, five hundred million years of evolution, stretched out to infinity.

CHAPTER THIRTEEN

My grandfather was a gambler and an adventurer. He was devilishly attractive, but unreliable; a restless man, who did not know what he was pursuing. My father was also attractive, but in a different way—everything about him was more austere, even his facial features. My mother was my grandfather's eldest child. He broke her heart when he left his family. I have only three photographs of him. In the first one he is standing with my grandmother and my mother in front of an obscure billboard in an open stretch of veld. This photograph probably dates from the early Thirties. It is small, only a snapshot, really. He is holding my mother; she is still a baby. She is wearing a little knitted bonnet that fastens under her chin with ribbons. My grandmother is wearing a fashionable dress with a broad sash around the hips, opaque stockings and pointed shoes. The second photograph, postcard size, must have been taken a good ten years later. He and my mother are in a boat on a lake; she is sitting on his lap. She is wearing a checked dress and a beret; she is a child of eleven or twelve, her hair in ringlets. It is a vulnerable age for a young girl to lose her father. He must have left his wife and four children shortly after this photograph was taken. He left them to work on the mines in Messina and the third photograph, also postcard format, dates from this period. The photograph, taken of him standing next to a baobab tree, was sent to his family with his best wishes. Initially he still sent money home, but as time passed, they heard from him less and less, and eventually not at all. Perhaps he had been swallowed by the mine. Perhaps he went to seek his happiness elsewhere—further north, on the lookout for other mines, other adventures, other gambling spots.

Twenty-three years later he returned. Or reappeared. By then he was in his late fifties, my mother was a grown woman with children of her own. Her mother—my grandmother, his first wife—had already died. She had gradually come to accept that her husband was dead to her. She had remarried. Her children had been adopted by their stepfather; they had accepted him as their own. When my grandfather returned, he wanted to establish contact with his children again, but the three younger children could hardly remember him. They had grown up with a different father. Only my mother remembered their father. She was the only one willing to re-establish contact with him. But she wavered. She was uncertain. Hesitantly she looked over her shoulder into the past. She remembered herself as a twelve-year-old girl with ringlets and a beret. She remembered how she and her father had gone rowing. She remembered how dark and opaque the water had been. From his wanderings of nearly twenty-five years he had brought her back a locket with a small inlaid stone. He had told her that he always thought of her as he went down the mine. In his thoughts he had always taken her down with him into the unknown darkness.

She was the only child who allowed their father back into her life, but she found the relationship a strain. Her father was only half familiar to her. During a crucial part of her life as a child, young adult and adult, he had been absent. My mother nevertheless tried her best to mend the relationship and to be on an amicable footing with his passive second wife.

Their renewed contact did not last long, as he died seven years later. My mother and the indolent wife buried him. On that day my mother was profoundly absent. I have difficulty recalling her presence among the funeralgoers. These were mostly miners, for after his wanderings my grandfather returned to the gold fields. (The names of the mines on the Witwatersrand peal like bells in my memory: Western Deep, West Driefontein, Harmony.) Of the cunning widow I have a much clearer picture, though. She hung like a huge black bell between the arms of two of my grandfather's mining companions: a Mr. Kronk and a Mr.

Schiller, or a Mr. Lessing and a Mr. Kratz. My mother was there, that I know for certain, but in her thoughts she was elsewhere. On that day she was like someone crossing the Styx in a small boat.

More than all his other children, my mother resembled her father. In his late middle age, when I came to know him, my grandfather's youthful, sensual features had already thickened, the finer planes and contours of his face had already coarsened and lost their definition. My father, on the other hand, retained his classic good looks all his life. He was an emotionally absent man, my father, an ironic man. He could laugh at the folly and blundering of others. (Joets's early marriage, the premature ending of her promising career, his bitterness towards the man she married, weakened him emotionally, although he would never show it openly.) Unlike my grandfather, he did not wear his heart upon his sleeve. My grandfather was prone to extravagant emotional displays, to tears and sentimentality. This caused my mother much embarrassment. As a young man, he had been fond of women, had drunk too much and had gambled. But all his life he remained one who hankered after mystery, and later that made him join a secret order. Our maternal grandfather was a Freemason. Like her father, my mother was a soul in need; she also yearned for revelation, ritual, mystery. This desire she had to suppress in her marriage, in her suburban home, in a suburban neighbourhood, in a conservative society, married to a man temperate in his habits and demeanour.

If my mother had unrequitable longings, my father could only watch her in silence and with detachment. Did he realise his own limitations? I would not know how powerless his wife's yearnings left him. Both of them were restricted—they kept each other within bounds.

Before his marriage my father worked for a while in Messina. He travelled on his own, something he did less of after his marriage. From Mombasa he brought back a fan. Perhaps the cowrie shell was also bought somewhere along the East Coast of Africa. Later the shell and the fan were the only mementoes of his earlier life, of the time when he was unattached. The years before this light, dry, sardonic man became entangled in the dense undergrowth of his marital relationship.

Was his association with Messina something that made my father attractive to my mother? A link to her own lost father? Messina. Ever since childhood the word has had an extra charge for me. It was only ever mentioned in passing, but never neutrally, always either with longing or bitterness. It was a place of betrayal and transgression, but it also held the promise of treasure and adventure, it was the door to another Africa. A place that appealed strongly to my child's imagination. A dark, fraught leitmotif.

•

For two weeks at the end of August, after Sof and I have returned from Ladybrand, I am depressed. Before two witnesses (Sof and Jaykie) I declared that I am letting go of my shells. But no sooner are we back than I look up Ozzie's name in the telephone directory.

Sof accompanies me. I do not have to explain. She grew up in a pastorie. She knows everything about depravity.

Ozzie's second-hand store in Pickering Street is clearly situated in a whoring neighbourhood. Lionel House is a derelict building; we climb stairs and go down narrow passageways, the smell of urine coming from the walls. Ozzie unlocks a steel gate for us. Two rooms with high ceilings are crammed from wall to wall and from floor to ceiling with the most incredible assortment of junk. I would not know where to start looking among the chairs and tables, fridges, stoves, household appliances, crockery, portraits, toys, trays, electrical wiring, floor lamps, bedside lamps, clocks, alarm clocks, magazines, and old LPs. What are the chances of finding the delicate *Harpa majors*, the precious nautiluses, the fragile *Argonauta*, the conches and the paper-thin tonnas among all this rubbish? In one corner Sof is leafing distractedly through a stack of *Hustlers*.

Ozzie's hair is white, his curly chest hair too. A blue ring covers the brown of his iris like a disc, an extra lens. That this assortment of junk reaching up to the ceiling does not drive him to distraction, is a miracle. I explain what I am looking for. Did anyone perhaps bring in some shells? They are of no value to anyone except me. (Not exactly true. To a collector they may be worthless, but to a ferreter with a finely honed aesthetic sense they may be an unexpected treasure.) Ozzie shakes his head. No, nothing of the sort. He nevertheless searches through the rooms and returns with a coffee jar full of small shells. No, I say, that isn't what I'm looking for. He writes my name down in case anyone arrives with something that matches the description of the lost shells. He is an honourable man, he says, a man of his word. When he promises something, he keeps his promise. He will be on the lookout.

As we leave, Sof remarks to me that Ozzie should burn everything in those two rooms as soon as possible, put in a few beds and start a brothel. She reckons that would be far more lucrative.

My mouth is dry and my insides are like lead. Never before have I found this city so unattractive. I cannot shake myself free from the atmosphere of Ozzie's place in that harlots' quarter. My shells seem contaminated, an extra dimension added to their violation by Ozzie's trashy setup. I feel polluted myself, as if it were I who came to an undignified end there. We drive back along the coast. The tide is low, the water oily. It is a grey, overcast day, dull and depressing. Sky and horizon are barely distinguishable from each other.

Sof clears her throat. "I don't want to meddle in your affairs," she says, "but don't you think that you've done just about everything possible to get your shells back? Shouldn't you let them go now?"

"Yes," I say. "I should."

At night I stare dry-eyed into space. I drink a glass or two of whisky, sometimes with milk. I sleep restlessly. Nothing delights me. Nothing appeals to me, there is nothing that I wish for or desire or set my heart on. The search for my shells has run its course. It has produced nothing. Constable Modisane is gone; Jaykie Steinmeier tried to help me, he took me as far as he could. The visit to Ozzie did not yield anything. There is no alternative but to resign myself to the inevitable. Because of a small error (a street address read or written down or memorised incorrectly), I lost my shells.

Frans de Waard, my lover and companion, wants us to meet more often. During the weekends we have spent together since I came here, I have been distracted. I lay in his arms with my eye steadfastly fixed on the death combinations. I have to admit, I have to grant him that—it is no satisfactory state of affairs. We have a solid relationship—I would even go as far as to claim that I feel a deep bond with him, in flesh as well as in spirit. Am I not always reassured by his familiar smell next to me in bed at night?

Why are you taking some of your most beautiful shells with you, he asked when I came here. Because I need their beauty to support me, I said, because without that I cannot survive. He said nothing. I could not take back my words. Their implication was clear: I can live without him but not without my shells. Like the dowager empress who took pleasure in lifeless things only. Of all living things, it was only her silkworms for which she had a strong affection. I was ashamed. I miss him. He has given me much pleasure. I often think of our times together. I think with appreciation of his body. Rosy from the shower, and lovely, swollen appreciably. He touches the mossy surface of my pubic area approvingly, as if wishing to test its resilience. Our pleasure has been considerable. But since I came here, I have been distracted.

Theo Verwey and I have moved on to the letters *E* and *F*, we are nearly done with *G*. Initially we progressed more slowly than we had planned, but we are now moving faster. My extended contract is for a year, it is already the end of August and we are not yet halfway through.

Edelaardig and *edeldenkend*—nobility of being and of thought (cultivating noble thoughts—like Theo Verwey). *Edelmoed*—magnanimity (unstinting, disinterested, unselfish). *Edog*—outmoded and rather grand intensive form of *dog*—yet, however, nevertheless. *Eedgebaar* and *eedgenoot*—gesture or action to seal an oath (*eed*), and confederate to an oath. *Eedgespan* and *eedhelper*—witnesses to an oath. *Oom Eelt die erdvark* (regional)—Uncle Wart the warthog. (*Oom Eelt*—I find that lovely. Would my father have known the expression? I never heard him say it. He liked unusual words.) *Eeltig*—calloused. *Eendags*—outdated form of ephemeral, of a day's duration. *Eendekooi*—duck decoy. All recorded, all entered onto the cards.

Ekshorteer, ekshumeer and *eksiel*—exhort, exhume and exile. All recorded.

"*Ekshorteer*? To advise a certain line of conduct strongly—a virtuous line, for example?"

"Yes, a virtuous code of conduct, for example."

It was already evident in July that the moles were active; now the entire lawn in front of my garden flat is porous from their subterranean labours. Even on my late afternoon walks in the park I notice their small unearthed mounds. It makes me think of the fifteenth-century

Dutch poem in which the king of moles, the prince of the underground, invites everyone to his feast. Everyone, regardless of identity or appearance, status or occupation; old or young, pretty or ugly, highly-placed official or humble clerk. He warns that it would be futile to demur, for when his messenger knocks, there is no way out. I am reminded of the court of the mole king, of the deep and labyrinthine passages of his underground kingdom, when I see these small mounds of earth everywhere.

The days are cool and the nights cold. A cool dampness rising from the ground (from the subterranean domain of the mole king) compels me to heed the dark underworld, decomposition and death.

I want to pause and reflect on *euwel*—all manner of evil. I want to linger on the denial of what is good, noble or virtuous. On the straying from the virtuous path and the frustration of the good. On evil-doing and the evil deed, on the evil I still hold against (the umbrage I take at) those who took my shells, whether on purpose or through unfortunate coincidence. I want to pause at the evil aftereffects of, among other things, my association with Abel Sonnekus.

But these days I get the impression that Theo Verwey wants to pick up the pace. I suspect that he has suddenly come to realise that the project is larger and more time-consuming than he had bargained on. We complete *F* faster than *E*, and *E* we had already completed faster than *D* (slowed down by the many combinations with the word "death").

We proceed rapidly through the cards: *faamskender*—one who defames, defiles another's reputation. *Faamrower*—a robber of someone's honour; one who robs another of his reputation. (Marthinus Maritz could never forgive Abel Sonnekus for criticising his second volume; he continued to regard him with rancour—as one who had robbed him of his standing.) *Faarhoutjie* as variant of *farohoutjie*, or *faraoshoutjie*—a small wooden device for keeping a pierced ear open. Theo explains that the *fabella*, the small, flat cartilege bone on the tendon of the calf muscle, is visible on an X-ray as a tiny shadow behind the knee joint. A *fabelliepie* is a street story, a colloquial fable. *Fahamtee*—tea used for the treatment of stomach and lung ailments, and *fahfee*—a gambling game. *Falie*—the rectangular black headscarf worn in earlier times to church and christenings and by those in mourning. It is only the manifold "factory" and "family" combinations that delay us. Factory literature for factory girls, who dress up in lovely festival gowns of *faillesy* and *fagarsy*—*sy* being silk. The countless family combinations which have fallen into disuse: *familieberig* and *familiebeskeide*—formal family notices and communications. *Familiebrief*—family letter. *Familiedeug*—family virtue. *Familietoneel*—the family scene. *Familietrou*—familial loyalty. The colloquial form *familjaar* for familiar. (I believe that Theo Verwey strictly maintains the distance of a restricted familiarity with me.) *Fatsoenlik* and *fatsoenshalwe*—decent and for the sake of decorum. I am enchanted by *flodder*—mire, sludge, or slurry as a noun, flounder as a verb. By *floers*—the genteel word for mourning crepe; figuratively something that covers, that veils like mist. By *flonkervlam* and *flenterfyn*—flickering, scintillating flame and smashed to smithereens. By girls and poets who idle about (*flaneer*) in streets, as did Baudelaire in his day. By *flouhartig*—faint-hearted, *fluim*—phlegm, and *fluisteraarster*—female whisperer. All recorded.

Fnuik. I permit myself the familiarity of asking Theo if he has ever been thwarted (*gefnuik*). (He smiles. Often, he admits. I wonder in what way he would have felt himself obstructed, or hurt in his pride.) *Foelieneut*—obsolete word for mace; *foemfaai* (recorded in the Bredasdorp district), *fomfaai* and *fonkfaai*—to set things out of kilter. *Foerneer* (obsolete)—to furnish, to provide, and *foepa*—finished (usage uncommon). *Foeterasie*—monkey business. *Folterbeul*—torturer. *Fomenteer*—foment, through application of *fomente*—warm compresses. *Foltersmart*—agony caused by torture. And, of course, Dame Fortuna: the blindfolded *Fortuin*—Fortune. *Fortuinlik*—fortunate; aided and abetted by Dame Fortune. We move on, Theo Verwey and I, but I do not want to let her out of my sight. Although Theo has taken hold of my arm, like Lot dragging his wife away from the depraved city.

Does anyone still practise the *fraaie lettere*—the belles-lettres? I ask Theo. He smiles and regards me, often and mostly still with a forced *fraaiigheid*—decorum. His factotum and famulus.

The many family combinations stir the submerged web of family ties.

I dream of Joets. I pick her up, I carry her on my shoulders, I swing her in a circle, and I say: The seasons were so beautiful when we were young.

Would you describe them with exclamation marks? she asks.

I reflect. Only winter, I say, summer is too slow. Come, I'll show you a river, I say, with snow on it.

It was bitterly cold in the dream.

•

My last conversation with Joets was over the telephone. I was in a hurry, on my way somewhere, when she phoned. We were living in different provinces. We had not seen each other for quite some time.

"I have become very thin lately," she says.

"What's the matter?" I ask.

"My flesh flaps loosely on my body." She laughs.

"What's the matter. Are you ill?"

She quotes a biblical text, and laughs.

"What's wrong? Have you been to a doctor?"

"I've been very ill, but I'm better now."

"But are you completely recovered?"

"I'm better. I'm scared of doctors. It's not a profession that I trust."

"It's better to go."

"I'm better. I've been thinking a lot lately."

"You've always thought a lot."

"Yes," she says. "Maybe. But lately more than ever. You know, our mother was not a good mother to us. Always remember that. She had too many problems of her own."

"The death of the child was perhaps more than she could cope with?" I ask.

"Yes. That too. But she had had a poor start. She was not well equipped. She had children and she was still a child herself."

"I realise that," I say.

"She had to bear too many responsibilities too early. She never came to grips with her father's desertion. There was never any space for that. And our father was not the right husband for her. He couldn't support her emotionally."

I look at my watch. I have to leave urgently. I shall be late. But I cannot cut this conversation short. It is not the kind of conversation that can be postponed. For some reason it is important to Joets to speak to me now.

"He was in need of emotional support himself," I say.

"That's right. They were both immature. They never grew up. People like that shouldn't have children. Too much responsibility too soon. I saw that when I had my first child. When I had Laura. I was too young to be a good parent to her."

"Joets," I say, "you've been a good mother to your children. You still are."

"I'm not going to make old bones," she says unexpectedly.

"Joets," I say.

"I know it. I've always known it. But it's not the worst that can happen. I'm preparing myself."

"Joets," I say, "we have to get together. It's been too long. We have to talk."

"Yes," Joets says. "Remember, you also had a hard time of it. For you it wasn't easy either. Don't be too harsh on yourself."

"Joets," I say. "We have to talk. I am coming to see you."

"Yes," she says. "I have to go," she suddenly says. "Don't judge yourself too unkindly. The book you wrote was very good. I didn't give you enough credit for it. I was still very bitter about my own failure."

"Joets . . ." I say.

"It took me a long time to make peace with the fact that nothing had come of my writer's dreams."

"Joets," I say, "it's not too late yet!"

Two months later she was diagnosed with a terminal disease. Four months later she was dead. She was a relatively young woman, a year or two older than I am now.

•

Joets is dead. Our infant brother, three years younger than she, died before he had ever had a life. As for our youngest brother, the child to whom my father had sung "Oom Kalie" in the dark, he turned away from everything and everybody. The genes of our grandfather resurfaced in him. He followed his own course. I have no knowledge of his welfare, of the body as well as of the spirit. He withdrew from the family circle. Family scene.

Our mother must have experienced great anxiety about the welfare—the survival—of her father, after he had left their family. Anxiety, longing, and sorrow. I now realise that it was a burden she could never lay down. Was there anyone to reassure her as a child, as a young girl? Early damage. Lifelong scarring. Is that what Joets referred to in our conversation? The sins of the fathers are visited upon the children unto the third and the fourth generation. If our grandfather's sins—his dubious morals, his heedlessness and irresponsibility—are to be visited upon the children of the third generation, will those be Joets's children and mine, will it be our children's children that they will be visited upon? And what about my grandfather? Was he himself not a child of the third or fourth generation, visited by the sins of his forefathers? Of what generation are we—Joets and I and our surviving brother? Whose sins are visited upon us? Is there nowhere a just generation, who kept His commandments, in order that the chain of visitation may finally be broken?

CHAPTER FOURTEEN

In September the first lovely spring rains fall. The heavens fan open dark and wet. Theo and I approach our task with renewed vigour. The letters *G* and *H* have to be completed this month. We should already have been busy with *K*, *L*, and *M*. It seems that the project will take much longer than Theo had anticipated. At the end of the year he has to give up his office here at the museum. The space was allocated to him when he was still a consultant for the Department of Regional Languages, but as he is no longer attached to it, the space will be needed for offices. I am grateful that his office has been situated here—for else I would not have met Sof, and my interest in evolution would not have been rekindled in this way.

We still often listen to Schubert.

"So beautiful and so sad," I say.

"He was apparently unknown in his lifetime," says Theo.

"He died young," I say.

"This music is the music of pathos," says Theo.

Pathos is the attribute that inspires sympathy or sadness. It is the music that Theo listens to when he is out of sorts, or when he returns in a manic or worked-up state from auctions, which happens these days. This is the music that restores his calm. Nothing like the mood of pathos to counteract the desire for the exceptional.

When relaxed, he sometimes softly hums a few notes to the music. I do not find this distracting. Rather, it causes my heart to go out to him. When he abandons himself completely to the music, the contours of his face become soft and harmonious.

I sometimes have to think of Constable Modisane—of how his skin formed one smooth, uninterrupted plane, in contrast with Theo's face, of which the forms are more broken, the colour more rosy, the skin more textured—and how each to me is appealing, each in his own way.

One afternoon Theo turns up with a piece of sculpture that he has bought. It is small, of yellow copper, not more than fifteen centimetres high. It depicts two copulating figures: the female figure sitting astride the male. Theo explains that it is a nineteenth-century copy of an eighteenth-century original from Rajasthan. It depicts the goddess Kali having sexual intercourse with Shiva, the male element—in the form of a corpse. Kali has four arms, her tongue sticks out, Shiva lies with one arm folded behind his head. She straddles the corpse of Shiva; his penis is clearly visible, entering her smooth, girlish vulva. The forms of the figures are stylised, their heads are large in relation to their bodies, their facial expressions are severe.

It is a remarkable little sculpture, powerful in impact, and Theo must have paid no small amount for it. He is both agitated and delighted. His face has an almost feverish glow. With his fingers he traces the smooth outlines of the female figure approvingly—with awe, almost. The expression on his face has the same intensity as when he is listening to music. I can see the powerful hold the beauty of the work has over him.

"I didn't know that you have an interest in Indian art," I say.

"It is only recently," he says, "that I've developed a taste for it."

In other regions of the country the first spring rains have also started to fall. It is the end of the dry season.

•

Just when I thought that Freek van As has taken to his heels, has vanished over the Gauteng horizon, that I have seen the back of him (that he has vanished without a trace; but what kind of trail would Freek van As leave anyway?), he phones again, shortly after Sof and I have returned from our second visit to Ladybrand. As on the previous occasions, he phones late at night.

Have I heard that Abel Sonnekus has had a serious relapse after his stroke, Freek wants to know. What an astonishing knowledge the man has of literature! There is little one can tell him. And a staunch language campaigner! What he hasn't done for the Afrikaans language is not worth doing! What a loss it would be for Afrikaans if he were no longer around. Who takes the rumours circulating about him seriously anyway? They are as unworthy of consideration as the rumours about Theo Verwey.

He must know that my defences are down at this late hour. By day I would have far less patience with him.

"But you've had the privilege of knowing Dr. Sonnekus personally, isn't that so?" he asks. "May I say the privilege to have known him intimately?"

The temerity of the man. The rank insinuation. But yes, indeed. The night Sonnekus wore his knees through on the bathroom mat, for instance. But known intimately? No, I believe not, Freek. *Eilaas!*— Alas! *Eilasie*—comically intensified exclamation of self-pity or remorse. Whorer, *dog, edog* (intensive form of however), his fornication (congress and coupling) was no expression of sexual exuberance or celebration of sexual abundance, but instead there had been something grim to his dogged pursuit of pleasure. A deed of aggression, the deed had been, I would rather claim. I remember the light in rooms and bathrooms, the axis of beds, the axial relationship of bathrooms to bedrooms, beds to windows, windows to doors, but I can hardly recall his face. The general mood of morbid fun, yes, that I remember well. How should I estimate the emotional damage I incurred through association with that least magnanimous, least noble-minded, least generous of souls? None, at first glance. Nevertheless and *edog*, how chilling the thought that I had coupled with him. That we shared—however briefly—a bed of love, love's joys and sorrows; that he entered me. Some deposit has remained. Something flaky, like skin dust. Corpse dust. Sediment that I cannot rid myself of. Like a toxic chemical accumulation that has become sedimented in the psyche. His hands were those of a manual labourer, a bricklayer or trench-digger, short and broad. He offered a plea for the sensitivity of his soul. On more than one occasion he proclaimed withdrawal from the world as ideal, and envisaged an ascetic life. Perhaps he saw himself as some contemporary Saint Jerome in the wilderness. (A Saint Brendan on his journey). A closet saint. (Saint of the closets.) As if Sonnekus could have any aptitude for saintliness. (Am I too severe in my judgement of myself and of him?) Who knows, on his deathbed the purified soul may be exposed radiantly—when some of the coarser self-promoting qualities have fallen away. Who can tell what kind of softening, deepening or ennoblement may have occurred in him over time? I ventured into that relationship wilfully and open-eyed, in a time of recklessness and delusion. In that time I was blind as a mole, and it might not have been the blindness of youth alone, but also, alas, a blind spot in the psyche.

"Goodbye, Freek," I say. "You'll have to excuse me, I still have something urgent to complete tonight."

·

One or two evenings later he phones again. Late again, when I have already drifted off to sleep. His voice sounds darker, more intimate. A dark man, pale as a fungus. Tall. (Or am I confusing him with the child psychiatrist, whom I dreamt of a night or two ago?) Why do you cut yourself off from good advice? he asks. Intimately, late at night, in my ear. Why exert yourself for Theo Verwey's project instead of focusing more on your own interests? If there is one thing for which there is no excuse, it is for wasting talent. Spilled seed, as it were. There is nothing wrong with Dr. Verwey's project, it is admirable in every way, but is it really the best way to utilise your skills and talents?

"I have started writing again," I say to justify myself. (Immediately I regret saying it.)

"Oh, really?" he says. "That I am so pleased to hear! Something large in scope—bigger than the previous little work? Something worthy of your talent?"

"What do you know about my talent?" I ask bitterly.

"Enough," he says. "Enough to know when and by what it is hampered."

(What had been the nature of the aberration: a mole, a club foot, or a cleft palate? Artfully veiled, veiled, veiled.)

"By the way," he says, "you probably know that Theo Verwey and Dr. Sonnekus—whose life is hanging in the balance at the moment—have been hand in glove for years?"

"I know that Sonnekus is sponsoring Theo Verwey's project."

"Ah," says the man. "If only that were all. All I can say of these two gentlemen is that both have always known from which alliances they can profit best. In my book this is not the first business transaction in which they have been partners."

"Theo Verwey would not describe his project as a business transaction. It is close to his heart."

"This," Freek van As says, "is what they all say. I'm not referring to his project anyway."

"To what then?" I ask reluctantly.

"Shall we say to a modest joint investment?"

To this I do not answer him.

"And you say your lovely sister has died?" he says.

"Yes," I say. "I have no desire to discuss her with you."

"That I can well understand," he says. "Your relationship was not without its problems."

I keep silent.

"Isn't it wonderful," he says, "when one looks back on a life, and you consider all the people you have crossed paths with, such divergent personalities, and yet they all have one thing in common—"

I put the receiver down. His lisping, midnight insights he can keep to himself from now on.

•

With the advent of the spring rains, the sky suddenly seems larger. In the early morning the clouds are wet and dark. They move rapidly, in large, stacked masses, as if driven by a polar wind. Lovely, uncharted spring winds from far-off regions. Here and there patches of dark-blue sky are visible. The heavens are in motion, with large forces gathering; the season is in transition.

Good, I say to Hugo Hattingh, I now grasp something of the formation of the earth's crust and the atmosphere. The sea and the earth have taken shape—the land masses and the water. The volcanic eruptions have abated for the time being. The earth has cooled down sufficiently. I am eagerly awaiting the appearance of the first forms of life. The primeval slime. I am ready. Please continue.

"Life as we know it," Hugo says, "probably began four thousand million years ago in the Archaean as a self-replicating organic molecule. These organisms originated in boiling hydrothermal fissures under the sea. The chemical imbalance between seawater and these fissures probably supplied the energy for the origin of life. All forms of life share the same blueprint—the genetic code. That is the DNA. The RNA, the simpler version, reads and executes this blueprint."

I interrupt him. "Could you please indicate the exact point," I say, "at which life originated?"

"At a certain level," Hugo Hattingh says, and gives a slightly deprecating laugh, "and that is something of which the lay person apparently has no grasp, there isn't all that much difference between what lives and what doesn't."

He laughs again. A caustic little laugh. "Lay people often ask these unanswerable questions," he says.

"Be that as it may," I say. "Just give some indication of the specific level you are referring to."

Freddie Ferreira, curator of mammals, laughs softly and shakes his head. Hugo and I always have our conversations in the tearoom, and apparently always in the presence of Freddie. He seldom lets on, but I suspect that he listens attentively.

"The molecular building blocks of life consist of simple chemicals," Hugo Hattingh says. "That was indicated by Aleksandr Oparin in 1924 already. The earliest—prebiotic—atmosphere did not contain oxygen. No oxygen, only ammonia, methane, water vapour, and hydrogen. People like Harold Urey—Harold Urey himself, to be precise—claimed that electrical emissions of lightning, or ultraviolet radiation, can form simple biological molecules from these prebiotic predecessors—molecules like amino acids and sugars."

Freddie tips his ash in the ashtray between his feet. His hair particularly oily again today. What would be going on inside his head—always averted and full of unfathomable cares? From where his constant perturbation?

"In 1952 Stanley Miller—"

"1953," Freddie says.

"In 1953 Stanley Miller, a student of Urey's, tested his ideas in the laboratory for the first time. In a test tube, under simulated atmospheric conditions, he was able to produce a wide range of biological molecules. Since then, all the building blocks of which life consists have already been synthesised. An indication that the distinction between life and non-life is not as great as is commonly assumed."

"By lay persons," I say.

Freddie smiles, shakes his head, lights a fresh cigarette.

"Yes," Hugo says, "both by lay persons and by experts. But it has not yet been determined how these molecules could organise themselves into a self-reproducing system. No blueprint could have existed for the first replicating RNA. It must have originated by means of some or other process. Miller and Urey's theory is one of many. It cannot yet be stated with certainty where life began, what the essential chemicals were, where they came from."

Freddie is tapping the tip of his shoe softly and rhythmically on the floor. Nathi has turned up in the meantime, with his Rasta dreadlocks and his irrepressible optimism, always ready for anything. Hugo does not greet him, and Freddie, not looking at Nathi, merely raises his right hand in acknowledgement of his presence. "Howzit," Nathi says. "It's okay," Freddie answers. Hugo is not looking well. Could it really have been he who let Sailor have it so vigorously the other day? (The day when the boys nearly sported themselves to death.) I am beginning to see him in a different light. Initially I thought him solid, impenetrable to the core. But his physical composition appears more porous now. He looks like one who has difficulty staying on his feet. Someone standing in a gale-force wind on a street corner. This wind is tugging at his clothes, his hair, even his cheeks. It looks as if the very flesh on his

176

body is constantly being plucked at—as if invisible torturing spirits are seizing him, snatching and clutching at him, tormenting and afflicting him. It looks as if there are insinuating voices continually whispering in his ear, undermining his grip on reality. His complexion is blotchy. His mouth is indecently red, as if the skin has been peeled off. His hands are trembling slightly. It must have been someone else going for Sailor. I gave Theo Verwey the wrong impression when I said that Hugo Hattingh and Sailor had found solace in each other's arms.

"What are these first forms of life?" I ask.

"The first life forms are archaeobacteria, single-celled organisms without a nucleus, also known as prokaryotes, that can survive under oxygen-poor conditions. Eubacteria developed from these archaeobacteria, with a different DNA structure. A branch of this family developed the ability to photosynthesise—probably as long ago as three thousand eight hundred million years. The oldest rocks, like those in Barberton, contain some of these fossilised bacteria. The most primitive form—anaerobic photosynthesis, did not release oxygen. But aerobic synthesis, developing later, does emit oxygen as waste matter, and through that the concentration of oxygen in the atmosphere gradually changed," Hugo says. "Life could now appear everywhere and these bacteria, the cyanobacteria, releasing oxygen, could multiply and colonise the oceans. Fossil evidence of this may be found in the Barberton rocks in the form of stromalites."

"The primeval slime."

"Stromalites—stroma. Bacterial colonies. Algae." His attention suddenly seems to wander. Perhaps these questions no longer interest him. "Some of the oldest fossils . . ."

"Please continue," I ask him. "I find it important to know these things."

He gives no indication that he has heard me, but continues nevertheless. "A new type of life developed approximately two thousand million years ago as a result of the heightened oxygen levels and a symbiosis between the archaeobacteria and eubacteria—the eucharyotes. These bacteria contain a nucleus, and they are the ancestors of animals and fungi. With plants, things developed somewhat differently."

Freddie stubs out his cigarette. Nathi, straight-backed, his lively eyes slightly oriental, takes a seat beside him with his cup of tea. He is also eager to learn from Hugo Hattingh's conversations.

"By one thousand two hundred million years ago the first sexually reproducing multicelled animals, the metazoa, appeared."

"The secret of their ability to reproduce sexually hasn't yet been plumbed," I say.

"No. By between six hundred and five hundred million years ago this macroscopic life already included an enormously extended variety of organisms with soft body parts—the Ediacaran and the Cambrian fauna, from which all modern life forms have developed."

"And when do the first organisms with hard body parts appear?"

"Organisms with hard body parts, which can therefore fossilise, only originated during the Phanerozoic, the period of visible life. There are few fossils in rocks dating from the preceding Archaean and Protero-zoic—at most only traces of very primitive single-celled organisms. The Precambrian fossil record is dominated by stromalites."

Later in the day I ask Freddie why Hugo Hattingh is looking so troubled.

"Unstable," he says, shaking his head, stubbing out his cigarette under his heel. "Most unstable."

•

As I am leaving the building during lunch a day or two later, I hear a strange sound coming from the basement. A low moaning, burbling noise. I hear the sound before I come across Hugo Hattingh. He is lying on the floor before the entrance to the men's toilet. The raw, inhuman sound is coming from him. His body is rigid, his eyes rolled back in his head. He is frothing at the mouth, his face already turning blue. I have enough experience of epileptic seizures to know that there is nothing I can do except to remove any objects in the vicinity that could injure him. I drag a steel table away—it seems he has already struck his head against it. I phone Freddie on my cellphone. I do not know how long Hugo has already been in the throes of the seizure. I look at my watch. After another minute or two he starts calming down.

Only now do I become aware of another presence. A worker in

a blue overall, unbuttoned at the front so that his naked chest is visible. Go and call someone, quickly, I say, this man is sick! The worker does not respond. I repeat the instruction in English, and then again in Afrikaans. The expression on the man's face is hard to fathom, difficult to describe. Bewilderment, agony, despair? He does not look at me or at Hugo Hattingh, who is now lying motionless. He looks over my shoulder, at some point in the distance, as if he is going towards a bloody sunset. Then he turns abruptly and walks away, a strange hobbling walk, his feet twisting awkwardly out to the sides.

I kneel down next to Hugo Hattingh, still following the other man with my eyes. Something about his dogged gait unexpectedly calls to mind the figure of the poet Marthinus Maritz. Marthinus redivivus— the wordsmith Marthinus, in a mute and hampered reappearance.

Freddie arrives. The museum's first-aid team arrives. Hugo Hattingh has injured himself badly against the table. His eyebrow is bleeding. He is carried away on a stretcher. How often does this happen? I ask Freddie. Freddie shakes his head, steps on his cigarette, looks at the floor and says: He is not well at the moment. Always a sign that he is severely stressed when he gets these attacks.

Freddie later informs me that the worker is called Chicken because of his hobbling walk. He speaks neither Afrikaans nor English, and apparently precious little of his mother tongue. A short while after Hugo's attack Chicken is discovered in the men's toilet, smearing the walls with his own excrement. With shit (*stront*). (*Stront*: between *stronsium*—strontium, and *strooi*—straw. Shit. Between shish kebab and shitbag. Shithead. Coarse slang for a contemptible or worthless person.) With much trouble and with the help of an interpreter it transpires that Chicken believes he was told to do what he did (evil whisperings and insinuations). The sick man did it, he says, the man who lay like an animal on the ground, that is the man who told him to do it.

•

I believe that I am beginning to sense a change in Theo Verwey. His restlessness seems to me unrelated to the slow pace of our progress, though I have no way of knowing this for certain. Perhaps it has something to do with the surging of spring. Perhaps with his buying mania. He has begun to attend auctions again. Something seems to be fermenting in him; I sometimes notice a feverish glint in his eye. He has devised a complex and time-consuming system for categorising words according to degree and phase of obsolescence. Archaic forms, dated words, regional and colloquial terms, words of which the original meaning has become worn down, words of which the meaning in the course of time has become garbled, botched, and bungled. In brief, a documentation of the origin, ascendancy, and decline of words. (What he actually has in mind, I suspect, is a large-scale cartography of the whole language. Not merely a record of what has become lost or obsolete, but a user profile and frequency profile for every word. A much larger, more ambitious project than the one we are working on at the moment.) He is a meticulous (as well as a virtuous) man, he has gleaned information over a long period, consulted his sources thoroughly, but I wonder if there is not a megalomanic aspect to his endeavours. (I am sceptical of grandiose and overarching systems, although I am not unsystematic myself—lexicography demands that of one.)

On a morning in early September his pretty wife comes to visit again. I see to it that I excuse myself promptly, in case the couple want to discuss something in private. When I return after a while, I hear their voices in what sounds like an argument behind the closed door. Again I turn on my heels. When I return later, Theo is visibly upset. I do not know if I have ever seen him like this. He looks as if the blood has rushed too suddenly and too feverishly to his face.

A day or two later I arrive at the office earlier than usual and I am surprised to hear voices behind the closed door. I knock. Inside I hear a shuffling before Theo answers. I am surprised to find Sailor visiting him so early in the morning. Theo is his polite self and Sailor a trifle coquettish, as always. He is sitting on the edge of Theo's desk, holding the Indian sculpture depicting the goddess Kali copulating with the corpse of Shiva. As I enter, he gets up, puts the piece back on the desk. He was on his way out, he says.

I have to think back to the morning when I came upon him and Hugo Hattingh robustly rollicking. Not a word said between Theo and myself about that again.

I notice that Theo is distracted these days. Maybe even out of kilter. On one or two occasions he addresses me with irritation in his voice. This temperate and noble-minded man. We do not have the kind of relationship that permits me to ask if anything is wrong.

Alverine phones me one night, roughly three weeks after our visit to Ladybrand. I can immediately hear from her voice that something is amiss.

"No, Miss Dolly, we are very worried about Jaykie."

"Why are you worried?"

"We think he's mixed up with the gangs again."

"Which gangs, Alverine? What do you mean, again? Has he been mixed up with gangs in the past?"

"No, Miss Dolly, I can't say which gangs. Some of the gangs around here. He's gone around with them in the past."

Would that be Fish, Flesh and partners? Is that the gang she is referring to? Sparrow, Alvin D, Rosencrantz and Guildenstern—aka Malone and Molloy? Could Jaykie be in cahoots with them, are they the hoodlums after all, the hooligans? Or was he referring to other gangs? Did Jaykie deceive me? Did I allow myself to be persuaded by him too easily?

"Jaykie has not been himself lately, Miss Dolly."

"In what way?"

"He doesn't sleep, he doesn't eat, he didn't go to work yesterday."

"What does he say?"

"He doesn't want to talk, Miss Dolly. He is as quiet as the grave. My mother wants him to talk to our minister, but he refuses, Miss Dolly, he just refuses to do it."

"I see."

"I think his conscience is bothering him about something, Miss Dolly."

"What would it be about?"

"No, mevrou, that I can't say myself."

"Alverine, is he on drugs?"

"That I can't say, Miss Dolly. But we are very worried about him."

(Clearly before my eyes the image of Hazel with the child on her hip, twenty years ago.)

"What do you know about Fish and company? Sparrow and the rest?" (Sparrow too stammering to commit any deed: be it wrongdoing, misconduct, offence, transgression, violation or sin. And the other two, Molloy and Malone, too deeply immersed in abstruse exchange, in oracular dabbling. That leaves Fish, or Flesh—whatever his name may be—accompanied by his Beatrice in her donkey slippers, his most blessed lady.)

"I don't really know about them, Miss Dolly. But we know Jaykie is not on the right path," she says softly.

"Does he have a job at the moment?"

"Yes, Miss Dolly, he has a good job. He runs the home-industry shop here in town for one of the mevrouens, who is away on holiday. But yesterday and the day before he wasn't at work, that's also the reason we worry so much."

The home industry. By day Jaykie runs the home-industry shop and by night he is on the prowl with the gangs, accompanying them on their unholy missions. He leads a double life. Here the possibility of a Dr. Jekyll and Mr. Hyde presents itself again. By day Jaykie has no memory of his nocturnal deeds, misdeeds, crimes, or misdemeanours. He awakes (comes to his senses) in the home-industry shop, with a gilded shell in his hand. Where does it comes from? he wonders. Meanwhile my shells are being recycled, reworked, artfully taken in hand: they are painted, their surfaces are decoupaged, they are skilfully glued together to form fancy articles of everyday use. The nautiluses are sawn through, magically transformed into glammed-up soap containers and lamp stands. The thought of this possibility makes me turn ice cold. The exact moment I thought the matter out of my hands, that Jaykie has done his best, that he has no part in the wrongdoing, that moment there appear to be reasons for my suspicions to flare up again: Jaykie on drugs, Jaykie mixed up with gangs. Jaykie is an unreliable witness—my initial suspicions regarding him were justified. I should have stuck to my guns, I should have trusted my intuition. He pulled the wool over my eyes thoroughly. He put the best (penitent) foot forward, but he spoke with two mouths. He beguiled me with his squint-eyed charm, with the suggestion of religious rapture, with his restless, winsome, youthful glance. I took pity on him too easily. Jaykie has gone astray, and Alverine is appealing to me. In what way does she think I can help?

"Alverine," I say, "I am very sorry to hear about this, but I don't believe there's anything I can do."

Then I suddenly realise. It dawns on me. The Bible Society. My supposed connection with the Bible Society is the link.

"Alverine," I say, "I will send him a booklet, but don't count on it to help much. Maybe you should consult a social worker."

"No, that's good, Miss Dolly," Alverine says. "My mother said that she *thought* Miss Dolly could send us something. She says if the books for Patrick arrived here earlier, he might still have been with us today."

I tremble when I reflect on the consequences of my own deception.

•

In the second week of September I betake myself for the second time to the bookshop in the big shopping mall. Too late to extricate myself from this. I now have to see my own fraud through to the end. I buy a couple of booklets. It takes me a long time to decide on suitable titles. One for Aunty Rosie to comfort her (*Blomme vir 'n moeder*—Flowers for a mother). One for Alverine to support her (*Vreugde vir vandag*—Joy for today). Two for Jaykie (*Hoop vir jou vertwyfeling*—Hope for your despair, and *Genade-oomblikke*—Moments of grace). He can make of that what he wants. He knows very well what my real identity is, and that I have no connection with the Bible Society. I will never underestimate him again. I proceed on the assumption that he knows more than he pretends to. He can view the booklets in whatever light he chooses—as a joke, as a serious reprimand, as an acknowledgement of reciprocal double-dealing and duplicity. With the booklets I enclose a card, the words chosen with great care. He must know that I am watching him.

This is the way I see it: my shells have disappeared into a labyrinth, an underground maze. They have become dispersed, entangled in a densely woven network, intertwined and enmeshed with the fate of Constable Modisane in Musina, with Jaykie and Patrick Steinmeier, with Sparrow and Fish and Rosencrantz and Guildenstern, and with the home-industry shop in Ladybrand—where they are subjected daily to multiple metamorphoses. Perhaps they are being destroyed at a deeper level. Perhaps their distribution and dissolution are happening on a more profound, darker level. At the level of total disintegration. Be that as it may. I cannot follow them any more. I have to let them go.

I am displaying my other shells again—those not stolen and those I got back. The fourteen that remain. I have to open myself to their beauty again, in spite of their desecration. I arrange them in a new formation on the small table next to my bed. They stand there as if lining up to be counted—the five that escaped unharmed, and the nine that came away with a negligible loss of vitality—like the survivors of a disaster.

•

In the third week of September the spring rains fall ever more penetratingly at night. In the early mornings I take a walk in the small park close to the house. Something is straining inside my head, like a flower wanting to open. The sky is large and wide and heavy with clouds. A spring wind plucks at my hair, at my clothes, it stirs the foliage in the trees. With excitement I breathe in the new air. I feel myself at one with cosmic forces and unharnessed energies.

Hugo Hattingh has since recovered sufficiently from his seizure to be questioned about the earliest fossil evidence of organisms with hard body parts. On his cheek the blue-green shadow of a bruise is still visible, as well as the scar of the cut he sustained when he struck his eyebrow against the steel table. He explains that the so-called snowball earth—a period during which the earth was practically covered with ice—caused an enormous acceleration of growth in the Cambrian (approximately five hundred and forty million years ago), with an increase in the occurrence as well as the complexity of multicelled organisms during this period.

Could there be any truth in Chicken's allegation, I ask Freddie Ferreira, the curator of mammals. Freddie shrugs, stubs out his cigarette butt beneath his heel and says: "Chicken is completely bonkers. He's been suspended for a month after the shit episode in the toilet."

"And Hugo Hattingh," I ask cautiously, "isn't he a little disturbed too?" (In the light of Theo Verwey's caustic insinuation.)

"Not so disturbed that he doesn't know what he's doing," Freddie says.

Sof has still not decided if she should let go of the paediatrician or accommodate him. She changes her mind every so often. Some mornings she arrives at work sobered and pale with resolve. On other mornings she will be glowing from the previous night's seductive SMS messages. Perhaps also under the influence of the rising sap of spring?

What do I really know about this woman with whom I have gradually become friends? What do I know about her, except that she grew up in a pastorie and that she has rejected the doctrine of predestination? I know how she envisages the virtuous way. I know that she was in love with Kafka at fifteen and mourned his death when she read his biography. Together we visited Ladybrand twice, and there she allowed me a glimpse of her parish persona. Only to her and to Theo Verwey have I mentioned that I have begun writing a book again.

Theo and I proceed energetically to the letters *G* and *H*. In a dream Abel Sonnekus wears a dark suit. He sits down. I shake his hand. I wish him luck. He addresses me with great tenderness. How strange.

Sometimes I turn my head towards Theo Verwey in anticipation. I want to ask him if he is also conscious of a renewed charge in the air. But I decide against it every time, for what good could it do? He is not the kind of man to whom I can put a question like that. (Just as I could not ask him if he really is hand in glove with Sonnekus.) I should rather direct my apprehensive energies toward Frans de Waard, my companion, with whom I have arranged to spend a couple of days in October.

On Friday afteroon at the end of the third week in September I take a walk along the beach. When I come home, I have a light supper. I am resolved to get a solid stretch of writing done this evening. The book is taking on an ever more definite shape. It is about a man travelling by boat up the coast of East Africa. He is undertaking this journey because of an interest in foreign countries, in geography, and because he is open to new experiences. Also because his heart has just been broken, and he wishes to turn the page on this chapter. He should have known that the woman would be his downfall, but this is precisely what made her so irresistible to him. It had been the first time that he had set his heart on someone in this manner. He undertakes the boat trip in the company of a friend. At night they watch the women on board; there are any number of them not disinclined to seduction and pleasure. But he has hardened his heart against their enticement—he will not make himself vulnerable to their charms and wiles again. He buys a shell once when they go ashore. Another time he buys a bamboo fan from a dark woman exhibiting her wares on the quay.

But my writing is interrupted twice tonight. First by Alverine, phoning to say that Jaykie is still on the errant path, and then by a light knock on my front door.

It is Theo Verwey. I immediately assume that he is drunk. His hair is dishevelled, his jacket is flung over his shoulder, his shirt is not tucked in properly. May he come in? He does not look at me. I stand aside for him to enter. He immediately sits down on a sofa, his elbows on his knees, his head dropped forward. Nothing was wrong with him this morning, and now he looks like this. Something must have happened. I am as surprised by his turning up at my house unexpectedly as I am by his appearance.

I sit down on a chair facing him. What is the matter? I ask. Did anything happen? (I expect the worst: his car has been hijacked, his wife or child has been assaulted, his house has burnt down, he has lost all his money.) He only shakes his head. Speechless. Would he like something to drink? Coffee may be a good idea. He shakes his head. No, he wants nothing to drink.

Music? I ask. Anything he wants to listen to? Bach's cello suites perhaps? Schubert? He shakes his head again. No, nothing. He will listen to nothing, drink nothing, and obviously also say nothing.

We sit together in silence like this for some time before he abruptly lifts his head and says: "The rich man, of whom you told me once. The book you read."

"Yes."

"The man's dogs. He talks to them."

"Before he leaves his apartment in the mornings. His apartment consisting of twenty-eight rooms."

"Where does he go again?" Theo's head is still drooping between his shoulders.

"He goes on a trip through the city in his limousine. There he encounters various things. He talks to his advisors. He has erotic encounters both inside and outside the car. Against the counsel of his advisors, he trades ever larger sums of money—he goes into a frenzy of divesture. He even shoots his bodyguard in the end."

"What happens to him?"

"At the end of the book he is dead. Someone else has shot him. He walked into an ambush with open eyes—almost wilfully."

Again Theo sits wordlessly for a while.

"Theo," I say, "what is the matter?"

Theo shakes his head. He is clearly not drunk, as I assumed initially. For that he is far too controlled. Even now, in extremis. He is in some or other state of psychic affliction, but he cannot or will not speak about it. I cannot force him.

"You spoke about the funeral procession," he says, "about the mendicant monks—the dervishes."

"Yes," I say. "The funeral procession is perhaps the most beautiful part of the book. I can't remember exactly, but first there is the motorcycle cavalcade, then the security vehicles, then cars with white roses, then the hearse with the rap singer lying in state, his body positioned at an angle to be clearly visible, surrounded by flowers—pink asphodel. You probably know that the asphodel is the flower associated with Hades?"

"It is the immortal flower growing in Elysium, related to the lily family," Theo says without raising his head. "Genus *Asphodelus*."

"Amplified by loudspeakers, the dead man's voice accompanies his own cortege. Next to the hearse wailing women walk, wearing headscarfs and djellabahs . . . djellabahs?"

"A loose woollen tunic, derived from the Arabic *jallaba*," Theo says, his head still in his hands.

"The women's hands are decorated with henna. Four bodyguards with rifles are positioned at each end of the hearse. Then come the break dancers. Then the family and friends in thirty-seven limousines, three abreast, I don't remember all that well. Then the high-placed officials, the rap singers, the media and delegates from various religious institutions. In the air above are the helicopters. Four, I believe there are four. Then follow the Catholic nuns, and then the dervishes. They are dressed in tunics and caps, and they whirl, they spin slowly. The rich man sees them whirling, and it occurs to him that they are spinning out of their bodies, towards the end of all possessions—for spinning is a gesture of shedding. Divesture is an important motif in the book. Then the rich man weeps. He pounds his chest with his fists as three buses pass by, followed by the unofficial mourners, on foot, of all races and persuasions, some of whom resemble pilgrims. Then come the ordinary cars—eighty, ninety of them. The rich man thinks of his own death. He could never command anything similar—all he can think of is himself lying powdered in his coffin, and everyone sniggering covertly as they express their condolences."

I pause.

"Please continue," Theo says.

"The man moves slowly through the city in his limousine. He is super-rich. This I have mentioned. Apart from the funeral procession, he encounters two other obstacles—one of them a protest march. At various points he comes across the woman he married two weeks before. They eat together once or twice. The rich man has a prodigious appetite. Sexually as well. He has sex with different women in different places, also in his car. On the way, also in the limousine, his doctor examines his prostate. Lovely portraits of all these characters, by the way. The writer is a master of dialogue, of characterisation and situation."

Theo nods briefly, indicating that he is still listening.

"At the end, as he is dying, he fantasises about the conduct of his mistresses after his death. One washes his entrails in palm wine during a ritual before his body is embalmed. One masturbates quietly where she is sitting in the back row of the funeral chapel. His wife shaves her head and wears black for a year. As he is dying, he thinks that he would like to be buried in a nuclear bomber aircraft, he wants to be solarised, he wants the plane containing his embalmed body to be flown by remote control, he wants to be dressed in a suit, with a tie and a turban, the bodies of his dogs accompanying him—his huge, silky Russian wolfhounds. The plane must plummet from a great height—when striking the earth it must form a fireball that leaves behind a landscape artwork interacting with the desert. This artwork must be placed in a trust and managed by his art dealer—also his lover of many years. Even in his dying moments he has monumental fantasies. He is fabulously rich. Everything he undertakes is larger than life."

Theo sounds as if he is blowing softly through his nose (it could also be a sob), his bearing still one of attentive listening.

"The story of this man," I say, "suddenly sounds like a biblical parable to me. A contemporary variation of one of the parables about the rich man." I say this with a smile. Slightly ironically.

He nods slowly and affirmatively, head still hanging.

"How many parables of the rich man would there be in the Bible?" I ask.

"Three," Theo replies without hesitation.

How should I interpret this visit from Theo Verwey? I see this man daily in a work situation; our relationship is strictly professional. He is the embodiment of respectability and decorum. Then he shows up unannounced at my door, dishevelled and clearly acutely distressed. Is there a reason that he turns to me specifically, or did he just happen to be in the vicinity, like Sailor a while ago? He cannot or will not say what is wrong with him. He is obviously a troubled man, but the only thing he wants to talk about is a fictitious character of whom I spoke on one or two occasions: a rich man. In that case, very well.

"Theo," I say, "do you want to be buried or cremated?"

He glances up and looks at me for a few moments. Only now do I notice that his face is puffy and his eyes red, as if he has been crying, or is suffering from lack of sleep. This impeccably dressed man's shirt is rumpled and stained at the chest. Were I not convinced that he has not been drinking, I would have assumed that he has an evening of debauchery and drunkenness behind him.

"Cremated," Theo says.

"And where should your ashes be strewn?" I ask.

He gives this some thought. His head is still raised. His gaze focused on an indeterminate spot behind me. I see that much is going through his mind at this moment.

"They are to be strewn in the Tugela River," he says, "from the bridge just outside of Colenso. A little further along the bank."

"In an eastern or western direction?" I ask.

"Eastern," he says. "In the direction of Bergville."

"You have thought this through well," I say.

He nods, looking at me again briefly, but does not answer.

"In my Children's Bible the rich man always wore a large, coiled hat. A kind of turban," I say. "The rich man in the novel has an asymmetrical prostate. That is the verdict of the doctor after he has examined him in the limousine, as I mentioned earlier. This examination takes place just before or maybe even while the rich man commits an unconventional sexual act with a female advisor."

Theo listens attentively, but with his head down.

"This matter of the asymmetrical prostate recurs later in the book. Can I make you a cup of coffee?"

"That would be nice, thank you," Theo says politely, almost as if there is nothing awry. We drink our coffee in silence. He looks less distressed, more preoccupied. When he has finished, he gets up and says that it is a good thing that tomorrow is Saturday.

"I have already taken up too much of your time," he says.

•

On Saturday I disconnect my telephone. For the time being I do not want to be kept informed about Jaykie's doings. Theo Verwey never initiates a conversation, and then he arrives at my house late one evening—in a disconcerted state—without giving the slightest indication of the reason for his visit. I can come to a few conclusions about this, not one of them necessarily correct. It is clear that he is in some sort of crisis, be it financial, marital, or spiritual. It could be anything from a crisis of faith to money lost on the stock exchange, or debts he has incurred through the buying of ancient Indian copulating figures at auctions. Or something could have gone wrong with his joint investments with Sonnekus—if I am to believe the lisping Freek van As. What it is that intrigues him about the story of the rich man, I can only speculate. It could be anything. It could be the man's fabulous wealth. It could be his casual sexual encounters. It could be the whirling dervishes. It could be the man trading and losing all of his and his wife's money in the course of a single day in a high-risk transaction. It could be the man fantasising about his own funeral. Although I do think that the story of the rich man is only a pretext for Theo Verwey to deceive both himself and me. I suspect that he has an equally strong need to reveal and to conceal. He wants to put me on a trail and at the same time throw me off the track. About that I can do nothing.

I ask Sof about him. Is Theo Verwey affluent? Ye-es, says Sof, if not, he could never have launched such a comprehensive project and virtually financed it single-handedly.

(I haven't yet told her that we receive financial backing from Abel Sonnekus. That the wheel has turned full circle, that life is unpredictable, that Sonnekus is now my benefactor. Even though I have lost my shells through his doing.)

"Would you go as far as to say that Theo Verwey is a rich man?" I ask. Yes, says Sof, she could think of him as rich—not super-rich, but rich enough.

"But he's a pretentious doos," she says.

"How can you say that?" I ask. "What do you have against him?"

"Nothing," Sof says. "I just find him a pretentious doos, that's all," and she clears her throat slightly.

"Has he done you any kind of disservice?"

"No," she says, "he is always politeness itself."

"And you hold that against him?"

"No, I hold nothing against him. I just don't like him. Neither do I like his wife. She's even more pretentious, if that were possible."

"What else do you know about him, Sof, other than that he's a pretentious doos?"

"Well," Sof says, giving it a moment's thought. "Nothing, really."

"His wife had a strange smell when she came to visit him the other day," I say.

"What did she smell like?" Sof asks, interested.

"As if there was something wrong with her feminine hygiene."

"It wouldn't surprise me at all if there was a great deal wrong with her bodily *and* mental hygiene," and she gives her little cough.

"Maybe she was simply wearing a strange perfume that day."

"Yes," Sof says. "Black Widow from Charnel House."

"Theo and I encountered the word *charnel* just recently! I even asked him about it. Both *charnel* and *carnal* are derived from the Medieval Latin *carnale*, and the Late Latin *carnalis*, from *carnis*—flesh. Of the flesh, fleshly intercourse in particular—sexual intercourse. We are busy with the word G." (Sexual intercourse—*geslagsgemeenskap*.)

"Sexual intercourse," Sof says. "I see. Is that what you busy yourselves with?"

(When I was a child, I remember, Joets asked what it actually means: *die gemeenskap van die heiliges*—literally the intercourse of the saints. I was too young, I think, to realise that the biblical phrase had a double meaning.)

"Amongst other things, yes. But we are actually focusing on words formed in combination with the word 'death'."

"Sexual intercourse and death, they are one and the same thing," says Sof.

"Possibly," I say. "But be that as it may, you grew up in a pastorie, you ingested the Bible along with your mother's milk. At a tender age you had insight into the concordance and into the lives of the judges and prophets. Tell me everything you know about the rich man in the Bible. But before you expand on the rich man as trope, please refresh my memory about the different parables in which he appears."

"Oh, hell," Sof says, and she blows her nose twice in rapid succession. She gives it some thought. "There is the parable of the rich fool, the parable of the dishonest manager and the parable of the great feast. Then there are related references to borrowed money, debts written off, implacable creditors, and so on—over and above the references to wealth in the Old Testament."

"I can see," I say to Sof, "that you were well instructed in the pastorie."

On Monday Theo and I continue our work, side by side. Not a word or a hint about his visit of Friday evening. As if it never happened. His mood is clearly in equilibrium again. I do not attempt to draw him out. How charming he looks this morning, how freshly pressed and manicured, how finely decked out—today he is wearing a pearl-grey silk shirt, lovely to look at. I can imagine its texture under my touch, and the texture of his chest underneath the shirt.

We are still busy with the letter G. We work through the different meanings of *gaar*. When you appeared drunk (*gaar*) in my doorway, I was completely (*gaar*) astonished, but totally (*gaar*) under the wrong impression. Because, kind companion (*gawe gesel*), you actually (*gaar*) had your wits about you, that much I noticed while observing you (*terwyl ek jou gadegeslaan het*). Nothing Gadarene (*Gadareens*) to be driven out of you, absolutely not (*glad en al nie*), so elegantly dressed (*geklee*) in gabardine (*gabardien*). Far from your wife (*gade*), close to your ruin; but your preference (*gading*) you sought away from home. Gallant (*galant*) as always, though bitter as gall (*galbitter*).

"*Gegabbat?*"

"Regional term for courting and love-making."

"*Gabbatjies?*"

"Weak coffee."

"*Greppel?* I'm not familiar with this word either."

Greppel or *grippie* or *grippe* is Early Afrikaans for a narrow, shallow trench or furrow, Theo explains.

"*Gulskop?*"

"Glutton."

(Abel Sonnekus.)

We work through combinations with the words *gal* and *galg*—gall and gallows: the pejorative *galasem*—gall breath and the improbable *galgbruilof*—gallows wedding. (Do you take this man, this woman, to love and honour, in the shadow of the gallows?) The criminal with his *galgetronie*—gallows mug. (Would that be a good description of the sneering face of Flesh, Fish—or whatever he is called?)

Die hele wêreld is ganselik en gansemal, glattemal en glattendal omgekrap. Trek dig die gardyne, dat ons die ganske nag, die gansgoddelike nag, onder gan-sveer, op liefde en gansmelk, mekaar in ons gansheid kan geniet—The whole world is wholly, entirely, and utterly out of kilter. Close the curtains, that we may for the whole night, and all night long, under goose down, on love and milk of goose, enjoy each other wholly and in our entirety. I have dreamt of Sonnekus again. Behind a fence he is cooing and warbling. In a garden (*gaarde*) of rose fragrance and moonlight. For the whole of the dream (*die ganske droom*) we are on our way somewhere, caught up in a (gallows) loop (*galge-lus*), which hampers our progress. He surprises me with gifts (*gawes*) of food and of song. He surprises me

193

with his friendliness (*gaafheid*), so utterly (*gans*) to my liking (*gewenste*).

Gebrokehartjies (little broken hearts: a shrub with red, heart-shaped flowers) and *gebrokenheid* (brokenness).

"Bring me a bouquet of little broken hearts, dear heart, to make amends for my brokenness," I say.

"For my broken heart," Theo says, and smiles.

Broken heart, I think. Is *that* what brought Theo to my door on Friday night?

Like the letter *D*, the cards for *G* are also extensive. We work in silence. We put our shoulders to the wheel. There are the many beautiful *gh* words, mostly of Hottentot origin. *Gha* (go). *Ghaai* (little Bushman apron). *Ghaaierig* (sticky). *Ghaai-ghaai* (a game). *Ghaaisa* (a dance). *Ghaaiwortel* (Ghaai root). *Ghaan* (girl). *Ghaap* (a kind of succulent). *Ghaapgrawer* (abusive name). *Ghaas* (elephant's foot, a plant). *Ghabba* (thorny shrub). *Ghabbe* and *ghawwerig* (bragging or showing off). *Ghabera* (sometimes also *ghaberietjie*, a lizard). *Ghaboe* (without taste). *Ghaip* (the erdwolf or aardwolf, the maned jackal, of which my father used to tell me). *Ghal* (sheep's fat, snot). *Ghannaghoetjie* (a kind of beetle). *Ghalli* (children's game). *Ghantang* (a suitor). *Gharra* (edible berry). *Ghibbie* (drizzling rain). *Ghillie* (mucus). *Ghnarrabos* (ghnarra bush). *Ghô* (wild almond). *Ghobbablom* (flower of the ghobba plant, an edible leafless succulent). *Ghoef* (onomatopoeia for thudding sound). *Ghoeghoe* (without value). *Ghoem* (something very large). *Ghoera* (girl, with your blood-red lips and braided hair). *Ghoetang* (edible bulb). *Ghoghogh* (sound of the bush crow). *Ghommaliedjie* (picnic song). *Ghong* (gong). *Ghonnel* (part of a boat). *Ghorghorra* (millipede). *Ghrokstem* (hoarse voice). *Ghwa* (gone). *Ghwalla* (worthless person). *Ghwano* (guano). *Ghwarra* (tease). *Ghwarrie* (shrub). *Ghwarrievlakte* (ghwarrie plain). *Ghwel* (phlegm). *Ghyl* (a glass marble).

My father would have taken pleasure in each and every one of these words, especially the animal names—the meerkat (*ghartjie*, *gharretjie*, *ghratjie* or *ghariemeerkat*), the maned jackal (*ghaip*) and the lizard (*ghaberietjie*), and in all the various imitations of bird and animal sounds.

In the meantime and for certain, but unrevealed and hushed, the shadow of the rich man lies between Theo Verwey and me.

•

September has four and a half weeks. In the fourth and last week of the ninth, the first month of spring, the heavens open. There are floods inland. Bridges are washed away along the coast. On television I see a house, a cow, a piano, a pram, borne along from the interior by the seething water masses. As a child we experienced something similar on holiday at the South Coast: I clearly recall that the sky was the exact colour of the brown mass of water; within hours the bridge we had been standing on had been washed away.

During this time I have a horrifying dream. A severed head is accidentally wrapped up in something resembling plastic or Cellophane—the transparent paper that bouquets are often wrapped in. This head is later sawn open to reveal its two inner halves. I try my best to disentangle the web of associations in which the dream could be embedded, but to no avail. I do not believe in premonitions, but the dream and the freak weather make me apprehensive.

After the heaviest rainfall has abated, Sof and I go for a walk on the beach one afternoon. After the storms of the past week the sea is calm, but there is the pungent smell of seaweed and washed-up bamboo. On the horizon is a ship. The air and the sea have the same dull, metallic sheen. We walk in silence, our heads bent forward. I search attentively among the algae and bamboo, among the empty plastic containers, the driftage and flotsam. What do I hope to find? The head of an angel in stone. A shell. Whole and undamaged. A fossil from the sea. An ammonite. A petrified nautilus or a mussel. Something from the Cambrian period. Something dating from the time of the earliest fossilised remains of organisms with hard body parts. But the ocean does not surrender her treasures. Sof finds a wreath of plastic flowers, which seems to have come from the grave of a child. Where is Patrick Steinmeier buried? I must pay a visit to his grave.

Sof tells me of a book she is reading. A man undertakes a journey on foot. At the end of each day's walk he arrives at an inn. He has a light supper, but cannot fall asleep at night, the greater part of which he spends listening to the sounds in the tavern beneath his room, or to the creaking of the floorboards and the occasional calls of nightbirds.

Only by morning does he fall asleep. The mood of the evening or night is always indicated very simply. A storm brewing over the sea. Dusk descending on a field of heather. The sky darkening and a wind rising abruptly. The sun becoming visible behind the clouds for a moment. A darkness moving in from the horizon.

Sof turns her face towards me. The late afternoon light is suddenly tinted pink, the brooding sky is reflected in the water. Her eyes are grey, the outlines of her face hardly discernible.

"That is how I would have liked to write," she says. "Without the writer's voice droning in the background. If I could write, I would want the same distance between myself and what I write about. Do you understand?"

"Not quite," I say.

She points to the horizon. Sky and sea are now one uninterrupted, brooding plane. The ship lies motionless in the distance. "That's how I would have liked to write if I could," she says, "with little happening ostensibly, but everything charged with meaning."

We walk back slowly. We do not speak much. We are both under the impression of the waning day, the sombre hour, the oyster-grey sky, the murky sea, gleaming dully, like a pearl.

Even in the half-dark I still cannot take my eyes off the water line. Little ghost crabs, barely visible, scurry towards the sea. I am still hoping, I am always hoping to find something. Hope maketh not ashamed. I distinguish between two kinds of shells: those that I collect, and those I pick up. Those that I collect are usually larger, unblemished specimens. With a single exception, I acquired all the shells in my collection through buying. This exception is the shell that Joets found more than thirty years ago as we were walking on the beach. I was visiting her. I was nineteen, Joets was twenty-five. She had two young children and she was in an unhappy marriage. She envied me my life. She did not want to be burdened with a husband and two children. She bitterly regretted having ended her studies. She told me that she had started to write, she had started working on a novel. She told me about an idea she had. I listened. I had my own ideas about what I would like to write. Half-formed ideas, spliced with free-floating longing.

We were walking along the beach. Joets spoke about her conception of time. Of the time bomb inside the moth. How one is in fact as solid as one's breath. Joets was smaller than I was, she took more after our mother's side of the family. (I, in turn, incline more towards our father's side.) She was a lovely woman, dark, with a soft, sensual face, like our mother and our wandering grandfather. (I am taller, lankier, blonder, like our father.) At that time she was still smoking heavily.

She does not believe in free will, she said; we are as helpless as a beetle that unsuspectingly lands in a braaivleis fire at night. Like a mantis on a jazz record, she said, and laughed. (Joets could *laugh*, she could be completely overcome with laughter.) She explained that time does not move horizontally, but that it is constantly rearranged, as in a kaleidoscope. She spoke about the Holy Spirit—she said that she imagined it as a winged egg on a cloud, or a seed with wings, like a pine seed—and that of all things it was the only thing that could become nothing and out of nothing recreate itself again: a miracle, like an aerial root. I listened. I did not understand everything she said. The beach was blue. The rocks a deep blackish blue (so different from the colours of rocks and beach along the Indian ocean). It was late afternoon.

Every little insect, every moth, Joets explained, carries within it the time bomb which will determine its death, and everything ticks together, each according to its own inner circular time with all its tiny cogs and wheels, and in this manner the end speeds closer for all beings, great and small, each appropriate to its own appointed time. Each according to its time bomb within. Only now, she said, does she understand the painting by Picasso of the girl holding the fan in her hand, so much like the rhythm of fate. (Did I not place the pack of photographs of the small building where the hanging corpse of Patrick Steinmeier was found like a fan in front of Constable Modisane?)

Then we found the shell. Joets picked it up and gave it to me. Quite a large shell, something almost fossilised about it, the colour of bone— smooth and polished, as if it were carved out of marble. It was my first shell, the predecessor of all the others. It was before I started to collect shells. I never felt the need to identify it, as if it had always had a separate status. Joets was my sister; I loved and admired her.

"The sea is so beautiful, it makes one long for a different life," Sof says. (Her face is sometimes severe and sometimes shy, but when she speaks, it is always with a disarming intensity.)

"I wonder if there are as many dead souls as there are shells on the beach," I say. "What does the Bible say?"

"I don't think there is any reference to shells in the Bible," she says. "Everything seems so sorrowful to me, and love brings only unhappiness and ruin. I've had enough of it."

"Love ruins and injures us, spoils and damages us; it is pernicious, detrimental, and fatal. Is that what you mean, Sof?"

"Yes," says Sof, "something like that. Whatever."

Joets told me during that holiday that she loved someone other than her husband, that she had always loved, and would always love that person. That she nurtured the pain, that it gave her the strength to write. Only once did she ever again refer to this secret love in a letter and then never again, as later she would never again refer to the book I had written. Except during our last telephone conversation.

"Did something happen?" I ask.

"No," Sof says. "Nothing happened. Every choice I made in my life was the wrong choice."

"Is it that bad?"

"Oh," she says, "it's actually okay. It's not that bad."

We walk in silence for a while. It is already deep twilight. "I've been wondering," she says, carefully clearing her throat, "whether it wouldn't help you to think that one cannot possess beauty. That one can only ever be its temporary custodian. Wouldn't that help with the loss of the shells?" She gives a slight cough.

I reflect for a moment. "No," I say. "No, it doesn't help me to think about it like that."

"In that case," Sof says, "I think we should buy you some new shells somewhere."

•

I am twelve, Joets is eighteen. It is December, we are on holiday in the Free State. It is a sultry evening. The black woman serving us at the table is in an advanced state of pregnancy. She is an attractive young woman. There is no electricity as yet; we eat by candlelight. The dining room is far from spacious and the ceilings are low. Even in the unnatural light of the lamp the woman's face appears particularly dark. It is covered in sweat and expressionless, perhaps from exertion or fatigue, for it is hot, and she has been on her feet all day. My uncle will take her in to town later that evening for her confinement.

That night the moon is full. I stand at the window and look out on the bright, moonlit yard. A shiver goes through me. A peacock cries. It is an unearthly sound. The moonlit nightscape touches me deeply. There is something newly awoken in me that the moon and the night speaks to. In my young girl's breast there are the first stirrings of an ache, a longing.

The next morning my uncle says that the woman died in the night during childbirth. The child also.

I sit at the breakfast table with misery welling up in me like nausea, and it remains with me all day long.

Joets attacks our father. Had that woman been white, she says, she would probably not be dead now. Our father keeps quiet. He will not be provoked. He does not want discord. (Oneness, unanimity, unity that is strength, that is what he aspires to.) He especially does not desire discord with his elder daughter, the apple of his eye. But Joets is unyielding. She does not give up easily. Her flushed, animated face is turned towards him; his he keeps averted.

My cheeks are burning, I am not hungry, I feel sick. I find it hard to believe. The woman who only last night was standing next to me at the table. A suspicion darkens my mind like the shadow of a cloud. With this my childhood is concluded and my turbulent youth ushered in by the cry of a peacock.

CHAPTER FIFTEEN

October is the loveliest month. Once again I am burdened with improper thoughts about death. Unseemly as ever. Theo shows me a set of crystal glasses he has bought. Exquisite craftsmanship and quite possibly fabulously expensive. He has not yet offered a single word in explanation of his unexpected visit to me ten or eleven days ago.

On Monday he shows me the glasses; on Tuesday he is particularly quiet. I am in no mood to strike up a conversation either. We work in silence. We have moved on to the letter *H*. Theo again mentions that we have to increase our pace—at this rate we will not make the deadline. He has planned to spend a year on the project and would like to keep to that.

Tarried too long at *D*, I think, with all the death words and combinations.

I am sitting with a small stack of *H*-cards in my hand. The many words formed with heart (*hart*) and expressions in which the word is used. *Hartbrekend* and *die aas van harte*—heartbreaking and the ace of hearts. *Hartebloed*—lifeblood. (Theo is giving his lifeblood to the project; he has set his heart on it; a virtuous man to the marrow—*in hart en niere*—but not a man to wear his heart on his sleeve.) Jack of hearts, knave of hearts. King of hearts (*harteheer*) and queen of hearts (*hartensvrou*).

"Do you play cards?" I ask.

"No," Theo says. "Not any more. I did play when I was younger."

"You have made the acquaintance of the queen of hearts?"

He smiles. He knows as well as I do that this is a trap of sorts. He does not fall for it.

Hartedief (thief of hearts, darling), *harteloos* (without heart—lacking compassion). *Hartepyn* (heartache), and *harteleed* (affliction of the heart; grief).

"What is the difference between ordinary grief and grief of the heart?" I ask.

"Grief of the heart," he says with the hint of a smile, "one experiences in the region of the heart," and he strokes lightly over his chest, in the proximity of the heart. (Would I not love to lay a hand on his chest as well.)

"Ordinary grief, on the other hand," I say, "is suffused throughout the body."

He merely smiles.

I could go further this morning, and ask him if he has ever experienced true grief, the grief that brings anguish to the heart. I could cautiously prod him—apropos of his remark about the broken heart—and in this way trick him into divulging the reason for his visit to me. But I have no desire to draw him out today. What he does not want to say of his own accord has to remain unsaid.

I am somewhat irritated with him at present, with him and his project. It looks more megalomanic to me than ever before. Is there not something obsessive about this frantic documentation and conservation? Does it not point to an inability to let things take their natural course? (The natural course of things being constant change and loss.) But who am I to talk—the loss of a few shells is surely of significantly less importance than the daily loss of so many words in Afrikaans. (Like ballast thrown overboard a sinking ship. Should the language fare in ballast—without cargo—the ship would perhaps not sink.)

But here I am—bound and contractually obliged to assist Theo for a couple of months more. Heartache (*hartewee*) and heartfelt (*hartgrondig*). Darling, my little heart (*hartjie*) and lamb of my heart (*hartlam*). Stirring the heart (*hartroerend*) and secret of the heart (*hartsgeheim*). Gladdening the heart (*hartverblydend*) and lifting the heart (*hartverheffend*).

Before lunch Theo suddenly turns to me and says: "Am I imagining it, or has it suddenly become much colder?"

"No," I say. "Not that I've noticed. I find it quite warm this morning." I look out of the window. It is a fine day. The sky is open, cloudless. I turn towards Theo. He suddenly looks tired to me. What could be harrying this man, causing him suddenly to turn so deathly pale? So ashen. Could it have been our reference to grief, to the woes of the heart? Shall I risk asking him what is wrong? I hesitate. Even in extremis he could not speak to me. Today I lack the desire, or daring, to keep provoking him. I am still hesitating when Freddie Ferreira puts his head around the door to say that Theo has left the lights of his car on. After lunch I do not see him again. He has left a note saying that he has an appointment this afternoon.

After work Sof and I sit in a café that looks out over the sea. We drink our coffee in silence. I think again of Mrs. C and her companion, the silent Vercueil, who sits with her in her car, both of them gazing out over the sea. Mrs. C and I are in no way comparable as characters, of that I am thoroughly aware, and it is hardly an appropriate comparison. And yet, how I admire the author, for in the same way that he takes the astonishing risk of having Mrs. C talk to the young boy in the hospital about Thucydides, he risks (and gains) much—indescribably much—by the improbable conversations between Mrs. C and Vercueil, in her car by the sea, underway, in her house. Later even in her bedroom. Later, when she comes to realise that there is no longer anything that claims her, that binds her to her life.

I arrive home later than usual. When I am about to unlock my door, I cannot find my house keys. The only place they could possibly be is at work. I have no option but to go down to the city again. My landlord is not in; I cannot get a spare key from him.

Reluctantly I get into the car. I park at the hotel across the street. With my card, I let myself in at the side of the building. I greet the night watchman. I walk up the broad staircase with worn red carpeting to the second floor. My footsteps leave a hollow echo in the deserted building. The stuffed giraffe looks shockingly dilapidated. The handful of shells in a single display cabinet hardly reflects the treasures stored away in the boxes and cabinets elsewhere in the building. For whose pleasure, I wonder resentfully.

The lights are on in Theo's office and I hear music. He must be working late tonight. I knock and call out his name. There is no answer. I knock more loudly and gently turn the handle. The door is not locked. Theo is sitting at his desk, motionless. No, he is not sitting. His upper body is slumped forward, his head twisted at a strange angle, his cheek resting on the desk. His right cheek, to be precise. His arm, the right arm, hangs by his side, the other arm, the left, is tucked at an odd angle under his body. There can be no doubt at all. My first thought is: Murder, most foul.

Janet Baker on the CD player. "Ach, zu schnell," she sings. Something aching and silvery in her voice. Like powdered metal. Something sharp and flaky. Incredible what a voice can do, Theo said when we first listened to this recording. I close the door behind me and lock it. I turn around and take a step forward, but there is a threshold that for the moment I cannot cross.

An intense repugnance, a feeling of disgust and misery—physically manifested as nausea—overcomes me.

I switch off the music. Too painful to listen to for one moment longer. Too heartbreaking. It breaks my heart. Theo's eyes are half open, from his mouth a little water has trickled. His face is a dark, purplish red, as if he struggled to breathe. I place my hand between his hand and his chest to feel his pulse, but as I have lost my composure, I fail to locate it. I feel only the accelerated beat of my own pulse. There are no signs of wounds on his body, I see no blood anywhere. He is cold to my touch. Under his shirt I feel the texture of his chest: its hairiness. It is the first time, I realise, that I have ever touched him, except to shake his hand.

I sit down. I phone Sof. She is shocked. "Fuck," she says, "it's *bad*." Does she think I should phone his wife first, or the police? First the police. On Theo's desk I see a crumpled ball of paper. After phoning the police, I open it carefully.

I can't come tonight. The cunt never showed up. Fuck him. S.

Theo Verwey's wife is called Suzaan. I take it that this is not the kind of language she would ever use. Not even in the privacy of the marital bed. Not even in a state of profound ecstasy or need. Of that I am convinced. It has to be Sailor. Sailor seated casually on the edge of Theo's desk. Did this message contribute to Theo's dismay? His hand upon his heart. There he lies, his left hand wedged awkwardly between the desk and his chest. A heart attack? Heart failure caused by the heart's affliction, my heart? My legs are shaky. Did he at least have the consolation of the woman's silvery voice in his hour of death?

It does not take the police long to arrive. And who shall I meet up with again? None other than the morose Constable Moonsamy, who arrived at my house with Constable Modisane when my shells were stolen. He looks at me suspiciously—as if I am responsible for the dead man's condition. As if he considers a woman who could carry on like that about her stolen shells capable of anything, even murder.

The crumpled scrap of paper I have in the meantime put away inside my handbag.

•

No foul play is suspected. Theo died from a heart attack. The state pathologist at the mortuary was able to establish that soon enough. It was massive heart failure and over quickly, the man states. Theo mercifully did not have a drawn-out suffering. At work the next day everything is in turmoil. Nobody is more stricken than Sailor. He weeps so profusely that threads of slime dangle from his nose and mouth. He stands in the door of Theo's office while I vainly try to clear up my desk. I do not know where to start, I do not know what to do.

"Mind that you don't weep like that in front of the widow," I tell him.

"He was like a father to me," Sailor says.

Behind him stands Vera Garaszczuk. She wipes her eyes with the sleeve of her jersey. This morning, more than ever, she looks like a rundown cleaning woman. Pretty, with the long, strong legs, the turned-up nose and the high Slavonic cheekbones. Could Theo have had a go at her also? Behind her stands Freddie. He keeps shaking his head in disbelief.

Mevrou arrives. We all stand respectfully aside. She appears remarkably dry-eyed.

She looks absently at Theo's desk, at the books on his shelf. "Poetry," she says. "Lieder. Theo had such refined taste." She runs her finger distractedly over the piles of CDs. She strokes the boxes of cards with her hand.

I stand somewhat aside. I notice that I am keeping my nostrils slightly flared, alert to picking up the tiniest odour from her side. Deviant, unsavoury, whatever—some or other sign or key to Theo's death. To his heart's affliction. As if her smell could put me on the trail of his closed, concluded life. But this morning she smells only of perfume. All signs meticulously concealed. Anything that might have given her away. Anything that could betray the secret of their relationship and of Theo's broken heart.

Only after a day or two do I start to feel sad. Not the grief one feels at the death of a loved one, but a dry, bitter grief, as if for the needless squandering of something of value.

•

Alverine phones the day after Theo has died.

"Miss Dolly, I've got a tip for you from Jaykie," she says. "There's a container in the docks with twenty thousand rand's worth of shells. Jaykie asked me to tell you. They are holding it back because there are illegal corals with it."

"Alverine, where does Jaykie get this information?" I ask.

"He's got lots of contacts, Miss Dolly. Jaykie has lots of contacts."

I tell Sof about it. What am I to do with this tip—hang out at the docks? You won't be the first woman to do that, Sof says. Yes, I say, but I shall be the first woman who does so in order to get hold of shells. Except for Miss Eva, perhaps, Sof says.

"What would I do with twenty thousand rand's worth of shells?"

"Oh," Sof says, "you'll think of something to do with them," and she gives her little laugh.

CHAPTER SIXTEEN

In the days after Theo Verwey's death my limbs feel heavy as lead. It feels as though a great weight is pressing down on my chest. At night I go to bed early, or try to read. I read poetry; the facts of evolution I put aside for the time being—my gaze wants to move inward, I want to focus on small, lyrical, human moments. I read Wallace Stevens for the sake of Marthinus Maritz, the deceased poet, my maligned erstwhile friend. So shockingly, so purposefully slighted by Abel Sonnekus.

As far as possible, I avoid any thoughts of Sonnekus—apparently lying on his deathbed, although I doubt if he will let go that easily. Sonnekus is the sort of person who will cling to life till the bitter end out of godless greed. (Like a praying mantis on a jazz record. Joets's words.) I do not see him departing this life peacefully, but rather holding on frantically, not giving God's judgement much thought.

During this time I have erotic dreams. Indecently, embarrassingly erotic. Inconsiderate towards the deceased, I would think.

Sailor, aka Johannes Taljaard, sits with me in the office and tires me with his tears and his prattle. He sits with one leg over the armrest of the chair. A cigarette between the fingers of one hand, his head supported by the other. Propped up like this, his broad face appears even broader. Sitting here with his lush blond chest hair and his expensive wristwatch. Staring in front of him. His expression completely disconsolate. He blames the fucking cunt for Theo's death. The cunt blackmailed Theo.

He played games with him. He kept him on a string. He played him off against another lover. He squandered Theo's money, while his own father is stinking rich. The margarine magnate. Made his fortune with common cooking oil. He blackmailed him. Who blackmailed him— the father or the son, I ask, but it is never clear to me from Sailor's incoherent narrative. The whore, he broke Theo's heart. Over and over he repeats it: The whore, the fucking dog broke Theo's heart.

(A bouquet of little broken hearts.)

"How do you know these things?" I ask.

"Theo told me."

"You were good friends?"

"He was like a father to me." Every time Sailor utters these words, the tears flow freely.

He brings me poetry he has written, poetry and page upon page of prose. I take it home in the afternoons. I page through it. I do not have the energy to read it attentively. The poetry offers little at first glance; the prose is one uninterrupted account of sexual adventures. I am not too sure what kind of feedback Sailor expects. Does he feel the need to pour out his heart to me, or does he want a literary assessment?

After Theo's death on Tuesday his wife arrives at the office on Thursday. She is still remarkably self-controlled. She begins to pack some of his belongings into boxes: the CDs and the books. She wants to know whether I would be willing to continue with the project. It was important to Theo, it was what he had always dreamt of doing. He had so much respect for my expertise. (I wonder what has happened to the little sculpture he bought. It was in the office for a while, and then it suddenly disappeared. Would he have taken it home? What would his wife have made of Kali and Shiva in stark copulation? Was it also, like the ring, intended as a gift to her? Why do I have my suspicions about this?)

I will have to rethink my plans, I say. I doubt if I will want to complete the project, or to stay on much longer than the end of the year.

His wife could hire someone else, I think. From now on she and Abel Sonnekus, my benefactor—whether or not on his deathbed—will have to put their heads and their funds together. They could use the proceeds from Theo's estate (her inheritance) and Sonnekus's millions (apparently he has amassed a small fortune over the years; he is undoubtedly a rich man) to put together and finance an excellent new team to complete the project. I believe my time in this city and in this province has come to an end. Theo's death has dampened my enthusiasm for the project. It has dampened my enthusiasm in general. His death put a damper (a pall and a gloom) on my mind and my mood. If only I could weep, if I could pound my chest, but all I have experienced yet is a barren grief, and a strange aggrievedness.

Only my missing shells are keeping me here. The day I leave this city I shall leave them behind for good. While I am still here, the possibility remains, however slight, that I will obtain some certainty about their fate. The day I leave here, I leave them behind like the graves of children.

I reflect upon the rich man. I told Theo on the evening that he arrived at my house unannounced and without explanation, that the rich man in my Children's Bible wore a turban. I was given that Bible as a present by my grandmother when I was ten years old. I liked the illustrations in colour more than the black-and-white ones. Ruth picking up sheaves of corn in the field of Boas—resembling my mother so closely when she was picking up shells—was a colour illustration. I liked it very much. Also the one of the little daughter of Jairus being raised by Jesus. I liked the way she kept her gaze fixed on Him intently.

The rich fool was a black-and-white illustration. The man sat on the roof of his house in the shade of a striped, woven covering, his fingers propped against his forehead. His head was covered by a turban. He was overseeing his slaves, unloading sacks from camels. A little picture insert showed his coffin being borne away to the graveyard. The parable of Lazarus and the rich man was also depicted in black and white. Here, too, the rich man wore an ornate turban—so much like a turban shell. There was a lesson to be learnt from every one of these parables, and these lessons did not interest me. The momentous, somewhat pensive gesture with which Solomon held out his hand to the queen of Sheba, dressed in a beautiful gown of yellow silk, on the steps of his palace, suggested more (promised more) to my child's mind than all the stories and parables about the rich man who could apparently never succeed in grasping the simple fact that his goods were worldly goods, and that he could not take his riches with him.

•

Theo Verwey died on Tuesday and is to be buried the following Tuesday, a week after his death. It has already been arranged that Frans and I will see each other over the weekend. It is too late to cancel his visit. Joylessly I lie in his arms, this time not mourning my shells, though. What will you do, he asks. Stay on till the end of the year, I say. Every time we see each other, your attention is elsewhere, he says. I can't deny that, I say. If it isn't the shells, it's the death of your colleague. Theo Verwey was more than just a colleague, I say. We worked together closely for seven months—his death came as a great shock to me. That I can understand, Frans says, and I am trying my best to be accommodating.

"As far as your shells are concerned," he continues, "I have to say that you are the only person I know who refuses so utterly and obstinately to confront the darker regions of your psyche. If you still haven't realised that the shells are a pretext, that they are not what your feelings of loss are about, I again recommend a few therapy sessions to put you in touch with your true feelings."

I remain silent. I lie motionlessly in his arms. I keep my body turned away from him. I stare into space. Next to my bed are the three rows of shells, like the wretched survivors of a catastrophe. How do I explain to this man what my shells mean to me? If he still does not know this by now—if he cannot imagine how they gladden and console me, how can I explain it to him? He is my lover, he is intimately familiar with my body, he is attuned to my emotions, how come he cannot grasp the way in which their beauty speaks to me and supports me? If he does not know how my heart swells and lifts, how a space opens in my head, how my mind is flooded with serenity and contentment—if he cannot know that, who could ever know? If he cannot conceive of the extent of my loss, how should I explain it to him? Constable Modisane showed more empathy, I think bitterly.

"You don't want to look," Frans says. "You don't want to face your own demons. You don't want to accept that what the shells represent is more important than the shells themselves."

No! I want to say, the shells represent nothing but themselves! But I maintain a rancorous silence.

He is a reasonable and empathic man, he is trying his best to understand how I feel, but he is becoming impatient with me. I am trying his patience.

I say nothing. My body is rigid and my expression is set. What am I averting my face from? What do I not want to open my eyes to? My mother's anguish? My father's remorse he could not articulate? Joets's thwarted life? The transience of our earthly existence? The vulnerability of everything of value? The pain of children, the suffering of nations? Our human insignificance, our precarious position in the universe?

"Why so stubborn?" Frans says. "Why not try to get to the root of your obsession with the shells once and for all?"

What do you know of what the shells have to offer me, I think resentfully, of the pleasure I experience in contemplating them—more than pleasure: a deep satisfaction, an equanimity that I seldom experience in any other sphere of my life?

"Do not expect of me," I tell him, "to problematise my relationship with the shells. Do not expect of me to judge it at more than face value."

Unreconciled, Frans and I part after the weekend.

CHAPTER SEVENTEEN

On Tuesday morning, the day of Theo's funeral, I awake with a feeling of apprehension. For a while I lie in bed, listening to the traffic on the highway far below, with its monotonous drone like the sea. Then I focus my attention on the harsh calls of the hadedas at a distance, and then on the sweet song of birds closer by in the garden. I feel no grief, only a dryness, like a constriction in my throat, and a feeling of indefinable physical unease.

I do not have good memories of funerals. This morning I have to think of my grandfather's funeral, the grandfather who went down the mine in the erstwhile Messina. He had a photograph taken of himself standing next to a baobab tree. This photograph he placed in an envelope and sent home. My mother, a young girl then, kept it in her Bible. Years later I came upon it at the bottom of her box of photographs. Stored away, its purpose served. My grandfather was not a man who was close to nature, but he spoke with awe about the baobab tree. I remember the exaggerated gestures with which he tried to conjure up an image of its circumference before our eyes, we children watching him in silence. A man of conflicting impulses: a hedonist, a gambler, and an adventurer, with a restless longing for mystery. My father also listened to him in silence. He always regarded this father of his wife's (this intruder) with ironic detachment. For my mother, her father's words never registered at a conscious level—only at an old, preverbal level. At the level of intuition and emotion. At the level of powerlessness and longing.

I do not remember how old I was the day he was buried. Perhaps in my last year of school? I cannot recall the presence of my father, or Joets, or our younger brother. They were there, but I no longer see them. The grave is on the left side in my field of vision. A small group of people approach from the right, stumbling over the clods. At the grave the apathetic, overweight second wife is supported by a group of friends. She has black freckles, like an overripe peach, and heavy eyelids. She wails and blubbers and dangles like a huge black bell between Mr. Kronk and Mr. Kratz (or Messrs Schneider, Lessing, or Schiller)—miner friends of theirs. But she is actually laughing up her sleeve, for she is the sole beneficiary of my grandfather's will. Soon she will vanish over the horizon with the loot, sail to Hawaii, to lounge in a canvas chair on a tropical island for the rest of her days, pineapple cocktail in hand.

Who supports my mother on this day? No one, I think. She remains hovering on the periphery. She received the news of her father's death like a sidelong blow. Her face remains averted. As if she refuses to allow her father's grave into her field of vision. She is like one rowing on a small boat at night. The water is dead still and leaden and she is making no progress. She does not know if she will ever reach the opposite shore. She is so locked into herself that day that she is virtually invisible. Her thoughts are so murky and deep she can hardly fathom them, not on this day, and not on the days that follow.

This is how I remember my mother at her father's funeral.

•

The previous week the municipal workers were on strike. In the city they ran through the streets, overturned refuse bins, committed deeds of vandalism. The situation is more or less under control, but there is still a feeling of unrest in the air.

Sof and I go to Theo Verwey's funeral together. It is an oppressively hot day. The sky is low, a warm berg wind has been blowing since the day before. Above the city hovers a cloud of smoke.

Sof says that she has slept badly. She finds the city particularly shrill this morning, almost brutal. She endures all this only for the sake of the sea. If it were up to her, she would live somewhere else. But her husband would never leave here, his practice is too well established.

"He is like a Venus flytrap or something," she says. "If his poor patients only knew what they were in for. Poor sods."

On the way to the church Sof has a constant little asthmatic cough (a sign that she is tense) and sucks on a peppermint. When we arrive, the church is packed. I had expected a large turnout, but nothing like this.

"Vultures," Sof whispers as we sit down. "Anything for a bit of excitement."

Immediately after us another small group enters. It is Freddie, Nathi, Mrs. Dudu, Vera Garaszczuk and Sailor. A dramatic entrance: from the corner of my eye I see that Freddie and Mrs. Dudu are supporting Sailor, who seems unable to stand properly on his feet. He is wearing dark glasses and is dressed in a white suit.

"Fu-uck," Sof whispers, "we're in for something."

During the service Sailor's deep sighs, groans, and restless shifting are clearly audible behind us. The text verse is 2 Peter 1 verse 14: "Knowing that shortly I must put off this my tabernacle . . ." It is stuffy in the packed church, and I soon lose the thread of the minister's argument. Then follow several eulogies. Theo Verwey was an honourable man, a pillar of the community, a respected academic, a devoted family man. Yes, I think: righteous, noble-hearted, noble-minded, magnanimous. You name it. For seven months we worked together almost daily, and all I know about him—apart from his commitment to the Afrikaans language—is that beauty had a firm hold over him.

When the family leave the church, the widow in all her well-clad glory is clearly visible for the first time. She is wearing a black dress and matching jacket of impeccably stylish cut.

"Indecently dressed for a widow," Sof says under her breath. "If she respected her deceased husband properly, she would have appeared in sackcloth and ashes today."

"It was his wish to be cremated, not buried," I say.

"Their marriage was probably based on lies and miscommunications," she mutters.

Outside the church Freddie, Sailor, and company disappear to their car before we have had a chance to greet them.

In the funeral procession, more or less halfway to the cemetery, the wave comes to meet us. We hear the swelling rumble before we see the people approaching at a distance.

"Fu-uck," Sof says.

As far as the eye can see, a mass of people, escorted by the police, are approaching slowly over the first hill. Wave upon wave they approach. First the striking municipal workers, running at a slow, rhythmic pace. They are singing. They are waving sticks with red flags tied to them in the air, as well as banners with painted slogans. Some are holding the lids of refuse bins like shields. They are wearing red T-shirts with the SAMWU emblem, and hats, caps, or berets on their heads. They come running up, singing, entirely occupying one side of the road, accompanied by supporters on the pavements and escorting riot police with firearms, batons, and helmets designed to protect the neck from behind and to be drawn down over the face.

SAM-WU, SAM-WU, SAM-WU, the men chant, and behind them the ululation of the women is becoming audible. Lovely, the sound, and the people approaching in waves. In hierarchical order, the legions of the aggrieved.

On the heels of the men follow the striking nurses. First the nursing sisters, with epaulettes flashing in the sun and cloaks billowing in the hot breeze, in a stately toyi-toyi. Then the rank and file, nurses in uniforms and sensible shoes, more exuberant, dancing and ululating, then the male nurses, then the cleaners, in blue and green uniforms with aprons and headscarfs, shrilly ululating, with mops and buckets and brooms, on which they beat like drums at times. Then follow the ambulance drivers with their fists in the air, blowing on shrill whistles, their vehicle keys tinkling on forked sticks.

In this way they approach over the hill, like the hosts of heaven. Surely the city must be brought to a near standstill by this procession—hospitals, emergency services, ambulances? Theo's long cortege is moving at a snail's pace, occasionally coming to a complete halt. In the stuffy heat Mevrou must be getting impatient.

Following the ambulance drivers are members of the TAC with large placards. Then men in traditional dress, and then women in traditional dress. Group after group passes us in rhythmic elation. They pass so close to the cars that it seems one could reach out and touch them. It is hot and the noise and throng of moving bodies make it seem hotter still. A cloud of dust hangs over the entire city, and above the singing and the drone and the sound of helicopters in the air the amplified directions given by the police are hardly audible.

Only the dervishes, Theo, I think, only the dervishes are missing today.

Sof and I watch silently as the groups pass us in huge rhythmic waves, some beating on the roofs of the cars with their flattened hands.

"Fu-uck," Sof says.

Theo would have had no cause for complaint about a lack of spectacle and fanfare, I think. (*Fanfare*, from seventeenth-century Dutch, Theo explained once. We did not accomplish much, I think, we could not even complete *H*.)

The procession arrives nearly an hour late at the cemetery. "What a blessing the undertakers didn't strike as well," I say.

"Mevrou must have bribed them," Sof says.

The funeralgoers move to the grave in a large group, slowly, in slow motion, it seems to me, as if, as in Zeno's paradox, we will never reach our destination. In the background linger echoes of the chanting and ululations of the protestors, of the deafening sound of the helicopters. In the cemetery it is quiet and dry, a wintry decorum to the surroundings, except for the lush palms, and the jacarandas, which have already started to bloom—so much earlier here than in other parts of the country.

Freddie and company join us. Sailor is looking even more frayed than he did in church—at times he all but dangles between Nathi and Freddie, with Mrs. Dudu and Vera Garaszczuk in a supporting capacity. As he embraces me fervently, pressing his damp, feverish cheek, slightly raspy with designer stubble against mine, I detect an overwhelmingly strong odour of aftershave. Hugo Boss? I wonder involuntarily. We move forward. Sailor stumbles repeatedly, the little group having to support him. Laboriously and at a slackened pace we move forward.

Did he use something? I covertly ask Freddie. Smoked something, snorted something, something stronger than alcohol? How would I know, Freddie says (at his wits' end) and Mrs. Dudu rolls her eyes heavenwards.

"Just keep him away from the grave," Sof says.

Mrs. Dudu is stylishly clad in a little black two-piece outfit, Freddie is wearing a suit, Nathi is modestly dressed in black jeans and T-shirt, Vera Garaszczuk (possibly not quite familiar with local dress codes) is wearing black stockings, high heels and a black minidress with revealing décolletage—an outfit which would not be inappropriate for a paid female escort. If Mrs. Verwey could be said to be dressed in Errol Arendz today, then Sailor's white linen suit is nothing less than Armani. With it he is wearing a tight-fitting black T-shirt. Far gone, however. Far gone in his grief and misery, his face flushed and puffy.

I feel dizzy. The earth is rising and falling underneath my feet, like the undulations of a grassy plain. Above our heads the sky is hard and pure and open, with a shimmering of gold leaf and undertones of indigo and scarlet. Full of signs and portents for those willing to take heed.

"I last saw such a turnout at the funeral of Saartjie Baartman on television," Sof remarks and coughs surreptitiously.

"What about Dr. Verwoerd's funeral?" I say.

"Yes," Sof says, "but that wasn't on television. We had to sit in the lounge with drawn curtains, listening to the radio all day. My father insisted on it."

From the corner of my eye I notice how Vera Garaszczuk hands Sailor a hip flask to drink from during their stumbling progress. "Come on, boy," she tells him, "stop behaving so miserably."

Sailor takes a gigantic swig, nearly stumbles one last time and says: "Christ, I very nearly landed on my cunt," and with that we finally reach the grave.

The funeralgoers are arranged in hierarchical circles around the open grave. The first and inner circle is formed by the widow and her two children as well as the nearest relatives. The second circle by close family friends and other relations. The third circle is formed by Theo's former colleagues, dignitaries and members of the Academy, executive members of the Department of Regional Languages and business associates of Mrs. Verwey's. The staff of the museum form the fourth circle: Freddie Ferreira, curator of mammals; Nathi Gule, geologist in training; Vera Garaszczuk, expert on fossils from the Cambrian; Sailor, the man in charge of exhibitions; Kleinjan Coetzer, curator of amphibians (with red eyes as if from swimming long stretches underwater, back for the occasion from the swampy regions where he is doing research); Bobbie Bester, curator of birds (also back from an extended field-work trip); Mrs. Dudu, chief librarian of the Natural History Museum and advisory member of the managing committee of the City Library. Myself, Theo's project assistant, and Sof, (unofficial) curator of languages. Also present are a large number of well-wishers and interested parties, and the press, for Theo Verwey was an important man, and his wife is a high-profile businesswoman. Only Hugo Hattingh is shining in his absence. One and all stand gathered around the grave, with the lovely gold-leaf heaven above our heads, the first tender signs of spring already visible, the echoes of the protest march still in the air.

"He wanted to be cremated and his ashes strewn in the Tugela River," I whisper to Sof.

"I told you his wife is indescribably backward," she whispers back.

Apart from Hugo Hattingh, the only absence is that of our chief sponsor, Abel Sonnekus, the man of good works, our great benefactor (mine in particular). For all I know, they may yet come, bearing him in on a stretcher, that he may bless, with a weighty gesture as from the Old Testament, Theo Verwey's departing soul and his impeded project.

In the middle of the first prayer Sof nudges me softly. She gestures with her head. On the periphery, on the outer rim of the crowd of mourners, a small group is standing at a respectful distance—three young men, accompanied by an older man. The tallest of the four is a fine-looking, slender young man, with an aristocratic face and bearing. Could this be the dog who allegedly broke Theo's heart? It has to be him, I think.

"Could that be the dog and his father," I whisper to Sof, "the margarine magnate and his blackmailing son?"

After the conclusion of the funeral oration a little choir of farm workers sing; they are from the farm where Theo was born. Their singing is exceptionally moving, and I feel a lump forming in my throat. But the last sad notes have hardly died away, and the coffin has just started to be lowered, when Sailor, to our left, begins to move forward, purposefully making his way through the mourners. It looks as if Freddie and Mrs. Dudu are trying in vain to restrain him.

"Fu-uck," Sof says, "he's going to jump into the grave."

Indeed it seems that nothing will stop Sailor. Purposefully he elbows open a path to the grave, where he is mercifully restrained by many hands. An unidentified duo support him, for his knees have apparently given way under him again. The little choir has started singing once more—probably at a signal from the widow—and to the mournful tune of their song, and the sound of a helicopter passing overhead, Sailor starts throwing white carnations, which he has conjured up from God knows where, on the coffin, one by one, with a histrionic gesture. The undertaker meanwhile has hastily begun to hand around a little basket with flower petals in order that Sailor should not be the only one to take leave of Theo in this passionately floral manner. Mevrou is also strewing for all she is worth, looking more determined than shattered (overcome with emotion), insofar as her expression is visible behind her dark glasses. She has taken hold of her two children by the arms and they are trying to work Sailor firmly but unobtrusively to the side. The press are taking photographs, the little choir is singing, the helicopter is circling above our heads, a flock of hadedas fly shriekingly over the cemetery, and as I look back, I see the small group of men turn around and vanish over the nearest hillock.

"Exit the margarine magnate," Sof says, who also saw them leaving.

"At least he had the decency to attend the funeral," I say.

"After having driven Theo to the verge of bankruptcy," Sof remarks. (She has obviously had to listen to Sailor's tattle as well.)

•

A large number of guests have been invited to Theo's house after the funeral proceedings. The house is stately, in a grand neighbourhood, and I am struck by the coldness of its atmosphere. Chintz, satin, and velvet; teak and yellowwood furniture; white floor tiles and expensive ornaments. I suspect that it does not quite represent Theo's taste.

The tables are laden with edibles, expensive china, heavy silver, crystal glasses, lovely flower arrangements. Young men and women have been hired for the occasion, stylishly but demurely dressed in black and white. The girls are serving snacks on silver trays, the men glasses of fruit juice and dry sherry. "Is one allowed to smoke?" asks Sof, knocking back two glasses of sherry in quick succession.

The food is splendid. There is a huge variety of sandwiches in the best English tradition—variations around the theme of the ordinary sandwich: thin rounds of lightly toasted bread with Parma ham and a quail's egg in the centre, delicate triangular sandwiches with a cucumber-and-herb filling, artfully rolled ones with spinach-flavoured butter and smoked salmon, dark rye and white bread in chequered slices. There are continental-style canapés—rounds, ovals and crescents, with toppings of mushroom and ham, chopped salami and olives, pieces of crayfish and sprigs of dill. Snacks and delicacies are colourfully displayed on large plates (heirlooms): strips of raw beef enclosing anchovies and olives, ribbons of raw ham round melon balls, spinach leaves enfolding mussels, speared lobster tails in a shellfish sauce, squid fragments flambéed in brandy. There is even a selection of delectable Indian morsels. As for the sweet things, there are puff-pastry milk tarts, hertzoggies, koeksisters. The cuisine is obviously an attempt to reflect the demographic composition of this cosmopolitan harbour city with its intermingling of cultures.

"She must have blown half of Theo's estate on this exhibitionist extravaganza," Sof says, and takes a delicate bite of an almond-soufflé sandwich.

Mrs. Verwey descends the broad staircase and hesitates for a moment before clapping her hands to get everyone's attention, the elegant cut of her simple black dress coming into its own only now. (A lovely, charming woman, despite the predator's eyes and the sharp, feral teeth.) Still remarkably composed, she bids everyone welcome.

"She's decided to combine the funeral with a debutante ball," Sof whispers beside me.

This is the way Theo would have wanted it, says Mrs. Verwey. Each one of his relatives, and every one of you, dear friends, was close to his heart. My life without him will be indescribably poorer; he leaves behind an emptiness that cannot be filled, but he would also have wanted me to continue with my life. Such a person was my husband, Theo. He was a dreamer, an aesthete, but also practical, with both feet on the ground.

"He wanted to be cremated," I say softly to Sof, "and drift in peace down the Tugela."

Freddie and company have in the meantime moved closer to us. I would not have expected Sailor to be among the invited guests, but here he is, more subdued now, still wearing his dark glasses. His plate is already piled remarkably high. Extreme affliction of the heart seems to agree with his appetite. As he puts a canapé (whole) into his mouth, I notice for the first time that he is wearing the ring. The antique ring of which I harboured the impression that Theo had bought it for his wife. He wears it on his little finger. Does this double-heartedness, this duplicity of Theo Verwey surprise me? No. I have already accepted that I knew very little about that noble-hearted man.

"My worst suspicions are being confirmed here today," Sof remarks, and gives her little cough. "The woman is a spendthrift and a show-off. Would Theo have approved of all this? Would funeral rice and bobotie not have been sufficient?" she says as she relishes a canapé with caviar and spring onion.

In April, shortly after I had arrived here, Theo and I worked on the letter B. (A we had completed in March already.) Tonight Mrs. Verwey reminds me of a *badmeesteres* (mistress in charge of a bathing house), who keeps a strict eye over the *badpawiljoen* (bathing pavilion). *Badhuis, badkuur*, and *badpak* (bathhouse, bath cure, and bathing suit). The word combinations formed with *begrafnis* (funeral). The B-words, all completed, all documented. Would *begrafnispraal* (funeral splendour) be applicable here today, or *begrafnisbanket* (funeral banquet)? I hardly see this as a *begrafnismaal* (funeral meal), for it is not a particularly sombre gathering—there is ample evidence of barely suppressed elation around me, the funeral guests are restrainedly enraptured by the extravagance and magnificence of the cuisine. *Begrafniseetgoed* (funeral food). *Begrafnisgerei* (funeral utensils). *Begrafnissilwer* (funeral silver). *Begrafnisblomme* (funeral flowers). Veiled funeral exuberance.

During the course of the afternoon I engage in several conversations. Mrs. Verwey, or Suzaan, is an excellent hostess. Not only does she keep an eye on the proceedings, she also introduces people to one another, facilitates interactions, sees to the refilling of empty glasses and plates, mixes with the guests (*begrafnisgangers*) so as to exchange an intimate word with everyone, receives condolences with a fitting expression of grief and resignation, and gives unobtrusive directions to the team of waiters and waitresses who continue to emerge from the kitchen with more delicacies. "It was God's will," I hear her say, and "I am grateful for the years Theo and I could spend together." Every time she passes me, she squeezes my arm gently and whispers in my ear that she is relying on me—Theo had such a high opinion of me as co-worker and assistant.

"Think it over well," she whispers urgently. "You don't have to decide immediately."

She introduces Sof and me to an ex-colleague of Theo's. It is a woman who has immersed herself in a study of Middle-Dutch literature, and has recently completed a book about the journey of Sint Brandaen. She has translated the Middle-Dutch text into Afrikaans, annotated and furnished it with a commentary. This house reminds her of the ninth circle of hell, Sof says, of the frozen lake of Cocytus, where the souls of the traitors dwell. It has the same icy-cold atmosphere. "It must be the white tiles that give me this feeling," she says, and gives her disarming laugh. The medievalist looks somewhat taken aback. She is a woman with lively eyes and short, unruly curls. I am reminded of the journey of Sint Brandaen by dint of my Afrikaans-Netherlands studies, and although that was many years ago, I can still recall the gigantic head washed up on a beach that Brandaen encounters. We talk about the origins of the Middle-Dutch text, about the texts that preceded it—the Irish from the seventh and eighth centuries, the Latin from the ninth century. We talk about the depiction of the devil in the text, about the manikin on the leaf, and the man on the clod of earth. The medievalist points out that each one of them is doing penance for a sin committed, and that this will never come to an end, that it will continue into eternity, or until the Second Coming, at any rate. Sof shudders. As a child, the idea of eternity made her hair stand on end, she says, and she still finds it a chilling thought. She motions to one of the handsome young waiters, takes a glass of sherry and tosses it back unceremoniously. She almost chokes, I slap her on the back, she coughs, gives an exculpatory little smile and says: "The Second Coming is an equally intimidating concept, but fortunately I am now finally rid of those obscene notions."

I encounter Hugo Hattingh. He has showed up after all. He is standing in a corner with a glass of sherry and a small plate of eats. He is staring absently in front of him, which makes me wonder for a moment whether he knows why he is here. I cannot engage him in small talk, for he has no aptitude for that, and I am in no mood for niceties anyway. I therefore come straight to the point and ask him what it means that there was nothing before the beginning of the universe.

I notice that he has difficulty placing me for some moments, before he answers. "There was no space," Hugo Hattingh says, "because there was nowhere for it to exist. The universe probably not only developed out of nothing, but also out of nowhere. Because space did not exist, time did not either." On his plate are a small assortment of canapés and a koeksister.

I am restless, strangely perturbed, and however much the subject interests me, I suddenly realise that I have no desire to pause and reflect on the unfathomable mysteries of the universe right now. Not today. I leave Hugo Hattingh to deal with his untouched delicacies and start talking to a young man, a former student of Theo's, unabashedly sorrowful in appearance, who is writing a thesis on the funeral motif in Afrikaans literature, and who shyly admits, while self-consciously ingesting an ornate puff-pastry tartlet, that he is working on his first novel. How well it fits his lugubrious countenance, I think, how in keeping with his field of study. What else can he do but make of it a huge success? I encounter Sof in conversation with Vera Garaszczuk. From her facial expression I can deduce nothing about the nature of their exchange. I move on. Between conversations I try to see as much as possible of the house. I ascend stairs, I walk down passages. I carefully open a number of doors. I am looking for something that could evoke the memory of Theo—something to unleash my emotions.

222

Eventually I get drunk on the sherry. Theo Verwey is extricating himself from this house and this city and this incarnation at the speed of light. I have not yet shed a tear about his death. There has been no opportunity for me to pound my chest like the rich man and weep passionately. The marching strikers did not provide that; at the graveside I was distracted by Sailor's obtrusive behaviour—even though the little choir sang movingly, and I could feel the first stirrings of grief rising in my throat. The atmosphere of this house is not conducive to emotional release; it is cold, as cold, indeed, as the ninth circle of hell, as Sof has justly remarked. From the corner of my eye I notice Hugo Hattingh moving on the periphery, disembodied as a ghost. I come across Sailor in a passionate embrace with a waitress, and still later in an even closer embrace with a waiter, his hand firmly on the younger man's crotch. Wherever I encounter Freddie Ferreira, curator of mammals, he is seated, smoking, his head down, always with a plate of untouched food at his feet. So much like my cynical, hard-arsed, defenceless uncle.

The afternoon gradually gets into its own crazy rhythm. I increasingly perceive everything from the corner of my eye (peripheral vision, surely on account of my reckless ingestion of sherry and canapés). Mevrou is darting around everywhere like a black butterfly; I think I still hear the afterdrone of helicopters and the rhythmic chanting of the protesting masses. One of the guests nearly falls into the swimming pool, someone vomits convulsively behind a hibiscus bush, and in one of the upstairs rooms Theo's daughter—a lovely dark-haired child, who closely resembles her father—is listening to heavy-metal music with friends. Sailor beckons Sof and me aside at one stage to ask if we want to cut a line with him. Barring his flushed cheeks and red eyes, he appears to be once again in fine fettle. "Are you out of your fucking mind?" Sof asks. "Are you asking to be thrown out of this house? Where did you get the stuff?" From one of the waitresses. One of the many faceless little girls with black dresses and white aprons.

Sof and I continue our search for Theo's study, and when we eventually locate it, we close the door carefully behind us. "Fu-uck," Sof says, "I'm as drunk as a fucking fruit bat." The room is clinically neat, so neat that I doubt whether Theo ever used it. Sof immediately lies down on the divan, covered with a kelim. I look at the books on the shelves. On the desk are photographs of the children and Mevrou. There is an amber paperweight with a petrified insect inside. Against one wall, half hidden, is a mounted poster, not very large: *Diable. Detall de la Davallada als inferns. 1470-1485. Bartolomé Bermejo*. It is from the Museu Nacional d'Art de Catalunya, and must have been bought in Spain, in Barcelona. It depicts a devil sitting with his elbows propped on his knees. His feet are birds' claws, one of which is gripped around the ankle of the other. He is naked. On his skin are patterns, like those of a snake or an insect; camouflage, as of a worm. He has black butterfly wings with glowing motifs in red and yellow, and breasts like a woman's, but with black veins. His body is hard and sinewy, the skin on his thin belly wrinkled. His forearms are segmented, like the limbs of a grasshopper, or like the apparel of a knight, with sharp protrusions. His naked testicles—the hairy black sac, with the vertical ridge in the centre and the horizontal transverse grooves beautifully visible—are conspicuous between his legs. Bartolomé Bermejo (an artist completely unknown to me) clearly had much pleasure in the depiction of the detail. The devil's short horns are visible amongst his short hair, and the skin on his face is darkly tanned, like that of a Catalan peasant. His eyes are yellow. He stares morosely in front of him. This is no active devil—in contrast with the restless, energetic devil and his devilish underlings who remorselessly harrow the poor bridle thief in Sint Brandaen—but a passive, disaffected devil. He is not a creature with supernatural, evil powers, but a mal-content peasant. Someone who has strayed from the virtuous path, who has made the wrong choice, and now has to do penance for all eternity in the fires of hell. I think of all the many devil words that Theo and I worked through. This portrayal must have made an impression on him—I can hardly imagine that Mrs. Verwey would have bought it; it does not strike me as something that would appeal to her taste.

The funeral festivities are in full swing when we go downstairs a while later; the celebration is now in its mature phase. Even the dour-est of mourners—the most sombre among the relatives from remote regions; the colourless, stuffy former and retired colleagues—all are warming to the spirit of things. Women with stiff coiffures and prim, tailored suits; aunts from distant provinces, related by blood as well as by marriage; staid ladies from the congregation—all of their tongues are beginning to loosen considerably around the table laden with sweets. "Only when that little woman—the little widow—comes to a standstill," says one of the women (puffed up hugely, clad in a billowing raiment with printed floral motif), dabbing her tiny, vindictive mouth delicately with a printed serviette, "will she realise what has hit her." The men have formed small groups at a safe distance and are risking rugby talk and cracking the odd little joke. Soon we shall be dancing the funeral reel. Nathi Gule is deeply immersed in conversation with the young writer. Hugo Hattingh is still meandering about on his own. The lights in the chandeliers are burning already, although the sun has not yet set. Before long the candles in the silver candleholders on the table are lit, and a small string quartet replaces the soulful little funeral choir. Bowls of steaming food are carried in and chilled white wine is served. Freddie Ferreira has moved to a different spot, his head still hanging, his plate of food still untouched. Now and then he looks up and shakes his head in disbelief. Mevrou has a deep glow to her pretty cheek. She squeezes my arm in passing, and for a moment I pick up a trace of her body heat as she says close to my ear: "Think it over well, Theo would have wanted it. It was his lifelong dream, that project."

I encounter Hugo Hattingh once again. For the first time ever he addresses me of his own accord. Against the funeral din in the background he explains the concept of inflation to me—setting out exactly what happened during the first fractions of a second after the Big Bang—after the beginning of space and time. On his plate are a stuffed egg and a koeksister.

The Big Bang was not a contained explosion, he says, it happened everywhere, there was no surrounding empty space in which it happened. The moment space came to exist, time started flowing. The two are intimately connected.

I am always interested in what Hugo Hattingh has to say—how I have badgered him with questions over the past weeks! But today, on the occasion of the deceased's departure, there is something else I want to know of him. Something more human, more intimate. In the presence of death I do not wish to fathom the mystery of time and space—I would rather concentrate on the personal. I want to cast myself into the

225

specific, the subjective, the small, transient human moment, that I may be deaf to the immense rushing of time passing in my ears. I want to know (though I dare not ask) how Hugo Hattingh feels about Theo's death, what he believes to have precipitated it, what his relationship with Sailor is, and what the nature of his paedophiliac longings are. What he experiences during one of his seizures, and whether it really was he who spoke to Chicken, who whispered scatological suggestions to him. But Hugo Hattingh does not notice my lack of enthusiasm today, he continues to explain the concept of inflation with relentless precision—the vast, but as yet uncoordinated interaction between gravity, radiation, and matter in the earliest formative moments of the universe.

He now attaches himself to me, as to a familiar chair or drinking utensil. He follows me as I walk, explaining that when this universe comes to its end, a succeeding universe could arise out of it, and this cycle could be repeated infinitely, with each cycle of longer duration than the preceding one. The stuffed egg and the koeksister remain untouched on his plate. From his neck a deep blush rises threateningly, the scar on his eyebrow looks red and tumid. He has long since ceased to register my presence, but he needs someone towards whom he can direct himself. I lead him to Freddie, and politely disengage myself. He continues his exposition as he sits down next to Freddie, who does not so much as lift his gaze from the floor. Over my shoulder I see Freddie lighting a cigarette and sporadically looking in Hugo Hattingh's direction, but how much he is exerting himself to listen, I would not know. I move on, away from the contracting universe and the end of time.

A Mr. Mdletshe from the Department of Regional Languages engages me in conversation. The smooth, chiselled planes of his handsome, middle-aged face remind me slightly of Constable Modisane, which immediately predisposes me positively towards him. He has a well-shaped forehead and an ironic glance (which I like in men). In welcome contrast with Hugo Hattingh, he makes solid eye contact and I think I detect an inviting glint in his look. He talks to me about the implications of the strike, about the policy of his department, and, do I imagine this, or is he steering me towards the garden with decidedly amorous intent. Yes, I think, this man pleases me well, I am not at all averse to being persuaded by him, I can feel my senses stir, somewhere my overwrought, pent-up emotions have to find release. I am involuntarily reminded of the rich man's wife clasping her legs around her husband at their last meeting (to his pleasant surprise) and how I told Theo about this. But Mrs. Verwey interrupts our conversation; she leads me away towards a nondescript man, who wants to clear up some lexicographic matter with me, and I leave the handsome, sexy man behind in the garden. I encounter Sof in conversation with the medievalist, who turns out to be a descendant of the Lion of the North (a former champion of the Nationalist cause). They are wrapped up in an intense discussion about Dante, surely as a result of Sof's initial comment about the icy atmosphere of the house.

As I seek relief from the throng in one of the upstairs bathrooms, I come upon Sailor, sitting by himself on a riempiesbank in one of the many hidden corners of the large house. He is staring pensively in front of him, one leg crossed over the other, a burning cigarette in his hand. I sit down beside him. His face is even more flushed than before. There is a wine stain on his expensive jacket. From his pocket he produces a half-jack of whisky and offers me a drink.

"For God's sake don't let Mevrou see you smoking and drinking like this in her house and snorting up whatever you can lay your hands on," I say.

"Fuck her," Sailor says tonelessly.

"Were Theo's troubles mainly financial?" I ask.

"I told you," Sailor says, "the cunt ruined him. He broke his heart."

"Did the cunt do both?" I ask. "Break his heart by ruining him, or break his heart by leaving him for someone else?"

Sailor looks at me uncomprehendingly. "Then he still had the fucking cheek to show up at the funeral," he says.

"I wasn't aware that you had seen him. You were too busy shoving the poor widow out of the way."

"Fuck her," Sailor says again. He toys distractedly with the ring on his finger. The antique Indian ring with the amethyst stones.

"Sailor," I say, "what brand of aftershave do you use?"

He looks at me. "Hugo Boss," he says. "Why, do you like it?"

On Sof's cheeks there are two flaming spots when I meet up with her downstairs, this time in lively conversation with a fervent academic.

This is where I realise that I have had enough. So much for Theo's funeral festivities. We are not staying a moment longer, I say softly to Sof. We are leaving right now.

In the car Sof says: "That woman—widow, whatever—certainly knows how to network. You can be sure that she's clinched quite a few business deals today."

I say to Sof: "I harried that man with my nonsensical prattle."

"What man are you talking about?" she asks.

"Theo Verwey. The deceased. The departed."

We are both out of sorts from the large quantities of sherry and white wine. I invite Sof for a drink at my house. I am scared of being alone. My feet seem weirdly close to my head, as if my body has been compressed. I pick up all kinds of perceptual disturbances on the periphery of my vision. The world appears to be pulled slightly askew—elliptically flattened. I keep hearing the afterdrone of the day's sounds: the thud of feet on asphalt, the roar of the helicopters, the singing of the multitudes and the heart-rending lament of the little funeral choir. My condition could be ascribed to all the sherry and canapés, or to suppressed emotions. I have a strong urge to shed tears, an increasing urge for an excessive, unrestrained display of grief. I want to be able to weep and tear my clothes and pound my chest with my fists. But my eyes remain dry, and my throat constricted.

"I don't know what prompted me," I say to Sof. "During the time Theo and I worked together I was constantly babbling away. I harassed him with the story of the rich man. You are familiar with the novel. I tried to provoke him. I set him cheap snares. I wouldn't leave him in peace. I was unstoppable."

"He was probably all too glad that you did so. He was grateful to you for speaking about all kinds of things on his behalf. He probably thought it bad manners to talk about death and about feelings—I know many people like that."

"Such a noble-hearted, such a virtuous man," I say. "My heart goes out to him, wherever he may be."

"Definitely on his way to heaven."

"Wherever. Heaven, hell, limbo. In strange tunnels of light. Between births. The poor man. Poor Theo, beneath the ground. I get claustrophobic when I think of that. He wanted to be cremated. He wanted his ashes strewn in the Tugela. Just outside Colenso. I suspect he identified with the rich man."

"You sensed it intuitively," Sof says. "You were probably finely in tune with each other. You probably had a better sense than his wife of what he wanted to hear, what he wanted to talk about."

"I obstinately stuck to my own agenda."

"Maybe he was on a self-destructive mission that made him increasingly reckless in his actions. Maybe he associated with disreputable types—not that I believe a word that Sailor says. Maybe he began to fantasise about his death because there were people who were not well disposed towards him, whom he knew to be plotting his downfall, which made him think—"

"Sof," I say, "I cannot reconcile this picture with Theo."

"Nor can I, really," Sof says, and gives her little laugh.

•

"What are you going to do now?" Sof asks a couple of days later. "Now that Theo is dead?"

"What should I do?" I say. "I am torn apart! The project is close to my heart. But is that because it was Theo's project? We achieved so little—we completed only nine letters of the alphabet! When I think of all the lovely, lost words that we never got to! Why did it take us so long? Why did we dawdle over it so long? Did we in fact dawdle? Were we delayed by the death words—should I see any significance in *that*? *H*—we stopped at *H*! Is it coincidence that we stopped at *H*? I know it is coincidence, and yet I still want to attach some meaning to it. Such a nondescript letter! What should I make of this?"

"Heaven and hell," says Sof, and clears her throat.

"Certainly. I lie awake at night wondering about the most significant letter of the alphabet. If I had to choose one, and one only. If I had to single out *one* to save from destruction."

"It's a fucking impossible choice," Sof says.

"I know. I tell myself that all the time. Heaven and hell. The hereafter. Sadness of the heart and grief of the heart. The afflicted heart was

229

Theo's undoing. Of that I am convinced. Heart—a significant word for the way I related to him. I often had the urge to pour out my heart to him. In his presence an unaccountable anguish from the regions of the heart often arose in me. When this happened, I sometimes spoke to him about the rich man. Theo tolerated this. More than that, actually—it interested him, it gripped his heart. Although I will never know what appealed to him most about the story. No, Sof, not without Theo. Theo and the project are inseparable to me."

"Then there's no problem," Sof says, and gives a small cough.

"In that case I won't remain longer than the end of the year," I say. "The project won't be anywhere near completion, but I can't do anything about that. Perhaps I will train as a conchologist and return to order the museum's shell collection."

•

I receive a call again one evening—later still than on the previous occasions. I had already fallen asleep, and had just awoken from a distressing dream in which my brother's body had been shattered by a fall. He lay stretched out on his back on some rocks surprisingly close to me. Around his mouth was an expression of bitter determination—the expression of one who has realised that human endeavour is futile, and has resigned himself to that. I turned away from the window and waited for the reality of his death to sink in.

It is Freek van As. His tongue moves more heavily tonight, more lispingly.

"Have you been drinking?" I ask admonishingly.

He gives his sly, vindictive laugh. Club foot.

"How far do you think you'll get as a writer with decency and compromise, with currying favour, with soft-soaping and sweet talk?" The line is not clear.

"What are you talking about?" I say.

The line crackles for a few seconds before his voice becomes audible again. Am I imagining it, or is he speaking with great difficulty. Pushing with the tongue. Heavy, dark, clammy.

"How far can you get with virtuousness and virtuous integrity, with respectability, seemliness, honesty, decorum? You name it, you are a woman with imagination."

It is raining. It has been raining all night and I have been conscious of that in my sleep.

"Enough of that," he says. "Enough of . . ."

But he fails to complete his sentence, for a fit of coughing overtakes him. His chest sounds dark and wet. Morbidly infected.

"Are you ill?" I ask cautiously.

Again he ignores my question. Merely gives an abrupt, mocking little laugh.

"Go for the jugular!" he says.

The line crackles and sputters. His voice is barely audible. I press the telephone closer to my ear. I exert myself to hear what he is saying.

His voice becomes clearer again. "Who do you want to shelter against the storm?" he asks. "Who do you want to be a stronghold, a citadel to? Who do you want to shield against the onslaught, give solace and comfort to?" He coughs.

I listen. The line buzzes.

"Who do you want to protect?" he asks. "Your mother, your sister, yourself?"

I cock my ears to catch his words.

"Cold," he says, and coughs. "Horrible. Cold."

"Freek," I say, "where are you?"

His voice disappears and becomes audible in turn.

"Show no mercy," he says, and gives a short little snicker before being overcome by a fit of coughing again (dark, slimy). "Expect no mercy!"

"Freek!" I say.

"Before you have not . . . cast off everything . . . that . . ." I hear him say, but the line comes and goes, becomes more indistinct, there is a last sharp crackle, and his voice disappears as if it has been sucked in by a thin, black tunnel.

"Freek van As!" I call after him.

Only the crackling of the line is still audible, and the sound of the rain dripping on the large leaves outside.

CHAPTER EIGHTEEN

In the days that follow, the mood in the tearoom is subdued. Everyone there knew Theo, and attended his funeral, even though he was not a staff member of the Natural History Museum.

Before I can tell Hugo Hattingh that I am ready for an exposition of the period of visible life, the Phanerozoic aeon, Freddie Ferreira informs me one morning that Hugo tried to hang himself in his office the day before. He was the one to discover Hugo there. Hugo was immediately admitted to an institution. A relapse, says Freddie, it happens from time to time, when Hugo does not take his medication regularly, when he is subjected to too much stress. The epileptic fit had already been a first indication, a warning signal.

"What precipitated it this time?" I ask.

Freddie shrugs. He would not know. It could be anything. With Hugo Hattingh one never knows. Theo Verwey's death might even have triggered it. The most unexpected, sometimes the most trivial things can throw Hugo off balance, Freddie says.

Trivial, I think, as Theo's death. As Hugo's fervid sporting with Sailor. As the possibility of a small confrontation with the disturbed Chicken. As the sustained contemplation of the inexorable laws of evolution. As the meticulous reflection on the timeless, spaceless void that preceded the advent of human time. Perhaps it is the sum total of such trivialities, I think, that makes him go off his head from time to time.

•

Ten days after Theo Verwey's funeral Sof and I sit looking out over the Indian Ocean. We have just swum in its lovely blue waters.

I often think of the manikin on the leaf that Sint Brandaen encounters on his journey. The manikin, hardly bigger than a man's thumb, tries to measure the sea with a slate pencil, with which he scoops up water, pouring it into a small bowl. He tells Sint Brandaen that it is as impossible for him in all eternity—or until the day of judgement—to measure the sea in this way, as it is to fathom the wonders of God. From this Brandaen has to learn that he too has had insufficient faith in God's wonders.

"Tell me about the life of shells," Sof says abruptly. "I know so little about it."

"The body of the snail that inhabits the shell," I say, "is unsegmented and divided into a foot, a head, a mantle and internal organs. The shell is the external skeleton—it supports and protects the soft internal body and the organs. The shell is secreted by the mantle and consists chiefly of calcium carbonate."

"A basic chemical substance," says Sof.

"Yes. A chemical substance already present in the earliest oceans. This calcium carbonate is secreted by cells at the side of the mantle, along with a protein mixture, conchiolin. The calcium is deposited in layers, and in this way the shell thickens during the growth process. The shape of the shell is determined by folds and ridges on the mantle. The colour of the shell is determined by the secretion of pigments and metabolic waste, influenced by the diet of the animal. Variations in colour among individuals of the same species are caused by differences in diet and by the salinity of the water. These pigments are mixed with calcium while the shell is still soft, and permanently embedded when it hardens.

"As in a fresco technique?"

"Yes, something like that. This is the way in which the shell grows. New layers are constantly added. The shell increases in size without changing its shape, for the growth of the shell is logarithmic. The growth curve is determined by a logarithmic spiral. A clean, predictable, mathematical process. Rhythmic and balanced. So different from our human lives, which are neither rhythmic nor balanced, but for the most part chaotic—far removed from order or regularity, tainted by madness and remorse. That has at any rate been the case with my life. Another reason that I like shells so much. Like Piero della Francesca in the poem by Van Wyk Louw, the nautilus exists in the pure realm of mathematics. I like that. You must understand that I am no true collector. And that I have no desire to be one. The place and date where the shell was found hardly interest me. My response is subjective. I respond to shells with my heart, with my kidneys, with my entrails. Some of the oldest fossils are shells. Molluscs have been around for much longer than vertebrates, and will survive long after we have stopped being here to collect them. When the continents once again join up into one huge continent, and the seas dominate the earth, and people no longer exist, there will still be shells—whether at the bottom of the great ocean, or in tepid pools, or in swamps, or in rivers—where they will be crawling or swimming, or jumping, with or without eyes, but always wearing their beauty as protection. Each with its own blazon, its shield, its own colours.

"From this I cannot but conclude," Sof says, "that the shell, and not the human being, is the crowning glory of creation. Or one of its crowns. Or one of the pearls in its crown. Perhaps you should think about it that way," she says, "that your lost shells are now in heaven, adorning the throne of God."

"I did indeed learn from Hugo Hattingh," I say, "that humans are not necessarily the apex of creation."

"I saw that quite early on in the pastorie," Sof says, and gives her little cough.

"You must understand, Sof," I say, "I am not a believer. I believe in the indifference of the universe, in the insignificance of human beings. I believe in coincidence, in the chance evolution of our particular human form. In the chance evolution of *all* forms, also those of shells. And yet I have to say—and here you, a child of the pastorie, could perhaps help me—I cannot look at the beauty and variation of shells without thinking in terms of the wonder of creation."

"It's a nasty habit," Sof says, and coughs. "Established early. It can be unlearnt."

A week after the funeral of Theo Verwey, Alverine phones me to say that Jaykie and his friend Bennie Fortuin are gone.

"What do you mean gone?" I ask.

"Gone as in missing, Miss Dolly. Missing for a week already." She is weeping softly on the other side. I can see her sitting, her head slightly averted.

"Did you notify the police?"

"Yes, we did, Miss Dolly."

"Who is this Bennie Fortuin?" I ask.

"A local guy, Miss Dolly, but he's always been a bad influence on Jaykie."

•

This is how I see it. Theo Verwey is dead. At the end of the book that I told Theo about, the rich man is also dead. Theo and I never spoke about the manner in which this man dies, I think I only ever mentioned it. We were too caught up in the funeral of the rap singer. Mrs. C dies at the close of *that* book. Vercueil folds his arms around her like the angel of death, but it brings her no comfort, no consolation. The writer does not see it as his writerly task or duty to console either Mrs. C or the reader. Resolution, yes, there is resolution at the end of that novel, but not consolation. Joets is dead, too soon, and she had to divest herself of much in this life. My mother is dead. My father is dead. My child is alive. My brother is alive; he is somewhere, I have no idea where; I have lost contact with him. I am alive, but my shells I shall never find again.

•

Joets's life, like my own life and that of my father and mother, can be divided into different periods.

I think of Joets as an eleven-year-old, when I was five. Fierce, un-yielding, unfriendly towards me, territorial. She mocked and teased me, she would not play with me, she would not take me along with her and her friends. I think of her as a fifteen-year-old, when I was nine, one afternoon in particular, one long, hot summer afternoon, while the grown-ups were sleeping, in the dark lounge with the low ceiling of my aunt's house in the Free State, of how she and one of our cousins conducted a long whispered conversation about their first, tentative sexual explorations, while I lay on the carpet drawing, listening to them. I drew in a lined, hardcover book with coloured pencils I received as a present from my grandmother. I drew little figures of women and of girls. My drawing skills still left much to be desired (unlike Joets's) and the eyes were drawn unnaturally big, set too wide apart and too close to the sides of the head. I drew girls with red hair, with black hair, with blond hair, with a wide variety of hairstyles. It gave me great pleasure, intense satisfaction, to lie like that, drawing and listening, unheeded, to their risqué conversation. Over a period of fifteen years we regularly spent our summer vacations there. It is there that I recall the youthful Joets most vividly. As if she acquired a form and definition there that she lacked for me elsewhere.

Joets had a couple of friends her own age in town, while I played with Engela and Moetsie. One of Joets's friends was the daughter of a minister, an unchaste child. Short, buxom, cheeky, forward. Her presumptuous way of speaking thrilled me. I hung on every brazen word emerging from her mouth. I begged Joets to allow me to join them. Joets was relentless.

Hence I had to roam as Tarzan and Jane with Engela and Moetsie among the fruit trees, the lumps of earth a pale brown, the clear, infinite Free State summer sky high above our heads. Or we played with paper dolls in the cool, dusky house. While their mother (with the hairy legs set a tad too far apart), for the whole of the long Saturday afternoon, roused and enticed the Afrikaans teacher during the mixed-doubles match.

When not playing with the little sisters in town, I amused myself during the endless afternoons in the warm, sleeping house with the closed-off front stoep, where the wires hummed like a slow whirligig, like the lamenting voices of ghosts. Or I played outside with small dolls, in the rock garden in front of the house. At Christmas we ate watermelon and on New Year's Day we played cricket with the uncles in the large yard. (Everyone, except Joets, who stayed in her room and read; she would not spend her time on trifling games.) The same yard that was flooded by moonlight on the night when the peacock cried and the woman died in childbirth—when I laid down my childhood and entered my turbulent youth. But that was later.

I think of Joets as an adult, in the back of the car, when I placed my hand between the legs of the man. Silent in the back of the car. I think of her at the time when she picked up the shell for me on the beach. When she spoke to me about her conception of time, about the time bomb within the moth, about the fan of fate, and about the novel that she had begun to write. She worked on this novel for a long time, but never completed it. Initially she still talked about it, but later no longer. From time to time I would ask our mother about Joets's progress. The book had to be perfect—nothing but perfection was acceptable to Joets, and in her own eyes she could never achieve that.

Twice during our adult lives I experienced in Joets the same relentlessness she had when we were children. The first time was when she turned her back on me for months after the publication of my novel (because she thought that I had been unkind to her and our mother in that work). The second time was when she decided to stop writing. Of this resolution she never told me herself—I had to hear it from our mother. Joets never went back on her resolution.

From what strange and improbable directions those two people— our parents—came to meet each other! After her father had left them, our mother never regained her trust in the world. Before his marriage my father had been an uncommitted, attractive bachelor. He travelled and had adventures. When he went home on holidays, his widowed sisters received their youngest brother with open arms. With his adult nieces and nephews there was plenty of entertainment: endless picnics and automobile excursions; local girls were in no short supply. (I saw the photographs—sepia photographs of girls with strange dresses and hairstyles and pointed shoes.) He had only one serious relationship with a woman that he took on holiday to Lourenço Marques, where she cheated on him with another man. In the wake of that, our father undertook a boat trip along the East Coast of Africa with his friend Swannie. In the evenings they danced with the girls on deck. They disembarked at every harbour and sometimes took day trips to the interior. (Of this my father never told us.) After his marriage he became less sociable. My mother once remarked to me that he was not a man capable of making conciliatory moves. A light, ironic man, who had difficulty with issues of faith, and laughed when I said that I would never listen to the devil again. It was a laugh from his belly, but soundless, pulling the corners of his mouth up high.

•

Joets draws beautifully and she can sculpt in clay. My efforts always seem primitive compared to hers. She can run fast and write lovely essays. She makes a small sculpture of a naked woman from clay that we found in the banks of the spruit. I find it more beautiful than anything I have ever seen. When it is dry, my aunt places it on the bookshelf made of stacked bricks and loose planks. The amenities in the house are primitive, the hygiene in the kitchen dubious, but my aunt, my mother's youngest sister, chooses the exact colour of every little cushion placed on the divan in the sitting room with the utmost care. (The sitting room with the low hessian ceiling.) When my mother and their other sister come to visit, the sisters drink tea endlessly. All day long the servants carry trays with cups of tea to and fro between bedroom and kitchen. Maria, a shy young black girl, sets my aunt's hair with large curlers. The sisters never stop talking, the milk is thick and creamy, there are dead flies in the half-empty cups of cold tea. The servants prepare pumpkin and mutton for dinner. In the evening, when my uncle returns from his work in town, he is tired, and impatient with his wife, who has apparently spent her day lying around, talking. His food has not been heated up, there is no hot water for him on the stove. The shower in the tiny bathroom is a perforated basin, a strange contraption he devised himself. One evening Joets announces that she wants to shower by herself. She has a pimple on her bum, she says. I am disappointed, but I accept it with resignation, although I find it puzzling that she does not want to shower with me for that reason.

It is only when she leaves home that our sisterly bond begins to knit. At university I often spend summer holidays with her. She talks to me about the Holy Spirit, whom she pictures as a seed with wings. About her concept of time. About the book she is writing. She quotes from

William Blake. I sit with her while she is having a bath; her hands are clasped around her bony knees, her large, near-sighted eyes are fixed on me. She tells me about William Burroughs' *Naked Lunch*. She laughs so much that she seems to be crying. Then she slowly stirs the cooled water with her hand. She is my sister, I have a boundless admiration for her. I see her talent as more significant than mine. Through an unfortunate conjuncture of circumstances the promise of her youth is never fulfilled. One day death overcomes her, before I have the opportunity to speak to her again for the last time.

CHAPTER NINETEEN

Sof announces one day: We are going to buy you some shells. I have an address.

I phone the woman. Her voice is flat and betrays scant aesthetic feeling. Does she sell shells? Ye-hes, she still has some shells, but she is now mostly doing (sic) teddy bears. Can we come and have a look anyway? Ye-hes, we can come. She will ask the boy (sic) to fetch the shells from the house and bring them down to the cottage.

On the appointed day Sof and I drive to the home of Mrs. Theodora Wassenaar, dealer in shells. When we arrive, she views us with suspicion through the iron bars of the gate—as if we were black of skin and ignoble of intention. In a corner of the garden is a birdbath in the shape of a sea horse. "She's going to barter with us through the gate today," Sof mutters. We are allowed to enter, but with little enthusiasm.

Mrs. Wassenaar takes us to the front room of the cottage. The teddy bears are displayed—shelf upon shelf—in colours, textures and patterns ranging from mauve plush to brown velvet, from dots to stripes—in cheery variety. She informs us that she supplies a beginner's pack consisting of a pattern, buttons, and thread. The buyer chooses her own material. These rolls of material are folded away in shelves underneath the teddy bears. Mrs. Wassenaar's small lapdog follows us around. He is wearing a little jacket—like the white dog sleeping on the couch beside Rosencrantz and Guildenstern, the evening Jaykie took us to Fish and

240

company. Despite her Afrikaans name, she speaks English to us, but with an Afrikaans accent. (Theodora! What a mockery she makes of Theo's name!)

When I remind her of the purpose of our visit, she reluctantly takes us to the next room. In the corner is a smallish bookcase with four shelves. On each of the shelves are a couple of baskets filled with shells. The largest shells are on top of the bookcase. The shells on offer are mostly tonnas, but with a surprising number of harpas, a rare shell, difficult to come by. Not a dramatic selection, but I know how difficult it is to get hold of shells nowadays. I know, for wherever I go, I keep looking out for them. Where do I start? May I unpack some?

On the table is a cloth decorated with a teddy-bear motif. Carefully I start making a provisional selection. It is hard to see the shells against the intrusive background of teddy bears. Sof suggests lifting the tablecloth on one side, but Mrs. Wassenaar is not open to this suggestion. She sits next to me, fixing me with a hawk's eye, in case I should be tempted to loot, to pilfer, to help myself to one or two of her wares. She is a short, buxom woman, puffed out like pastry. She is wearing a navy-blue tracksuit, gold earrings and a gold locket. I do not like the colour of her nail polish, or the design of her rings. Behind her glasses, her eyes are enormously enlarged.

While I carefully make my tentative selection (with trembling heart and hands), Mrs. Wassenaar talks. She holds forth about "the Blacks." This is the first and the main motif. The Blacks who, if given the chance, would strip the cottage, damage the teddy bears (defile them), take the shells and barter them (at black-market prices), steal the petty cash, rape the woman of the house. Who will, in short, plunder and rob, filch, snaffle and snitch until the blessed Second Coming.

"The Blacks, who don't know the difference between a teddy bear and a shell," Sof remarks softly to me, with Mrs. Wassenaar directing her immensely enlarged eyes suspiciously in Sof's direction. The woman watches me as if I am pretending to be someone I am not. (Not in this context, lady.) Her voice is toneless and without cheer, her basilisk gaze fixed on me—totally devoid of any sympathy, self-reflection, or irony.

Where are the shells from, and why are they so difficult to acquire nowadays? I ask.

Mrs. Wassenaar gathers momentum. The second motif is introduced. Her split (half-English, half-Afrikaans) tongue is loosened. Before our eyes she conjures up a vision of darkness and calamity: a spectral image of what is in store. It will be increasingly difficult to get hold of shells, until eventually they will become completely unavailable, or available only at black-market prices. Their numbers will decrease even more drastically because the ocean bed is being stripped, because the very oceans are drying up. The increased import tax on shells will furthermore make them unaffordably expensive. The illegal trade in shells—a growing black-market enterprise along the East Coast of Africa, as well as illegal caravan routes elsewhere—will make of shells a rare commodity, which will engender further criminal activity. And all of these things are mysteriously linked to the scandalous conduct of the Blacks.

Sof carefully clears her throat and asks Mrs. Wassenaar what her home language is, and if she is by any chance related to the Afrikaans poet. Her mother was Afrikaans, her father was English, she spoke Afrikaans at home, went to an English school, her husband is Afrikaans, they speak English to each other. She doesn't really read Afrikaans— the last time she had to do that was at school. (Shuddering slightly at the thought.) A Babylonian bewilderment—a profound confusion at the level of language is probably the cause of Mrs. Wassenaar's inability to choose between teddy bears and shells. She keeps talking as I make my final choice. Under no circumstance must the Blacks see from the street that there is something going on here, for that reason she always keeps the curtains (with dancing teddy bears) closed. The Blacks must not know that there is money here, and she turns her huge eyes knowingly towards me. The teddy bears on the tablecloth acquire a frenetic rhythm. When I am done and Mrs. Wassenaar is calculating the amount on a pocket calculator, I whisper urgently to Sof: Let's not stay here one moment longer.

Her own shell collection, Mrs. Wassenaar tells us as we depart, is exhibited in a display cabinet in the house. I imagine that she has a preference for the more fanciful forms—the lambisses and the ornate bivalves. This collection is probably kept under lock and key, in a cabinet with ball-and-claw legs, with a Black instructed to dust it daily.

After that, Sof and I go for tea. "How would you describe the colour of that woman's nail polish?" I ask.

"A kind of prostate-piss pink," Sof says contemptuously.

"I thought it an ordinary pearl pink," I say.

I barely taste what I am eating or drinking. I have just bought fifteen new shells, and I am both excited and anxious. These fifteen shells have to compensate for my shells, stolen by some thug as a result of a bizarre misunderstanding and an unfathomable convergence of circumstances. (Jaykie probably knows who the person or persons are, but he will never tell.)

"What do you think," Sof asks, "should a novel come to a final conclusion? Should it pitch towards resolution?"

Resolution: decision, solution, conclusion. The tea is too weak. The light is too bright.

"I refuse to see it like that," Sof says. "Am I deluded in this matter as well?"

She becomes increasingly heated. She bangs with her fist on the table so that the cups rattle. Two red spots appear on her usually pale cheeks. Her glasses flash. "Does life move towards resolution?" she asks. "Is anything ever concluded? Has that been your experience?"

A word occurs to me, from the depths of my confused being. "Bellerophon," I say. "An extinct species of gastropods with a thick shell curled up in a symmetrical spiral." The word has broken off its murky stem. I have on occasion picked up similar fragments of loose coral from the seabed.

Sof regards me intently.

"Also the letter of Bellerophon, fatal to the bearer."

"Fatal in what way?" she asks cautiously.

"Bellerophon was sent to the king of Lycia with a letter in which his death is requested," I say.

More words come unstuck and bubble to the surface. *Bogterig* (cowardly). *Bontprater* (babbler). *Boeteling* (penitent). All of these words, I tell Sof, Theo and I put on cards. Also *bedot* (fool or trick), *bemantel* (cloak or sheathe), *belas* (burden), *belemmer* (impede), and *beminnaar* or *beminner*.

"*Beminner*?" Sof asks carefully, eyeing me intently.

"Yes," I say. "Obsolete. Not only in the sense of someone who loves another, a lover, but also said of a person with a passionate taste, an intense hankering for something. Like Theo for beauty."

Sof still watches me closely.

"I think I'm hallucinating," I say.

"Oh, hell," she says.

I lean forward on the table and take both her cool hands in mine. I press them against my hot forehead. Would that I were able to weep.

"I am actually overcome," I say. "Overcome with joy."

Sof, slightly flustered, tactfully disengages her hands from my grip and suggests that I go home immediately and get some rest—I am clearly in need of it. I take my leave of her. On the way home I am suddenly uncertain of my direction, despite being well acquainted with the area.

At home I set out the new shells in rows on the coffee table in the lounge. They stand rigid and subservient, like members of a congregation, like small votive statues in Sumerian temples—offering intercessory prayers to the gods on behalf of certain individuals: all taut attention, with great, fixated eyes and hands clasped together.

I am overwhelmed by exhaustion. I turn away from the shells, which suddenly look like nothing to me. I might as well not have gone to the trouble. They seem to me a feeble reflection of what I have lost and a ridiculous attempt to rectify that loss. Mrs. Theodora Wassenaar confused me. Her basilisk gaze disoriented me. I lost my sound judgement as a result. I made the wrong choices. I see that I should have concentrated more on the harpas, and less on the small murexes (crinkled like the skin of a chameleon) that I do not care for much.

I sleep deeply for three solid hours. When I awake, I have no clear idea of where I am—not the city, the province, the phase of my life. I think I heard my child's voice, but I do not know for certain.

Only after I have risen from that deep sleep, am I able to turn my attention to the shells again. They are substitutes, and can never take the place of the stolen shells. Alike in colouring—mostly soft, unremarkable brown ochres and pink ochres. They can never compare with the dramatic *Murex nigritus* (with black and white stripes like the proud zebra), or the cool, weighty, beautifully whorled conches, the prancing nautiluses, the flecked burnt-orange mitres, like pointed bishops' hats.

For a considerable length of time I sit at the little table in the lounge, gazing at the small group of new shells. I regard them with displeasure, with a relentless stare.

Child, I think, I wish to call up your presence today. I have a need to be with you. Behold your mother's bitter folly. You too are well aware that my despair (my attenuated life) is not bound up with the indifference of the universe or the loss of the shells.

I can hear you saying: Surely you know that the shells are but a pretext? You do not need the shells to survive. Why cling so obstinately to your loss? Why attach yourself to your loss in this way? There will always be losses. Life continues. Stop this—stop this foolishness!

And I will answer: I know. I know it all. There is no explanation for human short-sightedness.

Life is so short, my mother said with wonder at the end of her life. Had she realised this earlier, I asked, would she have led her life differently? She would, she said passionately, she would! She tried to moisten her dry mouth with the tip of her tongue. She was out of breath, for she was dying.

"The world is charged with the grandeur of God," she quoted. She fell silent.

I waited.

"You don't have to be a believer to see this," she said. She averted her gaze; there was no imputation in her voice. "If only I had focused more on that and less . . ."

She kept quiet and again tried to moisten her lips slightly. "Less on the small disappointments," she said, completing her sentence.

Soon afterwards she was dead. My brother read the poem by Gerard Manley Hopkins at her memorial service. Not much later he was gone, and in the five years that have elapsed, I have barely had any contact with him.

•

At work I try to round off and complete everything as best I can. In the evenings I watch television. I borrow a video from Vera Garaszczuk—a reconstruction of what the earth might look like in a hundred million or two hundred million years from now—based on research done in palaeontology and evolutionary biology.

A hundred million years from now there will no longer be human life on earth, to start off with. The programme posits that we have removed ourselves to other regions of the Milky Way. That seems to me overoptimistic. It seems more probable that by then we will have blown ourselves off the globe, or have perished from the effects of a cataclysmic natural disaster—a sixth or seventh great extermination.

Antarctica is now situated at the tropics, it has changed into a tropical rain forest. Hot trade winds sweep the globe. There is more oxygen in the atmosphere. Insects of monstrous size abound. Australia has collided with the southeastern part of Asia, and the impact has caused high mountain ranges to form. These mountains are higher than any that existed previously. Winds of a hundred and ten miles per hour blow across the high plateau formed by the mountains. At night temperatures drop to minus thirty degrees Celsius. The dominance of mammals has come to an end. A small rodent, the last remaining mammal, burrows deep in the dark crevasses and caves of a mountain. Mountain ranges, seas and the climate are unstable, and volcanic eruptions occur regularly.

In two hundred million years from now all the continents have again been fused to form a supercontinent in the northern hemisphere. The remainder of the earth's surface is covered by a single giant ocean, occupying three-quarters of the earth's surface. (I have to think of the medieval world view—two cold zones at the poles, two temperate zones, and in the middle, at the tropics, an unbridgeable watery zone, which divides the known world from the unknown. According to certain medieval conceptions, this unknown southern world would be the inverse of the known.) Because there are fewer coastlines with a moderating influence, the seas are subjected to vast storms of long duration. Winds attain unprecedented speeds and waves reach heights of nearly a hundred feet. The immense continent is a huge desert, undergoing drastic shifts in temperature.

A successive great extinction has in the meantime destroyed ninety-five percent of all existing species—in the sea, on the earth, and in the air. The species that have survived have evolved into new forms—into fish that fly, supersized sharks that hunt in packs, enormous octopuses with highly sophisticated colour-camouflage systems. The humble worms, so well adapted since the origin of life, are still around, but they have also had to make certain adaptations to survive. In cool, subterranean caves a deadly killer worm hunts. Another species has developed algaelike protrusions, transforming the worm into a self-supplying, photosynthesising creature. Highly evolved ants, of which the class system has been further refined, inhabit tunnels deep underneath the earth and erect giant towers above ground, towers serving as reservoirs for the cultivation of algae, and offering shade against the red-hot desert wind.

An inhospitable landscape. The landmass is a virtually uninhabitable desert and the ocean a seething mass of water. Nowhere a sign or trace of anything human. Everything that was humanlike or human or created by humans has gone (through our own efforts, or assisted by uncontrollable natural forces). Everything reduced to ashes, to bone, to stone: unrecognisably ground to fine powder, decomposed. Buried, sunken, reduced to atoms and dispersed over the wild and empty globe.

What has survived is hypereffective, hyperaggressive, hyperadaptable. Whatever used to be defenceless has become extinct. It seems that not even God has been able to survive here in this desolate corner of His creation. Gone is He, disappeared, passed from sight like imprints in sand, come to an end, or removed Himself to a more grateful (more human?) environment. Gone is He and all thought of Him: sanded over, silted up—as is every trace of human presence or human folly.

CHAPTER TWENTY

Alverine phones me one afternoon at the end of October. Jaykie is in hospital, he has been wounded in a shoot-out with the police.

"What happened?" I ask.

"No, Miss Dolly," she says, "he and his friend Bennie were trying to get away from the police when they were shot."

"What happened to the friend?"

"He was shot, Miss Dolly."

"Is he alive?"

"No, Miss Dolly. He's dead. The police shot him dead."

"What were they doing, Alverine?" I ask.

"I can't really say, Miss Dolly. But Bennie was a bad influence on Jaykie. He had a police record. Theft. He was a gang member also. The Bitter Boys."

"Was Jaykie also a member of this gang? The Bitter Boys?" I ask.

"No, Miss Dolly. Jaykie was never a member of any gang. He and Bennie were just friends. Since they were young."

"I'm glad that Jaykie is alive, Alverine. It could so easily have been different. It would have been very hard on your mother if he also came to harm."

"Yes, Miss Dolly," Alverine says.

But what does she keep quiet about, I wonder. What are the sighs and reservations that I seem to hear in her voice? I see the fickle hand of fate at work here (the capricious, inconstant shaper of destinies). In my mind's eye I see the mother: Mrs. Fortuin, the mother of Bennie. Large, weighty, forbidding, a shadow on her cheek and upper lip. I imagine Bennie slipping out as fully tattooed Bitter Boy from between her immense, dusky thighs. I see him lying in state in her house on a white candlewick bedspread, a fly perched on one corner of his mouth. The members of his gang, the Bitter Boys, demurely pass by, one by one. Bitter youths, with vengeful and uncouth thoughts. I am sorry, I mutter in her ear, my deepest sympathies, Aunty Fortuin, Missus Fortune.

I picture Jaykie lying in hospital with a white bandage wrapped around his head—like Marat in his bath. His Spanish priest's eyes cast upwards, with the whites visible. Full of sweet talk and feigned remorse. Aunty Rosie moved to tears beside his bed. I like Jaykie, but I do not trust him. Perhaps I should visit him in hospital. I have to think again of Mrs. C's visit to the young black boy in hospital, the child with whom she spoke of Thucydides. She did not like him. She reproved herself for that; she tried to overcome her resistance, she touched his hand, he drew it away. The boy was later shot and killed in her back yard. Her illness took its course. Vercueil moved in with her; she allowed him congress with her. In her dying moment he embraced her. But for her there was no more hope of consolation—that was the author's conclusion.

Jaykie knows what became of my shells, I believe, but he will never admit it. Maybe it is better that way. Bennie Fortuin lies in his coffin, a shell placed on each of his closed eyelids, in each of his armpits, in his folded hands, in the groin on both sides, on his sex. The heavy conches at his feet. These shells were slipped in unseen at the funeral parlour, placed on the body before the lid of the coffin was closed. My shells accompany him on his last journey to decomposition and dissolution. With him they perish, and pass into oblivion. With him they return: dust unto dust. Further than that I cannot follow them in my imagination.

•

I continue with the novel I have begun to write. How unexpectedly Theo's death came over us! Over his wife, over me, over Sailor, over the

Indian dog (with his hot opium arse, according to Johannes Taljaard). Every one of us who imagined that we shared a privileged understanding with Theo. I know as little as does the shell what tomorrow holds in store for me. I am a more complex and sensitive being, but I have as little control over my fate—although I (like the rich man) can contemplate and fantasise about this fate. I do not see my destiny as determined by providence, but rather as the convergence of a hundred, of a thousand and one minor coincidences.

My telephone rings one night, four weeks after Theo's death.

"Helena, sister," a voice says.

"Yes?" I say, slightly uncertain, but with rising expectation.

"I am back. Your lost brother. Back in the land of the living. Back from my wanderings."

"Where on earth have you been?" I ask.

"You might say I've been eating husks with the swine."

"Our parents are dead," I say. "Our father can no longer run to meet you and fall on your neck, and kiss you."

"I know," he says.

"When we were children, he sang to us. I don't think I ever knew him—our father," I say. "A good part of his life was concealed from us."

"That is so," my brother says. "He was not a man who let himself be known easily."

"He sailed up along the coast of Africa before he married our mother. He had experiences there, adventures," I say.

"I have often thought of that, these past years," my brother says.

"Our mother confused him with someone else," I say. "She thought that she was seeing him, but over his shoulder her gaze was fixed on another person."

"He was not the kind of man to impose himself upon her," my brother says.

"No, that was not his nature," I say. "But I am glad to hear your voice today. While you were eating husks in the company of swine, I have experienced much."

"I've had time to think things over," my brother says. "We must talk. I have much to tell you."

"I want to hear," I say. "I want to hear everything that you've been thinking. It is about time. We haven't seen each other for a very long time."

That evening I think back to how our father sang to us in the dark when we were children, to me and to my younger brother, who has now returned after eating husks with the swine. We are in bed in our children's room, painted blue—my bed is beneath the window, opposite the half-open door, casting a wedge of light into the room. My brother is lying in his pram. I see my father and the pram etched in profile against the light. I am six years old, my brother is two, we are both lying with our eyes open in the dark. I know this, for I can sense his attention, and he asks for another song as soon as my father has finished the last one. Our father is pushing the pram and he is singing. He is in no hurry, he is not impatient, he has all the time in the world. *Wat maak oom Kalie daar*—what is Uncle Kalie up to, he sings softly in his fine, deep voice, and I am amazed that Uncle Kalie's roguish adventures can make me feel so sad.

CHAPTER TWENTY-ONE

It is the beginning of November, more than four weeks since Theo Verwey's funeral, and I am still unable to pound my chest and weep like the rich man in an extravagant display of grief about Theo's death. I still experience no more than a dry anguish, and a strange sense of aggrievedness—resembling indignation.

I continue with the letters *I, J* and *K*. Certainly not with the same thoroughness and extensive overview as under Theo's expert guidance, but at least not completely and utterly (*gans en gansemaal*) incompetently.

I draw a scheme of the alphabet: three lines of eight letters each, and a fourth line with two letters. Theo and I completed the first line. A third. I find a certain consolation in this symmetry.

Sometimes Mrs. Verwey stands behind me in the doorway. She wants an answer from me; she expects of me to commit myself to the completion of the project. She wants me to realise Theo's dream.

At the end of the working day Sof and I often sit wordlessly, looking out over the ocean. Sometimes we see prancing dolphins in the water. I find sisterly consolation in her presence.

I tell her: "You are not the first minister's daughter to cross my path, but you are the most exemplary."

Suddenly there are few distractions. Theo Verwey is dead. Everything that welled up from the regions of my heart in his presence—that I often cast in the form of talk about the rich man—has to sink back of its own accord, to be absorbed back into the murky waters of the subconscious from where it surged upwards.

Vera Garaszczuk is still on leave. Hugo Hattingh still in an institution. (Still in the grip of pestering spirits, at the mercy of tormenting voices.) Sailor keeps quiet as the grave about him. I have never heard him make a single remark concerning Hugo, and Sailor is one who seldom watches his speech. (Though Sailor knows how to lie, and deception is second nature to him, Sof maintains.) Freddie Ferreira says Hugo Hattingh sometimes sat talking to him in his office for hours. A taxing man, Freddie says, and shakes his head. Someone with whom one needs to have endless patience. Frightful mood swings, terrible things that harry the man. Freddie shakes his head, grinds out a cigarette butt beneath his heel. I now realise that his feeling of responsibility towards Hugo Hattingh makes up a fair share of his tribulations.

Perhaps I should visit Hugo at the institution and tell him about a dream I had. A humble worm, of an uncommon blue-green colour, is at first working its way laboriously forward as I watch, until gradually two brightly coloured growths like small flippers start protruding from the sides of its body, so that the worm slowly begins to resemble a salamander. Further than that I could not progress in the dream. I am surprised by the glimpse my sleeping unconscious granted me of the evolutionary process. For the time being I cannot speak to Hugo Hattingh about coincidence, about Darwin's study of worms, about the astounding outburst of growth in the Cambrian. I hope to talk to him still about the possible origin of the universe from the void—as a quantum shuddering, slighter than a sigh, than the fluttering of an eyelid.

My shells I have laid to rest. I have become resigned to their disappearance. An uneasy resignation—for any day I expect feelings of loss to flare up acutely again. I no longer talk about it to Frans de Waard, my lover and companion, and he does not enquire. When we spend a weekend together, he is grateful that I am more receptive to the pleasure he wants to give me.

The orbital paths of my mother and Joets move closer to me again, although my mother turns herself to me ever less frequently. She averts herself from me in my dreams, as if she has forgotten that she ever gave birth to me. Joets and I still attempt to reach each other, but there is a boundary neither of us can cross. It is like a burning ring dividing us—she is on one side, I am on the other. I speak to her. Look! I say, do it this way! But although she is so close to me that I can see her wringing her hands, she does not notice me.

Soon I shall see my brother. He will tell me how he ate husks with the swine; he will tell me of his adventures, of everything that he experienced.

ACKNOWLEDGMENTS

I wish to thank Margaret Lenta and Sally-Ann Murray for their invaluable comments on the manuscript;

Elsa Silke for her steady editorial hand and sound judgement;

And Alida Potgieter for her professionalism, commitment and care.

Ingrid Winterbach is an artist and novelist whose work has won South Africa's M-Net Prize, Old Mutual Literary Prize, the University of Johannesburg Prize for Creative Writing, and the W.A. Hofmeyr Prize. *To Hell with Cronjé*, also available from Open Letter, won the 2004 Hertzog Prize, an honor she shares with the novelists Breyten Breytenbach and Etienne Leroux.

Open Letter—the University of Rochester's nonprofit, literary translation press—is one of only a handful of publishing houses dedicated to increasing access to world literature for English readers. Publishing ten titles in translation each year, Open Letter searches for works that are extraordinary and influential, works that we hope will become the classics of tomorrow.

Making world literature available in English is crucial to opening our cultural borders, and its availability plays a vital role in maintaining a healthy and vibrant book culture. Open Letter strives to cultivate an audience for these works by helping readers discover imaginative, stunning works of fiction and by creating a constellation of international writing that is engaging, stimulating, and enduring.

Current and forthcoming titles from Open Letter include works from Argentina, Catalonia, China, Czechoslovakia, Poland, Russia, and numerous other countries.

www.openletterbooks.org